SUSAN MALLERY

is the bestselling and award-winning author of over fifty books for Harlequin Books and Silhouette Books. She makes her home in Los Angeles with her handsome prince of a husband and her two adorable-but-not-bright cats.

CAIT LONDON

is an avid reader and an artist who plays with computers and maintains her Web site, http://caitlondon.com. Her books reflect her many interests, including herbs, driving cross-country and photography. A national bestselling and award-winning author of category romance and romantic suspense, Cait has also written historical romances under another pseudonym. Three is her lucky number; she has three daughters, and her life events have been in threes. Cait says, "One of the best perks about this hard work is the thrilling reader response."

Lassoed Hearts

SUSAN MALLERY
CAIT LONDON

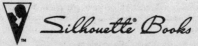
Silhouette Books

Published by Silhouette Books
America's Publisher of Contemporary Romance

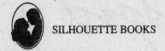 SILHOUETTE BOOKS

ISBN 0-373-23022-2

by Request

LASSOED HEARTS

Copyright © 2004 by Harlequin Books S.A.

The publisher acknowledges the copyright holders of the individual works as follows:

COWBOY DADDY
Copyright © 1994 by Susan W. Macias

THE COWBOY
Copyright © 1993 by Lois Kleinsasser

CONTENTS

This book about a mother's love for her daughter could only be dedicated to my mother. For listening and encouraging me. For giving me the freedom to try and the support to risk failing. For never judging me. For always being there when I needed her.
With love.

COWBOY DADDY
Susan Mallery

Dear Reader,

I really appreciate the opportunity to have *Cowboy Daddy* back in print. It's been (gasp!) ten years since it was first published by Silhouette Books and I confess I love the story as much today as I did when I first wrote it.

Most of my books are about family—what it takes to be part of a family and how we all long to belong— and this one is no exception. The idea for this book came from several news stories about the impact of unsealed adoption records on the children given up and the mothers (and sometimes fathers) who had made the heart-wrenching decision in the first place. Thrown in the middle of this emotional turmoil was the adoptive families and their unique combination of joy and pain.

As a writer, I can't help asking, "What if?" From that single question came this story. I hope you enjoy it.

All the best,

Susan Mallery

Chapter 1

"**Y**our two o'clock is a hunk."

Anne Baker stared blankly at her assistant. "A hunk?"

"Yeah!" Heather clutched her notepad to her chest and sagged against the door. "Tall, dark, with big brown eyes that could melt you faster than..." Her voice trailed off. "I assume by the way you're looking at me that you're not happy with the news."

Anne fought the urge to bury her face in her hands. "It doesn't matter what he looks like. The fact is he's here. What am I supposed to do with him?"

"Talk?" Heather grinned. "You aren't scared of him, are you?"

"Me?" Anne firmly shook her head. "Of course not. I've worked with company presidents, relocated Fortune 500 companies."

"Leapt buildings in a single bound. You *are* scared."

Anne sighed. "Terrified."

"Should I send him away?"

Anne almost wished that was possible. No, that wasn't true. She didn't want to send him away; she desperately wanted to meet Jake Masters. With one phone call and a few carefully chosen words, the man had turned her world upside down. For the past two days she'd thought about nothing but his call. Now he was here, waiting to see her. She'd hoped for a connection—a way to undo the past—but she hadn't thought it would happen like this. Or happen this soon.

Anne glanced down at the slim gold watch on her wrist. It had been a gift to herself last month, celebrating both the completion of the electronics firm's contract and her birthday. Thirty-one. The day had made her think about many things, most of them revolving around her eighteenth birthday. Funny, less than a month later Jake Masters called. Had her thoughts been a premonition? She shook her head. Of course not. She thought about the same thing every birthday. She tried not to of course, but it was inevitable.

Anne looked up and forced herself to smile. "Is he really a hunk?"

Heather smiled back. "We are talking heartthrob city. Long, lean and luscious."

Anne's forced smile became genuine. "You are a wicked woman."

"It is one of my best qualities." Heather winked. "He's pacing back and forth like a caged lion. Do you want me to send him in?"

Anne's stomach lurched as if she'd just taken the last heart-stopping drop on a roller coaster. "Waiting is only going to make it worse." She drew in a deep breath. "All right. Here goes nothing. Tell Mr. Masters he can come in."

Heather nodded. Her blond hair bounced with the movement. "One hunk, coming right up." The oak door closed quietly behind her.

Just keep breathing, Anne told herself. She sat straighter in her chair and rested her hands on the desk. Her fingers shook. She thrust them onto her lap. She touched her hair to make sure it was still neatly smoothed in place, then wished she'd told Heather to give her a couple of minutes. She wanted to freshen her lipstick, to check the mirror for the hundredth time and make sure there was nothing in her teeth. She wanted to catch her breath and think about something other than Jake Masters and why he was coming to see her.

A knock on the door brought her out of her seat. She straightened, tugged at her suit jacket and called, "Come in."

Heather pushed the door open. "Mr. Masters to see you, Ms. Baker." She stepped back to let the man enter.

Anne's heart was already pounding in her chest, but at the sight of the tall, dark-haired man standing in front of her, it leapt into high gear and tried to lodge in her throat. Her palms grew damp.

The panic threatening to swamp her had a little to do with the reason for his visit and a whole lot more to do with the way he was dressed. Boots, jeans, tailored white shirt rolled up to the elbows and a black Stetson he'd removed when he came to her office. It took all her strength to remain standing. Jake Masters was a cowboy. She avoided cowboys at all costs—not an easy thing to do in Houston, Texas.

It shouldn't matter what he wore or did for a living, she reminded herself. But why did he have to be a cowboy?

"Would you like me to bring coffee, Mr. Masters?" Heather asked.

He turned to her assistant. "None for me, thanks." His voice was low and controlled with only the hint of a Texas drawl. He was a native, but not local. Dallas, maybe.

When Heather glanced at her, Anne shook her head. The younger woman gave her a thumbs-up sign and retreated.

The door closed. Anne returned her attention to her guest. His shadowed eyes held hers. Brown, she thought, with odd flecks of gold, but no expression. He might have been a hunk, as Heather had promised, but Anne couldn't judge from the impressions she gathered. Tall, brown hair, a firm mouth with no hint of a smile. Broad shouldered, slim hipped. Younger than she would have thought. Midthirties. Handsome? It didn't matter. Her gaze drifted back to his face and she saw he returned her close inspection. Her hands tightened into fists. What was he seeing? She resisted the urge to smooth her hair.

"Mr. Masters?" she said, raising the pitch of her voice so it came out as a question.

He nodded. "Thank you for seeing me, Ms. Baker." Those cool, oddly flecked eyes searched her face. "I still have the picture you gave us. You've changed."

Anne flushed. She knew the hot color would flare brightly on her cheeks, giving away her embarrassment. She ducked her head and pointed to the leather chair in front of her desk. "It was a long time ago."

"Thirteen years," he said as he sat down and set his

hat on the edge of her desk. His hair was short, barely brushing the collar of his white shirt.

Anne lowered herself into her seat. She looked at the bookcases against the right-hand wall, at the sofa on the opposite side of the room, at the closed door, and suddenly wished she'd asked for coffee. She could use the momentary rescue, if not the caffeine.

"I know how much time has passed," she said. "It's not the sort of thing I would forget."

His eyes narrowed and his mouth drew even straighter. "I'll have to take your word on that."

She leaned forward. "You know nothing about me or my circumstances, Mr. Masters," she said curtly. "You have no right to judge me. If that's what this meeting is about—"

"It isn't." He cut her off, then rubbed the bridge of his nose with his thumb and forefinger. "Look, it's been a hell of a summer. First the move, then this whole situation with Laurel."

"Laurel?" Her voice quavered as she spoke the name.

He dropped his hand to the armrest. "Yes. My daughter."

Laurel. Anne blinked several times. She had often wondered what they'd called her child. Now she knew. No matter what, she would always know. Laurel. She pictured a towheaded toddler in a frilly pink dress. No, that wasn't right. Thirteen years had gone by; Laurel was a teenager now. A milestone in a child's life. Maybe that's why their shared birthday had struck a nerve this time. "It's a beautiful name."

"My wife picked it out." He watched her carefully. "Is she here with you?"

"My wife passed away two years ago."

"I'm sorry. But I was asking about…your daughter."

He caught the slight hesitation. "I thought we should speak alone first," he said.

She hadn't known how much she'd hoped to meet her—to meet Laurel—until this moment. To have come so far, to be so close. It was more than she'd ever dared to hope for, and yet she *had* hoped. The chance had been snatched away and she wanted to cry out her pain. She rose slowly and walked around her chair to the floor-to-ceiling window.

Downtown Houston stretched out before her. The double-glazed glass protected her from the weather and the noise, but she could see the August heat shimmering on the streets and sidewalks.

Heather had opened the vertical blinds that morning. Anne stared out at the city. "You have the advantage here, Mr. Masters."

"How?"

"I don't understand why you're here or what you want from me. From your reaction a minute ago I would guess you might not want to believe me, but I'm having a difficult time with this. When you called, I agreed to meet with you because—" She paused. The ache in her chest deepened. She drew in a breath and told herself she was strong enough to get through this. She had no choice; she was in this alone. "Because I couldn't say no. I've spent thirteen years wondering about her. The private adoption arranged by the attorneys meant you could have contacted me at any time. Why now?"

"She wants to meet you."

The opposite of pain was joy. Happiness flooded her, chasing away the darkness and the fear. Tears she'd managed to ward off before filled her eyes. She covered her mouth with her hand to hold in her cry of relief. The window in front of her blurred as she remembered a day thirteen years ago.

It had been summer then, too, but July instead of August. Paradise was too small a town to have a hospital, so her mother had driven her the forty miles to the nearest community facility. On her eighteenth birthday, surrounded by strangers, with only her mother's hand to hold, she'd given birth to a daughter. She remembered little of the pain, although the smells stayed with her, as did the cold stare of the nurse who had taken the baby from the doctor and carried her from the room. Later, the woman had returned, her arms empty. Anne had cried out to see her child. The woman had refused. "If you give 'em up, you can't see 'em. Hospital policy."

She had begged for hours. The stern-faced woman refused to budge. Later, the night nurse had taken pity on her and told her the baby—her child, her daughter— was already gone. The new parents had whisked her away.

Anne wiped at the tears on her cheeks. "She wants to meet me," she whispered, barely able to believe her good fortune.

"I think it's a mistake."

She spun to face him. Sometime while she'd been lost in the past, he'd risen from the chair and approached her. He stood only a foot away. She had to tilt her head back to look into his eyes. Coldness radiated from him. And anger.

"Why?" she asked, fighting the urge to step back.

"Laurel is having some problems right now and—"

"What's wrong? Is she sick? Tell me what I can do."

"It's nothing that concerns you."

"But it does. I'm her—"

He grabbed her shoulders. Strong fingers bit into her. "Don't you dare say it. You're *not* her mother."

She wanted to contradict him, but she knew he spoke the truth. She'd given up all rights to that title the day she'd given up her child. Another tear rolled down her face.

He briefly tightened his hold on her, then released her. He cursed under his breath. "Ms. Baker—"

She turned away and fumbled for the box of tissue in the bottom drawer of her desk. She glanced at him.

Jake Masters looked as uncomfortable and confused as she felt. "I need a drink."

She wiped her face, then glanced down at the streak of makeup and a black smudge staining the white tissue. "Me, too." She pointed to the center cabinet in the bookcase. "Please pour me one of whatever you're having. I'll be right back."

She escaped through the door opposite the bookcase and into the small powder room off her office. When she was safely alone, Anne braced her forearms against the vanity and exhaled. Her whole body ached, as if she'd been beaten and left for dead. Her eyes burned and her hands still trembled. She'd thought she'd been prepared for this meeting.

"Not very," she muttered softly as she forced herself to stand upright.

After clicking on the overhead light, she stared into the mirror. The summer humidity had already done its damage to her hair as the sleek pageboy crinkled into an unruly mass of waves. Mascara and eye shadow

collected below her eyes, and what was left of her lipstick didn't begin to cover her mouth.

"Good thing he didn't bring Laurel. Seeing me like
this would probably scare her back to—"

She paused in the middle of turning on the faucet.
Back to where? She didn't know where her daughter
lived. Didn't know where she'd grown up or what she
looked like or if—

She closed her eyes. To see her, to hold her, just
once, she prayed silently. One time. To look into her
face. To know that she was all right.

Anne swallowed and blinked away fresh tears. After
opening the single drawer on the right of the sink, she
took out her emergency makeup kit and used a headband to pull her hair away from her face. She always
got red and puffy when she cried, but it could all be
cured with a little cold water and a lot of denial.

Jake stared at the shot of brandy, swore briefly, then
tossed it back with a single gulp. The fiery liquid
burned down to his stomach. He filled the snifter again,
but this time he carried it over to the coffee table in
front of the leather couch. He set the glass next to the
one he'd poured for Anne, then looked around the
room.

He knew all about executive offices. She was one
step away from the prized corner slot. A high-powered
lady on her way up. She'd come a long way from that
tiny west Texas town. She'd probably forgotten all
about her little mistake in high school. He must have
shocked her when he'd called. The tearful scene today
had been a nice touch. He shook his head. If he had
his way, he would walk out that door and never come

back. She didn't deserve to know his daughter. But Laurel wasn't giving him a choice.

Why now? he wondered for the hundredth time. Why this? He'd asked Laurel, had argued with her, but she'd refused to listen. Meeting her birth mother—he hated that phrase—had become the only thing she cared about. He didn't know how to talk to her anymore. Laurel wasn't grown-up yet, but she wasn't the little girl who had spent so many evenings curled up on his lap. Was he making a mistake?

He paced the area between the coffee table and the window. She was his daughter. And Ellen's. Only Ellen was gone. It was up to him to do what was right and to protect her. Especially from Anne Baker.

The side door opened and Anne stepped out. She'd cleaned up her face. Except for the slight redness around her eyes, no one would know she'd been crying. Probably had it down to an art form.

She walked over to him. "We have a lot of things to learn about each other. Laurel wanting to meet me must have been a shock for you, as well. I know I haven't been a part of her life, but you must believe I only want what's best for her. Let's start over." She offered him her hand.

Jake stared down at her. Unlike Ellen, who had stood only four inches shorter than his six foot one, Anne Baker's head barely skimmed his chin. He didn't want to shake hands, he didn't want to be friendly, he didn't want to do a damn thing but get the hell out of here.

He hesitated long enough to make her uncomfortable, but she didn't back down. Light blue eyes met his, refusing to look away. She'd put mascara on her top lashes, but the bottom ones were pale. He could see freckles across the bridge of her nose.

It wasn't politeness or his mother's training that caused him to reach out and engulf her small fingers in his. It was the memory of Laurel staring up at him, confused and scared and desperate to find something—and someone—to belong to.

As he took her hand, he felt it. A jolt of electricity flashed up his arm, igniting a spark that flared low in his belly. He fought to steady himself. The anger inside fed on the heat and burned hotter. She pumped his arm once. He withdrew from her and retreated to the edge of the couch.

When she sat at the far end, he lowered himself down to the leather seat and picked up the drink he'd poured. Instead of gulping down the brandy, he stared at the liquid.

He'd sensed it—the attraction. From the moment he'd walked into this room. Whether it was scent or instinct or some great cosmic joke, he didn't know. But he did know the meaning of that jolt. Ellen had been gone two years. In all that time, he'd never felt the surge of need, had never wanted to—

He looked at Anne Baker. She sat in the corner of the soft leather sofa. The supple material surrounded her, the light peach color highlighted the pale red of her hair and made her skin appear translucent. Oh, she'd planned this right down to the slight gap in her navy suit jacket that allowed him to see the lacy edge of her blouse.

"How much do I have to pay you to meet with Laurel?" he asked abruptly.

She gaped at him. "What?" Fury straightened her spine and darkened her pale blue eyes. It shot out at him, heading straight for his heart.

Unperturbed, Jake took a sip of his drink and rested

one arm on the back of the sofa. He didn't trust her. She'd disappeared from her daughter's life once already. Why should anything be different now?

"Mr. Masters, you don't know what you're talking about. I agreed to see you because I care about—"

He stiffened, but she stumbled on without saying "my."

"—your daughter. I don't see what money has to do with it." The fury abated. Her full mouth trembled slightly. "I just want to see her and t-talk to her."

"You expect me to believe that?"

"Why would I lie?"

"You took money easy enough the last time."

She flushed. The bright color didn't complement her freckles or her hair. "It was necessary. I needed it to pay the medical expenses. My mother couldn't afford insurance."

A poor girl with a struggling single mother. He didn't want to buy into the lie. The point was she had taken a large sum of money. He frowned, trying to remember the report he and Ellen had read so many years ago. Had Anne Baker had a father? He vaguely recalled the mention of the man running off. Ellen had said that was why she'd gotten pregnant in the first place. Jake had told his wife it was more likely that Anne Baker hadn't bothered to say no some night in the back of a pickup.

He leaned forward. "Just so we understand each other. I've checked with my attorney. You have no legal or financial rights to me or my child."

She reached for her glass of brandy. When she picked up the snifter, her hand shook so badly the liquid sloshed up the sides. She set it back down and looked at him. Pain straightened her mouth. "I know."

"And?"

"And what, Mr. Masters? You're the one who contacted *me*. You had to go through several people to get my name and number. I'd left the channels open because I wanted Laurel to be able to find me if she ever wanted to." She smoothed her pleated navy skirt, then clasped her hands together to stop their shaking. "So far you've bullied me and accused me of wanting your money. Anything else you need to get off your chest before you tell me about the problems you're having with Laurel and what I can do to help?"

He would have walked out the door. He was in fact ready to leave, except she raised her head and her chin jutted forward defiantly. Recognition clawed at his gut and with it, pain. Laurel stood up to him much the same way. She squared her shoulders and tilted up her head until her chin thrust out. With her hands planted on her hips, she would say, "Dad," stretching the word out to two syllables.

Until this past summer, he'd thought the gesture cute. But now, between the tears and stormy arguments, the door slamming, the threats, he didn't know what to do anymore. Ellen could have guided him, but Ellen was gone. He'd come here because he had nowhere else to go. And because he would do anything for Laurel, no matter the cost to him.

He rose to his feet and walked to the window. The view of the city stretched out before him. He ignored it. Turning to face the woman, he shifted until the afternoon sun hit her full in the face. He knew the light at his back would keep his expression in shadow. That's what he wanted. For Laurel's sake he had to know everything Anne Baker thought, dreamed or lied about.

"I told you my wife passed away two years ago," he said abruptly.

Anne watched him warily but didn't speak.

"Laurel took her death pretty hard. They'd always been close. She started running with a bad crowd."

The corner of Anne's mouth twitched slightly, as if a spasm of pain had caught her off guard. This was hard for her, he realized, then squashed any thought of compassion.

He folded his arms over his chest and continued. "We moved recently. It seemed the best solution for both of us. Laurel hasn't adjusted to our new home yet. She misses her friends. I'm sure that's why in the past couple of months she's started talking about her birth mother. She wants to meet you."

"As easy as that?" She rose to her feet and approached him. "Why don't I believe you? It's been thirteen years. Tracking me down is obviously the last thing you wanted to do. Why did you agree to this?"

She was close enough that he could feel the heat of her body. He told himself to ignore it, but he couldn't. Something flickered in her pale blue eyes. It took him a minute to identify the emotion, then he realized why. He'd never seen an open wound before—nothing as raw and exposed as the haunted emptiness that flashed through her eyes. She looked away quickly, then back, and by then, the feelings had been shuttered. But he'd seen them. It was her pain that allowed him to speak the truth.

"I didn't handle Ellen's death any better than Laurel did," he said. "Her grandfather, Ellen's father, also fell apart." He thought about his last conversation, then forced the older man's harsh words from his mind. "We've all spent the past two years missing her. I thought moving would make it better for Laurel and me. Get her away from those kids and bring the two of us closer together.''

"But it hasn't?" she asked.

"No. If anything, it's worse. She didn't want to move and now she hates the new place. About two months ago there was some program on TV about adopted kids finding their birth mothers.'' He shoved his hands into his pockets and walked over to the bookcase.

"She knew then?''

"Yeah. We talked about it from the beginning. She probably doesn't remember not knowing. Anyway, after this show, she started mentioning that she wanted to find her—you.'' He studied the titles of the books, seeing the words, but not really reading them or understanding what they said. Just thinking about Laurel made the knot in his gut double in size. She was his baby—he couldn't lose her. But she was slipping away before his eyes. Day by day she pulled back until he worried he wouldn't be able to reach her ever again.

"She seems a little young to make that kind of decision,'' Anne said, from somewhere behind him.

He didn't bother to turn around. He didn't want to see the look on her face. Compassion would be more than he could handle, and triumph, well, he didn't want to distrust her any more than he did.

"She ran away.''

Silence.

"She was gone overnight. Hid out in a neighbor's barn. When we found her, she was fine, but it made me realize she wasn't kidding. That's when I called the attorney.'' He fingered the thick volumes. Something about zoning laws, he noticed. "Just meet with her one time. That's all she wants. Then we'll be out of your way."

"I'll do anything I can to help."

"How about dinner tomorrow night?" he asked.

"W-where—" she had to clear her throat "—where would you like to meet?"

Not the hotel, he thought, knowing he was being a jerk but not able to help feeling he had to protect his own turf.

"How about my place?" she asked.

Why not? he thought. At least he would be able to see where she lived. There might be some clues as to the kind of person she was. Despite his claims of a single meeting, he knew Laurel wanted more. He could only pray the two of them wouldn't hit it off.

"That's fine." he said.

She scribbled her address on a piece of paper and handed it to him. He took it from her, careful to make sure they didn't touch. But she didn't let him escape that easily. She rested her hand on his bare forearm. Hot need bubbled to the surface. He tried to ignore the sensations, tried to step back away from her. He didn't want this in his life, not from a woman like her.

Her eyes held his, their gazes locked until the entire world faded leaving only the sound of their breathing to fill the silence. Her scent teased him. It was just a popular expensive fragrance. It wasn't special. But on her the perfume became something different, more tantalizing. He tore his gaze away from hers and studied the pale red of her hair. Strawberry blond? No, that wasn't right. Definitely red, but a lighter color. The thick blunt cut had begun to curl slightly, spoiling the smooth style. He could see the freckles on her nose and cheeks. He didn't like freckles. Never had. But he couldn't help wondering if they stopped at her chin or continued down farther toward her—

He wrenched his arm free of her light touch. Stop! he commanded himself. It had been too long since Ellen passed away. It wasn't Anne Baker, it was the fact that she was female. Dammit, it couldn't be her.

"Seven o'clock?"

"Seven o'clock," he said curtly, and turned to leave.

"Mr. Masters?"

He paused, his hand on the door.

"Do you have a picture?"

A simple request. Reasonable. But his irrational anger returned. He didn't want her to see what Laurel looked like. It was too much like giving in. That made no sense, he told himself, even as he knew it made perfect sense. He wanted to put off the inevitable as long as possible. Fate, and his teenage daughter, were forcing his hand.

He reached into his jeans pocket and pulled out his wallet. The front slot contained her seventh-grade school photo. Without looking at the sweet smiling face, he extracted the snapshot.

"Here." He half turned and thrust it out toward her.

Anne stepped forward and took it. He told himself to leave now, while she was occupied. He shouldn't watch this private moment. But he couldn't stop himself.

He stared at her small hand. It shook slightly. He raised his gaze. She stared down at the photo. Her lips trembled and her white teeth worried her lower lip.

A single tear fell on the picture. She carefully wiped it away. "She's very beautiful."

"Yes."

"She has my mother's eyes."

The simple statement caught him like a pistol shot. He grabbed his Stetson, then blindly reached for the door and yanked it open. He heard Anne call his name, but he didn't stop moving. Past the curious secretary, into the main foyer, then to the elevators. When the bank of doors remained stubbornly closed, he sprinted for the stairs and out toward the street.

Chapter 2

"What does she look like, Daddy?" Laurel practically skipped with impatience as they walked along the street.

Jake brushed her bangs out of her eyes. "You need a haircut."

"Da-ad!" Laurel shook her head. "You're avoiding the question. Is she pretty?"

He didn't want Anne Baker to be anything. Especially not important to his daughter. But it had already happened. Yesterday, Laurel had pounced on him when he'd returned to their hotel suite. He'd told her he'd met with her birth mother and that the three of them would be having dinner tonight. Now, walking along the wide street in front of Anne's high-rise condo, Laurel continued the barrage of questions that had flowed since the moment he'd announced the meeting.

"Does she look like me?"

He glanced down at his daughter's upturned face.

She'd sprouted in the past couple of years, and almost
reached his shoulder. Her hazel eyes, wide and framed
with dark lashes, gazed up at him.

She has my mother's eyes.

Anne's phrase echoed over and over again in his
mind, as it had since he'd escaped from her office. He
didn't want the reminder that Laurel wasn't completely
his. With her medium brown hair, easy smile and tall,
lean body, there'd been enough physically to let him
and Ellen pretend she was really theirs.

Now, he took his daughter's arm and tugged her to
a stop. He cupped her face in his hands. He studied her
wide full mouth and the dusting of freckles on her nose,
then the dark hair hanging long and straight down her
back.

He wanted to lie and say she and that strange woman
had nothing in common. Only he'd never lied to his
daughter. He wanted to tell her it didn't matter, but her
determination told him it did.

"Do you look like her? A little I guess," he said.
"Not so much your coloring, but other things. She said
you have her mother's eyes."

As soon as he spoke the words he wanted to call
them back. "You showed her my picture?"

He nodded.

Laurel's smile faded. "Did she like me?"

"I didn't discuss that with her. I left right after I
gave her the photo." He bent down and kissed her
forehead, then pulled her close for a hug. She was still
young enough to allow the embrace, but he knew that
in a year or two it wouldn't be cool to hug her dad in
public. "She can't help but like you, Laurel."

"Promise?"

Those wide hazel eyes he'd always thought so beautiful stared into his. He watched the shifting colors of blue and green and brown and knew that he would never look at them again without hearing Anne Baker's words. Another woman had given her those eyes. Another family's blood coursed through his child's veins. Another—

He forced the thoughts away. "I promise," he said, squeezing her briefly, then releasing her. "Everything is going to work out."

As they approached the high rise, Laurel craned her neck to see to the top. "I wonder which floor she's on. Do you think she can see us?"

He shrugged and buzzed the button by the glass door.

"Hello?" a soft voice said.

Beside him, Laurel froze. "It's Jake Masters. I've brought—" He had to clear his throat. "My daughter is with me."

"Come in."

The door buzzed and he pulled it open. Laurel walked in beside him. When they stood in front of the elevators, she reached for the button and pushed.

"Do I look all right?" she asked, glancing down at her dress, then up at him.

It had taken her the better part of the day to choose her outfit. Last night, after he'd told her about meeting Anne, Laurel had insisted on going shopping to find something to wear. The huge Galleria was just off their hotel. She'd tried on dozens of outfits, only to reject them all and decide on something she'd brought with her.

He'd hated to see her so frantic to please, but told himself she was only a little girl. Her desire to make a good impression was natural under the circumstances.

Yet it didn't feel natural, he thought as he gave her a quick smile.

"You look terrific."

"Thanks." She smoothed the skirt of her green dress. The drop waist made her look taller. There weren't any sleeves, but a ruffle began on each side, above her waist, and went up over her shoulders and down the back. A matching headband held her hair away from her face. Small gold earrings glittered from her ears. They'd had an on-going fight about makeup; he wanted her to wait until she was twenty-five and she wanted to wear it all today. Their compromise showed in the pale gloss on her lips.

When the elevator doors opened, he stepped inside. Laurel hesitated. He had to push the button to hold the doors open.

"Laurel?"

She shifted her weight from one leg to the other. Her mobile mouth straightened, then one side tilted down.

"I'm scared."

"We can leave, if you'd like." Oh, God, had he sounded too eager?

She didn't notice. "No. I want to meet her. It's just—" She shrugged and stepped inside.

As the elevator began to rise, Laurel slipped her hand in his. The warmth of her small hand and the trust behind the gesture eased the knot in his chest.

She watched the flashing numbers above the door. When the light reached fifteen, the elevator stopped. They walked out into a long hallway.

Anne's door was on the end. It would have a perfect view of the city, he thought as he reached up to push the bell. It sounded loud in the silence.

Laurel squeezed his hand tightly, as if she'd never let go. "I love you, Daddy."

"And I love you."

The door opened.

Anne stared at the tall man and the young woman beside him. She wasn't sure what to expect. Nerves had kept her stomach jumping all day and she hadn't been able to form a coherent thought since noon. She offered Jake a quick smile and wasn't surprised when he didn't return it. The man didn't like her, but that was the least of her problems. She drew in a breath and turned to the teenager.

"Hello, Laurel."

Even prettier in person, she thought with pleased surprise. A couple of inches shorter than her own five foot four, her daughter stood stiffly at her father's side, her hand holding on to his. Anne could see the white around her knuckles and the worry in her hazel eyes. Her mother's eyes.

She'd studied the picture for hours last night, searching for something of herself in the snapshot. She had found it in the way Laurel held her head as she looked at the camera.

Laurel gave her a smile that faded quickly. "Hi."

Anne fought the urge to pull her close and hug her. Laurel was obviously nervous. They all were. But none of that mattered. Her child, *her* beautiful child. The thought echoed over and over until she was afraid she would say it aloud. After all this time, she could see her and speak to her. It was more than she'd dared to dream.

"Come in, please." Anne stepped back and searched her mind for small talk. "Did you find the building easily?"

"Yes," Jake said curtly. He held on to his daughter's hand as if he had no intention of letting go.

The trio paused awkwardly in the foyer of the two-bedroom condo, then Anne ushered them toward the living room. At 7:00 p.m. in August, the sun was just beginning to slip below the horizon. Heat and haze created a shimmering blanket that separated the light into all the colors of a kaleidoscope. She'd opened the blinds, but left the sheers closed to diffuse the glare.

She glanced around her decorated living room and wondered how it looked to Jake Masters and Laurel. As she waved them toward the overstuffed white sofa, Laurel at last released her father's hand and stepped past him to one end of the sofa. She perched on the edge of a cushion. Jake walked over to the window and stood in front of it, a trick he'd used on their previous meeting to hide his expression from view. Anne hovered uncertainly, wondering what she was supposed to say. Part of her had foolishly hoped to be welcomed with open arms. She held in a sigh. It was too soon.

"Would anyone—"

"This is—"

Anne and Laurel spoke at the same time. Awkward silence followed.

"Would you like anything to drink?" Anne asked.

"A soda, please."

Anne looked at Jake. He shook his head. She walked toward the wet bar in the corner of the living room. After filling a glass with ice, she opened the small refrigerator. "What kind?"

Laurel glanced at her father. When he didn't say or do anything, she rose slowly and approached the wet bar. She offered Anne a shy smile and pointed at the red-and-white can. "That one, please."

"Sure." Anne poured the drink and handed her a glass. "You're very polite."

"Thank you. My mom—" Laurel stopped talking and took a sip of her drink.

Anne felt the flash of pain deep inside, then told herself she was being foolish. Laurel was right. The other woman—Ellen Masters—*had* been her mother. Ellen might not have given birth to the girl, but in every other way, she'd been her mother.

"Yes," Anne encouraged. "Your mother what?"

Laurel shrugged. "She always made me say things like please and thank you. You know, dumb stuff like that."

Anne studied the teenager. In her green dress with her dark hair swirling around her face, she looked more like a changeling than a young lady. All long legs and big eyes. She would grow to be a beauty. And she was *here*. Close enough to see and hear and touch.

Laurel looked around the living room. "This is nice," she said. "I like the white. Do you like it, Dad?"

"It's very nice."

He sounded thrilled, Anne thought sarcastically, then glanced at the bleached wood floor and white over-stuffed furniture. "I had a decorator do it. I was so busy at work that I never got around to unpacking boxes after I moved. As much as I love decorating, I never found the time. Finally I gave up and called someone to get the place together for me."

"We just moved," Laurel said, then took a sip of her drink. She ran her fingers along the metal sink. "I haven't finished unpacking. We don't have a lot of furniture yet." She shifted her weight from foot to foot.

Compassion flared in Anne. She wanted to make the

teenager comfortable. She leaned toward her slightly.
"It's not much fun, is it?"

"No." Her expression brightened then, and she
grinned. "I have a horse. I mean, I've always had a
horse, but now I take care of her. I'd rather be riding
or reading than unpacking—" The grin faded. "But
there's not much else to do. I used to spend a lot of
time talking with my friends, but they're so far away."

"Where do you live?"

"Colorado. It's pretty, but—"

"It's not home," Anne said.

"Yeah." Laurel looked surprised. "How'd you
know?"

"I left home once."

Those hazel eyes so like her own mother's met and
held hers. "You ever go back?"

Anne shook her head. "Just to visit sometimes. I live
here now."

"I'm going back." Laurel darted a glance at her father. Anne suspected the girl was trying to look defiant,
but only succeeded in appearing young and lonely.

"I'm sure you'll make new friends," Anne said.

"Maybe. But they won't be the same."

"Different doesn't mean they won't be as much
fun."

Laurel didn't look convinced. Jake stepped away
from his place by the window and approached the wet
bar. Anne looked up at him, then quickly turned away.
The anger flaring in his eyes was hot enough to burn
wood. He stopped behind his daughter and rested his
hands on her shoulders. The possessive signal came in
loud and clear. He didn't want or need her running
interference with his child.

Anne tilted her chin up a notch. She refused to be

intimidated by the likes of him. But the sensation of her heart's rapid pounding told her that as with Laurel's attempt at defiance, her bravado was only a facade. Still, *he* didn't have to know that.

"Would you like a glass of wine?" she asked.

He nodded. Despite his obvious ill temper and combative stance, he was, Anne had to admit, attractive. Perhaps not the hunk Heather had claimed, but certainly a man easy to look at. Yesterday, she'd noticed his appearance, but simply as a collection of features. Now she saw his sharp cheekbones and strong jawline made him look aristocratic. His well-shaped mouth that had yet to smile in her presence suggested a sensual nature, although she didn't want to think about that. He wore his brown hair short, not touching the collar of his pale blue shirt. New jeans skimmed over slim hips and hinted at muscular thighs concealed by the denim. All in all, a very impressive package. He'd left the Stetson home tonight so no shadows diffused the intensity of his gaze. She shook her head and fought the urge to sigh. A cowboy. Just her luck.

She managed to open the bottle and pour without spilling more than a drop or two. When she handed him the glass, he took it carefully, as if he were trying to make sure they didn't touch. The tension between them was obvious. Anne glanced down at Laurel. The girl stared up at her.

"Do I pass inspection?" Anne asked, forcing herself to speak with a teasing tone.

Laurel smiled slowly and nodded. "I wondered what you would look like. Sometimes I'd like stare in the mirror and think about if we had the same hair or something. Daddy says I have your mother's eyes."

"That's true. You and I both have freckles."

Laurel wrinkled her nose. "Do you hate them, too?"

"All my life." Anne grinned, then walked over to the entertainment unit and picked up the small photo she'd been given the day before. "I think you and I have the same smile."

Laurel moved to her side and glanced down. "Really?"

"Yes." Anne could feel the teenager's warm arm casually brushing hers. She wanted to pull her close and hold on forever. She forced herself to act calmly, all the while fighting new and wonderful maternal urges.

Laurel looked at her. "You have to smile now so I can see if we do."

Anne laughed.

"Gee, you're right." Delight flashed in her eyes. She sipped her soda. "I can't wait to call my friends and tell them about meeting you."

Anne caught her breath. This moment, more perfect than she had ever imagined, made her want to cry out with gratitude. She'd never thought she might actually meet the child she'd given up all those years ago. She'd never allowed herself to do much more than mourn. Of course she'd left information available so that Laurel could find her. But she'd half feared her child wouldn't be interested in her birth mother. She'd never thought she'd be with Laurel any sooner than her eighteenth birthday.

Laurel looked at her father. "What do you think, Dad? Same smile?"

"I see the similarity." His words sounded stiff.

"Similarity." Laurel chuckled. "I know that one, but he's always using big words to improve my vocabulary." She shook her head. "I have to ask him what they mean and he tells me to look them up in the dictionary. But I can't spell the words enough to find them, and I *never* learn what they mean." She rolled her eyes.

Anne returned her conspiratorial grin, then made the mistake of glancing at Jake. He stood beside the wet bar, clutching the glass of wine so tightly she feared he would snap the delicate stem. Their gazes locked and his cold rage threatened to freeze her into oblivion. His intensity shocked her and her laughter died. She fought the urge to step closer to Laurel and protect her from her father's wrath. She understood his need to stake his claim, even as she resented his selfishness. Would it be too much to ask him to share her for an hour?

"I should see about dinner," she said, then ducked into the kitchen.

Once alone, she pressed her hands against her flushed cheeks. She didn't want to know that this was difficult for Jake Masters. Just thinking about his assumption that she would expect to be paid to see her own daughter made her want to march right back into the living room and tell him to leave.

But she couldn't. Partly because she *had* taken the money they'd offered thirteen years ago. Even knowing that she'd had every right to accept the payment and that she had needed it to pay her medical bills didn't stop the feeling of shame.

Anne checked the oven. Despite the summer heat, she'd chosen to make a roast. The built-in rotisserie made the entrée foolproof, and the way her apprehension had shattered her concentration, she'd been concerned she wouldn't be able to handle anything more complicated. The meat was almost ready. She sniffed the pleasing scent and closed the door.

From the refrigerator, she pulled out green salad and the vegetables she wanted to steam. She'd already prepared her mother's famous potatoes and had them simmering on the back of the stove. After putting the vegetables into a pot, she walked into the dining room and set the salad in the middle of the table, then returned to the living room.

Jake stood by the window again, staring out at the view. She wondered what he was thinking. Laurel bounced up from her perch on the sofa.

"You don't need any help in the kitchen, do you?" she asked, obviously hoping for a refusal.

"It will just be a few more minutes," Anne answered. "I have it all under control. But thanks for asking."

Laurel looked at her father as if to show him she'd done as he requested, then turned back to Anne. "It sure smells good. Back home—Dallas, I mean, not where we live now—we had a housekeeper who did the cooking. She was okay, but she wouldn't fix any good stuff. You know, like cookies. My mom—" Laurel suddenly stopped talking and stared at her empty glass.

Anne drew in a breath to fight the unexpected tightness in her chest. Silence filled the room. Laurel fidgeted. Damn. She was obviously uncomfortable. This was difficult for all of them, but as the child, Laurel was the least equipped to handle the situation. Anne glanced at Jake, but he had his back to them. Apparently she was on her own. She took Laurel's glass and walked over to the wet bar. The teenager trailed along behind.

"Ellen Masters was your mother in every sense of the word," Anne said as she popped the top on another can of soda. "I don't mind if you talk about her."

She handed the girl her drink. They looked at each other. Pain flashed through Anne as she stared at eyes so much like her mother's. The older woman had been gone eleven years, but she still missed her. Laurel must feel even worse about Ellen. "I know that you loved your mother very much," she said.

Laurel blinked in surprise.

Anne perched on the end table between the sofa and the wet bar. The teenager took a step closer. Anne drew in a deep breath, then reached forward and briefly touched the girl's arm.

"I'd like us to be friends, Laurel," Anne said. "We don't know each other very well so we're both going to say things that make us feel funny. I think we should keep trying until we get it right. What about you?"

"Okay." Laurel gave her a quick smile, then took a sip of her soda. "I'm glad you're not mad or anything. I don't talk about her much, but sometimes things just kinda slip out." She darted a glance at her father. Her voice dropped to an audible whisper. "Daddy gets upset if I talk about her."

Anne followed Laurel's gaze. Jake Masters remained in front of the window, staring out at the city. The sun had slipped below the horizon and lights twinkled all around. With his hands shoved into his pants pockets and his legs braced, he seemed more conquering hero than mere visitor in her home. At his daughter's words, his shoulder's tightened, but he didn't turn around or otherwise acknowledge that he'd heard the confession.

Anne decided it was best to return to a safe topic of conversation. "I'm not much of a cook," she said. "I don't get home from work before seven, and by then it's so late that I don't want to bother.''

"Mom cooks—" Laurel glanced at her father and worried her bottom lip. Then she took a deep breath and spoke very quickly. "My mom *used* to cook a lot. She made special things. You know, like gourmet foods? I didn't like all of it, but it was fun to try. There used to be parties with lots of people and I'd help sometimes. Once for my birthday, my mom decorated a cake with—"

"Laurel, I'm sure Ms. Baker doesn't want to hear this," Jake Masters said, without bothering to turn around.

"But, I—"

"Laurel." The tone of his voice made even Anne sit up and take notice.

The girl shrugged. More silence. Anne searched her mind for a topic of conversation. She didn't know very much about teenagers. Most of her friends had chosen the career path rather than marrying and having children. A few had recently changed their minds, but they were still in the pregnant stage or had infants and toddlers. Her cousin, Becky Sue, had teenagers, but Anne couldn't ask her for advice without getting a lot of questions in return. Questions she wasn't ready to answer. Anne didn't watch much TV, and she had a feeling her taste in music and movies was light-years away from the girl's.

In the kitchen, a timer rang. Anne sprang to her feet and raced toward the other room. "Dinner is almost ready," she said. "I'll be right back."

But her escape was short-lived. Laurel followed her into the kitchen and leaned against one of the counters. Like the other rooms in the condo, this one had been professionally decorated and the predominant color was white. The counters, floors and appliances gleamed. Copper pots provided contrast, while the bleached wood cabinets softened any glare.

Laurel watched with interest as she poured the steamed vegetables into a serving bowl. ''Daddy called you Ms. Baker.''

''I know.''

Anne thought she was lucky that was all he'd called her. His distrust and anger radiated like a giant beacon, circling through the room and lighting up all the corners. She felt so exposed having him in her house. It was difficult to act normally knowing he sat in judgment of every word she said. She half expected him to decide that she was an inappropriate role model and march his daughter out of her presence. If it were up to him, there never would have been a meeting at all.

Anne looked at the young woman glancing around the room. Curiosity brightened her hazel eyes, turning the multicolored irises more green. Long brown hair bounced and swung with each turn of her head. So alive, Anne thought. Bright and pretty and interested in everything. Pride swelled within her. She savored the sensation before allowing her practical nature to firmly squash it. Laurel was her child by birth, but not by environment. She had no justification for her pride; she'd done nothing to earn it. And yet—

She stuck a serving spoon into the bowl of vegetables and handed the container to Laurel. ''Put this on the table, please. Through there.'' She motioned to the dining room, off the opposite end of the kitchen.

And yet, she didn't want to lose her. Not after just meeting her. One meeting, Jake had said. But was that Laurel speaking or was it his own agenda?

Laurel returned. "Should I call you 'Ms. Baker'?"

"My name is Anne," she said.

"Anne," Laurel repeated. "Okay." She said it again. "Does anyone call you Annie?"

Anne smiled. "My mother used to. My cousin still does. Just family members I guess."

Laurel propped her elbows on the center island and rested her chin in her hands. "Can I call you Annie?"

"It's 'may I.' Not 'can I.'"

Anne hadn't heard Jake enter the kitchen, but he stood just inside the room, leaning against the cabinets.

Laurel straightened. "*May* I call you Annie?"

Anne hoped she didn't look as flustered as she felt. She understood that Jake wouldn't want her to be alone with his child for too long. Heaven knows what sort of corrupting influence she could be in two or three minutes. But did he have to be so obvious about it?

"I'd like that, Laurel." She thought about telling Jake Masters he could continue to call her "Ms. Baker," but figured he wouldn't appreciate her minor attempt at humor. "Here. The potatoes are ready to go into the dining room. Then if you'd like to wash your hands, the powder room is down the hall on the right."

"Be right back."

Laurel moved forward and picked up the dish. As soon as the swinging door closed behind her, Jake straightened. "You're handling this very well."

Anne pulled open the stove and shut off the rotisserie. "If anyone else were saying that, I'd think it was a compliment."

"It's not?"

She slid the rack out toward her, then began to move the heavy roasting pan closer to the edge. "I know it's not. You made your decision about me thirteen years

ago. There's nothing I can do to change your mind."
She lifted the pan and placed it on the counter. She
stepped back and glanced up at him. The bright overhead lights caught the gold flecks in his brown eyes.
She'd been right. Anger flared there, right alongside
distrust and a few other emotions she didn't want to
name.

"My main concern is Laurel."

"That much is obvious."

He raised his eyebrows, as if surprised she'd admit
that.

"Oh, you don't make it *easy* to dislike you, Mr.
Masters. You're judging me based on some very out-
of-date information. Even this minute you're standing
over me waiting to pounce in case I say something
inappropriate." She tossed her oven mitts onto the
counter and rubbed her hands on her silk trousers.
"Your only saving grace is that you obviously love
Laurel very much." She took another step back.

"Look out!" he said. "The oven is open."

He leapt forward and grabbed her arms, jerking her
hard against him. One of her hands got caught between
their bodies and she felt the cold metal of his belt
buckle. Her breasts flattened against his hard chest. His
thighs brushed hers. Their breath mingled as she exhaled sharply with the impact.

"What are you—?"

Their gazes locked. Something dark and hungry
flared to life in his eyes, and the flames turned the
flecks of gold almost iridescent. The fingers holding
her arms tightened their grip. It hurt and she told herself to pull away but she couldn't. Whatever had exploded in him sparked a response deep within her body.
The need, the want, raced through her like a fire storm

consuming dry brush. Everywhere they touched—his hand on her arm, her breasts mashed against his chest, their legs trembling against each other—electricity arced. The scent of his body—clean, masculine, he was not a man to wear cologne—made her wonder what he would taste like if she were to kiss him.

"Oh, my God." Gathering the last of her rapidly dwindling strength, she slipped free of him and leaned against the counter. The cool tile contrasted with her overheated body. They were both breathing heavily, as if they'd run five miles.

As if they had kissed.

Kissed. Involuntarily, she licked her lower lip. His mouth pulled into a straight line. No, she cried silently. Not him. Not now. Not like this. She swallowed and forced her eyes closed. Only then was she able to break the spell.

"You almost stepped into the open oven door," he said. She opened her eyes. He pointed. "You would have been burned."

She shook her head to clear it. "Thank you," she murmured. "I appreciate what you…" Her voice trailed off as she looked up at him. The fire continued to burn inside him, but the heat of flames had changed from desire to hate.

She saw the contempt steal across his expression. He blamed her for that moment between them. He thought she'd done it on purpose.

"Everything smells so great," Laurel said as she entered the kitchen. "When do we eat?"

Her presence dispelled the last of the tension between them. Anne turned her back on Jake. It didn't matter what he thought of her, she told herself. This night was about Laurel, and not about the handsome stranger who had adopted her.

Chapter 3

"The beach house is really big, with lots of windows and stuff. We lay around by the ocean. My dad and great-uncle go fishing sometimes, and my great-aunt takes me shopping." Laurel paused long enough to take another bite of potatoes.

"Sounds lovely," Anne said.

Jake remained silent. Anne told herself she shouldn't be surprised. He'd been nothing but silent since they'd sat down to eat almost an hour before. Laurel had chattered on about school and the friends she'd left behind in Dallas. Anne had explained a little about her job, but Jake hadn't said a word.

"We'll spend a week there," Laurel said after she'd wiped her mouth with her napkin. Her smile faded. "Then we're going back to Colorado."

"You make it sound like you're going back to prison," Anne teased.

"Worse. At least in prison you get time off for good behavior." Laurel stared at her plate.

Anne toyed with her wineglass. "I think you might surprise yourself," she said at last. "And you do have that great week by the beach."

"Do you like the ocean?"

"Sure. I love the smell of the salt water, and seeing all the people on the sand." She wrinkled her nose. "Hot dogs always taste the best on the beach, don't you think?"

Laurel laughed. "Yeah. And ice-cream sandwiches. At home, I never eat them, but there—" she shrugged "—I get one every day." Her hazel eyes widened and she turned to her father. "Daddy, can Annie come with us for a couple of days? You said I could bring a friend."

Anne was glad she'd spent the evening toying with her wineglass rather than drinking from it. If she'd been swallowing at that moment, she would have choked. She looked at Jake.

His tanned skin darkened, and his mouth pulled even straighter. She hadn't known it was possible for a man to look completely furious and devastatingly handsome at the same time. She clenched her hands into fists and waited for the explosion. Laurel stared hopefully, never realizing what she asked.

"I don't think that would be a good idea," he said, calmly.

Anne didn't know she'd been holding her breath until she exhaled it in a loud rush.

"But why?" Laurel asked. "They've got extra bedrooms. You *said* I could bring someone."

"No."

The teenager sprang to her feet. Her brown hair

swirled around her face and she brushed it back impatiently. "You're *always* like this. I never get to do anything I want. You *always* decide. I didn't want to move. I didn't want to leave my friends behind. You say it's for me, but it's *always* what's easiest for you." Laurel threw her napkin on the table and stormed out of the room. There were a few seconds of silence, then Anne flinched as she heard the bathroom door slam shut.

"I'm sorry," she said softly. "I didn't mean to start anything."

"Yeah, I'll bet." He stood up. "It takes her about five minutes to cool down, then she'll be out. I'd appreciate it if you wouldn't encourage her. We're spending the week with Ellen's aunt and uncle. I don't think they would understand if you came along." With that, he turned and left the room.

Jake was off by two minutes, but Laurel did finally emerge from the rest room. Her eyes were puffy and her face blotchy, but other than that, she seemed to have recovered from her outburst.

"I'm sorry," she said as she walked into the kitchen.

Anne put the last plate into the dishwasher. "It's okay, Laurel, but I'm not the one you hurt."

"I know. It's just he's so—" She scuffed her white flats against the wood floor. "He makes me so mad, sometimes. He doesn't understand."

"Maybe you don't understand so well, either."

Laurel looked at her. "You think so?"

"He's your father. He loves you."

The mouth so much like her own tilted slightly at one corner. "Then why's he always telling me what to do?"

"That's what dads are for. He's doing what he thinks

is best.'' She looked at the young woman who, except for a decision made thirteen years ago, could have been hers. Funny, she would have thought she'd give up missing her a long time ago. She'd been wrong. ''From where I stand, he's doing a fine job.''

''Thank you.'' Laurel flushed at the compliment. ''Maybe I should go tell him I'm sorry.''

''Maybe you should.'' Anne wiped her hands on the dish towel and gave the girl a gentle push toward the door. ''Now is a good time.''

''I can't.''

''You can. I know you can.'' Anne held open the door.

Jake had returned to stare out the window. At the sound of her voice, he turned and looked at them. She'd lived in her condo long enough to know that noise and conversations traveled fairly easily from the kitchen to the living room and that he'd probably heard everything they'd said. Not by a flicker of his thick lashes did he give that away. He stood, waiting. Laurel hovered by the door.

Anne gave her another nudge. The girl stepped forward. ''I'm sorry, Daddy.'' Then she flew across the room and into her father's embrace.

Jake pulled his daughter close and held her tightly against him. ''I know, sweetie.''

From her place in the doorway to the kitchen, Anne looked at the two of them. Jake knew he should be grateful that she'd been so generous with his child, but he couldn't bring himself to say anything. She stared at him, at the way he held Laurel, with all the intensity of a starving person staring at bread. He read the hunger in her eyes, and the loneliness.

Laurel stepped away and gave him a brilliant smile.

He forced himself to return it. When he looked up, Anne had returned to the kitchen.

Damn. He didn't want to like her. He sure as hell didn't want to feel sorry for her. And he certainly didn't want to remember what had happened that moment when he'd pulled her away from the stove.

"It's late," he said. "We should probably be going."

Laurel looked like she was about to protest, then seemed to think better of it. "Okay. When can I see Annie again?"

He should have been prepared. All the signs had been there. But he'd pretended that it would only happen this one time. Refusing another meeting was the best solution for all of them, but he couldn't. Not only because Laurel would fight him, but because he couldn't tell her why she couldn't see Anne Baker. He didn't trust the woman, but more than that, he didn't want to risk losing his daughter. Not when he'd just found her again. Neither of those reasons would make sense to Laurel. He had to decide what to do based on what was right for her, not what was easiest for him.

"We're leaving for the beach early in the morning," he said.

Laurel nodded. "I know Annie can't come with us to the beach, but I have to see her again, Dad. She's my birth mother."

That fact had haunted him ever since Laurel had first said the words. As long as he lived, he'd never forget the slash of pain when she'd told him she wanted to contact her "real" mother. He was grateful Ellen hadn't ever heard Laurel say those things.

"Can't we stop before we go back to Colorado? Just for a couple of days." Hazel eyes pleaded.

"One day. We'll stay overnight, then head back home."

"Thanks, Daddy." She reached up and kissed his cheek, then scurried toward the kitchen. "Annie, Annie."

Anne came out of the kitchen. She looked from the teenager to him and back. He tried not to notice how the pale peach silk shirt she wore brought out the color in her cheeks and darkened her hair to a more auburn shade of red. He looked away from the hopeful expression in her pale blue eyes, and the way her hands balled into fists at her side. If he'd been able to hear her conversation with his daughter when they'd been in the kitchen, it stood to reason she'd heard what Laurel had said. But she still looked nervous, as if she was afraid he would take it all away.

"We're coming back to Houston after our week at the beach," Laurel said, bouncing from foot to foot. "I can see you again." She became very still. "If you want to."

Anne smiled. "Of course I do, Laurel. I'd like very much to see you again."

"Great."

"We need to get going," he said. "It's late and we have to get up early tomorrow."

"Okay." Laurel hesitated, then ducked toward Anne.

Jake forced himself to watch the two women embrace. He saw Anne's eyes close as emotions chased across her face. He saw the tender smile, the brief kiss on the cheek, heard the promise to not forget their plans. He saw Anne scrawl her phone number down, Laurel take it and stuff it into her pocket. He saw his daughter approach him, happiness shining so brightly from her face, it almost blinded him. He saw it all and knew that he was close to losing everything to a woman whom he didn't like, or trust.

"Wait for me by the elevator," he told his daughter.

She waved once, then disappeared out the front door. Anne stared after her.

"You can be busy," he said.

Anne stared at him. "I don't understand."

"When she calls you don't have to see her if you're not interested."

A spot of color flared on each cheek. "I *want* to see Laurel again."

He shoved his hands into his pockets to make sure he didn't give in to the temptation to strangle her, then moved forward until he was directly in front of her. The kitchen door prevented her from backing up, although she didn't seem inclined to give any ground. The soft light from the lamps made her freckles stand out. He stared at the random pattern and told himself he'd always hated freckles.

"Why do you care?" he asked. "If Laurel is so damn important to you, why did you give her up in the first place?"

He might as well have slapped her. The color drained from her face and her eyes widened with disbelief.

"That's none of your business," she said, her voice low and angry.

"If it's about my daughter, it's my business."

"Get out!" She pointed to the door.

"If I leave now, I'm never coming back."

She parted her lips to draw in a breath of air. He didn't like the man he'd become these past few days. He was beginning to believe that Anne Baker's pain was as real to her as his was to him. He almost wanted to take it all back. But he couldn't. Laurel was his responsibility. The bottom line was this woman had once given her child away. Who was to say she wouldn't get involved with Laurel, only to dump her a second time when the relationship became inconvenient?

"What do you want to know?" Anne asked, her voice resigned.

"Why did you give her up, and why do you want anything to do with her now?"

She seemed to collect herself. The color returned to her face and this time she was the one to step closer. Less than a foot separated them. She had to lean back to look him in the eye.

"You're quite a bastard, Jake, aren't you?" She folded her arms over her chest. "You can threaten me all you want. You're the one holding all the cards anyway. I can't make you let Laurel see me. There's nothing I can say to explain my actions to you. There's nothing to justify what I did. You've already passed judgment on me. If I'd known the name of the family adopting my daughter, I would have gotten in touch with them, with you, right away. I didn't know. Not a day went by that I didn't hope and pray Laurel would want to follow the trail I'd left and find me." She walked to the front door and gripped the knob. "You go ahead and believe what you want. Just don't be too surprised when you find out you were wrong."

With that, she swung the door open. Laurel stood in the doorway. "Dad, the elevator's come and gone. I thought you said we were in a hurry."

He stared at Anne. From the rapid rise and fall of her chest, he could see that she was still furious.

He brushed past her as he walked through the door. Sparks flew between them, sending liquid need pouring through his blood. He gritted his teeth and kept walking. Behind him, he heard Laurel say goodbye again and promise to call. As the elevator doors opened, he swore Laurel would never have any contact with that woman again.

"Then we need to see to the executive homes. I think three should be—" Anne put down the papers she was holding and glanced at Heather. Her assistant continued smiling. "Why are you grinning at me like that? Do I have lipstick on my teeth?"

Heather shook her head. "You gave me this information two hours ago, Anne. What *is* the matter with you?"

Anne groaned. "My concentration is completely gone. The RCR Company relocation committee will be here at the end of the week and I'm not even close to prepared."

Heather leaned forward from the seat opposite Anne's desk. "Man trouble?"

"Don't sound so excited. No, it's not man trouble. At least not the way you mean it." She pushed her chair away from the desk and slumped against the back. "Laurel called me again last night." In spite of herself she smiled. "Told me all about this movie she'd seen. Boy meets girl. Girl turns out to be a vampire. They don't make movies like they used to."

Heather tilted her head and frowned. "But if your daughter is calling you every other night, what's the problem? I thought you wanted to stay in touch with her."

"I do. I love hearing from her. We talk about movies

and clothes and she tells me everything she's doing.''
Anne picked up a pen and fiddled with it. Just thinking
about Laurel was enough to give her a warm feeling
inside. She wasn't sure if it was genes or the way she'd
been raised or both, but Laurel had turned out to be a
fun, sweet, charming young woman. Their phone conversations were equal parts pleasure and pain. Pleasure
at the relationship they were building and pain at what
she'd missed all these years. ''It's not her, it's her father. He doesn't trust me. The worst of it is, I almost
don't blame him. If she were my child—''

''Isn't she?''

''Good question. I've been wrestling with the same
one for almost a week and I still don't have an answer.
All I did was give birth. Jake and his wife raised her.''

''So where does that leave you?'' Heather asked.

''Confused.''

''What are you going to do?''

Anne tossed the pen back on the desk. ''The only
thing I can do. Keep working on the RCR bid. Try not
to let the situation destroy my job performance.''

Heather placed her hands on the desk. ''When Wilson retires in four months, you're right in line for the
vice presidency.''

Anne nodded. ''I know. If I can get RCR to sign,
I've got the promotion. If not, Tim the Turkey gets it.''
She jerked her thumb to the office next door. ''He's
always hated the fact that I've done better than him
and I'm just a woman.''

Heather chuckled. ''That does make him cranky,
doesn't it? I'll go get you the figures for the RCR project.''

''Thanks.''

''When do you see Laurel again?''

"Day after tomorrow. I'm hoping Jake will have cooled off enough so that I can arrange to visit her in Colorado from time to time. I'd like to stay in touch. She's important to me."

"Sounds like everything is going to work out."

"I hope so." Anne shrugged. "I wish I knew how much of her wanting to be with me is because she needs a mother figure in her life and how much of it is to get back at her father. If I get too involved before I figure out the situation, I could really get hurt. I want a second chance with Laurel, but I'm not sure how reasonable that is. Or if I even deserve one." She rose to her feet and straightened her white linen jacket. "I know that my real life is here, with the company. Work is the only thing I can count on. I'm so close to that promotion, I can't afford to let it go."

Heather looked at her. "You've got it under control."

"It only looks that way." Anne smiled. "Still, I'm going to keep pretending I know what I'm doing until I figure it out."

"I think denim is going to be very hot this year," Laurel said as she fingered the cropped jacket.

Anne looked at the price tag and winced. "This isn't very practical, honey. It snows in Colorado and this isn't even lined."

Laurel grimaced. "Now you sound like my dad."

"Maybe your dad has a point."

Jake didn't bother entering the discussion. He didn't like shopping and given a choice, he would have stayed in the hotel bar and watched the football game on the big screen TV. But Laurel wanted to go shopping with Anne, as part of their day together. He was determined not to let the two of them spend any time alone. He wasn't concerned about Anne kidnapping the girl, or anything that extreme, it was more an issue of trust. Or lack of trust.

After the way they'd parted company a week ago, he'd expected Anne Baker to be uncivil, or at the very least, ignore him. She'd done neither. Except for a slight tension in her body and the way she paused before speaking, as if considering her words carefully, she'd treated him as if they were old acquaintances. She included him in the conversation, spoke highly of him to his daughter and consulted him on every clothing purchase. It was driving him crazy.

"But it won't be cold during the day. Not for a couple of months. And I'll be taking the bus to school, so I won't need a warm coat. Besides—" Laurel pulled the jacket off the hanger "—it goes great with that skirt we saw at the other store."

"The one that's too short?" Anne asked.

"I'm thirteen."

Anne grinned. "That doesn't make the skirt any longer."

"But it's in style."

"But you're still not buying it."

Laurel looked mutinous. "I'm the one who has to wear these clothes to school. You probably don't even own one denim skirt."

"True, but if I did, it would be bigger than a bandage." She touched Laurel on the nose. "Give in graciously. It's easier for all of us." Her smile remained teasing.

Laurel turned to him. "Da-ad."

He hated to agree with Anne, but he had no choice. He shook his head.

Laurel sighed heavily. "You guys have no sense of style."

"I know." Anne took her arm and steered her over to a selection of jeans. "How about something like this to go with the jacket?"

Laurel frowned. "You said it was impractical."

"Compromise."

"You're the best."

Laurel rose on her toes and kissed Anne's cheek. The older woman flushed with pleasure, then darted him a glance. "I hope you don't mind," she murmured.

He didn't know if she meant the jacket or the kiss, but it didn't matter. He was too busy trying to remember how to breathe again. Laurel had accepted Anne so easily.

The kicker of it all was that Anne was either a superb actress or not the bitch he'd thought her to be. In the last—he glanced at his watch—six hours, Laurel had run the gamut of her emotions. Anne had handled them all well. Not always easily, but well. Even the potential squawk about the short skirt had been averted by the judicious use of humor.

They came to a kiosk selling fudge. He bought three pieces and passed them out. The rich chocolate required drinks and by the time everyone had finished their snack, they were too tired to do more than sit on the level above the ice skaters and watch the antics below.

Anne picked up her purse. "I have to call the office," she said. "I'll be right back."

He watched her walk away. Laurel chatted on about clothes and accessories, but he didn't pay attention. He was mesmerized by the sway of Anne's hips and the way her tailored cotton trousers outlined her generous curves. The soft silky shirt she wore clung to her breasts and emphasized their fullness. So different from Ellen who'd had the height and figure of a fashion model.

He preferred long and lean to petite and curvy, he told himself. Besides, whatever it had been that had sparked between them was nothing more than nerves. They'd both been tense about that first meeting. Today, nothing like that had happened.

He leaned back on the bench and nodded at what Laurel was saying. Of course he'd been careful to never touch Anne, so his theory remained untested, but he was confident the problem had been solved.

"Oh, Dad, look at the girl down there." Laurel pointed to one of the skaters. The young girl jumped into a high turn, then landed and spun around several times. "She's so good. Can I go down and watch?"

Jake glanced around the rink, then nodded. "Stay by that bench there," he said. "No shopping."

"Okay." Laurel piled her purchases on the seat next to him. "I won't be long." She gave him a quick kiss, then hurried to the stairs. By the time Anne returned from making her call, Laurel had already found a seat in front of the skaters.

"Where's Laurel?" Anne asked.

"Down there." He pointed.

"Oh, aren't those kids incredible? I always wanted to learn how to skate but there wasn't an indoor rink where I grew up and we certainly never got cold enough weather to freeze a pond."

He shifted the packages and made room for her on the bench. Anne glanced anxiously from him to the seat, then carefully sat down on the far end. She held her purse on her lap. He could see the apprehension in her pale blue eyes. He didn't blame her; now that they were alone, he could feel his own concerns returning.

He shifted until he was facing her. "Everything all right at the office?"

She nodded.

Most of her lipstick was long gone. He studied her mouth, especially her full lower lip. The corners trembled, then curved up. He found himself smiling in return.

He raised one arm and rested it on the back of the bench. "What do you do?"

"I would have thought you'd have had me investigated."

He shrugged. "I did a little checking. I was mostly concerned about a criminal record."

The trembling stopped and she grinned. "Just from that bank robbery last year."

"So what do you do?"

"I work for a relocation firm. We help other companies move to the Houston area. We handle everything from permits to housing." She shifted toward the center of the bench, sliding one leg under the other. "Once I've signed a company, the whole team takes over to make the relocation flow smoothly." She moved her hands as she spoke and leaned forward. "There are all sort of details to be worked out."

"I can imagine."

Her eyes glittered with enthusiasm. "The hardest part is recruiting the company. A lot of them are moving out of the Northeast and California, but they don't all think of Houston as their first choice."

"You convince them?"

"I do my best. There's nothing like a little Texas

hospitality to persuade the unbelievers.'' She raised her eyebrows. ''Doesn't everyone want to live in Texas?''

He glanced down at the rink. Laurel perched on the edge of her seat and watched the skaters. ''My daughter sure does.''

''I know the move has been hard for both of you, but it'll get better.''

''I'm not so sure.''

''Once school starts and she makes a few friends, everything will change.''

He rubbed the bridge of his nose. ''I hope you're right. I couldn't take another summer like this one.'' He sensed she was about to start asking questions he didn't want to answer. ''How long have you worked for the company?''

''Since I graduated from college. There's been a lot of opportunity for advancement. I'm up for a promotion. To vice president.''

He glanced at her. Now, with her red hair curling to her shoulders, with the casual silky blouse draping the curves of her breasts, with most of her makeup worn away and a tentative smile tugging at her lips, she didn't look like anyone's example of an executive on the way up. But he remembered her cool confidence in her office, and the way she'd stood up to him. No doubt Anne Baker could play hardball with the best of them. And win.

''Good luck,'' he said sincerely. A hard-won promotion would keep her firmly located in the Houston area and away from his ranch in Colorado.

''Thanks.'' She moved her purse off her lap and onto the bench. One of the packages went sliding toward the ground. She grabbed it and set it back on the pile. ''Do you think Laurel is going to need anything else?''

Jake eyed the bags. "I can't imagine anything, but I'm sure she'll think of something. I still have to buy her a decent jacket and some boots, but we'll do that back home."

Anne nodded. "I, um, I had a good time today. Thank you for letting her call me."

"Look..." Jake cleared his throat and glanced around at the crowds in the shopping center. Teenagers walked together in groups. Rich matrons clustered around the expensive boutiques and young women pushed strollers through the open walkways. Conversation filled the multistory center, but their bench, tucked in front of the railing overlooking the ice rink, offered an illusion of privacy. "About last week—" He cleared his throat again. He'd been thinking about it for days, but that didn't make saying it any easier. "I was out of line. You've been great with Laurel. You could have made me pay for some of the things I said, and you didn't. I appreciate that."

Instead of looking pleased, or at least superior, Anne surprised him by flushing and staring at her lap. "Don't thank me. I want to see her again."

Jake stiffened. "We're leaving in the morning."

"I know." The words came out as a whisper. "I can't let go. I've spent all these years wondering about her, and now, to have met her and spent time with her..." She drew in a breath. "She's wonderful."

"Yes, she is."

Anne leaned forward. Her hair swung out and shadowed her face. "I don't mean big visits. Not alternating weekends or anything. I understand that I have no legal rights, but maybe just a couple of days over Christmas break or in the summer. A phone call now and then. Just to stay in touch."

The fear deep inside him grew with each word. He wanted to grab Laurel and disappear into the crowd. He wanted to take back ever meeting this woman, ever letting Laurel know she'd been adopted. But he couldn't. Not for Anne, even though he was finding it harder and harder to hate her, but for Laurel. She would want the same thing Anne did. Laurel would want more.

He looked down at his daughter. She was talking to another girl her age and they were pointing at the skaters. As if she sensed his gaze, she looked up, smiled and then waved at him. He waved in return. He couldn't refuse her what she needed simply because he was afraid of losing her. But by God, he wanted to.

"I'll let Laurel call you," he said slowly, not looking at her. "I would appreciate it, however, if you didn't initiate the calls or talk about a visit. I believe it should be Laurel's decision."

"Yes, of course." Anne smiled brilliantly. Her pale blue eyes practically glowed with happiness. She tilted her head. "Why are you being so accommodating?"

"Do I have a choice?"

"I think so." She folded her arms over her chest. "Oh. I get it. You're hoping that by giving Laurel what she wants, she'll get tired of the whole thing. By taking away the forbidden, you eliminate one of the attractions."

"Maybe."

Her smile faded, and with it the light in her eyes. "You could be right."

"Look, Anne, don't take this personally."

"Hard to take it any other way." She shook her head. "Jake, I know you don't like me very much. I understand that. I even understand what you're doing and why. If Laurel was my daughter—'' She stared at him for a second. "If I had raised Laurel, I'd probably be doing the same thing. That doesn't mean I have to like it.''

It was a victory of sorts, and he could afford to be generous. "This isn't about you, Anne," he said.

"But if you had your way, I'd disappear from her life, never to be heard from again?"

He looked at her. "Do you want me to lie?"

"That answers the question."

"I guess it does. If it makes you feel any better, you've changed my opinion some."

Her delicate brows raised slightly. "For the better, I assume. You could hardly think worse of me."

Now it was his turn to feel a little uncomfortable. He resisted the urge to shuffle his feet. "Maybe if you'd robbed that bank."

"Right." She held out her hand. "Truce?"

"Truce." He reached out and engulfed her small fingers in his.

Immediately electricity shot up his arm, through his chest and down into his groin. He wanted to jerk his hand back, but that would mean admitting she affected him. Yeah, right, as if he was supposed to ignore the practically visible sparks flying between them.

Her smile faltered, then faded altogether. They stared at each other. Awareness flashed between them, and a growing horror that they were both experiencing the same physical reaction. He released her hand. She pulled her arm close to her chest and massaged her fingers as if they'd been burned.

This wasn't happening, he told himself. It couldn't be. Not with Anne Baker. Ellen had been gone two years. In all the time he'd been alone, hell in all the time he'd been married, he'd never felt like this with anyone. Never. Not even with Ellen.

"Jake, I—"

"Don't say a damn thing," he commanded. He turned until he was facing straight ahead and rested his elbows on his knees. It didn't make sense. It wasn't anything. Just weather, or static electricity or—

"I'm sorry," she said softly.

"There's nothing to be sorry about."

"Are you denying—?"

"Yes." It was, he decided, an aberration of nature. He didn't care for curvy women, he hated freckles, except for Laurel's, and had never been attracted to a redhead. He glanced at Anne. Her hair wasn't even red. It was a paler color.

She folded her arms over her chest. "Have it your way."

"Can you explain it?"

"No, but at least I'm willing to admit it exists."

Before he could answer, Laurel came up the stairs and walked over to them.

"How was the skating?" he asked, grateful for the interruption.

"Terrific." She spun in a circle. "I wish I could do that." When her turn was complete, she leaned against the railing and stared at him. "Dad, I've been thinking."

Ever since Laurel had mentioned wanting to find her birth mother, he'd been carrying around a knot in his gut. At her casual phrase, the knot tightened a notch.

"About?"

"I'm not ready to leave."

He glanced at his watch. "It's not even six. I thought we'd have dinner here before—"

She slowly shook her head. "I'm not ready to leave Houston."

He shot Anne a glance, but her confused expression told him this was as much of a surprise to her. "School is starting in a few days," he said. "We have to head back."

"I don't want to go back. I love you, Daddy, but I want to stay here. With Annie."

Chapter 4

Anne told herself to close her mouth. She could feel it hanging open. No doubt she looked as shocked as she felt. She couldn't move or speak. Good thing, because the malevolence in Jake's gaze was enough to send her running for cover. Laurel wanted to stay with her?

"Please don't be mad," Laurel said to her father and twisted her hands together.

"I'm not." The anger faded from his expression, leaving behind intense pain, then he blinked and there were no emotions at all. "What brought this on?"

"I just met Annie, and now we're going to leave." Laurel gave her a smile that quivered a little at the corners. "I know you have to go back because of the ranch and all, but I could stay. I could go to school here. I know you didn't like my friends back home, but I'd be getting new ones here. Just for a little while, Daddy. Just so I can spend some time with Annie."

She spoke quickly as if she could convince her father by the volume and speed of her words.

Anne stared down at the pile of packages, then at the people walking by, and finally at Jake. She waited but he never jumped up and accused her of having planned this with his daughter. She was grateful for that. Laurel wanted to stay with her. She had to bite down hard on her lower lip to keep from grinning like a fool. Her daughter wanted to stay with her. It was a dream come true. Better than a dream because it was actually happening.

She glanced over at Jake and saw he was leaning back on the bench as if everything was fine. Her gaze dropped to his lap where his hands rested on his worn jeans. His fists were clenched so tightly, she thought his skin might split. Confusion, hurt and a desperate need radiated out from him. She could feel his emotions pounding against her like waves against the shore. Suddenly her own lighthearted joy began to fade. What would Laurel's staying do to Jake?

"Anne has a full-time job," he said, his voice low and controlled.

Work. Anne shook her head. She hadn't thought about that.

"So do you," Laurel said. She shifted until her feet were spread, then placed her hands on her hips. "Da-ad," she said, drawing the word out to two syllables. "I'm old enough to stay on my own until Annie gets home from work. I've done it before."

"It's more than just child care," Jake said. He ignored the way his daughter huffed at the phrase. "She probably goes to her office early and stays late. Who's going to take you to school? Cook your dinner? Help you with homework? What about your horse?"

What about me? He didn't ask that question, but Anne heard it all the same. What about him? What about her taking in a thirteen-year-old who she knew nothing about? The sense of responsibility overwhelmed her. Yet even as she thought of a hundred reasons why it was a bad idea, a part of her screamed *Yes, I want the chance to get to know my daughter.*

"Your father is right," Anne said, speaking for the first time since Laurel's announcement. "There are a lot of practical considerations."

"You have a spare bedroom," Laurel said. "I know. I checked when we were at your place for dinner." She looked pleadingly at Anne. "Don't you want me to be with you?"

"I—"

Jake cut her off. "Laurel, I've tried to explain why it's not possible for you to stay with Anne Baker. We're leaving for Colorado in the morning. End of discussion. Now finish your shopping or go up to the room. I don't want to hear any more about it."

The cold anger in his voice made Anne want to cower back against the bench, but Laurel was unaffected. She leaned closer to her father.

"I'm not going back with you," she said loudly. "You can't make me."

A couple of shoppers gave them odd looks, then hurried past.

"Dammit, Laurel." He rose to his feet. "Stop acting like a child."

"You just *said* I was a child. That I needed someone to take care of me after school." Tears threatened. "Annie, you want me to stay with you, don't you?"

Father and daughter turned to look at her. Brown eyes flecked with gold dared her to interfere and promised swift, angry retribution if she did. Big hazel eyes framed by thick lashes begged for a hint of caring and support. Slowly Anne rose to her feet. She told herself she was the stranger here, and it was up to her to remain calm. It wasn't easy. Part of her wanted to pull Laurel close and admit she would love the girl to stay with her. Part of her was practical and wondered what on earth she was going to do with a thirteen-year-old. And a small part of her, a piece of her heart, back in the place that was familiar with pain and loss, ached for Jake.

"Laurel, this isn't something we should be discussing right here and now. Let's go back to your room and we can—"

Laurel turned on her father. "You're making her say those things. I know you are. She *wants* me to stay with her. I know she does." Tears streamed down her face. She brushed them away impatiently. Several people stopped to stare.

"Laurel, he's not making me say anything."

"I don't need your help," Jake said, glaring at her. "You've done enough." He moved close to Laurel and put his arm around her shoulders.

She shrugged it off. "You're doing this on purpose, Dad. I know you are." Her voice caught. She sniffed and wiped her face again. "I know the truth. You didn't think I would figure it out, but I did. Annie loves me. She's always loved me. You stole me from her. She didn't want to let me go, but you made her. You and Mom." She stood stiffly, with her arms at her sides. Fresh tears flowed down her cheeks. Her skin was blotchy and her freckles stood out like painted dots.

Anne's heart went out to her. So much pain in one teenage child. They were all hurting in different ways.

Jake spun toward her. "Is this what you tell her when my back is turned? What the hell kind of lies are you—?"

"Don't talk to Annie that way," Laurel said, coming to stand in front of her father. "She didn't have to tell me. I figured it out on my own. You stole me from my birth mother."

The crowd around them was getting larger by the second. Anne felt a heated blush climbing her cheeks. She didn't like being the center of attention. She bent toward the bench and grabbed an armful of packages. "Here." She thrust them at Laurel. Quickly she picked up the rest, then slipped her purse strap up over her shoulder. "Can we please continue this upstairs in your hotel room?"

Jake glanced around as if just realizing the interested group hovering nearby. He took Laurel's arm and led her through the crowd toward the elevators. Anne followed behind.

The ride up to the room was accomplished in silence, except for Laurel's muted sniffs and the rustling of paper bags. Jake opened the hotel room door, then stepped inside. He walked over to the window overlooking downtown Houston and stood there, his back to the room.

Must be a favorite position of his, Anne thought, dropping her packages into a wing chair. Staring out into the great beyond like some cattle baron of the 1800s. Damn. Now what was she supposed to do?

Laurel let her bags fall to the floor. "Annie?" she said, then burst into tears.

Anne reacted without thinking. She opened her arms

and, when Laurel threw herself against her, she hugged the girl close. "It's going to all work out," she said softly, hoping she wasn't lying.

"No, it's not," Laurel said between sobs, her voice muffled against Anne's shoulder. "It's not. He won't let me stay with you. But I have to." She raised her head. Those familiar hazel eyes, her own mother's eyes, stared back at Anne. "Don't let him take me away *again*. Please."

"Oh, baby." Anne brushed her fingers against her daughter's cheek. For the first time in her life, she felt the warm skin and the dampness of Laurel's tears. She squeezed her tight, loving the lankiness of her daughter's growing body. She was going to be a beauty, but right now she was a confused, overemotional teenager.

"You look like a wet chipmunk," Anne said, teasingly.

Laurel raised her head. "My eyes and mouth get all puffy when I cry, huh?" She wiped her face with the back of her hand.

"I get puffy, too," Anne said. She touched her arm, briefly. "You've really dropped a bomb here, kid. I need to talk to your dad. Why don't you take your new clothes into your room, wash your face, then try everything on again to make sure you really want to keep it."

Laurel's eyes started to fill with tears again. "You're going to make me go back with him, aren't you?"

"I'm going to talk to your father."

Laurel gave him a quick glance, then gathered her bags together and escaped through a door at the end of the room. When she was gone, silence filled the elegant salon.

While she was trying to figure out what on earth to

say to Jake, Anne glanced around. The suite was obviously expensive. She figured a three-night stay would be more than her mortgage payment for an entire month. The huge parlor held two couches, a large entertainment unit, a wet bar by the powder room, two blue wing chairs and a dining room set in the far corner. Big windows filled one entire wall, giving a perfect view of downtown Houston. She stared out past Jake and figured if she was standing right by the window and looked to the left, she would be able to see her office building. She wondered if he knew that.

"I had no idea what she was thinking," she said when it became obvious he wasn't going to speak.

Jake turned away from the window, but he didn't answer. He walked over to the wet bar and pulled open the refrigerator. After removing two cans of soda, he popped the tops on both of them, then handed her one and sat on the floral-print sofa across from the entertainment center. He stretched out his long jean-clad legs and rested his cowboy boots on the coffee table. He hadn't worn his Stetson for their shopping trip, but despite the omission, he still looked like a cowboy come to the city.

She'd always been a sucker for a man who could fill out a pair of button-fly jeans. There was something lethal about the combination of hard man and soft denim. Even with the crisis Laurel had thrust upon them, Anne found herself itching to rub her hands up and down his thighs. Denim could transfer body heat just about better than any material she knew. That's why she never wore it. The fabric was too much of a reminder of her weakness. Cowboys. She took a long drink of the cold soda and wondered if the day could get any worse.

"She's only thirteen," he said at last. He leaned his head back on the sofa and closed his eyes. Lines of stress and pain tightened around his mouth. "I can't let her go."

"I'm not asking you to. I swear I didn't know what she was going to say."

He tilted his head forward and looked at her. Something dark and untrusting swirled in his brown eyes. "You'll have to forgive me if I don't believe you."

Anne turned away and started walking around the room. A couple of teen magazines lay scattered by the dining room table. Pumps and athletic shoes formed a pile by Laurel's bedroom door. An oversize T-shirt bearing the likeness of a popular cartoon cat was slung over one of the wing chairs. Anne touched it.

"I don't know her," she said, stroking the nightshirt. "We've talked on the phone three or four times. We've met twice. I don't know why she thinks you and your wife stole her from me." She looked at him. "I never said anything about that. We've never even discussed the adoption. I give you my word."

"I don't know you well enough to know if your word means a damn thing."

He wasn't making this any easier, but then he wasn't trying to. She drew in a deep breath and tried to stay calm. "I'd wondered why Laurel wasn't asking any of the hard questions. Now I know the reason."

"Hard questions?"

"You know. Why did I give her up for adoption? Why didn't I try to find her? That sort of thing. I was pleasantly surprised she was so accepting."

"At least one of us is happy," he said sarcastically. "Guess it's all going your way. Don't expect it to last. I don't know where Laurel got her ideas, but you and

I both know she wasn't stolen out of her mother's loving arms. You decided to give her up.''

He spoke the truth, but that didn't make it hurt any less. Still her discomfort would have to wait. Laurel was what mattered. She walked over to the sofa and sat on the far end. "Laurel must have seen something on TV or read it in a book," she said, ignoring his bad temper. "I know you don't like me or trust me. I know you didn't want me to meet her in the first place. That's okay. But I'd never ever do anything to hurt Laurel." She stiffened. She'd almost said "my daughter." That would have sent Jake over the edge for sure. "I'm sorry you have to go through this."

He grimaced. "I'm sure you'll understand if I don't believe that one, either."

She resisted the urge to throw something at him. "I'm *not* the enemy." She tucked one leg under her and shifted until she was facing him. "We have to work together and decide what's best for Laurel."

"We don't have to work together at all. You don't have any rights here. She's coming home with me."

"You're just going to tell her that?"

"Yes."

She put her soda down on the coffee table. Leaning toward him, she said, "Then you'll lose her. Don't let your anger at me and your fear cloud your judgment." She reached out to touch his arm. "Please, Jake—"

Without warning, he grabbed her wrist and held it tightly. She could feel the strength of his fingers and the heat from his body. He turned toward her, his brown eyes blazing with fire.

"Don't you tell me what to do with my daughter. You lost that right the day you gave her up."

Despite the anger and dark emotion swirling between

them, her body responded to his touch. Her quivering skin betrayed her. Sparks arced between the two of them. She could feel the individual imprints of his fingers as if the fire in his gaze reached down to sear her wrist.

He hated her more than he could say, he thought she'd conspired to turn his daughter against him, he correctly reminded her that she'd lost all claims to Laurel. And he could turn her on with the slightest touch. In her belly, wanting swelled, flowing higher to her breasts, and lower between her legs.

He dropped her wrist as if the fire that had been consuming her suddenly turned on him. Before she could say anything, the bedroom door opened and Laurel stepped out.

She'd washed her face and tied her hair back into a ponytail. With her scrubbed skin, and wearing a matching shorts set, she looked more like a child than a young lady. But there was a knowing sadness in her eyes.

"Daddy, don't be mad at me."

"I'm not mad," he said, sounding weary.

"But you don't want me to stay with Annie."

"No, I don't."

Laurel lifted up her chin. "You don't understand. And you won't give her a chance." She looked helplessly at Anne. "Can you explain it to him?"

"Come here, honey." Anne beckoned the girl over. Laurel stepped between them and settled on the coffee table. She angled her body away from her father. Anne straightened in her seat and took Laurel's hands in her own. She studied the short nails and stubby fingers. "You have Bobby's hands," she said without looking up. "He was a boy I liked in high school."

"My—" Laurel glanced at Jake. She couldn't say the word, but Anne knew what she was thinking.

"I dated him for almost two years. I thought we were in love." She gave Laurel a quick smile but didn't dare look at her father. "He was three years older than me. He rode in the rodeo."

"Really?" Laurel sounded pleased. "A professional cowboy. Cool. What did he do?"

"He rode bulls."

"That's dangerous."

"I know." With the telling, the memories threatened. It was easy to keep them locked up day after day, until she almost forgot she had them in storage. Now they came forward into her mind, a kaleidoscope of moments. Bobby so tall and handsome, laughing. His hot, eager young body. Her inexperienced desire to please. The devastating pain when he'd left her.

"He started doing well at local events," she continued, "so he left to go on the national circuit. When I found—" She cleared her throat.

Laurel squeezed her hands, then released her. "It's okay."

The sofa cushions shifted. Anne risked a quick glance and saw Jake leaning forward to grab her soda, then he handed it to her. His brown eyes gave nothing away, but the set of his mouth was kind. He, too, was handsome. But where Bobby had still carried the soft lines of youth, Jake was a man. Hard muscles defined his broad chest and arms. Lines fanned out from his eyes. Scars marred the male beauty of his large hands, and five o'clock shadow darkened the unyielding line of his jaw.

"Thank you," she said, taking the can. They didn't touch and she was grateful. The soft drink soothed her throat. "When Bobby left Paradise, he also left me. Us." She touched Laurel's leg. "I had a full scholarship to Vassar. I'd always promised my mother I'd make something of myself, use the opportunities that she'd never been given. I promised her I'd have the life she couldn't provide. Nobody stole you, Laurel. I gave you up."

The girl seemed to fold in on herself. Her shoulders drooped and she rested her forearms on her legs. Jake surprised Anne by scooting forward on the sofa, picking up his daughter and pulling her onto his lap. Laurel snuggled against him, but didn't cry.

Now Anne fought the tears. The lines had been drawn and she'd been left on the outside. Still, there was more to the story. Laurel deserved to know the entire truth.

"My mother had a friend who was an attorney. He told me I could choose a private adoption. That way I'd get the chance to know who was taking my baby, plus it would be easier to leave information so that if you wanted to get in touch with me when you were eighteen, you could."

Laurel raised her head and smiled hopefully. "Really? You wanted me to find you?"

"Of course."

Jake kissed the top of Laurel's head. "When you're not being a brat, you're an okay kid. Why wouldn't she want to know you?"

"Da-ad!" His daughter gave him a mock punch in the arm, then wiggled out of his embrace. "I understand now, Annie. Thanks for telling me."

She looked surprisingly calm, Anne thought, and wondered when the other shoe was going to fall. "What did you understand?"

Laurel grinned. "I know my mom and dad didn't steal me. You had to give me up. You didn't want to, though." She turned to her father. "See, Daddy, Annie needs me to stay with her. She's been waiting all this time for me."

Anne stared helplessly at Jake. "I'm only making this worse. I'm sorry. You're her father, you tell her."

"Tell me what?"

Jake rose from the sofa and walked over to the wet bar. He opened the small refrigerator, but instead of soda, this time he pulled out a beer.

"Laurel, you're too young to understand this."

She spun to face him and planted her hands on her hips. "I *am* not. You just don't want me to stay here with Annie."

She had him dead to rights with that one, he thought. He didn't want her to stay. He didn't want her out of his sight ever, but that wasn't an option. He could try to keep her safe, but he couldn't keep her from growing up.

He took a long drink, then set the can on the counter of the bar. He had to be honest—it wasn't her growing up that scared him, it was her growing away. These last two years. Damn.

"I know the move has been hard for you, Laurel," he said finally "It's been hard for me, too. But staying with Anne Baker doesn't solve any of that."

"Why do you have to say her name like that?" Laurel asked. "'Anne Baker,'" she said, her voice low and mocking. "Why don't you like Annie?"

Because she scares me, he answered silently. Anne Baker could finish what his two years of emotional withdrawal had started. She could steal away his child. His guilty conscience told him that Laurel's actions were a punishment for not being there when she needed him. But it had been so hard to keep it together after Ellen had died. On top of those feelings had been the nagging need for the one thing he could never have: a child of his own. What the hell kind of a man couldn't even father a child?

"Your dad is being cautious with you, Laurel," Anne said, rising and standing behind the girl. She rested her hands on his daughter's shoulders. He hated the possessiveness of the gesture. "You should be pleased he cares so much."

Jake was about to inform her that he didn't need her help when Laurel twisted free. "He doesn't care about me. If he cared he wouldn't have taken me away from all my friends. He wouldn't take me back to that horrible house. He wouldn't take me away from you. I'm staying with Annie, Daddy."

"You're not and that's final." He slammed the can on the bar.

Father and daughter stared at each other. His heart broke in the face of her anger, but he wouldn't let her see how she was tearing him apart. How in God's name was he going to raise a teenage girl on his own? When had loving her more than anything ceased to be enough?

"You can't make me," she cried. "I'll run away and keep running away until you can't find me." She tore across the room and slammed her door shut behind her.

He closed his eyes at the harsh sound. He'd earned her wrath, he acknowledged to himself. The shock of Ellen's death, his guilt at being free of their failing marriage, the second-guessing about what he could have done differently had taken their toll. Too many nights he'd stayed alone in his study wondering, mourning, not paying attention to his growing daughter. She'd become a stranger to him. She was the only thing good and decent in his life, and he'd lost her.

"I can fix this," Anne said. She crossed the carpeted floor to the bar. With her head held high and her chin thrust out defiantly, she looked like a warrior preparing for battle. "I'll tell her that I don't want her to stay with me."

"Is it the truth?"

"No." Anne gave him a faint smile. "But as you pointed out earlier, there is a lot of work involved with raising a child, even a half-grown one. It would require me to make changes in my life. I'd like to think that I would handle it all beautifully, but that's not true."

"I appreciate the offer," he said, "but it won't work."

"Why? She won't want to come if she thinks she's not welcome."

"Laurel doesn't need another rejection in her life. Especially not from you." He grimaced. "As her birth mother you've been vested with almost magical powers. If that image was destroyed, I don't know what would happen to her. Whatever my feelings on the matter, Laurel comes first." He was tempted by her offer, but he owed his daughter better than that.

"The problem is time," Anne said. "If only it was the beginning of summer rather than the end. I'm sure that after a few weeks of hanging around with me, Laurel would see that I wasn't the answer to all her problems."

"You start to wear a little thin after the honeymoon stage, Baker?" he asked.

She folded her arms and leaned one hip on the bar.

''Not always, *Masters*,'' she said, then grinned. ''But I think I might lose my magical powers.''

He relaxed a little. She was right. Laurel wouldn't take all that long to become disenchanted. It didn't even have to go that far. He was willing to compromise and let Laurel visit Anne. She just couldn't live there permanently.

''Why would you be willing to lose status with her?'' he asked, resting his forearms on the bar.

''Because I want a real relationship with Laurel. Not a pretend one. She has fantasies about me. I'm bound to disappoint her.'' She shrugged. ''Once that happens and is behind us, then we can get on with the business of being friends.''

He wanted to believe her, but he couldn't. There was too much at stake. ''That's all you want?''

''That's the only place left in her life. Ellen was Laurel's mother. I know that.''

''You're ignoring the fact that you're everything Laurel wants to be. Attractive, successful and independent.'' He'd spoken without thinking and now wanted to call the words back.

Instead of taking advantage of his slipup, Anne blushed. ''Maybe we can work something out.''

He was angry at himself for complimenting her. He let the energy of his displeasure fuel him. ''There's no time. Laurel's school starts in a week. I have horses being delivered and a ranch to run. I can't wait around for a thirteen-year-old girl to get her head on straight.''

''All right,'' she said, leaning toward him. Her pale blue eyes flashed with defiance. ''What do you plan to do about our little problem then?''

''Take you with us.''

Chapter 5

"You're going to *what?*" Heather asked, staring at Anne as if she'd lost her mind.

Anne smiled at her. "Take a two-month leave of absence."

"From work? You? I can't even remember the last time you took a vacation."

"I went to Cancun last year."

Heather shook her head. "That was over a long weekend. Taking off two extra days doesn't count as a vacation. What about the RCR contract?"

Anne glanced down at her notes, then looked back at her assistant sitting in the leather chair in front of her desk. "I've got most of the information mapped out. I'm going to have you meet with them in my place."

"Me?" Heather looked horrified. "Alone?"

"You'll be fine."

"But I've never done anything like that alone. I can't—"

Anne held up her hand to silence her. "I've spoken with Mr. Wilson and he's in complete agreement. We both think you're ready. Besides, if I get offered the promotion to vice president, don't you want a shot at my job?"

Heather wrinkled her nose. "I guess."

Anne grinned. "I'm overwhelmed by your enthusiasm."

"I'd like the big raise and the office," Heather said, looking around. "But I don't want to work the hours you do, Anne. I have a little boy who wants to see his mother now and then."

"I understand. You wouldn't have to put in all the hours I do. You have different priorities. I've always wanted to get to the top." Anne leaned back in her chair. Her need to get ahead wasn't just about earning more money or the prestige of being a vice president at the firm. She worked hard because work was the only place she ever really fit in. Now all that was at risk. Of course she was pleased about spending two months getting to know Laurel, but she had a sense of ambivalence about the whole situation. What price was she going to pay career-wise? Was she a horrible person for even thinking that? She told herself that of course Laurel had to come first, but that didn't mean she wasn't worried.

"Two months is a long time to be gone," Heather said, as if she could read her mind.

"I know." Anne sighed. "But the choice is between my career and my child. How can I choose my career? Laurel needs me, and I welcome the opportunity to get to know her. Selfishly, I can't help wishing all of this could have taken place in Houston.''

Heather winked. ''At least you'll be spending two months with her hunky father.''

''He doesn't like me very much.''

''Why?'' Heather sounded shocked. ''Everyone likes you.''

''Except Jake Masters and Tim the Turkey,'' Anne said, jerking her head toward the next office.

''Tim's scared he's going to lose the promotion to a woman.'' Heather stood up and smiled. ''For what it's worth, I think you're doing the right thing, Anne. You're getting a second chance with your daughter, and that's worth any price. I know your career is the most important part of your life, but maybe these two months will show you there's more to living than convincing companies to relocate in Houston.''

''Bite your tongue.'' Anne laughed. ''I'll be checking in regularly. You have the phone number there if you need me. Don't be afraid to call.''

Heather walked to the door, then turned back. ''Have a good time finding out how the other half lives. It wouldn't kill you to let a man into your life.''

Anne waved her out of the room. ''Get back to your desk before I give the RCR account to someone else.''

''I'm trembling with fear.'' Heather chuckled, then pulled the door shut behind her.

Anne turned her chair until she was staring out the large window. Ten days ago if someone had told her she would be taking a two-month leave of absence from her job so that she could get to know the child she'd given up for adoption thirteen years ago, she would have assumed that person was crazy. Now she was starting to question her own sanity. Was she making a huge mistake or was she setting everything right?

She still remembered the shock she'd felt when Jake had told her she was coming with them to Colorado. She'd started to tell him that it was impossible for her to leave work and just pack up for two months. But she hadn't. Maybe it had been because she'd thought about what Heather had said. She was getting a second chance with her daughter. Maybe it was because she wanted to store up memories for the times when she was alone. But mostly it was because of guilt. Although she'd missed Laurel and had never stopped thinking about her, giving up her child had allowed her to get on with her life. She'd never had to balance a baby and school, or a toddler and a career. She'd never had to worry about working late, child care, measles, or any of the problems of being a single mother. She'd taken the easy way out. She owed Laurel, regardless of what it cost.

She swiveled around to face her desk, then picked up the phone. After punching in a familiar number, she waited until she heard a voice say, "Hi, hold on," followed by a stream of instructions that included telling her youngest to stop chewing on the dog, and promises that yes, they were having hot dogs for dinner.

"Hi, Becky Sue."

"Annie. How are you darlin'? I haven't heard from you in forever. You callin' me from that fancy office of yours?"

"Yes."

"I bet you've got the air-conditionin' set just right. Out here it's hotter than a— Little Joey, I told you to stop chewin' on that dog. You're gonna make yourself sick. Stop it before I paddle you good. Sorry. These kids are driving me crazy. I can't hardly wait for school to get started.''

Anne leaned back in her chair and smiled. Becky Sue, her only cousin, had stayed behind in their small west Texas town. She'd married a local boy and had five children.

"I have some news," Anne said.

"You've gone and got yourself another promotion?"

"No. I've heard from my daughter."

She heard a loud thump as something was knocked over by one of the children, then Becky Sue's voice laced with excitement. "Why, darlin' that's just wonderful. I'm happy for you. You must have been surprised. What happened?"

Anne quickly explained about Jake's visit and the subsequent meetings with Laurel.

"Stolen," Becky Sue said. "I wish someone would come and steal some of my kids."

Anne laughed. "You know you don't mean that."

"It's true, but some days, I sure wouldn't mind. So you gonna live with this man and your little girl? What about your fancy job?"

"I'm taking a leave of absence." Anne picked up a pencil and toyed with it. Becky Sue would do anything in the world for her, she knew that. Anne wasn't afraid her cousin would say no to the favor she was about to request. She was afraid of what she would hear along with the agreement. Becky Sue had the disconcerting habit of telling everyone exactly what she thought of a situation. "We're driving from Houston to his ranch in Colorado. I thought we could stop by for a bit."

"You're always welcome here, Annie Jo. You know

that. There's plenty of air mattresses if you all want to spend the night.'' Her voice grew muffled. ''Joey, I'm gonna smack your behind. Leave that dog alone! You hear me?''

A loud squawk of displeasure followed by a woof from the oversize dog filled the receiver. Anne grinned. It was almost like being there. Sometimes she missed her old home.

''You sure you want to come back to all this?'' Becky Sue asked.

''I'm sure. I was forced to give her up. I thought if I brought her to Paradise, she might realize I made the best decision for both of us.''

''You know, darlin', I think the world of you. I've always been so proud of your education and your job. You've been real generous with clothes for the kids. And I know you're putting money away for trade school, or even college, but only little Dolly seems to have the brains. Stop it,'' she screamed, then sighed. ''I doubt little Joey's gonna live to grow up if he keeps chewin' on that dog. Anyway, you're a good friend, just like a sister to me. I've always wanted you to find some happiness. I'd like to meet your girl. But you be careful, Annie Jo. You say you want to show her that you made the right choice. Seems to me you're the one who needs convincin'.''

The knot in her belly was from nerves and the early hour, Anne told herself as she zipped up her suitcase. It was completely normal and would go away as soon as they got going. A sharp buzz made her jump. She hurried over to the security panel and spoke. ''Yes?''

''Annie, we're here,'' Laurel said, sounding awake

and cheerful despite the fact that it wasn't even seven o'clock a.m. "Are you ready?"

"Sure. Come on up." She pushed the release button.

After taking one last look around her bedroom, Anne pulled the suitcase off the bed and rolled it into the living room. Her makeup, a change of clothes and a nightshirt were in a carry-on bag. She rubbed her damp palms against her shorts and tried to stay calm. It wasn't working.

After what felt like an eternity, there was a knock. She pulled open her door. Laurel practically danced into the room.

"You're really coming with us," she said, grinning. Her brown hair was pulled back into a ponytail that bounced with her movements. She wore white shorts with a bright neon orange tank top.

Anne pointed at the suitcase. "Looks that way."

Laurel stepped close and gave her a hug. Jake followed his daughter into the room, but his greeting was more controlled. Anne knew he wasn't happy about the situation. She had just as many reservations as he did, but for different reasons. Still, they were going to be spending the next two months together. They had to find a way to get along.

"Where's your luggage?" he asked.

She motioned to the single suitcase standing in the center of the room. "I have this and that overnight case." She pointed.

"That's it?" He sounded surprised. "Have you changed your mind about staying for two months?"

"No. I don't have any cold weather clothes, so I'll get a couple of sweaters there. It's a horse ranch, right?

There's not going to be any fancy parties in town, so I didn't think I needed much."

Jake didn't say anything; he simply nodded and picked up the suitcase. "I'll take it and wait for you downstairs."

Laurel wasn't so circumspect. "Gosh, you hardly have any luggage. Whenever we went anywhere, Mom brought tons of stuff." She grinned. "She had this set of matching suitcases. There were four of them. The really big kind. Once, when we went to New York for a week, Mom brought twelve pairs of shoes. Dad and I counted. She had lots of pretty dresses and jewelry." Laurel's smile faded and her expression turned sad. "My mom was beautiful. Daddy and Grandpa always told her she could have been a fashion model."

Anne glanced down at her generous bust and wide hips. She wasn't overweight, but at five foot four and almost a hundred and twenty pounds, she wasn't anyone's idea of a fashion model. She picked up her carry-on bag, then her keys and ushered Laurel out of the condo. "She sounds lovely," she said, and locked the door.

"Oh, she was." Laurel pushed the button for the elevator. "She had dark hair, like Daddy's. It was long and pretty. She used to wear it up and then put on diamond earrings." Laurel looked at Anne. "Daddy says I'll get the earrings when I'm old enough. I want to wear makeup, but he doesn't like it." She grimaced. "Mom wore a lot of makeup all the time. She always liked to look put together."

She said the last two words with an affectation, as if playfully mocking her. When she giggled, Anne smiled with her. The elevator doors opened and they stepped inside.

On the trip down, Laurel continued to chatter on about the charms Ellen Masters had possessed. Anne started feeling more dowdy and inadequate by the minute. Maybe she should have packed some better clothes, she thought as they stepped into the foyer of the building. She didn't own much jewelry. A good portion of her extra income went to Becky Sue to help with the five kids. She'd thought about packing that silk dress, but had decided against it.

They stepped into the sunshine. Jake was waiting at the curb. Her suitcase had already been stored in the back of his black Ford Explorer. He took her carry-on bag and stowed it in the back seat. Laurel climbed in after it. He held open the passenger door and Anne stepped up into the vehicle.

Jake walked around the front, then slid in next to her. As always he wore jeans. Today his broad chest was covered by a polo shirt that hugged his hard muscles. The bright red knit fabric brought out the deep color of his tan. The Stetson shaded his eyes, but she didn't mind that. He had invited her to join them because there wasn't any other easy solution. It didn't matter what kind of clothes she wore or the fact that she would never be as pretty or well dressed as his late wife. She would only ever be a thorn in his side.

They pulled out into traffic, then headed for the freeway that would take them west. Laurel continued to talk about clothes. Anne glanced down at her own outfit of cream-colored shorts and a pale peach T-shirt. She had broken down and bought jeans for her stay at the ranch. They were the only practical attire for that sort of environment. After all, she was going to be living with a cowboy.

She shot Jake a glance. He concentrated on the road.

Mirrored sunglasses hid his eyes from view, but she suspected he was staring straight ahead. He drove confidently, relaxed, but with both hands on the wheel. There was something about the set of his head. It gnawed at the back of her memory. What was it?

Suddenly she had to turn and glance out the passenger window so Jake wouldn't see her smile. He reminded her a little of Bobby. She looked over her shoulder at Laurel. No wonder they looked like father and daughter.

They stopped for an early lunch. Laurel continued to keep the conversation going. Anne nibbled at her hamburger and salad. She had to talk to Jake, but didn't know how to get him alone. She didn't want to get Laurel excited about stopping to see Becky Sue and cousins she didn't know she had, only to have her father veto the idea.

In the end, fate and Laurel intervened. "I'm done," Laurel said, pushing away her plate. "Dad, I need some new batteries for my Walkman and video games. May I have some money?"

He reached in his front pocket and pulled out some bills. "Buy plenty of batteries," he said, then winked.

Laurel rolled her eyes. "Dad *hates* my music," she told Anne. "He makes me listen to tapes using my headset."

"I like that," Anne said. "I think my taste is a little closer to your father's than to yours."

"That's 'cause you guys are old." Laurel took the money he offered and headed for the convenience store that shared the parking lot with the gas station and restaurant.

Anne watched her go. "She's a good kid."

"I know." Without his sunglasses and Stetson, Jake

looked more approachable. He'd even joked with his daughter. But whenever he glanced at her, he iced up.

"You're going to have to do a better job of pretending," she blurted out.

They sat across from each other in a booth at the back of the restaurant. He raised his dark eyebrows. "Pretending what?"

"That you don't hate me."

Jake leaned back in the booth. He stretched one arm across the red vinyl seat. "I don't hate you."

"You don't trust me."

"In my position, would you be any different?"

"No," she admitted. "But we're going to have to learn to get along. Otherwise the two months will be unbearable."

"Agreed."

This would be the time to say something conciliatory, she told herself. Instead she was about to throw the fat into the fire. She glanced at him. He looked casual and in control. A lock of dark hair fell onto his forehead. The hollows of his cheeks emphasized the firm lines of his mouth and jaw. He was much too good-looking. If he ever turned his charming smile in her direction, she would melt. Not only because she found him attractive and they seemed on the verge of starting a fire every time they touched, but because he was a cowboy. Everyone had a weakness, she just wished hers could have been ice cream or gin.

"I'd like to make a detour," she said, then stared at the table. She began folding her paper napkin back and forth, pleating the white square into a long thick length.

"A historical site?" He sounded faintly amused.

"Paradise. It's a tiny town near El Paso. My cousin Becky Sue lives there."

Both his hands slammed onto the table. She jumped. "What the hell are you up to?" he growled.

She risked looking at him. Fire leapt from his eyes, but these flames weren't caused by casual contact. They were fueled by rage.

"I thought—"

"I won't allow you to manipulate my daughter for your own purpose. If you think introducing Laurel to a bunch of relatives will further your case, you're dead wrong. The only reason you're here today is because I care about my daughter. But don't push me, lady. I have the law on my side."

She fought the urge to shrink back in her seat. Instead she forced herself to stare him directly in the eyes. "Have you ever been to west Texas?"

He frowned. "What does that have to do with anything?"

"Paradise is miles from anywhere. The population is about a thousand. It's hot, dusty and poor. Most everybody lives in a trailer. Some of them are lucky, because theirs is a double wide." She paused and glanced down at the table. She was systematically shredding her napkin. She let go of the paper and pushed the mess to the side of the table. "Laurel is still confused about what happened when she was born. I thought if I showed her where I grew up, if she could see that it was poor and ugly, she might be grateful for what she has now."

She folded her hands in her lap and looked at him. He leaned his forearms on the table. "That sounds good, but I don't believe you. There must be another reason you're doing this."

His assumption that she had something to gain pushed all her buttons. Her temper overrode her desire to get along with Jake. "Who dumped on you so badly you can't recognize a decent act for what it is?" she asked hotly. "What could I possibly gain by this? Even if Laurel falls in love with Becky Sue and her kids, there's no way *I'm* going back there to live. I worked damn hard to get out of that town." She shook her head. "I'm tired of you judging me. You've had months to get used to the idea of Laurel wanting to meet me. I've had less than two weeks. My entire life has been turned upside down. I've risked a promotion that I've worked toward. I've tried to be fair and do what was best for everyone. I've put up with your innuendo and bad temper. Yes, I gave Laurel up for adoption. Yes, I have a certain responsibility to her. I am doing the best I can with what I have. If you can't see that, you're a bigger fool than I thought, and you deserve to lose your child."

With that, she started to slide out of the seat. Before she could, he reached out across the table and grabbed her arm.

"Wait," he said. "Please."

Jake didn't release his hold until she settled back in her seat. Only then did he let go. But even after he'd propped his arm up on the back of the vinyl booth, he could still feel the softness and heat of her skin. As always when he touched her, need flared to life inside him. He hated his body's betrayal. If only he'd returned to the land of the living with any woman other than her. But he hadn't. And she was right. He was going to have to get over his problems with her or it was going to be a long two months.

He shifted to ease the pressure in his crotch. "I don't mean to be a complete jerk," he said.

"Only half a jerk?"

Her smile was tentative. She was always willing to meet him partway. He had to give her that.

"Only half," he agreed, letting go of his anger.

"I know you're afraid."

"It's hard not to be."

"You're not going to lose her."

He rubbed the bridge of his nose. "She might already be gone."

"No." Anne shook her head. "Laurel loves you. You're a good father."

If only that were true. But Anne didn't know about the last two years. She didn't know about how he'd withdrawn from his child so that he could mourn Ellen and figure out a way to deal with his guilt. She didn't know about how he wanted a son to carry on the Masters name. She didn't know that he was the reason they'd had to adopt in the first place. She didn't know he wasn't enough of a man.

"Not good enough," he said bluntly, "or she wouldn't have gone looking for you."

"Maybe it won't be such a bad thing."

He studied her. "Maybe not."

She wasn't unattractive, he admitted to himself. Just different from Ellen. Anne had let her strawberry-colored hair go wavy today. A headband held it away from her face with only a fringe of bangs falling on her forehead. Her pale peach T-shirt brought out the color in her cheeks. She had freckles on her arms. Maybe they weren't so bad, either. He'd noticed her legs were nice. She was more curvy than his late wife had been. His gaze lowered to her full breasts. A lot curvier. The clinging knit of her shirt outlined her shape. She would fill his hands. The thought made his fingers curl into his palm and the ache in his groin deepen. He sighed. There were a few single women not far from the ranch. He was going to have to consider taking up with one of them. He might not hate Anne Baker, but he sure as hell didn't trust her. The last thing either of them needed was to complicate their relationship with sex.

"You really think letting Laurel meet your cousin and her family is a good idea?" he asked.

Anne shrugged. "I don't see how spending the night in Paradise is going to make anything worse. Hopefully she'll see that I made the best decision at the time."

"You sound as if you regret that decision now."

She slid out of the booth. He followed. Before heading for the door, she looked up at him. "I've always regretted it. That doesn't mean I've figured out if I did the right thing or not."

"You've got the job you wanted, and soon you'll have your promotion."

"I know."

She started walking. The scent of her perfume trailed after her like a seductive call. It whispered against his skin, making him break out into a sweat. He tried to ignore the sway of her hips in her shorts and the way her hair bounced as she moved. He had a sudden desire to know if her creamy skin tasted like peaches.

When they stepped outside, Anne slipped on her sunglasses. "I'd like to get sodas for the next leg of the drive."

"Fine by me." He moved into step beside her. "There's a cooler in the back. We can buy a bag of ice and keep them cold."

Before they entered the convenience store, Anne stopped. "What about Becky Sue? Are we going to go by there?"

He was torn between wondering if it would help or somehow make things worse. "When the two months are over, you're still going back to Houston."

It wasn't a question. "I know."

"She's my daughter, Anne. Nothing can change that."

Her mouth twisted. "I know that, too."

"Then we'll stop."

"So Becky Sue's five kids are my cousins, too?" Laurel asked from her place in the back seat.

"I'm not sure. They might be your second cousins," Anne answered. "I've never known how that works."

"Dad, do you know?"

"Nope."

"Well, I guess it doesn't matter, just so long as they're relatives. I haven't had many relatives before, have I, Daddy?"

"Just your grandparents," he said. And now, not even all of them. He didn't want to remember what Ellen's father, Michael, had said and done, but he couldn't forget.

They were miles from any large city, in the dusty west part of Texas. Instead of the dirt and scrub stretching out on both sides of the road, he saw the look on Michael's face when he refused to spend time with Laurel on her birthday.

"Why would I care about some bastard brat? I only dealt with her for Ellen's sake. She's your problem now. Keep her away from me."

Jake had been stunned by his father-in-law's dismissal of his only grandchild. But Laurel wasn't his by blood. Michael had taken great pains to remind Jake of that fact. So Jake had lied to his daughter and told

her that her favorite grandparent was out of town on
business the day of her birthday. With his father dead
and his mother remarried and living in Florida, it had
been up to Jake to make the day special for his daughter. There'd been a pool party with friends, but the
happy event had been marred by sadness. It had also
been a going-away party. He and Laurel had moved to
Colorado the following week.

Even as he listened to Laurel and Anne talking about
her "new" relatives, he wondered what kind of reception she would get from Anne's family. Would they
welcome her with open arms or would they hold back
and hurt his child?

Laurel leaned as far forward as her seat belt would
let her. "What about—?" She paused. He glanced in
the rearview mirror and saw her troubled expression.
"What about your old boyfriend?"

What about my real father. She didn't have to say
the words. He heard them pounding in his head. His
hands tightened on the steering wheel. Anne looked at
him, but his sunglasses hid his pain from her. He swallowed. What if that boy—no, he would be a man
now—staked some claim on Laurel? He didn't want to
hear what she would tell Laurel, didn't want to know
that another man was his baby's real father.

"He didn't have much family," Anne said. "I think
they're all gone. Either passed away or moved somewhere else."

That was something, Jake thought grimly. That only
left the man himself. He shook his head. Funny how
all this time he'd been grateful that Ellen wasn't around
to hear Laurel talking about her birth mother. He'd
never thought about himself. About the man who had
given life to his child. About the man who might now

take her away. What good was the law when this stranger might steal her heart?

He should have left, he thought with sudden clarity. He should have left the marriage and taken Laurel with him. Those last years with Ellen had been horrible for all of them. The fights, the stony silences. Her bitter accusations that he had better not leave her, not after she stayed all those years, not when she'd adopted a child when she could have easily left him and had her own baby with another man. How many times had she thrown his sterility in his face? How many times had he raged at God for depriving him of a son?

"Is B-Bobby still there?" Laurel asked quietly, stuttering over the name.

Anne turned in her seat and smiled gently at Laurel. "A couple of months before you were born he was killed by a bull at a rodeo."

The relief was sweet. Jake let out the breath he'd been holding and relaxed.

"Oh."

Jake watched Laurel in the mirror. She dropped her chin to her chest and flopped back in the seat.

"At least I've got you," she said.

"And your dad," Anne said quickly.

"I'll always have him," she said matter-of-factly, then slipped on her headset. She flipped on the tape recorder and started bouncing with the beat of the music.

Anne shifted to face front. She reached out her fingers and gently touched his forearm. "You okay?"

"Fine." Except for the heat boiling between them.

"I probably should have told you about Bobby sooner. I didn't think that you'd worry."

"I wasn't worried."

She chuckled. He glanced at her.

"You're a lot of things, Jake," she said. "But not a very good liar."

He checked the mirror, but Laurel was involved with her music. "Maybe I *was* a little concerned about having to fight some rodeo cowboy for my kid."

"Bobby burned too bright to live very long. I always thought he was destined to die young. I think that was part of his appeal." She looked out the window. "The turnoff is in about twenty miles."

"We're really in the middle of nowhere."

"Tell me about it. I grew up here."

As they got closer to Paradise, he could feel her tension growing. Soon they turned off the highway onto a two-lane road. It was late afternoon, but the sun beat down unmercifully. The car's air-conditioning was set to high, but the temperature inside continued to climb. Up ahead he could see a cluster of tired buildings, surrounded by dirt and a few low-lying bushes. There was an elementary school, a diner, a gas station. The general store looked about a hundred years old. An old couple sat on their front porch rocking. Several of the side streets were paved, but some weren't.

"Welcome to Paradise," Anne said. She held herself so stiffly, he wondered if she would snap if he touched her.

"You want to keep going?" he asked when he saw a sign pointing back to the highway.

"More than you know. There's something about coming back that makes me feel—" She gave him a quick smile. "Ghosts. Can't seem to shake 'em. It's through here." She pointed to a narrow lane that dead-ended in a trailer park.

A few limp trees grew in the dust. Rusting cars sat

on blocks. Barefoot kids played around a scraggly bush. His new Ford Explorer was as out of place as a Thoroughbred at a mule sale.

He heard a burst of music as Laurel pulled off her headset. "You grew up here?"

"I spent seventeen years in Paradise. All I ever dreamed about was getting away. Becky Sue's trailer is at the end."

He drove slowly to avoid the children and dogs crowding the dirt trail. Jake had assumed Anne wanted Laurel to see where she grew up as part of some master plan to steal her away. Now staring at the sun-bleached trailers, the frayed curtains and dirty children, he knew he'd misjudged her. He thought about her big office and her hopes for a promotion. He thought about her white-on-white condo, another lifetime from here.

"Park over there," she said, pointing to a spot past the last mobile home. A lone tree provided a fair amount of shade. As he came to a stop, a group of people rushed out of the trailer. A woman about Anne's size led the way followed by several children and two mangy-looking dogs. He opened the door and got out slowly. Anne and Laurel followed suit.

The woman stopped a couple of feet away. Her hair was several shades darker, a true auburn. It was pulled back in a braid, revealing features much like Anne's, but a little older. Her smile was wide and genuine. A clean but faded sleeveless blouse had been tucked into a loose skirt. He wondered if she'd dressed up to meet them. "Annie Jo Baker, you are lookin' mighty pretty. Is this beautiful young lady your little girl?"

Anne took Laurel's hand and led her forward. "Laurel, this is my cousin, Becky Sue."

"Laurel. Ain't that a lovely name." She moved

closer, then touched her cheek. "Oh, my. You've got Aunt Rose's eyes." She held open her arms.

Laurel looked at him for guidance. He felt as if someone had sliced his belly open and was now twisting the knife. He wanted to drag Laurel into the car and drive so far that they both forgot about Paradise and Anne Baker and birth mothers and being adopted. But he couldn't. He nodded his approval and his daughter stepped into Becky Sue's embrace.

"Welcome home, Laurel Baker. Welcome to the family."

Chapter 6

"Now are you sure you don't want another piece of pie?" Becky Sue asked, rising from the table.

"Not for me," Anne said. "I'm stuffed. Jake?"

The man beside her shook his head. He'd been silent through their meal. Not that she blamed him. It was hot and sticky; even talking was an effort. The air conditioner in the mobile home had long since given up. Even though she'd showered and changed before dinner, Anne could feel the sweat dripping down her back. Her normally curly hair was lying flat from the heat. Jake's tailored white shirt clung to him in patches. Only Becky Sue looked comfortable in her loose floral print skirt and blouse.

The three adults sat at the old table in the kitchen. The six kids were scattered throughout the trailer. Two dogs and an assortment of cats wove between their legs and generally added to the heat and din.

Anne glanced at the cherry pie sitting in the center

of the table. Becky Sue would have gotten up early to
bake it herself. The fried chicken and biscuits had been
from a family recipe, the corn picked that morning.
This was the home she remembered. It was all the
same; she was the one who had changed.

"I'm sure sorry J.T. couldn't get home early,"
Becky Sue said as she cleared the table. Anne rose to
help, but her cousin pushed her back in place. "Now
I know you're family, darlin', but today I'm gonna treat
you like company."

Her familiar open smile eased the pain in Annie's
heart. Becky Sue could always put her world right.

"Anyway, he wanted to meet your little girl, but he
can get to it in the morning. He's got an extra half shift
down at the gas station." She looked around the trailer.
"We sure could use the money to fix up this place."
She moved efficiently around the small but clean
kitchen. When one of the dogs walked in front of her,
she easily stepped out of the way.

"Annie Jo and her mother had a real nice mobile
home," she said, then gave Jake a wink. "'Course it
was only the two of 'em. Kids have a way of wearing
a place out."

Anne shifted uncomfortably in her chair. She wasn't
ashamed of where she'd grown up. There might not
have been a lot of luxuries, but there'd been plenty of
love and understanding. Still, what did Jake think of
all this?

"You must be very proud of Anne," he said, taking
the cup of coffee Becky Sue offered.

"Oh, we are. She's got that important job of hers.
And her place. Have you seen it?"

He nodded.

"Ain't it pretty? All white." Becky Sue gave her a

grin. "She tried to buy us a new mobile home, but I wouldn't let her. This one might be a little worn, but it still works for us."

"I'm sure Jake doesn't want to hear this," Anne said, starting to get uncomfortable.

Jake ignored her. "That was very generous."

"She is. She gives me money for the kids. College, she says, if they want to go." Becky Sue glanced over at her brood. "I think only little Dolly will take advantage of that, but the others might want to learn a trade." She sat down and patted Jake's shoulder. "Your little girl comes from strong stock. We ain't fancy, but we're good folks."

Anne felt the blush climbing her cheeks. She glanced down and smoothed her skirt. If Jake was half as uncomfortable as she was, he'd probably pay her to get him out of the sweltering kitchen. She looked at her cousin and smiled. "It's going to be a pretty night. Would you mind if we took a walk?"

"Go right ahead."

"Jake?"

He looked over at her. A puzzled expression wrinkled his brow. "Sure. I'll tell Laurel." He headed for the big family room.

"He's nice," Becky Sue said before Jake was out of earshot.

"He's Laurel's father. Don't get any ideas."

"But you haven't been out with a man since before my youngest was born."

Anne tried glaring at her cousin, but it was impossible to get or stay angry at her. She grinned instead. "Don't go matchmaking."

"I'm not. But you must admit, he's nice lookin'."

"I'll admit to that, but nothing else."

Becky Sue started to speak, but Anne saw Jake returning and jabbed her in the side with her elbow. She led the way outside. Here the temperature was about ten degrees cooler than inside the trailer. The night sky hung low.

"I'd forgotten about the stars," she said, staring up at the thousands of twinkling lights. "I never could wish on that first star. As the sun set, there weren't any, then I'd look up and the sky would be like this." She waved her arms toward the heavens.

"It's like this on the ranch, too," Jake said as he walked along beside her.

"But not so hot." She fanned herself with her hand.

"You got that right."

By silent agreement, they headed away from the trailer park. Quickly the sounds of the children and the dogs, the bang of pots on the counter and the blare of the televisions faded. Soon all Annie could hear was the soft hooting of an owl and the crunch of Jake's boots on the small rocks underfoot. Her own sandals were quieter as she stepped on the familiar, uneven ground.

The smells of cooking faded more slowly, but soon she could inhale the scent of the desert, the clean air and the musky fragrance that belonged to Jake. Her arms hung loosely at her sides. They moved in the same direction to go around a small boulder, and they brushed together.

Hot skin seared hot skin. The slightly sweaty contact sent excitement rippling through her body. The waves of need alerted all her senses, then settled low in her belly. She fought the urge to fold her arms over her chest. She didn't want him to know he got to her.

She cleared her throat. "So tell me, is Paradise what

you expected?'' she asked, more to distract herself than because she wanted to start a conversation.

"Not exactly. You said the town was small, but I was expecting—"

"A little more life?"

"Yeah."

His voice sounded friendly. She wanted to know if he was smiling at her, but she was afraid to turn her head and look at him. What if he was smiling? How would she control the impulses that flooded her? Worse, what if he wasn't? She would rather die than make a fool of herself in front of Jake Masters. He already had her at a disadvantage.

"It's not a bad place," he said, stopping beside a large rock the size of a dining room table. When she would have followed him close to the boulder, he held her back with a raised arm. "Wait a minute." He walked around the rock, then kicked at a small burrow. "Okay, you can come closer."

"What were you doing?"

"Checking for rattlers. I'm wearing boots, you're not."

She knew the desert snakes thrived around Paradise, but she was surprised Jake had thought of it.

"I might have grown up in Dallas," he said, as if he could read her mind, "but I've always been a country boy at heart."

"I never thought of you as a boy at all," she blurted out, then could have cheerfully thrown herself off a cliff. Unfortunately there weren't any around for hundreds of miles. She settled for sitting on the rock and staring at the stars. At least it was dark and he couldn't see her blushing.

"I like your cousin," he said as he sat next to her.

They weren't touching, but she could feel the heat from the rock, and the heat from the man. The temperatures were about the same, but her reactions were very different. She was hyperaware of her body. Of the dampness of her skin and the way her breasts swelled uncomfortably against her cotton bra. Her nipples puckered. Between her thighs the ache grew. She could feel her damp panties. He hadn't even touched her, but she was ready.

"Becky Sue is very sweet," she said, hoping the conversation would distract her. "She's only ever wanted to get married and have kids."

"Then she sure got what she wanted."

"I'm not going to apologize for her," Anne said sharply.

"No one's asking you to. I meant what I said. I like her. She's very straightforward."

"Sorry." She sighed and folded her hands on her lap. "I guess I'm a little tense about being back. There are so many memories." She studied the familiar stars. "My mother and I used to sit out on our porch at night and look at the sky. We'd wait for the moon to rise and talk about the future. She had so many dreams for me. She used to tell me that I'd leave Paradise and find something better."

"And you did."

"Sometimes it feels like I never lived here at all."

He leaned back on the rock and supported himself on his elbows. "I'll admit I have trouble reconciling you with the girl who grew up here."

"Oh, I was here." She half turned until she was facing him. She tucked one leg under her and smoothed down her light cotton skirt. "I graduated top of my class and seven months pregnant. Imagine what everyone thought of that.''

"Tell me about Bobby."

She laughed. "He was the hottest thing around. Bobby was going to be a champion bull rider. That's all he aspired to in life." Her smile faded. "I thought he was perfect. I didn't even care that we were doing it in the back of a pickup. My mother didn't like him, but she wasn't angry when I found out I was pregnant. She just held me and told me she wasn't going to let Bobby interfere with our plans for my future.''

"Did you want to marry him?"

"I don't know." She shrugged. "In a way, I think I did. But I'd always known I was going to college, and by the time I was willing to admit to myself I was pregnant, he'd left me for another woman. Guess who?''

"I can't imagine."

"A barrel racer. They met on the circuit."

Jake chuckled. His low laugh seemed to find its way into her belly and curl up into a soothing glow. She wanted to capture the sound and hold it close to her heart. She turned away and faced the horizon.

"Did he know about the baby?" he asked.

"Yes, but he didn't care. A friend of my mother's, an attorney, arranged for a private adoption. I never knew the name of the couple." She paused. "I never knew your name, but he promised you were nice and that you'd take care of my child. So I gave her up. It wasn't too horrible," she said, wondering if he heard the lie. Her throat tightened, but she forced herself to go on. "I had a full scholarship to Vassar. The baby was due in the middle of August, and I wasn't showing that much. Everybody knew, but no one said anything.

After Laurel was born, I went off to college, acting like nothing ever happened.''

But something had. And she'd carried around that hole in her heart for thirteen years.

"You've done very well for yourself," he said. "Your mother must be very proud."

"She was." She thought of how her mother had sat listening each summer break. She'd made Anne tell her everything she could remember about her year at college. "She died my last semester. She never saw me graduate, but at least she knew I was going to make it." She drew in a deep breath and forced herself to sound cheerful. "So, where did you say you grew up?"

"Dallas."

She felt him shifting on the rock beside her, but she didn't look. If he said something nice to her, she would break down completely. All the memories were hard to resist. She could hear her mother's gentle voice telling her that a baby would only get in the way. In her head, she knew her mother was right. It was only now that she realized her heart had never been convinced.

"My father was in construction," he continued. "He was very successful."

"Let me guess. A big white house with a swimming pool."

"And horses."

She looked around. The moon had risen. In the distance she could see the lights from the mobile homes. Some laundry hung limply in the warm night. A dog barked.

"That's a lifetime from here," she said.

"About as far from Paradise as you are now. You've come a long way yourself."

"That I have." But what was the price? Giving up

her child had been so logical. Her mother had always told her she didn't have to pay for that one mistake for the rest of her life. But was getting pregnant the only mistake she'd made? "You moved away, as well. Why Colorado?"

He shifted on the rock until he was sitting up next to her. His long legs swung back and forth. She heard the *thunk* as his boots hit the rock.

"My grandfather had a ranch there that he left to me. I always wanted to try to make it successful, but I was expected to go into my father's business. I never thought about trying to make a living with horses. I told myself it was a dream."

"You're doing it now."

"Yeah, and it's a lot more hard work than I'd realized."

He grinned. The flash of white made her own lips curl up. In the faint light of the moon, the details of his face blurred until she could forget he was good-looking enough to make her nervous. She could forget why they were here, and the distrust and awkwardness between them. Maybe this was their chance to become friends.

"You love it," she said, hazarding a guess.

"That I do. I should have done it years ago."

"Why didn't you?"

She felt him stiffen. She wanted to grab his arm and keep him with her, but she didn't. He had to make the decision on his own. He stared straight ahead into the darkness of the desert. The stars twinkled overhead. At last he exhaled and relaxed.

"Ellen and I were best friends in school. Both our families encouraged us to marry. There I was with a

wife and a child. Chasing dreams wasn't an option. I
had responsibilities.''

''Do you always do the responsible thing?''

''Don't you?'' Jake asked, and wondered when he'd
stopped hating her. Maybe it was the night, or seeing
how she'd grown up. But sometime in the last couple
of hours, Anne Baker had ceased to be the enemy.

''I try to do what's right,'' she said.

''Is that why you send Becky Sue money?''

She shrugged. The movement brought her shoulder
in contact with his arm. The faint brush, gone almost
before he registered the sensation, made him want to
haul her close to him and press his hard body against
her soft one. Being next to her, smelling the scent of
her perfume, knowing that if he could just bury himself
inside her he could get rid of this damn need, made
him half crazed. He wanted to touch her and taste her.
He wanted to forget himself inside her—he wanted to
forget she ever existed.

''She's my family. I want to help her. I do as much
as I can.''

It was a hell of a lot more than his family had done
for him. Or Ellen's father. He pushed away the
thoughts of Michael. ''It shows.''

She turned toward him. ''I think that's the first nice
thing you've said to me.''

''What have I said that hasn't been nice?''

She laughed. ''How much time do you have?''

''Okay, maybe I've been a little difficult.''

''A little? Oh, please. You've practically accused me
of harboring all seven deadly sins.''

She was teasing, but her statement made him uncomfortable. He stared out into the desert. ''I protect what's
mine.''

"Don't ever stop doing that."

He looked at her in surprise. "I would have thought you'd get all huffy and accuse me of being a male chauvinist or at least a barbarian."

"No. There were a lot of times I wished for someone to protect me. Mama tried, but she was gone so much. She worked two jobs to support us."

The moonlight reflected in her eyes turning the light blue irises to the color of sapphires. Her skin glowed as if lit by candles. He couldn't see the freckles anymore. Her hair brushed against her shoulders with each turn of her head. Would the strawberry-colored waves be soft against his fingers? He had to ball his hands up into fists to keep from finding out.

He forced himself to think of other things. Of a young girl waiting alone in a trailer for her mother to get home from work. Of the studying it must have taken to get a full scholarship at a prestigious school.

"You didn't fit in here, did you?" he asked.

"No."

"And at Vassar?"

She laughed, but it sounded hollow and sad. "I was a country hick with homemade clothes. I sounded just like Becky Sue," she said, falling back into the accent. "'Hi, ya'll, I'm Annie Jo Baker, from Texas.' You can imagine how well that went over." She stopped talking and swallowed. He watched the movement of her throat and wondered if she fought against tears. "The farthest I'd ever been from home was to the county hospital to give birth to my illegitimate child. I'd seen exactly five movies, I'd never eaten in a restaurant that had tablecloths. I'd never owned a hardback book."

For the second time in as many minutes he wanted to touch her. But this time the urge was about comforting rather than sex. Still he kept his hands on his lap.

"How many do you own now?" he asked.

"A lot." She smiled. "I have a whole bookcase of them in my bedroom at home."

"So you made it."

"I did. At work I've finally found a place to fit in. I'm successful and I know where I'm going."

She pulled up her knees close to her chest. Her full skirt reached down to her ankles so she was completely covered, but there was something provocative about the pose. And something painfully young. She might have made it financially, but in her heart she was still that young girl from Paradise.

"It must be hard for you to come back here," he said.

She looked at him. "I wanted Laurel to see where I grew up. I don't want her to have any fantasies about me. I want her to care about me. I want to be a part of her life, but she's too young for regrets."

"What about your regrets?"

"Do I get to have them?"

"I don't know. Do you?" he asked.

"Don't you hate me too much to care about my regrets?"

"I don't *hate* you."

She sighed. "You don't like me much. I suppose that's an improvement over being hated, but not one I can get excited about."

The night allowed them to speak freely. Perhaps he would regret telling the truth, but she deserved to hear it. "I don't trust you. There's a difference."

"Not a big one." She rested her head on her knees. "The trick is," she said, her voice slightly muffled, "that you never get to know what could have been. How would my life have been different if I hadn't gone to Vassar? What would have happened if I'd given up the scholarship and kept the baby?"

He didn't want to think about that, but she forced him to examine the alternatives. "I wouldn't have been Laurel's father." Or stayed married to Ellen.

The thought caught him off guard. But it was true. He would have left his wife. Without the responsibility of a child and her tearful claims that he owed her because she stayed when she could have left and had a child of her own, their marriage would have ended after a couple of years. If not for missing Laurel, that scenario would have been better for both him and Ellen.

"It's hard, isn't it?" she asked. "Trying to figure out what would have been. I could have gone to a local junior college, worked somewhere. You would have—" She looked at him. "What would you have done, Jake?"

He couldn't tell her the truth. She wouldn't understand. Besides, he'd only admitted half of it. The other half was that he would have still wanted a child of his own. A son. The one thing he couldn't buy, earn or achieve, no matter how hard he tried. He was sterile, and no wishing in the world could change that fact.

"I would have moved to the ranch sooner," he said at last.

"Did Ellen want to go there, too?"

"No. She liked Dallas and being in the city. After she was gone, I stayed for Laurel and because of my obligations to my father-in-law."

"What changed your mind? Laurel's new friends?"

He was surprised she'd remembered that conversation. "She was getting into trouble, but it was more

than that. My father-in-law, Ellen's father, didn't
want—'' He hesitated. Anne might as well know, in
case Laurel ever mentioned her grandfather. ''After Ellen passed away he decided he didn't want anything to
do with Laurel. She wasn't a blood relative and he
disowned her.''

Anne gasped. ''His own granddaughter?''

He nodded. He could still feel the rage swelling inside him. It had taken every ounce of his self-control
not to beat the crap out of the older man. Only his
respect for Ellen's memory had kept him from attack-
ing her father.

''Does Laurel know?'' she asked.

''I don't think she's figured it out,'' he said. ''He
didn't come to her birthday party, but I told her he was
out of town on business. I bought a gift and said it was
from him.'' He shrugged. ''That was probably a dumb
idea, but I couldn't tell her that her grandfather didn't
want anything to do with her. She would never understand. I'd already started the move to Colorado. What
he said that day convinced me that getting away was
the best thing for both of us. Even if Laurel doesn't
believe it right now.''

''She'll understand,'' Anne said. She leaned closer
and smiled up at him. ''One day she'll realize she has
a wonderful father who loves her very much.''

''I haven't been much of a father at all,'' he said,
turning away from her. ''After Ellen was killed in a
car accident, I had a hard time dealing with her death.
I pulled away from everything, including her.''

''I'm sure she understands.''

''Dammit, she was eleven. How could she understand?'' He pushed off the rock and stood up. ''I don't
understand. She's a stranger, Anne. I have a thirteen-

year-old daughter and I don't know what the hell she's thinking most of the time. She hates me for taking her away from her friends. Her grandfather has turned his back on her. She wants to live with you in Houston. The best news I've heard all day is that her real father is dead. I was glad when you said that. I don't need any more competition. What the hell kind of bastard does that make me?''

He shoved his hands into his pockets and started walking away. He'd barely gone two steps when he felt her hand on his arm.

"Wait, Jake."

He froze in his tracks. Her palm burned his skin. The scent of her body, the soft fragrance of her perfume, filled his senses.

"You're a good man," she said.

"Not by a long shot."

"You are," she insisted, moving closer. "You've done a fine job with Laurel. She couldn't turn out to be as sweet and loving as she is if you weren't decent."

He spun toward her so quickly she didn't have time to move back. In the moonlight he could see the shape of her head and body, but not the individual features. He couldn't see the expression on her face or read what was in her eyes.

He told himself he was a fool, that it wasn't about anything other than sex and that come morning he would regret acting on the impulse. But that didn't stop him.

"If I'm so decent," he said, grabbing her arms and hauling her up against him, "why can't I stop thinking about this?" He lowered his mouth to hers.

Chapter 7

His kiss was as sweet and hot as the Texas summer. His firm mouth softened when it touched hers. He moved his lips back and forth as if testing her, then his hold on her arms loosened. Anne knew if she pulled back, he would let her go in an instant. She told herself that she *should* pull back, or at the very least be angry with him. But she didn't, and she wasn't. She couldn't be. Not when every inch of her body cried out for his touch. Not when she trembled within his gentle embrace. She had longed for this from the moment they'd first met. Damn that cowboy curse.

But even as she leaned against his broad chest until her breasts flattened against him she knew it was more than her weakness for cowboys. It was her weakness specifically for this man.

One of his hands reached up to cup the back of her head, the other moved down to the small of her back. She raised her arms to rest them on his shoulders and buried her fingers in his hair. The coffee-colored strands felt like cool silk, contrasting with the warmth of the night and the heat of their bodies.

He angled his head and pressed more firmly on her mouth. She tried to hold back, but it was no use. Her body clamored for him. Before she could think that she shouldn't, her lips parted, begging for his invasion.

He didn't disappoint her. His tongue swept past her lips, pausing only to tease the delicate skin with a quick swipe. A shudder rippled through her. At the first brush, a moan started low in her throat. His hand on her back moved lower to the curve of her derriere. The tiniest hint of pressure caused her to flex her hips forward. Her hips and stomach cradled his pelvis. The rigid proof of his excitement surged against her.

She told herself this was wrong, or at the very least, insane. She barely knew this man. There was already so much going on between them. Sex would only complicate a difficult situation. But when his tongue circled through her mouth, she ceased to care about anything but the sensations he created.

She clutched at his shoulders. His fingers touched her jaw then moved to her ear and traced the curves there. He pulled back from her mouth and licked her lips around and around. Her breasts ached with need. Between her thighs, the dampness grew as her cotton panties clung to her.

He lowered his arm so both his hands cupped her rear. He squeezed and pulled her against him. She rotated her hips, needing more, so much more. He kissed her jaw, her neck, down to the first button of her shirt. His hot breath seared her skin. She arched her head back, begging silently for more. She needed this. It had been too long. More than that, no one had ever made her feel this way before.

"Annie," he murmured against her skin. He spoke the word as if it was an endearment. He'd never called her Annie before. Maybe he didn't hate her.

Oh, God, he was Laurel's father. It was all too complicated. She had to stop. They had to stop. Now, before it became too late.

He touched her breasts. She bit her lip hard to keep from moaning aloud. His big hands cupped her sensitive flesh, taking their weight in his palms. He brushed his thumbs over her hard nipples. Through the blouse and bra, the contact burned. And it was too late to think.

Even as he fumbled with the buttons of her blouse, he stepped back the way they'd come, bringing her with him. As he pulled the thin cotton free of her skirt's waistband, her thighs touched the rock they'd sat on. Jake grabbed her by the waist and raised her up onto the flat surface, then he pulled off her blouse and lay it down behind her.

Her thighs parted and he stepped between them. His denim jeans rubbed against her bare skin. She told herself this wasn't happening, but she knew it was. Maybe it was those damn jeans, she thought as she reached for his shirt. She'd always been a sucker for a man in jeans. And his were button fly, the style that made her weak in the knees.

She quickly worked his shirt buttons, but before she could touch his chest, he reached for the center clasp on her bra. She caught her breath in anticipation.

He bent down and kissed her again. This time there were no preliminaries. He plunged his tongue inside, sweeping around her mouth, tasting every part of her, letting her taste him. She closed her lips in a tight O and sucked. With her hands on his shirt, she felt his muscles stiffen. He groaned. His fingers toyed with her nipples, flicking quickly over the hardened tips until her gasp released him and he, too, let her go.

He pulled back and opened the clasp. Gently he drew the bra back. The cups caught on her nipples. He bent over and with his tongue, freed each side. Then he drew the straps down her arms, leaving her bare to him. He stared for so long, she started to feel self-conscious. She glanced down and saw the way the moonlight reflected off her skin. Her nipples were dark tips on alabaster skin. In the darkness, her freckles didn't show. She almost felt beautiful before him.

He moved closer and his groin brushed against her damp panties. She wanted him, wanted this, more than she'd ever wanted anything. He lowered her back onto the rock. Her shirt protected her from the rough surface. He kissed her mouth, then licked her ear. He trailed a wet line down her collarbone toward her breasts. She arched up toward him, impatient for his touch.

He cupped her in his hands and held her still for his tender assault. He licked the sensitive nubs over and over until her world consisted only of fiery sensation and a need that burned so hot, it threatened to consume her. She rocked her hips against him. Her hands clutched at the rock, but she couldn't get any hold on the stone. She eached for his warm chest and felt a light dusting of hair. She rubbed her fingers against him, finding the flat male nipples and teasing him as he teased her. He punished her with a gentle bite. She moaned.

Everything felt perfect. The night. The heat of the

rock below her, the fire of Jake's body above her. His hands and tongue continued to ply their magic. She wanted him, she could feel how he wanted her.

He nibbled along her midriff to the waistband of her skirt. She raised her hips. He reached down and began pushing the filmy fabric up her legs. His hands were hot on her thighs. His work-roughened skin grated deliciously. She could hear the soft rasping sound and it excited her more. She brought her arms back to brace herself and banged her elbow. The sharp pain made her cry out.

"You okay?" he asked, his voice gruff with passion.

"I just hit the rock. It's being outside. I haven't done anything this wild since..." Since she was seventeen. Since Bobby and doing it in the back of his pickup. Since she got pregnant.

Remembering that was like being doused in cold water. She struggled to sit up. What on earth was she doing? Was she crazy? They both had to be. His hand continued to climb her legs. His thumb brushed perilously close to the apex of her thighs and she stiffened against the pleasure that flooded her.

"Jake, stop."

"Why?" The night caught the flare of his lazy, self-satisfied smile. He touched her panties, and she knew he felt the moisture. "You feel ready enough to me."

Oh, she was ready. Too ready, and far too willing. "We don't have any protection."

"Is that all?" He bent down and nibbled the inside of her knee. "I haven't been with anyone in over two years. About six months ago I had to give blood to a friend. They checked and I'm fine."

"I'm okay that way, too," she said. "What I meant

was, I'm not on any birth control. I'm right in the middle of my cycle and probably as fertile as a rabbit.''

He reacted as if she'd slapped him. He straightened up and glared down at her. The moonlight caressed the skin exposed by his open shirt. She wanted to touch him and feel his warmth again, but he held himself stiffly, as if in terrible pain. She folded her arms over her bare breasts.

''Jake?''

''You don't have to worry about getting pregnant,'' he said grimly. ''I'm the reason we had to adopt a child instead of having one of our own. I'm sterile.''

Now it was her turn to be shocked. Sterile? She stared at him. She'd never given much thought to why Jake and Ellen had adopted. She supposed that if she had, she would have assumed it was Ellen's fault. Which was foolish. She had no way of knowing why they couldn't have a child.

He stood silently before her, his chest rising and falling with each breath. She had time to become aware of herself, of what they were doing. All she wanted to do was put her bra and shirt back on and escape to the safety of Becky Sue's mobile home. She didn't want to be out here like this. It was a huge mistake. But she couldn't just walk away and leave Jake in such emotional pain. She could feel it radiating from him. It showed in the set of his shoulders and the tilt of his chin. He was waiting for her to scorn him. She had to tell him it didn't matter to her, although inside she ached for him.

He was such a proud man. Finding out he couldn't father children must have devastated him.

He started to turn away. Without giving herself time to think, Anne reached out and grabbed him. The only

thing she could reach was his belt buckle. She pulled
him hard against her. He moved forward reluctantly.
She wanted to tell him she was sorry, but he wouldn't
want to hear her words. There was nothing she could
say, so when he was close enough, she wrapped her
arms around his waist and pressed her lips to his chest.

He tasted all male with a combination of sweat and
the unique flavor of his skin. What started out to be
comfort rapidly became something else. She kissed him
gently at first, moving her mouth across his chest with
hard, hot kisses, then she began to lick him. She found
his nipples and caressed them until his breathing became as rapid as her own.

His hands reached for her breasts. He touched her
sensitive skin, kneading and rubbing until she quivered
again with need. She'd had a half-formed notion that
this was for him, to help take away his pain, but the
second he reached under her skirt and touched her
moist center, all thoughts of altruism fled, washed away
by a flood of passion.

He jerked off her panties and pulled her skirt up
around her waist. She undid his belt buckle and reached
for the buttons on the fly of his jeans. To torment them
both, she worked slowly, savoring the feel of his hardness against the back of her hand. Her knuckles
brushed him with each button and his erection flexed
at her touch.

At last he was free. She stroked his smooth length.
He felt hotter here. Hard and ready. He quickly pushed
down his jeans and briefs and moved between her
thighs.

The velvet tip of him rubbed against her center,
causing her muscles to clench rhythmically. When she

was panting and desperately close to her release, he entered her.

She hadn't had a lover in several years and she was tight inside. He pushed forward slowly, stretching unused spaces, forcing dormant feelings to flare with sensation. She braced herself on her elbows and watched him move in and out of her body. She glanced at his face. He was looking at her. Their eyes locked.

They didn't speak, they didn't have to. Communication flowed between them as if they'd spent their whole lives waiting for this moment. Her hips flexed in time with his thrusts. She was closer, so much closer, but not close enough. She wanted more. He reached between them. With his thumb he gently stroked her. Up and down, double time to the movement of her hips. She felt him tightening, getting ready to explode and it was enough to send her to the edge.

He breathed her name and made her fall. Her muscles convulsed in release. It went on and on, forever it seemed. She felt his final thrust, heard the guttural cry, then he was still. He pulled her up against him, cradling her in his arms. She listened to the thundering of a heartbeat and wondered if it was his or hers. Perhaps now they only had one heart between them.

Reality gradually intruded and she could hear the night creatures around them, feel the hard rock jabbing her bare behind. She kissed Jake's chest and tasted him, but now her tongue was coated with the bitterness of regret. She sighed.

"That sounded pretty serious," he said, placing one finger under her chin and forcing her to look at him.

She flushed and was glad the darkness hid it from view. "You're Laurel's father."

"I know."

"This was all a mistake. I don't even know you. And you hate me."

"I don't hate you." He dropped his hand to his side. "I don't trust you."

"We just made love and you don't trust me?"

He stepped away. She pulled her skirt down and reached behind her for her bra.

"How did this happen?" she asked.

"I don't know." He didn't sound any happier than she did. "It was just hormones or circumstance." He pulled up his jeans and started fastening them. "We've both been without for a long time."

She slipped off the rock and grabbed her shirt. "So it was like taking a drink of water because you're thirsty?"

"Yeah."

The warm lover who had touched her was gone. Even his voice was different. Jake Masters was back. The man who, despite what he said, really didn't like her. And she'd just made love to him. In the desert. About fifty yards from Becky Sue's mobile home. On a rock. She wanted to die.

"I can't believe we did this," she said frantically. She tried to button her blouse, but her fingers weren't working. "We've never even been out on a date. I've known you less than two weeks."

"This isn't any easier for me," he growled. "Dammit, woman, I was married for fourteen years and I was never once unfaithful to Ellen."

"Golly, maybe you deserve an award for that," she snapped. "Blame it all on me, why don't you? That seems to be your favorite method for dealing with your problems anyway. Everything with Laurel is my fault, so make this my fault, too."

She was close to crying, so she clamped her mouth shut. By concentrating very hard, she managed to do up her shirt and stuff it into her skirt. She was about to walk away when he touched her arm.

"What?" she snapped.

Silently he held out his hand. He had her panties. The white cotton contrasted with his tanned skin. She covered her face with her hands.

"I just want to die," she whispered.

He pulled her close. "It's going to be okay," he said, his voice low and comforting. "We both reacted. I've never done anything like this, either. I'm not blaming you. It's no one's fault, Anne. Maybe it was for the best. We were both wondering about it. Now we know. It'll make the next two months easier for both of us. All we have to do is to pretend it never happened."

She stepped back and took her underpants. While he turned his back, she slipped them on. He was right. They had both wondered how it would be, and now they knew. But he was wrong, too. This wasn't going to make it easier. She knew that as surely as she knew he'd called her Anne again, instead of Annie.

They left Paradise early the next morning. Becky Sue got up before dawn and baked cinnamon rolls. After she'd filled them with coffee and the gooey confections, she gave them fifteen minutes of advice about the local highway.

Jake hovered in the background as Anne hugged her cousin goodbye. Laurel exchanged last frantic whispers with Becky Sue's oldest daughter and the two girls giggled together. He waited patiently while everyone got settled, then he headed toward the highway and home.

In the back seat Laurel fumbled with her portable radio. "I had a great time, Dad," she said, and yawned.

"I'm glad you enjoyed it. How late did you and Dolly stay up talking?"

She leaned back and yawned again. "Not late."

"Yeah, sure." He looked in the rearview mirror and winked.

She grinned at him. "Okay, maybe kinda late. But you know, not much past two."

"Yikes," Anne said from the seat next to him. "You must be tired."

"Maybe a little," Laurel answered. She slipped on her headset and started nodding to the beat. "I liked meeting everyone," she said. "Dolly's cool. We're going to write each other."

Jake's first impulse was to tell her that she would do no such thing. He didn't want his daughter corresponding with Anne's relatives. It was a knee-jerk reaction that would only get him in trouble with both Anne and Laurel. It was also unreasonable.

He rubbed his face with one hand, then shifted in his seat. He hadn't gotten much sleep, either. Not because he'd stayed up talking, though. He and Anne had immediately returned to the house. They hadn't bothered to linger in the desert. There had been awkward, mumbled "good-nights," then they'd fled for separate quarters. But even though she'd been out of sight, he hadn't been able to stop thinking about her or what they'd done. He was still thinking about it.

If it wasn't such a big mess, he'd have to laugh. After all he'd been the one saying they should just forget it. Yet every time he closed his eyes, he could see her naked body moving beneath his. He could feel her soft skin and taste her sweetness. Despite the release they'd shared, his body tightened over and over again in response to the memories. Even now, in the car, his groin hardened painfully, pressing against the button fly of his jeans. He prayed Anne wouldn't notice.

He glanced over at her. She was wearing a green tank top and matching shorts. Freckles dotted her skin. The shirt dipped low until he could see the hint of the valley between her breasts. Her perfume whispered through the interior of the Explorer.

She stared out her window and nibbled on her lower lip. He had a view of the elegant line of her neck. Last night he'd traced that line and tasted her skin. Not quite peaches, he remembered, but hot and sweet enough to drive a man to want more.

She drew in a deep breath, her breasts rising then lowering slowly. He could see the faint outline of one nipple. The tiny bud taunted him.

He glanced in his rearview mirror. Laurel had fallen asleep curled up on the seat, her head resting on Anne's carry-on bag. Thank God, he thought. Bad enough to have these kinds of thoughts, but it was disgusting when he considered his daughter was in the car with him. Her headset covered her ears. He could see the tape player was on. He thought about asking Anne to turn it off but he didn't want to wake the sleeping girl. She listened to the music all the time, anyway. It wouldn't kill her to sleep with it.

"What are you smiling at?" Anne asked.

He jerked his head toward the back seat. "She's out like a light. I was debating whether or not to ask you to take off her headset."

Anne twisted and looked over her shoulder. "I'm afraid I'd wake her."

"My thoughts exactly. She'll be fine."

"You're surprisingly cheerful." She faced front and smoothed her seat belt.

"Why wouldn't I be?"

"I saw the way you stiffened up when Laurel said she wanted to write Dolly. Don't you want to yell at me and get this off your chest?"

Nothing got by her. He resisted the urge to glance down at his erection. Maybe she hadn't noticed that. "Is that what I do?"

She shrugged. "I don't know you well enough to make a judgment. Let's just say that's what you've been doing with me about Laurel."

"This isn't easy for me," he admitted.

"It's not easy for me, either."

She looked at him. He quickly glanced over at her and their eyes met. Awareness flashed between them. The temperature in the car seemed to climb about twenty degrees. He swore silently. So much for forgetting. He returned his attention to the road.

They passed the next two hours in silence. Laurel slept on. Jake found a country station. The sound of steel guitars blended with his daughter's steady breathing. Anne stared out the front window. Occasionally he caught a glimpse of an emotion flickering across her face. He told himself he should ignore her. It wasn't any of his business. But he asked anyway.

"You're awfully quiet. What are you thinking about?" Part of him hoped she'd say "last night." Mostly because it was all he could think about.

"Becky Sue."

Jake shook his head. Guess he hadn't impressed Anne as much as he'd thought he had. "Why?"

"I was thinking about her life. Five kids in a double-wide trailer in the middle of nowhere. She couldn't be happier."

"You sound surprised."

She shifted until she was facing him. After adjusting her seat belt, she looked up and smiled. "I suppose I am. I spent most of my time trying to get away from there. It never occurred to her to do anything *but* stay. I'd always thought she was wrong."

"And now?"

"Now I'm not so sure. It was all so easy back then. I didn't even think about keeping Laurel." She glanced back at the sleeping girl. He saw her wistful smile. "I'm sorry, Jake. You're the last person I should be dumping this on."

"I don't mind," he said, and was surprised to find out he meant it. "I guess it's because all the wondering in the world isn't going to change the fact that you gave her up and we adopted her."

"I know." She leaned her head against the edge of the seat. "I always used to think that living in that tiny town and having just a few dollars above the legal poverty level would be a horrible life for a child. I didn't want that for my baby. Because I grew up that way. But so did Becky Sue. Her kids are doing it now. They all seem fine."

"Except for Joey chewing on the dog."

She chuckled. "Yeah, there is that." Her humor faded. "Don't be mad at me, but I can't help wondering if Laurel could have been happy there, too."

"Maybe she would have been."

She raised her head, her eyes wide with surprise. "I was sure you'd jump down my throat at that one."

"I'm not a complete jerk."

"I remember. Just half of one," she said, her voice low and teasing.

He gripped the steering wheel tighter. He liked this side of Anne Baker. He liked the quick mind and the gentle teasing. He liked the way her warm breath tickled his arm. He liked the sun catching a strand of her hair and turning the pale red color to auburn. He liked the feeling of family and it scared him to death.

"So you're having second thoughts," he said, returning to their original conversation.

"Maybe. But then I think about my career."

"And your promotion?"

"That, too. It's between me and this other guy." She sighed. "Tim the Turkey."

"Interesting title. Does it mean he's in management?"

She laughed. "Yes. And that he has a reputation for cornering secretaries in the supply room. No one's formally complained about sexual harassment, but the rumors have been running wild. He hates that I'm his competition."

"He doesn't like you?"

"He doesn't like the fact that I'm a woman." She looked up at him. "What kind of boss were you?"

"My dad made me work my way up through the ranks, so I knew what it was like to be forty stories up on a steel beam. I tried to be fair, to listen, then make the best decision. Pretty much an average kind of boss."

"Sounds a little better than average to me," she said, shifting until she was sitting straight in her seat. "I've worked so hard for this promotion. It was my goal from the time I hired on with the company right out of college.''

''How is the leave of absence going to affect your chances?''

''I don't know. I'd like to think it won't matter, but I'd be kidding myself. Tim will be there every day, getting his work done.''

Jake was surprised to find he wanted Anne to get the promotion, not because it would make his life easier, but because she'd worked hard and it was something *she* wanted. He was still a little wary, but the distrust was easing.

''I appreciate you taking the time to see this thing through with Laurel,'' he said.

''I want to spend some time with her, but I'm so scared.''

''Of what? She thinks you're the hottest thing since hand-held video games.''

''That's it, exactly.'' She glanced over her shoulder at the sleeping girl. Her lips curled into a smile. ''Every day I spend with her, I grow to care more and more. Laurel is in the honeymoon stage. It's working now, but we're heading in different directions. Her case of hero worship is going to wear off. I think she'll still like me, but it won't be the same. I don't want to get my heart trampled by a thirteen-year-old girl, but I can't find a way to stop it from happening.''

He'd never thought about Anne's risk in all this. He'd spent the past few days worrying about how Laurel's relationship with Anne affected him. But she was right. Laurel would get over her intense feelings and then life would settle down to some semblance of normalcy.

''She'll never want to let go of the relationship,'' he said. ''She needs a woman in her life.''

''She needs a woman, but that doesn't necessarily mean she'll need me. What happens if you remarry?''

''That'll never happen,'' he said without thinking.

''Why?''

''It just won't.''

Get married again? He shook his head. Not in this lifetime. He'd barely recovered from his last marriage, and Ellen had been gone for two years.

It had all started out so well. He and Ellen had been best friends. Marriage had been a natural extension of that relationship. Everything had been fine those first couple of years. Until Ellen had decided she wanted to have a baby. They'd tried and tried, but nothing had happened.

Jake gripped the steering wheel more firmly. He could still remember the look on his father-in-law's face when he'd sat Jake down in his study.

''I've got some bad news, son.'' Michael had taken to calling him ''son'' when Jake's father had passed away. ''It seems the problem is with you.''

He'd gone on with an explanation about low sperm and lack of production, but none of it had made sense. He hadn't been listening, didn't even remember leaving Michael's large house. The next thing he knew, he was home and Ellen was crying. She hadn't said a word about it to him. She hadn't had to. He'd seen the sorrow and pity in her eyes. There would be no Masters son to carry on the family name. No child of his own to love and watch grow. That night Ellen had spoken to her father about adopting a child and within two weeks he'd arranged something private through a lawyer friend.

Jake glanced in his rearview mirror. Laurel shifted in her sleep. Her long brown hair hung over her shoulders. He couldn't see her eyes, but he knew they were hazel. Like Anne's mother.

Anne. He looked at her. She was staring at him. Their eyes met, then she quickly turned away. Bobby had given Anne what Jake could never give any woman. A child of her own.

He remembered the last years with Ellen. The arguments, the silences. Laurel's pale face as she witnessed her parent's marriage fall apart. He remembered last night and the sound of Laurel's laughter as she had played with her cousins. He remembered her insistence on spending time with Anne. With her birth mother. He remembered the last two years and the way he'd pulled back from his daughter. The nights he'd spent alone mourning his late wife and the future they were supposed to have had. He remembered the times he raged against God for denying him a son.

Anne was right. They were all heading in different directions. He could only pray they weren't on the road to disaster. He clenched his jaw. No matter what, he wasn't going to lose Laurel. She was all he had left.

Chapter 8

The house stood in a shelter of pine trees. Behind it was a large barn and several corrals. Past them, Anne could see more buildings and a young man exercising a horse on the end of a lead.

"We're here," Jake said, turning off the engine. He glanced at her expectantly.

"It's beautiful," she said, staring at the peaked roof and wide bare windows. A big porch wrapped around the front of the house. The lawn looked new and a painfully bright green.

She stepped out of the Explorer. Her legs were stiff. She shook them and stretched. Jake hadn't rushed to get them back, so the drive had taken three days. Laurel unfolded herself from the back seat. She ripped off her headphones and tossed them back into the truck.

"Give me the key," she said, dancing around her father. "I want to show Annie *everything*."

He handed her his key ring. Laurel found the correct

one, then took Anne's hand and pulled her toward the house.

"Come on," she said. "You've got to see the inside. It's *so* big. But empty." She climbed the porch stairs, let go of her hand and stuck the key into the lock. "I've been working on decorating it, but I don't know very much, and it's not that fun to do alone. You can help me now."

She got the door unlocked and pushed it open. She dragged Anne across the threshold. Laurel had been right. The house was huge. A stone fireplace dominated the living room. A couple of couches were pushed up against bare walls, but other than that there wasn't any furniture. Laurel showed her the dining room. Again, bare walls and floors, no window coverings. Just a tattered old table and four chairs.

"Dad says we should replace this," Laurel said, running her hands over the pitted wood. "Through here is the kitchen."

Modern appliances gleamed from their built-in spaces. Unlike her white-on-white, this kitchen was filled with color. The tiles were cream with a pale blue pattern. The oversize center island continued the theme with alternating blue and cream tiles. The bleached cabinets contrasted with the bright floral wallpaper. Plants hung in the corners. A cow-print table with four matching chairs sat in front of the bare window.

"I ordered this from a catalog," Laurel said proudly, standing behind one of the chairs.

Anne stared. The furniture was wood, all right. But it had been painted white with black marks. Like a cow. "Oh, my. What did your father say?"

"He wasn't very happy," Jake said, coming into the

kitchen. He had her luggage in one hand and Laurel's bag in the other. "Where did you want to put Anne?"

"There's an extra bed in my room," Laurel said hopefully.

"Not a good idea," Jake said, before she could answer.

He shot her a glance as if daring her to defy him, but she had no intention of doing so. As much as she adored her daughter, she wanted her own room.

"How about that front bedroom?" Laurel said. "It's big and it's right next to me."

He looked at her for confirmation.

"Sounds fine," she said.

"I'll go ahead and take these up." He lifted the bags a few inches, then turned and headed toward the stairs.

Laurel took her hand and pulled her across the hall and into a library. "Daddy and I both like to read. Mom did, too. She liked to collect first editions. We've got bunches." There were piles of boxes, some of them open. Anne could see the books inside. The walls of the room were floor to ceiling bookshelves.

She remembered telling Jake that before she'd left Paradise, she'd never owned a hardcover book in her life. Had he thought of his library then? Had he secretly laughed at her or had he understood her desire to be more than she'd been born to?

A pair of leather wing chairs stood in one corner with a table and a reading lamp between them. Scattered throughout the room were smaller tables covered with framed photographs. Anne stepped closer to study the pictures.

The first one she picked up showed a much younger Jake and a beautiful, elegantly dressed dark-haired woman holding a baby. A newborn, from the look of the infant's scrunched-up face. The pain caught Anne like a blow to the chest. The air rushed out of her lungs and she had to gasp to breathe.

''That's when Mom and Dad brought me home from the hospital,'' Laurel said, blithely unaware of the hurt her words caused.

Anne stared. Her child. The baby they wouldn't let her hold that horrible day over thirteen years ago. She traced the cool glass, but she couldn't touch the infant's face, feel her warmth or inhale her baby scent. She wanted to weep and scream against a fate that had been so unkind. But it wasn't fate, she reminded herself. It was her. She'd made the decision to give Laurel up, and now she had to live with the consequences.

She swallowed hard and exchanged that photo for the one that had been next to it. This was a wedding portrait. Ellen looked stunningly beautiful in yards of white lace. The gown showed off her fashion-model's figure to perfection. She carried a cascade of flowers. Next to her, Jake stood tall and handsome. The look on his face as he stared at his bride made Anne's heart clench even tighter. There was so much love between them. It was as tangible as the cool silver of the frame.

The rest of the photographs showed the happy couple together. Some with Laurel, some just the two of them. Anne glanced down at her rumpled shorts and T-shirt. At her freckled arms and generous breasts. She was nothing like Ellen Masters. Even on her best day, she could never compete with the tall, slender beauty.

She told herself it wasn't a competition. She reminded herself that Laurel didn't care what she looked like, and that Jake hadn't minded her curves that night they'd made love. But it had been dark, a little voice whispered. Their joining had been about circumstance and mutual need. She had a bad feeling that he hadn't specifically been making love to her. Any woman would have done.

She took a moment to compose her features, then turned away from the photos. "I don't see any of your school pictures," she said to Laurel.

"Oh, Dad keeps those in his bedroom." She wrinkled her nose. "I hate some of them. There's a photo album of me somewhere in one of these boxes." She motioned to the stacks. "Maybe we can find it later."

"I'd like that." Anne drew in a deep breath to compose herself. "What's next?"

"Through here are all the catalogs and stuff." Laurel led the way into a smaller room. A long table stood against one wall. Decorating magazines, paint and carpet samples and catalogs from dozens of home furnishings manufacturers covered the surface. "I've been trying to figure all this out, but I don't know where to start." She brushed her bangs out of her face and sighed. "Dad told me I could do anything I wanted with the house, but everything is so expensive, and I *am* only thirteen."

"Oh, you are, are you?" Annie walked over to the table and gave Laurel a smile. She forced her feelings of inadequacy into the back of her mind and concentrated on her daughter. "A couple of days ago you were trying to convince us all you were grown-up."

"Maybe I am still a little, you know, young," Laurel said, then grinned. "Can you help me with this stuff?"

"I'd love to." If she really stayed for two months there wasn't going to be much else to fill her time, Anne thought as she stared at her daughter. "I used to do a lot of crafts when I was growing up. I also sewed."

"Really?" Laurel couldn't have looked more shocked if Anne had told her she was a spy for a foreign government. "With a sewing machine and everything?"

"It's a lot faster than doing it by hand. Why are you so surprised?"

Laurel shrugged. "I've never known anyone who could sew before."

Anne thought about the pictures of Ellen. In all of them she was wearing expensive designer clothes. It made sense that Jake's late wife hadn't taken the time to sew anything.

"I haven't done it in a while, but I think I could whip something up."

"Can you teach me crafts and stuff?"

"Sure. Next time we go into town, we'll find a crafts store and I'll get you started on counted cross-stitch. It's easy and the results can be beautiful."

"Cool." She motioned to the piles of catalogs. "Can we do my room first? I saw something in Dolly's room I'd like to do here. So can we?"

"If your father doesn't mind." Anne picked up a ring of paint samples. "Let's ask him tonight and then get started in the morning."

"You're the best." Laurel came up to her and wrapped her arms around her waist. "I'm glad you're here with me. We belong together."

Anne set down the samples and hugged her back. Despite her misgivings, it felt right to be here. She closed her eyes and concentrated on memorizing everything about this moment. When she opened her eyes again, she saw Jake standing in the doorway. From the look on his face, she figured he'd overheard Laurel telling her that she was glad Anne was here. A stark expression swept through his eyes, and she knew their fragile peace had once again been destroyed.

"Mom didn't do much regular cooking," Laurel said as she rinsed the green beans. "We had a house-keeper. Mom was really busy with her charity work a lot of the time. She didn't have a job. Mom said it was important for people with money to give something back to the community."

"That's a good philosophy," Anne said, and bit down on her lip to keep from screaming. While Laurel avoided mentioning Ellen around her father, she didn't feel that same restriction with Anne. In the past hour, she'd included the word "Mom" in almost every sentence.

They'd finished their tour of the house. Anne had a brief impression of large rooms filled with small amounts of furniture. In Jake's room, a king-size bed had dominated one wall. There had been a few scattered garments and his still-packed suitcase, but little else. Her guest room suffered the same fate. A bed, a small dresser and her suitcase. At least she had her own bathroom and some much-needed privacy. She adored her daughter, but she'd spent the past three days in close contact with Laurel and could use some breathing space.

Which probably makes me a crummy parent, she thought grimly as she searched for a casserole dish.

"They're in here," Laurel said helpfully, pointing at a shelf in the center island.

"Thanks." She rinsed off the chicken she'd de-frosted in the microwave. On the way to the house they'd stopped at a local vegetable stand for fresh produce, but everything else in the meal would have to be either canned or frozen.

Anne dug around in the pantry for a package of rice. "I can't find the rice, Laurel."

"We don't have any. Mom didn't like it."

Anne started to stand up, but she bumped her head on a pantry shelf. The sharp pain brought tears to her eyes.

"I heard that crack," Jake said, silently appearing at her side. "You okay?"

"Fine," she said curtly, and turned away from him. She rubbed her head and willed herself to ignore him.

He'd been doing that since they'd arrived. Drifting in and out of rooms. Showing up in the middle of conversations, then leaving. She knew what he was doing; she knew he was checking on her. He didn't trust her not to say or do something in the presence of his daughter. Anne fumed. He just plain didn't trust her. But he could sleep with her.

She wasn't completely upset that they'd given in to the sexual tension between them. She wasn't happy about it, but it wasn't a total surprise. The attraction had been too powerful for their vulnerable states. It almost made sense. Almost. But what really steamed her was the fact that he was actually able to do as he'd suggested and put that night out of his mind. She hated that he was able to engage her in casual conversation as if nothing intimate had ever occurred. It took all her mental power and self-control to keep from blurting out something inappropriate, or reaching to touch him. Now that she'd tasted his male passion, she wanted more.

Laurel hovered nearby. "Do you want some ice for your head?"

"I'm fine," she said again. If there wasn't rice, she'd have to come up with something else. She remembered seeing a frozen potato dish in the freezer. She rummaged around until she found it and set it on the counter.

Laurel looked at the package. "Are we having that with chicken?"

Anne drew in a deep breath. "Is that a problem?"

"Well, Mom always served that with pork, didn't she, Dad?"

The threat of tears returned, but not just because her head was hurting. Ellen had been gone two years. Shouldn't Laurel have let go of all these little traditions? Anne rubbed her swelling bump. She didn't have a clue as to what was going on with Laurel. Maybe she clung to the rituals because they were all she had.

"I think we can have them with chicken this once," Jake said.

Anne didn't dare turn and look at him. She didn't want to see anything like compassion in his eyes.

"I don't expect you to take the place of a housekeeper," he said, leaning against the island.

Anne moved around him and picked up the chicken. She placed it in the dish and sprinkled on the spices. "I don't mind cooking," she said. "I never have much of a chance at home."

"Are you sure?"

No, she wasn't sure about anything. "Of course."

"I've put a call in to an agency. Because of our location, it may be a little while until I can get someone full-time. I appreciate your help."

She put the cover on the chicken dish and popped

the casserole into the oven. After setting the timer, she forced herself to smile then turn toward him.

He leaned against the island, one hip resting on the tile with his opposite leg crossing over in front and the toe of his boot touching the floor. He'd folded his arms over his chest. The blue polo shirt hugged his broad shoulders, snuggling up to skin that two nights ago she had touched and tasted. His brown eyes studied her with equal thoroughness, and she wondered what he was looking for. Would he be pleased with what he saw or would she again come up short?

She thought about the pictures in the library and how perfect Ellen had looked in each of them. Even the candid shots. Anne became aware of her wrinkled shorts and T-shirt. She'd been in her clothes all day on the road and she looked like it. She brushed a stray strand of hair out of her face. No doubt her makeup had long since faded. She was a mess.

Laurel set the table, then excused herself from the room. When she was gone, the tension in the kitchen cranked up noticeably. Anne became aware of her breathing, of the heat from the oven, which was nothing compared with the heat from the man in front of her. And he was a man. Every lean inch, every masculine line. Her body cried out for what she had known. He might be able to forget what had flared between them, but she would remember long after these two months were over.

She wondered if he would take advantage of the moment of privacy. She wanted him to pull her close and claim her mouth. She wanted him to touch her and love her and— "What time do we eat?" Jake asked.

"About seven."

He nodded. "I need to go talk to my manager and

see how the horses got along." With that he, too, left
the room.

She stared around her, at the unfamiliar room and
furniture. She thought about the need filling her body.
Apparently she'd been wrong about the tension. How
could it have been there if only she could feel it? He
didn't remember their lovemaking. He didn't trust her.

Anne checked the oven, then headed for the stairs
and her room. She wanted a long shower before dinner.

As she stepped into the spray of hot water, she told
herself she'd been a fool. Of course she'd expected
some problems during the two months she'd planned
on spending here. But it was even worse than she'd
imagined. She'd forgotten what it was like not to fit in.
She felt awkward and self-conscious about everything
she said or did. She didn't know the right food or
where anything was. She was entering another
woman's domain. It didn't matter that Ellen Masters
had been dead for two years and had never even lived
in this house. Every item and every person in this house
bore her mark. Everyone except Anne.

As the water poured down her face and mingled with
the tears, Anne wondered if it was too late to go home.

Jake stared at the open ledger in front of him. Several of the mares were going to be ready to breed soon.
He was still mentally debating about whether to cover
them with his own stallions or go outside the ranch.
He weighed the expense with the value of fresh blood-
lines.

He leaned back in his wooden chair and glanced
around the office. It still looked the same as it had
when his grandfather had lived here. Trophies and ribbons covered most of one wall. The large window that

overlooked the paddock gleamed from its weekly washing. Like the old man before him, Jake wanted to be able to see what was going on with his horses. The battered desk was close to a hundred years old. Only the computer equipment and table were new additions. He was a long way from his penthouse office in his father-in-law's executive suite. A long way from Dallas and the life he'd known before.

He heard a knock on the door.

"Come in," he called.

Anne stepped into his office. She was carrying a tray, which she placed on the corner of his desk.

"You've been in here all morning," she said. "I thought you might be hungry."

He glanced at the plate of sandwiches, the cut-up fruit and the pot of coffee. He already had a mug of his own, but there was a second one beside the pot. In the two weeks that she'd been at the ranch, they'd settled into a sort of routine. It consisted of him avoiding her and her letting him. He knew that she was spending her days alone now that Laurel was in school. He told himself he should encourage her to fix up the house if she wanted to. God knows he wasn't interested in picking out wallpaper. He even felt guilty about leaving her every morning while he came out to the barn or to his office beside the tack room. But it had been easier to stay out of her way and try to forget what happened every time they were in a room together. Now she had made the first tentative move toward a normal relationship and he couldn't throw it back in her face.

He picked up his mug. "Looks like you brought an extra cup. Why don't you sit down and keep me company." He motioned to the leather chair in front of his desk.

"I don't want to disturb you," she said, nervously wiping her hands on her jeans.

"I wouldn't have asked if I didn't want the company."

"Thanks." She smiled and took the seat.

She didn't wear much makeup. Just something around her eyes and a little lipstick. Still, when she smiled, her whole face lit up. He liked that. He was also starting to like the freckles. He noticed there were exactly eleven on her nose. He'd caught himself counting them at odd times. Like when she sat across from him at dinner or when she earnestly asked if it was all right for her to bake a cake to celebrate Laurel's first day at school.

Even in southern Colorado, late September meant the arrival of fall, so she'd exchanged her shorts for jeans. The soft denim hugged her generous curves. Jake kept trying to picture Ellen in jeans, but he didn't think his late wife had ever worn them. He tried to remember her in any trousers so that he could use the memory of her slender hips and long legs as a talisman against Anne's sensuality. But he couldn't summon her to his mind. He was forced to admire the swell of Anne's hips and the way her breasts filled the front of her blouse. At least the table shielded him and she wouldn't be able to see the result of his erotic thoughts.

Anne poured herself a cup of coffee, then refilled his mug. She stared around the room, glanced quickly at him, then away. He sensed her apprehension. It made him feel like a complete bastard. It wasn't her fault he couldn't put the memory of their lovemaking out of his mind, so instead of continuing to try, he chose to avoid her. It wasn't her fault he couldn't bear to watch his daughter grow to love her more and more each day, so he hid out in his office. It wasn't even her fault that Laurel had wanted to meet her in the first place. For that last one, he only had himself to blame.

"This is really—"

"How are you—?"

They spoke at the same time. "Go ahead," she said shyly.

"How are you getting on?" he asked. "Do you miss work?"

She shrugged. "Some. The pace is certainly different. In Houston I generally work about sixty hours a week. With that woman coming in to clean twice a week, there's not much for me to do here." She grinned. "I can only bake so many cookies without all of us getting fat."

"I—" He drew in a breath. Hell, just ask her, he told himself. She deserved a little cooperation. "I'd appreciate it if you'd consider helping Laurel decorate the house."

"She'd mentioned wanting to do that," Anne said, staring at him intently. "But I didn't want to step on any toes."

He raised his hands in a gesture of surrender. "Don't sweat my toes. I don't know anything about furniture or color schemes or Berber carpet from shag. I'd prefer not to wake up to daisies in my bedroom, but other than that, I'm pretty easy to please."

She shifted in her chair and bit her lower lip. "If you're sure?"

"I am. Really. You'd be doing me a favor."

"Okay." Her blue eyes glowed with pleasure. "No daisies, I promise."

"Good, and I'd prefer to avoid any more cow-colored pieces of furniture."

She chuckled. "I'll admit I was a little shocked when I saw the table and chairs in the kitchen, but they're kind of growing on me."

He reached for the tray and pulled it closer to him. "Don't even try," he said with a mock growl. "You should have seen the look on my face when I opened that damned crate. I'm sure it was priceless." He took a bite of the sandwich.

"What did Laurel say?"

He finished chewing. "She was thrilled. I didn't have the heart to tell her it was the ugliest thing I'd ever seen. Who in their right mind would decorate their kitchen with cow-patterned furniture?"

She giggled and leaned forward, resting her forearms on his desk. "It's very trendy. All the best people are doing it."

"I've never been very trendy."

"Well, your daughter sure is. We had a 'discussion' this morning because she wouldn't wear a blouse. She'd had it a whole year and was convinced it was out of style."

He put down his sandwich and wiped his hands on the napkin. "How is she doing in school? She's told me she'd made some friends, but I worry she's just saying that to make me feel better."

Anne grew serious. "From what she's told me, I think she is fitting in. The students here are from a more rural background than she's used to, but she knows about horses and that makes a difference. I don't think she's hiding any big secrets. I know she's a little lonely, but a new girlfriend has invited her to a slumber party this Friday, so she's getting along."

"I appreciate your hand in all this," he said.

"You've gone out of your way to help Laurel. You didn't have to."

"I wanted to." Anne drew in a deep breath. "This has been hard for both of us, I know. I didn't know what to expect when you asked me to spend two months here."

He grinned. "I don't recall asking you."

"All right. When you *ordered* me to spend two months here. Is that better?"

"Much."

Her soft giggle made him want to laugh in return. He'd been a fool to avoid her, he realized. The kicker was he'd been trying to punish her, but the person who had suffered the most was himself. She wasn't half bad. In fact, she was pretty okay. Not that he was going to tell her that. At least, not yet.

Anne reached over for the plate of fruit. Her hand hovered above a slice of cantaloupe. "May I?"

"Help yourself."

She picked it up. "I'll admit that I didn't expect to spend two months here. I thought I'd drive up with you two, fix whatever needed fixing, then fly home and get on with my life. I thought I'd see Laurel every few months, maybe for a week or so during the summer, and that would be it." She took a bite and chewed slowly. "It's not like that at all, is it?"

"No. You're building a relationship with her, and a bond. That's hard to ignore."

"Do you still hate me?" she asked.

"I told you I never hated you."

"I know, you say you just didn't trust me. But the truth is you did hate me. Admit it, Jake. Why wouldn't you? I would have hated you if the situations were reversed. But do you still?"

He thought about the sound of Laurel's laughter and how much he heard it these days. He remembered the look on Anne's face every time his daughter talked about her late mother and how she never told Laurel to stop mentioning Ellen. He stared down at his half-eaten sandwich and remembered how she consulted him before trying a new dish. She was always careful to, as she put it, not step on any toes.

What was in it for her? In a few weeks she would go back to her real life. Laurel would miss her and want to keep in touch, but the reality of the situation was that Laurel would probably now be content to stay with him. Anne would find her condo lonely without the chatter of a thirteen-year-old underfoot. He'd learned that in the few hours Laurel had been missing.

"Truth?" he asked.

"Truth," she answered.

"No, I don't hate you, Anne." He couldn't. She'd given too much unselfishly. She was going to pay a big price for that giving. He could afford to be generous. He didn't only understand what she was going to feel, he realized he, too, was going to miss her when she was gone.

"Do you think we can be friends?" She stared at him as earnestly as a schoolgirl.

He smiled. "I'd like that."

"Even if I decorate your bathroom with cow accessories?"

"That would put a strain on the relationship."

She grinned. "Okay. I just wanted to know where the line was."

He chuckled. Anne loved the sound of his laughter. He could make her knees quiver and her thighs go up in flames. Down, girl, she told herself. This was about building emotional bridges, not passion. In fact, in the past two weeks Jake had done nothing to indicate he was the least bit turned on by her. Apparently their little roll in the hay—more like their little roll on a rock—had been enough to appease him. He was calm, competent and completely impersonal around her. He couldn't have treated her any more asexually if he had been her brother. She, on the other hand, had all the subtlety of a cat in heat. Every time she saw him, she wanted to rub against his body and purr.

On that cheerful note, she was going to leave. She stood up. "I should be heading back to the house. I have to get dinner in the oven. Then I'm going to pull out those catalogs and think about ordering furniture. Is there a budget?"

He reached for the second half of his sandwich. "Try to spend less than it cost to build the house."

She raised her eyebrows. "That's it?"

"You seem surprised."

"Let's just say it's a long way from Paradise."

The humor left his eyes. The gold-flecked irises darkened with compassion. "It is, Anne. But not so far from Houston."

"That's true. I'm not little Annie Jo Baker anymore."

His smile turned wistful. "I think I might have liked her just as much as I like Anne Baker."

Maybe even more, Anne thought as she waved goodbye and headed back toward the house. Annie Jo would have stayed in Paradise and kept her daughter with her. She would have tried to make it on her own. Anne sighed. Who's to say what would have been right? She could make herself crazy thinking about it.

She entered the kitchen. After collecting the vegetables she would need, she started chopping onions. A quick glance at the clock told her that if she was in Houston instead of on Jake's ranch, she would probably be knee-deep in meetings right about this time.

"If they could see me now," she said as she peeled the second onion. The pungent smell began to burn her eyes.

Where would she be if she'd stayed in Paradise? She would never know if she'd made the right decision or the easy one. But she was here and she'd better make the best of it. Not everyone got a second chance.

Her stomach lurched, surprising her. She stopped chopping and swallowed. Suddenly she didn't feel so great. She washed her hands, then drank a glass of water. If anything, the liquid made her feel worse. Almost nauseous. Was it the onions? She stared at the cutting board. They'd never bothered her before.

She started to take another sip of water when her stomach heaved. She set the glass on the counter and ran to the bathroom.

When she was done throwing up, she washed her face and sat on the closed toilet seat lid. Could it be the flu? Anne pressed a hand against her midsection. She hadn't felt this bad in years. She blinked. Thirteen years. She blinked again.

No. It wasn't possible. It couldn't be possible. Jake had said he was sterile. But it had been the middle of her cycle, at her most fertile time. Oh, God.

She ran through the kitchen and into the hallway. The Explorer keys hung on a hook. Jake had told her she could use his truck anytime she wanted. She grabbed the keys and her purse and headed out the front door. The closest drugstore was about five miles down the road. She had a couple of hours before Laurel got home from school. She could pick up the kit and be back in plenty of time. Then all she had to do was wait until morning. Then she would know for sure.

Chapter 9

Jake drew the razor along his jaw. The master bath off his bedroom was big enough not to get steamy. The eight-foot-long mirror reflected his image, the double sinks and the stall shower in the corner. Behind him was the Jacuzzi. He glanced at the tiled monstrosity and wondered what on earth his grandfather had been thinking of when he'd ordered that. Jake had never bothered to fill it up and turn on the jets. For all he knew, the sucker didn't even work. There were a lot of luxuries in the house he considered unnecessary. But his grandfather had passed away about three weeks after construction had started. Jake had been too devastated to do more than let the contractors continue with their work. It had been easier than planning a new house. He realized now that in the back of his mind he'd always figured on coming here and building up the horse ranch.

He adjusted the towel around his waist before wiping

away the shaving cream. He'd barely finished drying his face when the door to his bathroom flew open.

"You bastard!" Anne said as she stormed into the room. "You damned bastard." Her voice was low and controlled but there was no mistaking her anger.

"What the hell is wrong with you?" he asked, as confused by her rage as by her presence in his bathroom. It was barely six in the morning. "Don't you believe in knocking?"

"Interesting choice of words," she said. In her left hand she held a slender plastic wand. She raised her right and pointed her index finger at him. "How dare you? How *dare* you? Was it fun, like playing a game? Did you think you would risk it and let me pay the consequences?"

Her emotions flooded the room. He leaned one hip against the counter and folded his arms over his chest. "Are you going to tell me what you're talking about or do you want to rant some more?"

Her skin was pale, but her eyes flashed fire. Under her white cotton gown, her breasts rose and fell with each breath. He realized the filmy fabric was see-through. The darker circles of her aureoles and her puckered nipples were clearly visible. He hoped the towel was thick enough to hide his instant reaction.

"What is it about cowboys?" she asked, as if he hadn't spoken. She lowered her hand to her side and started to pace the room. She walked to the shower, then back in front of him to the closet door. On the return trip she glared at him. "Is it the jeans? Is it the button fly? Why can't I resist a tight butt in denim? Am I cursed or just stupid?"

"If you're looking for an answer, I sure as hell don't

have one. I don't know what you're talking about. And
keep your voice down. You'll wake Laurel.''

"Wake her? As if you thought you could keep this
a secret?''

She stopped in front of him and leaned close. He
could feel the heat of her body and smell her scent.
Her short hair was tousled from sleep. He wanted to
touch the shiny strands and run his fingers through her
curls. He wanted to pull her close and kiss away her
anger. He wished she would get to the reason for her
tirade because his groin had swelled past the point of
uncomfortable, and his daughter's alarm wasn't scheduled to go off for another half hour. It wasn't as much
time as he wanted to make love with Anne, but it
would be enough to ease whatever ailed her.

"Fine," she said, poking his chest. "Play dumb. Just
answer me this. Why? Why did you do it?''

"Do what?" he asked, his patience beginning to
evaporate. "What are you talking about?''

"This." She tossed the wand onto the counter. It
rolled until it came to rest against a box of tissue. He'd
been wrong. It wasn't all white. One end was bright
blue.

He looked from the device to her. "This is supposed
to mean something?''

She stared at him as if he were as dumb as a stone.
Then she shook her head. When she spoke, she enun-
ciated each word carefully. "I'm pregnant.''

He knew they didn't have anything close to a relationship, but his first emotion was heart-stopping betrayal. She'd told him it had been years since she'd
been with someone and he'd been fool enough to believe her. His gaze dropped to her belly, and the tri-
angle of reddish curls below.

"You lying bitch," he said softly. "What's next? You have some disease that you forgot to tell me about?"

"Disease?" Her brows drew together. "Lying? You're the one who lied. You're the one who promised you were sterile. Did you get a kick out of playing God? I even told you it was the middle of my cycle. What were you trying to prove?" She poked him in the chest again. "What is it? That you're too macho to use a condom? This is the nineties, buster. Only fools are unprotected. Okay, I was a fool. I admit that. But I'm pregnant!"

He tried to control his breathing, but he couldn't do anything except feel the red thick rage that flowed through him. His hands tightened into fists. He fought to relax them because he was afraid he would have to pound the wall over and over until she stopped torturing him. A child. She taunted him with a child.

Michael's words returned to him. "I'm sorry, son. The problem is with you. The problem is with you. With you. With you." The words echoed.

"No!" Jake said loudly. "No!" he roared. "Dammit, no!"

Anne backed away from him. He advanced on her. She grabbed for the door, but first she accidentally bumped it with her heel and it slammed shut. Her blue eyes widened with fear.

"Stop it," she commanded.

He froze in his tracks and fought the demons. With conscious effort he relaxed his muscles one by one. He turned from her and returned to lean against the counter. Slowly sanity replaced rage. With awareness came humiliation. She'd used him.

"You will not pawn another one of your bastard children off on me," he said softly.

A gasp was her only reply.

He didn't wait for more, he simply continued. "I don't know if this is what you did with Bobby. Was he Laurel's real father or did you try to trick him, too? Or are you such a slut you can't remember who knocked you up?"

"What's wrong with you?" she asked, coming up and standing next to him. "Why would I lie about this? Why would I pass another man's child off as yours?"

"So you could stay here, with Laurel." He turned suddenly and grabbed her arms. "It won't work." He shook her. "By God, it won't work."

"Stop it," she cried. "Just stop it."

He let her go and stared at his hands. What was wrong with him? In all the years he'd been married to Ellen, he'd never been this angry before.

"I'm not lying," she said. A lock of hair fell into her face. She brushed it back impatiently. He saw the tears in her eyes. "I swear, Jake, I'm not lying. My last relationship ended about four years ago. I haven't been with a man since. Why are you doing this? Why won't you believe me? You were there. You know what happened."

"Because I'm sterile," he said. "I can't father children."

The tears spilled over and ran down her cheeks. She squared her shoulders. Strength flowed through her. He could see it in the way she raised her head and tilted her chin. She defied him. "I've been honest with you from the beginning. I've been willing to accommodate myself to you and your wishes. I've tried to be fair with Laurel and with you. Not once have I lied or used my position against you.'' She wiped her face with the back of her hand. ''You and I made love almost three weeks ago. We were irresponsible and didn't use protection. I'm pregnant. The child is yours, Jake. Believe me or not. There's nothing more I can say to convince you.'' She walked over to the bathroom door and opened it. Before she left, she turned back and stared at him. ''Did it ever occur to you that the doctor made a mistake?'' The door shut behind her.

He looked around for something to throw. He needed to vent the rage inside him. How dare she try to pawn off some man's bastard. What kind of a fool did she take him for?

He gripped the counter, squeezing tight until his hands ached. The doctor might be wrong. Hell, what other piece of goods would she try to sell him? Maybe she wanted him to start digging for gold in the paddock. The doctor might be wrong. Why not say the doctor lied? He closed his eyes and exhaled sharply. Even as he tried to forget, Michael's words returned, getting louder and louder. ''It's your fault. Your fault. Yours.''

God, it was a waking nightmare. He couldn't escape from the past. That lying, cheating, no-good bastard. Of all the people to give him the news. Why had he been the one?

Michael lied whenever it suited him. That was one of the reasons Jake hadn't wanted to continue doing business with his father-in-law. Michael had been willing to cheat anyone out of a buck. The only person in the world he cared about was Ellen. He would have done anything to protect her. Anything at all.

Suddenly Jake straightened and met his own gaze in the mirror. Disbelief and the desire to make it true battled with reality. It couldn't be that simple, could it? Just one lie in a long line of lies? He walked out of the bathroom and headed for the phone sitting on the floor by his bed.

Anne washed the red apple, then wiped it dry. She placed it in the paper bag and folded over the top. "Laurel, you're going to be late," she called.

The teenager slowly entered the kitchen. Anne glanced up at her. "You're going to be late," she repeated, then realized Laurel's eyes were red. "What's wrong?"

"I heard you and Daddy fighting," she said softly.

Anne's heart stopped. Oh, no, anything but that. She swallowed hard. "What did you hear, honey?" she asked, praying it wasn't as bad as she thought.

Laurel shrugged. "Nothing you said. I just heard you yelling at each other." She blinked several times, but the tears still escaped. "Don't fight with my dad. Don't go away."

"Oh, baby." Anne moved close to her and wrapped her arms around her slender body. "Hush. I'm not going away." At least not yet, she thought, wondering what on earth she was going to do. "We were just arguing. Grown-ups often do that. Sometimes it gets loud but it doesn't mean we hate each other." Anne gave her a reassuring smile even as she knew she was lying. Jake thought she was a slut, and she thought he was a weasel bastard. Not a great basis for a relationship. Still, none of that had anything to do with Laurel.

The teenager moved away and went to pour herself a bowl of cereal. Anne didn't want to think about food. Not this early. She couldn't even face coffee, she thought, turning away from the pot. Good thing because caffeine probably wasn't healthy for the baby.

Baby. Her knees grew weak and she had to grab a hold of the counter. She was going to have a baby. All last night she'd been frantic with worry, wondering if her suspicions were correct. She'd had to wait until this morning before she could take the test. Then she'd been so furious with Jake for lying to her that she hadn't had time to absorb the news. She was going to have a baby...another baby. She pressed her hands to her stomach as if she could already feel the fragile life growing inside of her.

"You okay?" Laurel asked from her place at the table.

"What?" Anne stared blankly at her. "Oh, sure." She was going to have a baby. A second chance to do it right. On the heels of joy came confusion. What was she going to tell Laurel? What was she going to do with a newborn? What about her promotion? What about her career? What about Jake? Why did he continue to lie to her? Why didn't he think the child was his? Had he been telling the truth when he said he was sterile? But he couldn't be—she was *pregnant,* and he was the only man she'd been with. What if he never believed her? What if—

"Annie, you're not listening to me," Laurel complained.

"I'm sorry." Anne forced herself to take a seat at the table. Questions swirled through her head. She tried to ignore them and concentrate on Laurel. "What were you saying?"

"School pictures are next week. I need you to help me pick out something to wear."

The request was light-years away from what Anne

wanted to think and talk about. Scratch that, she thought suddenly. She certainly couldn't tell Laurel she was pregnant. Not yet. And certainly not until she'd figured out what was going on with Jake.

"Okay, a school picture. What about that red blouse you bought in Houston? You could wear it with your black pants."

Laurel shook her head. "I don't like the collar. It puffs my hair out."

"Then your cream sweater with the pink flecks. That would photograph well."

Laurel slumped in her chair. "What would I wear with it? It only looks good with jeans."

"The pictures are from your chest up, aren't they?" Anne asked, struggling to keep her patience. "What's wrong with wearing jeans?"

Laurel rolled her eyes. "It's picture day. We're supposed to dress up. Mom always told me to wear a dress."

Mom this, Mom that. Anne drew in a breath. She was trying to be understanding. Really she was. But every time she turned around she heard yet another truism from the sainted lips of Ellen Masters, as voiced by her daughter. *My* daughter, Anne thought defiantly.

"I can't deal with this now," Anne said, standing up.

"But the pictures are next week."

"Fine. Then we have the weekend, don't we?" She pointed at the paper bag. "Your lunch is ready. The bus will be here in about ten minutes. Please don't be late for it." She started walking up the stairs.

"Where are you going?" Laurel asked, trailing after her.

"My room."

''Why?''

Anne didn't bother answering. Why was she going to her room? Because she was tired, pregnant by a man who refused to acknowledge even the likelihood of his paternity, in a strange house, possibly risking her job, definitely risking her promotion, and sick to death of hearing what ''Mom'' would have done about any situation imaginable.

Anne taped several wallpaper swatches next to the window in Laurel's room. She'd promised the girl she would help her there first. The delicate floral prints belonged to different color schemes. One was rose, the other a pale blue. She'd already narrowed the selection down to several bedroom sets. Laurel could pick the one she liked best.

Anne walked across the room and looked at the samples, trying to get a feel for which would be more attractive. It was possible that Laurel would hate all of them. She stared at the patterns, then hurried back and touched their smooth surfaces. Pink and blue. A boy or a girl. She swallowed. She was having a baby.

Her legs grew weak and she sank to the bare floor, pulling her knees up close to her chest. A baby. She closed her eyes and allowed the feelings to wash over her. Regret. There was so much regret. She remembered the terror almost fourteen years ago when her period had been late. She'd waited and waited, praying every night and morning that God would make her not be pregnant. She'd waited until her clothes hadn't fit anymore before going to her mother and confessing her horrible secret. By then she'd been over four months along.

Anne hugged her knees closer. Life grew inside her.

Precious life. A tiny being who would grow into her child.

She could remember the pain of labor. Of how she'd tried not to cry out. She'd been young and healthy, and it had ended quickly. But they hadn't let her hold her baby. They'd whisked the infant away, then judged her—the unwed mother—with their cold stares. Most of all, she remembered the emptiness of her heart. How she'd cried all night after her own mother had gone to the motel next door to rest. She'd tried to console herself with thoughts of college and a new life. She tried to imagine what the young couple would be like and how they would treat her baby. But it had been hard to think of anything but the pain inside her and how her arms had ached to hold her child.

She raised her head and looked at the posters Laurel had on her walls. There were a couple of young men from a popular TV show and a few of rock stars. Teen magazines lay around the floor and across the bed. Tubes of lipstick, the only makeup her father let her wear, were scattered on the single dresser.

Laurel was almost grown-up. Soon she would be entering high school, then college. Anne picked up a small tattered teddy bear and held it in her hand. The poor thing had lost most of its fur. One eye was gone and the threads that made up the nose were coming loose. She hugged the bear to her breast. This toy was as close as she would come to the child she'd lost that summer. She would never know what Laurel had been like as an infant or a toddler. She would never see that first step, hear those first words. She would always wonder.

She clenched her stomach tight. Was this new life an exchange for what she'd already lost? Or was it more punishment? How could she be happy about being pregnant now? Her world was turned upside down. What was she going to do with a baby? What about her job and her promotion? What about child care and labor and maternity leave? How could she live in Houston if Jake lived in Colorado?

What about Jake? He was acting crazy. What if he never believed it was his child? Did that matter?

She looked at the bear and smiled at its worn face. No, she told herself firmly. It didn't matter. She would have this child on her own. She would figure out a way to make it work without Jake. She would find her own answers and go forward.

But what was she going to tell Laurel?

She dropped the bear and lowered her forehead onto her knees. How could she explain to the child she'd given up, that this time she wanted to keep her baby? There were plenty of logical reasons why she could now keep her child, but she had a feeling none of that was going to matter to Laurel.

The sound of a car stopping by the house followed by a door slamming shut brought her out of her reverie. Jake was back. She hadn't seen him leave, although Laurel had mentioned something about it when she'd yelled her goodbye.

Anne scrambled to her feet and walked out into the hallway. She didn't know if she should go into her room and lock the door behind her or go confront him. She shook her head wearily. What was she going to say to him? She'd told him the truth. If he didn't believe her before, no new words were going to change his mind.

She was almost to her room when she heard him

calling her. She walked to the top of the stairs. He stood at the bottom, his black Stetson in one hand.

He looked different, she thought, wary of his intense gaze. The lines of his face had deepened and his mouth pulled straight. There was an aura of controlled energy about him. Something hiding just under the surface, as if he fought with an emotion he couldn't quite control.

"Would you come down and join me?" he asked, pointing to the living room. His voice gave nothing away.

Anne hesitated for a second, then placed her hand on the cool wooden railing and slowly walked down the stairs. When she reached the bottom, Jake held out his hand, indicating she should precede him. She walked to the far couch and sat down on the edge of the cushion.

He tossed his hat on the other sofa, then stood in front of her. He braced his feet apart and rested his hands on his hips. Even with all that had gone on between them that morning, it was difficult to ignore the way he made her feel. Just seeing his long, powerful jeans-clad legs made her glad she was sitting. The proud set of his shoulders and head made her want to cling to him and borrow his strength. A fierce feeling of gladness stole through her. It didn't make any sense at all, but she was pleased he was the father. Her child would be strong because Jake was strong.

The silence between them lengthened. She glanced around the empty room, but there wasn't anything to look at so she found herself returning his intense stare. She wanted to ask what he was thinking, then realized she was too chicken to really want to know. What if it was awful? What if he still thought she'd lied?

At last she cleared her throat. "You took off without

giving the men instructions," she said. "When they came looking for you, I didn't know when you'd be back. I told them to take care of their normal chores, then continue with what they were doing yesterday."

"Thank you for that," he said, never taking his eyes from her face.

"It's nearly noon," she blurted out. "I didn't know how long you were going to stay gone. I didn't know what to tell Laurel. She heard us fighting this morning." Concern flashed across his face. "Not what we were saying," she added hastily. "Just the loud voices. I told her it was an argument and it didn't mean anything."

Jake shoved his hands into his pockets and paced to the window. When he reached the wide expanse of glass, he turned and walked back to her. He reached down and pulled her up next to him.

She stood reluctantly, prepared to step away if he started yelling at her again. But he didn't say a word. He touched her face with the back of his hand. His knuckles moved up and down against her cheek. His thumb brushed across her mouth. The softness of the brief contact made her want to lean forward into his embrace. But she held herself straight and waited.

He rested his hands on her shoulders and looked down at her.

"You're pregnant," he said quietly.

"Thanks for the news flash, but I believe I already told *you* that."

He smiled and reached down toward her stomach. She started to back up, then stood still. Slowly, tentatively, he pressed his hand against her belly. She felt the warmth through her jeans and panties, all the way to her quivering skin. Heat flared and traveled with her blood until every part of her body hummed from the contact. Her breasts tightened. She didn't dare look down to see if her nipples were betraying her state of arousal. He was treating her with all the reverence of a worshiper at a shrine, and all she could think about was having him touch her more.

His hand moved back and forth, creating delicious friction. She glanced at his face. He had the strangest expression, as if he'd just discovered something wonderful. Their eyes met, and he smiled.

"You're pregnant," he repeated. "And I'm the father."

Chapter 10

Jake heard the cursing even before he entered the kitchen. He grinned. Anne swore again, then something hit the floor. He walked to the entrance and leaned against the doorframe.

Bowls and dirty utensils were scattered on all the counters. Pots covered the stove. The sink was filled with dirty dishes. Anne stood with her back to him. She wore an oversize shirt and jeans. Thick socks covered her feet. A headband held her hair off her face. She turned to grab something and he saw a streak of red sauce on her cheek.

"You want to talk about it?" he asked.

She shrieked and dropped the spoon she'd been holding. "Don't do that," she said, spinning toward him. "You scared me to death. I didn't hear you come in."

"That's because you were cussing too loud."

She flushed and stared down at the counter. "I'm

having a little trouble with this recipe,'' she said, motioning to an open cookbook.

"So it would seem."

"Oh, stop it," she said, and went back to her mixing. "I know what you're thinking, and you're wrong."

He moved into the kitchen and pulled out one of the cow chairs. After turning it around, he sat straddling it and resting his hands on the back. "What am I thinking?"

Her shoulders raised and lowered in an exaggerated sigh. "That I'm trying to compete with a paragon. Sainted Ellen." The spoon clattered into the bowl again. She turned toward him and covered her mouth with her hand. Her eyes widened in horror. "Oh, Jake, I'm sorry. I didn't mean to say that."

He waited, wondering if he would get angry with her. Nothing. He prodded his heart, the broken part that still missed Ellen. There wasn't any pain. He knew he would mourn her always, but the woman he missed had died so long ago. The wife he'd lost two years before had little in common with her save name and appearance.

"It's okay," he said, and was pleased to find out he meant it. "Ellen could be a little intimidating for all of us. She had this thing about her world being perfect."

Anne glanced around at the disaster that when he'd left that morning had still been a kitchen. "She probably kept things clean, too. I just never learned how to cook neatly. I know you're supposed to wash as you go. Put things away when you're done with them." She picked up a jar of spices. "I try to, but then I get caught up in the recipe or something boils before it's supposed to and then I can't do anything but handle the crisis."

She frowned. "You probably think I'm completely incompetent, but really, I'm good at my job."

"I believe you," he said, liking this flustered woman much better than the controlled, competent stranger he'd met in Houston. He liked her in jeans instead of tailored trousers. He liked her sleepy in the morning because she'd stopped drinking coffee. He liked the way she started projects and didn't complete them.

Laurel's room was almost finished. The walls were done, but the furniture hadn't been delivered. Anne had already tackled the living room and the library together. Samples of wallpaper were tacked up in the front room. Between the bookshelves she'd dabbed bits of paint so they could "live" with the color. She'd taught Laurel some needle craft and pieces of embroidery floss littered the floor. She'd found an old sewing machine and was making curtains for the kitchen. He glanced at the scraps of fabric on the far counter and cringed at the cow print. She'd convinced him that they would blend with the table and chairs, but he sensed that he'd been had.

Ellen had kept his house orderly. Rooms had been decorated one by one, and kept closed off while the work was being done. She'd rarely appeared out of their bedroom without makeup. He liked the chaos; it reminded him that he was alive.

"What are you cooking?" he asked.

"Lasagna," she said, then looked at him. "Let me guess. You hate it."

"It's one of my favorites."

"Ellen had a secret family recipe?"

He shook his head. "To the best of my knowledge, she never made it."

"Thank God." She motioned to the mess on the

stove. "I decided to make the sauce from scratch. Then I wanted to use fresh tomatoes instead of canned and well, it all got out of hand."

"This isn't a competition," he said softly.

"I know. I tell myself that. Most of the time, I almost believe it."

"I was worried when I moved out to the ranch. I didn't think I'd measure up to what my grandfather did."

"Really?" She looked over and smiled. "You hide it well. I can't picture you not being the best." She bit her lip and ducked her head as if she regretted the compliment.

"Michael told me I was a fool for leaving the company. That I'd never amount to anything." He shrugged. "I tried not to let it get to me. There was plenty of money, so I didn't have to make the ranch pay, but it wasn't about finances. I wanted to build something of my own. My grandfather talked about his dreams for this place. He never saw them realized. After hearing about them, they became my dreams, too." He stopped, suddenly, feeling self-conscious. "That sounds pretty dumb, huh?"

"Not at all." She pulled a lasagna noodle out of a large pot and placed it in a casserole dish. "I think it's wonderful. I hope you get everything you want. I just don't understand your father-in-law's part in all this. Why was he so creepy?"

"I don't know. I tell myself it doesn't matter anymore, except as it relates to Laurel."

"Do you think—?" Anne concentrated on layering the cheese.

"What?" he asked.

"I— Don't get mad, but do you think Ellen knew? About the sterility thing, I mean?"

"No," he said quickly. She looked at him. He squeezed the back of the chair. "I don't know. I want to believe she was an innocent party in all this. The woman I loved would never have been that dishonest." But the woman he'd loved had been gone so long, it was hard to remember what she was like. The other Ellen, the woman she'd become in later years, she would have kept that kind of secret if it had meant holding her perfect world together.

"I'm sure you're right," Anne said, spooning sauce into the dish.

He studied her, trying to see if she was humoring him. She gave him an impatient glance.

"I mean it," she said. "You and Ellen grew up together. You knew each other very well. If she'd been hiding something that big, you would have been able to sense it. Besides, she would have been devastated by the news. I doubt anyone would be able to hide that kind of pain."

"Did you hide the pain of losing Laurel?" he asked without thinking.

She slowed in her work, then stopped all together. "I don't know." She placed her hands on the counter and stared at the casserole dish. A spot of sauce lay on the tile. She wiped it with her finger, then cleaned herself on her jeans. "I gave birth in August, and I was leaving for college about four weeks later. I don't remember much about that time except sitting in the shade and reading book after book. I just wanted to get lost and forget everything that had happened. My mother knew of course, so I didn't bother hiding it from her." She reached in the large pot and drew out a lasagna noodle to start the second layer. "At college—" she shrugged "—it took me a while to make friends, so I didn't have to hide it from anyone because they wouldn't have known in the first place." She looked at him and smiled. "You're right, Jake. Ellen couldn't have known. As much as you and Laurel loved her, she couldn't have been that cruel."

"Thank you for that," he said, rising to his feet and walking over to stand next to her. He leaned on the counter. "I know this hasn't been easy for you."

"If you tell me that you appreciate me, I'll attack you with this sauce spoon," she said, waving the utensil in the air.

"I do appreciate you."

"I warned you." She reached into the smaller saucepan and scooped up a spoonful of thick red sauce.

He backed up, holding his hands out in front of him. "I take it back," he said, and smiled. "I don't appreciate you at all."

She eyed him for a moment, then dropped the spoon into the pan. "Better," she said. "At least we're a little closer to the truth."

"What does that mean?"

"You're being nice to me because of the baby."

"I—" His denial died before he finished speaking it. Was he? "I'm excited about the baby, Anne. I'll admit that. I've never had a child before. If I'm a little crazy and overprotective it's because I'm concerned."

"About the baby?"

"Yes."

"I'm the one who wanted you to be honest." She reached for the cheese and began smoothing it in place. Her shoulders were hunched as if she carried a heavy weight.

He tried to figure out what he'd said to upset her. "I'm not like Michael. I won't say or do anything to hurt you. I haven't lied to Laurel about you or tried to influence her against you."

"I know that. I appreciate it." She chuckled. "I can't seem to get away from that word."

"Then what did I say?" he asked, confused by her sudden change in mood.

"Nothing, Jake." She looked up at him. "Forget it. I understand that you're feeling protective. I am, too. I worry about Laurel, about what's going to happen when she finds out about the baby."

He glanced at her stomach, but the oversize shirt she wore hid it from view. "Were you big with Laurel?" he asked, trying to picture her swollen with his child.

She shrugged. "Not huge, but it did get pretty uncomfortable. Especially in Paradise in the summer. We didn't have an air conditioner. I lived in front of the fan. My feet puffed up like water balloons." She grimaced at the memory. "I was a lot younger then. It probably won't be so easy this time."

He moved closer to her, eyeing her waistline. "How long until you felt the baby move?"

"I don't remember. Four or five months, I think. I'll ask the doctor when I see her."

"Have you made an appointment?" He moved behind her.

"Not yet. I thought I'd wait until— What are you doing?" she asked as he nestled against her and slid his arms around her waist.

"Nothing. Just go on with what you're doing."

"I can't."

She tried to twist away from him, but he wrapped

his arms around her and held on. She felt warm and smelled like flowers and Italian seasonings.

"Jake, what on earth are you—?"

He slipped one hand under her shirt. "Hush. I want to feel my baby."

"Don't be silly. There's nothing to feel," she said, but her voice had gone strangely soft.

He rested his cheek against her ear and murmured soothingly, as if gentling a skittish mare. Her body stiffened in his arms, then relaxed. He ran his fingers up her jeans to the snap. After unfastening it, he pulled the zipper down, then slipped his hand inside. He rubbed back and forth against her cotton panties. Her breathing increased slightly. He, too, was becoming aroused, but this wasn't about sex, he reminded himself. It was about the baby.

He moved his other hand down so both his palms cradled her stomach. Her cotton panties were too much of a barrier. He pushed them away so that he was touching her soft skin.

"You're having my baby," he murmured.

"If you start singing that damn song, I'll slug you. I hate that song."

He chuckled. "You are one feisty woman, aren't you?"

"You got that right."

He squeezed her tight. "I wish I could feel him moving," he said, rubbing back and forth along her skin.

"That'll happen soon enough. Then I'll look like I swallowed a basketball. My skin will stretch, my back will ache. I won't be able to sleep."

"Is it really going to be that bad?"

She drew in a deep breath so that her back pressed more against his chest. Her round buttocks brushed his groin. He was as hard as a rock, but he reminded himself this wasn't about sex.

"N-no."

It was the stutter in her voice that warned him his roving fingers had slipped lower on her belly. He felt the tickle of soft hair. It had been dark when they'd made love. Suddenly he wanted to see the color of the curls protecting her female secrets.

Don't be a fool, he told himself. But one finger moved lower to the dip at the apex of her thighs. Heat enveloped him. He wanted to plunge in and feel her moistness. He wanted to touch her most sensitive place and bring her pleasure. He wanted to raise her up on the counter and bury himself inside of her.

Before he could do any of that, she grabbed his wrist and pulled his hand up from her jeans.

"Let's hold off on the baby feeling until there's something more there, okay?" she said, her voice controlled.

But he heard the quiver underneath and knew somehow it had become about sex. What was there about Anne Baker that turned him on? He had to figure it out. When he could think straight.

He backed up. While he was trying to think nonarousing thoughts, she fastened her jeans and pulled up the zipper.

"Annie, I didn't mean—"

"It's okay," she said curtly, and went back to work on the lasagna.

"But I don't want you to think—"

"It's *okay*. I understand."

He wished he did. Instead of resuming his seat on the chair where his straddled position would flaunt his erection, he leaned against the counter. Her face was flushed bright enough to blend with the tomato sauce on her cheek.

"What are we going to do?" he asked.

"About what?"

"The baby? What else?"

"Oh." She swallowed. "I don't know. Our first concern should be for Laurel. I don't know how to tell her. She's going to hate me when she finds out."

"She won't hate you."

Anne laughed, but the sound wasn't pleasant. "That's easy for you to say. You get to come out perfectly in all this. I, on the other hand, am going to be the bad guy. Thirteen years ago I gave her up for adoption. Here I am, a single mother once again, but this time, I'm keeping my child. How is she going to feel about that?"

"Our child," he said, not liking her possessive tone.

"What?"

"The baby is mine, too."

She dropped the spoon she was holding and turned toward him. "It's not even real yet. The baby, our baby, if that makes you feel better, isn't going to be here for over eight months. Laurel is here right now. I don't want to have to lose her because you finally figured out you were fertile." She glared up at him, apparently unintimidated by the discrepancy in their size.

"So what do you want to do?" he asked.

"I don't know." She picked up the lasagna and put it into the oven. "But I'm not losing her now. Not after getting this second chance. You may not want to admit it, Jake, but Laurel is as much my daughter as this baby is your child."

He didn't have to like it, but she was right. "I know."

She raised her eyebrows. "That's quite an admission. I expected more of a fight."

"Why? It's true." He started to walk out of the kitchen, then paused by the doorway. "You don't want to lose Laurel, I don't want to lose my son."

Anne watched him walk toward the barn and his office. Great. Now what were they going to do? Part-time parenting? She would keep the baby for six months, he would have Laurel, then they would switch? That wasn't going to work. Would he give up his precious horses and come live in Houston? She shook her head. Of course not. She didn't want to move, either. She finally had the promotion she'd been working for since the day she graduated from college. As much as she enjoyed her time being in the house, decorating, baking, even sewing again, she couldn't move to Colorado. What would she do here? Act as the housekeeper?

The perfect solution, she thought sarcastically, wondering how many fights they could possibly get into each week. She started carrying the dirty pots and pans over to the sink. There was another reason living near him would never work, at least not for her.

Passion. Pure, simple, animal passion. When he'd touched her... She braced her arms against the edge of the sink and bit back a groan. She couldn't believe how quickly she'd gone from embarrassment to desire. She'd been ready to make love with him right there on the kitchen floor. She glanced over her shoulder toward the cow table. That would have worked as well.

Her stomach clenched tightly as she thought about his gentle hands on her belly. He'd stroke her reverently, searching for a hint of their growing child. Then he'd moved lower. Her hips flexed involuntarily. If he'd brushed against her center just once, she probably would have climaxed right there. Even thinking about it was making her blood hum through her veins.

"So stop thinking about it," she ordered herself and started cleaning the kitchen.

She'd almost finished washing up when she heard the school bus stopping in front of the driveway. About three minutes later the front door opened and slammed shut.

"I'm home," Laurel called.

"So I hear."

The teenager flew into the kitchen. "Something smells good. What are you cooking?"

"Lasagna."

"Great." She gave Anne a hug, then reached for the cookie jar, in one fluid motion.

"How was school?" Anne asked.

Laurel shrugged. "Good. I talked to Terry and that party is still on for tomorrow night."

"This is another sleep-over, right?"

"Uh-huh," Laurel mumbled, her mouth full. She filled a glass with milk and gulped down half of it. "But first there's a real party. With boys." Her hazel eyes gleamed with excitement.

"Boys?" Anne felt faint.

"Don't panic, Annie. Terry's parents are going to be there."

"That's something at least. Does your father know about boys being at the party?"

Laurel nodded. "He threatened to send me to a convent until I'm twenty-five, but I told him to lighten up. I'm a teenager now."

"Oh, well, that would make all the difference in the

world.'' Anne smiled. "So you're excited about this then?''

"Sure. Lots of people are going to be there. The best kids, you know.''

"So you're part of the 'in' crowd.''

Laurel sat at the table. She rolled her eyes. "You are so old. 'In' crowd. That's dumb.'' She sat up straight and raised one shoulder. "If you're asking me if I'm popular, the answer is—'' She paused dramatically. "Yes.'' She dissolved into giggles.

Anne filled a glass with water and took the seat next to her. When Laurel offered her stash of cookies, Anne refused. Her stomach hadn't recovered from Jake's tender caresses.

"Is this the same girl who kicked and screamed about moving away from Dallas?'' she asked.

"I never kicked.''

"But you did scream.''

"Maybe a little.'' Laurel's smile faded. "I still miss my friends, but it's kinda okay being out here. I get to ride my horse a lot. Most of the kids are nice. Some of the boys are cute.''

Jake walked into the kitchen. "You're not allowed to think boys are cute,'' he said. "I thought I explained that to you.''

"Da-ad.''

"See, you're already too grown-up to call me Daddy.'' He bent down and kissed the top of her head, then gave Anne a wink.

Laurel flipped her long hair over her shoulder. "Dad, you're so immature.''

"And you're the queen of maturity. How was school?''

"Fine. We're talking about the party. I have to have something perfect to wear."

Anne held her hands up in front of her. "I'm not getting involved with that one again."

"What one?" Jake asked.

"We had a slight disagreement about what Laurel would wear to school pictures."

"I was thinking about my red dress," Laurel said. "The one with the lace sleeves."

"Isn't that a little dressy?" Jake poured himself a glass of milk, snagged the cookie jar with his other hand and sauntered over to the table.

He often joined them in the kitchen when Laurel got home from school. Anne told herself it didn't *mean* anything. But she couldn't help remembering how his hands had felt on her body. Of how his chest had burned into her skin, and the hardness she'd felt when her rear had brushed against his pelvis. A heated blush climbed her cheeks and she quickly looked down. As the conversation flowed around her, she traced the outline of a black spot on the table.

"When will the curtains be done?" Laurel asked, pointing at the window beside the table.

"In a couple of days," Anne answered.

"Cool. I can't wait to see them up. It's going to be totally together looking, don't you think, Daddy?"

He shook his head. "I never thought I'd have a cow kitchen."

"Yeah, Mom would have croaked, huh?" Laurel grinned. "Everything was always so perfect in our old house. It looked nice, but—" she shrugged "—sometimes I just wanted to mess things up a little."

Glory be, Anne thought, staring at her. Would wonders never cease? She'd been compared to the Sainted

Ellen and actually come out ahead. Who could have thought?

"I liked Becky Sue's trailer," the teenager continued. "It was a place you could have fun in. You didn't have to worry about breaking stuff."

"It is a long way from Dallas," Anne said, risking a glance at Jake. He was studying her. Something in his gaze rankled her, as if he were weighing the factors of her life and finding them wanting. She squared her shoulders. "What are you staring at?"

"You. We come from very different worlds."

"You've just now figured that out? We've never had anything in common."

She wanted to bite back the words as soon as she said them. Jake's gaze instantly dropped to her stomach. She resisted the urge to fold her arms protectively over her midsection.

"You have me," Laurel piped up.

Anne broke free of Jake's intense gaze. "You're right, honey. We have you."

"And I have a party." Laurel stood up. "Come on, Annie. Help me pick out what to wear. I *promise* I won't get yucky this time."

It was as close to an apology as she was going to get. Anne rose to her feet.

"What time does it start?" Jake asked. "I have the vet coming out tomorrow afternoon. If I'm not done with him in time, Anne, would you drive Laurel?"

"I have a ride," Laurel said. "Brad is picking me up."

Brad? Anne struggled to keep her jaw from dropping. "You are friends with a boy old enough to have his driver's license?"

"No." Laurel shook her head as if she was dealing with morons. "His dad is taking us."

"I'm taking you," Jake said. "You're too young to go to a party with a boy."

"But boys are going to be at the party."

"I know that. I've already talked with Terry's mother. The boys are all going home at ten-thirty, then you girls are having your sleep-over. That's fine with me, but I'm driving you."

"Da-ad. Come on. Everyone else is going with a boy." She bit her lower lip and tried to look pitiful.

"No." Jake stood up and folded his arms over his chest. "Either I drive you or you don't go."

"Annie, would you please explain to him that he's going to make me look stupid in front of all my new friends?"

Anne had been hoping to escape without having to choose sides. She didn't look at either Laurel or Jake. She placed her hand to her stomach and prayed to be anywhere but here. God was busy.

"Jake, I—"

"See!" Laurel said, triumphantly.

Anne touched her daughter's arm, hating to see the hope in her hazel eyes. Hope that was about to be dashed.

"I was going to tell your father that I have to agree with him on this one, honey. You're too young to drive to a party with a boy."

Laurel's victory faded into bitterness. Her dark eyebrows drew together and her mouth started to tremble. "Annie, no. That's not fair. Everyone will make fun of me. You have to let me go. You have to."

"The decision is made, young lady. Either accept it gracefully or you're not going to the party at all."

"Laurel, I'm sorry," Anne said, gently squeezing her arm. "I hope you can understand—"

"Understand?" She jerked her arm free. "Understand?" she shrieked. "No, I don't. You can't do this to me."

"I'm sorry."

"No, you're not. You don't care about me at all. I hate you. I hate you." Tears flowed from her eyes and a spot of color stained her cheeks. "You don't care about me. You never cared about me. That's why you gave me up. You never wanted me. I'll always hate you."

She spun and raced out of the room. Anne stared after her. The words echoed over and over until she knew she'd hear them forever.

Chapter 11

Jake stared after his daughter. His first impulse was to catch her and shake some sense into her. His second was to pull Anne close and hold her until the pain was gone. Before he could make up his mind, Anne turned and started picking up the dirty glasses from the table.

"I'm sorry," he said, and realized he meant it. A few weeks ago he would have been grateful that Laurel wasn't getting along with Anne. He'd been so afraid of losing his daughter. But he'd changed in the short time Anne had been with them. He'd learned that as much as he might deserve otherwise, Laurel would love him forever. She would also love Anne. "She didn't mean it."

"I know that," Anne said as she put the milk back into the refrigerator. She sounded surprisingly calm. "She's just a child. She's lashing out at me because I'm convenient. Next time it might just as easily be you."

"I think I can handle it easier than you can," he said, coming up behind her and placing his hands on her shoulders.

She jerked free. "Don't touch me, Jake. Not again. I can't take any more today."

"I'm sorry," he repeated, and wished he knew the right words to say. "I mean that. Not because you and I have things to work out, but because you've made a real effort with Laurel. I know she means a lot to you."

"Of course she does. She's my daughter."

She moved around him and picked up the cookie jar. After returning it to the counter, she rested her elbows on the tiled surface and her head in her hands. He wondered if she was going to cry. He wouldn't blame her. He moved closer so that he would be ready to comfort her, but she surprised him by turning around and glaring at him. Her eyes were dry, her chin set in a determined tilt.

"She misses her mother, Jake."

He didn't want to hear that. "It's been almost two and a half years. She's gotten over it."

"My mother's been gone eleven years and I still miss her." She turned and in one fluid motion pressed against the counter and raised herself until she was sitting on the tile. "You miss Ellen. You told me you've never loved anyone the way you loved her. Laurel will never get over her loss. I think you know that, deep inside. But hiding away your feelings, pretending it never happened, not letting her talk about her pain isn't making her better. Don't you think it's odd that when she's with me all she does is compare me to Ellen?"

He shrugged and wished he'd stayed in the barn. He didn't want to talk about this.

Anne pulled off her headband. Her pale red hair tumbled into her face. She brushed it back impatiently. She wasn't wearing any makeup. The color had fled her face, except for the freckles dotting her complexion.

"At first I thought she was subconsciously telling me I would never be as good as her 'real' mother." She pulled one knee up close to her chest and hugged it. "God, that hurt. I just wanted to fit in. I didn't expect to take Ellen's place, but I thought there might be room in Laurel's heart for both of us."

"There is," he said. "I know Laurel loves you."

She went on as if he hadn't spoken. "I've finally figured out the problem. It's not about me at all. She was talking about her mother because I had given her permission to. I told her it was okay. You made her bottle everything up inside. That's the reason she started in with that bad crowd. I'm convinced of it. She wanted to get your attention. She wanted you to see she was hurting. She wanted you to let her deal with her pain."

He leaned against the sink. "I don't know what to say."

"Good. Then listen." She jumped off the counter and approached him. She raised one hand and poked him in the chest. "Ellen is dead. Nothing is going to bring her back. Not guilt or silence or hoping it's all going to work out. Your wife is gone, but you still have a daughter who needs you very much. Don't abandon her anymore. Deal with it, mourn, do whatever you have to, then get on with your life. Please. For all our s-sakes." Her voice got more and more shaky until it cracked on the last word.

She backed away suddenly and covered her mouth with her hand. Before he could catch her, she sank to the floor. He was beside her in an instant.

"Talk to her," she said, clutching his shirtfront. "Please. You've got to talk to her about Ellen. Otherwise she *will* hate me forever." Tears flowed down her cheeks.

"I'm sorry," he whispered, pulling her close. "It's all my fault."

It was. He'd known for a long time that Laurel was trying to make him see her pain. He'd ignored it and her because he didn't know what to do. He didn't have the words. He was so raw inside, he could barely hold himself together.

Anne was wrong about one thing, though. He wasn't missing Ellen. At least not Ellen as she'd been in the end. Maybe that was why he'd shut down. Maybe it had been guilt instead of mourning. Maybe some of it had been anger and disgust with himself for holding on to a relationship that had long been over. He should have left years ago. He'd always told himself he stayed because he couldn't leave Laurel, but maybe it was more than that. Had he stayed because Ellen had stayed? He'd hated the way she would throw his sterility up in his face every time he talked about a separation, but maybe he'd agreed with the logic of her arguments. Maybe he'd secretly believed that he did owe her for staying with someone who was only half a man.

Anne's tears soaked through his shirt. Shudders racked her body. He murmured soothingly and held her close. Slowly the tears slowed.

"Why are you being nice to me?" she asked, her voice muffled against his chest. "You don't even like me."

"You always say that. But you never say the second half of the sentence."

She sniffed and looked up. Her eyes were red and her face was blotchy. He used his thumb to brush away the moisture on her cheeks.

"What second half?" she asked.

"That you don't like me, either."

"Oh." She sniffed again.

One of her hands rested on his shoulder, the other lay on his thigh. She was half leaning against him and her breasts brushed his chest. "Do you like me, Annie?"

"I'd better start to if I'm having your baby." Her watery smile broke as a sob caught her unaware. "I can't do this much longer," she said.

"What?"

"Pretend it's not eating me up inside. Pretend I don't care about being compared to Ellen. I hate it." She rubbed her face with the back of her hand. "I know that makes me a horrible person."

"I don't think you're horrible."

"Not now." She sniffed. "You called me Annie again. But soon you'll shut down and I'll be alone in this house, with Laurel hating me, and you wishing me gone. I'm falling apart here. Why is all this happening now?"

"I don't know." He kissed the top of her head, then moved her bangs off her forehead and kissed her skin. "We'll figure something out."

"Like what? What are we going to do? Jake, I'm pregnant."

She looked weepy and fragile and in need of comforting, but he couldn't help grinning.

She glared up at him. "Stop it. You always get that look on your face when I mention the baby."

"What look?" he asked, even though he knew.

''The one that says 'look what I can do.' It's disgusting.'' She wiped her cheeks.

''Disgusting?''

''Well, maybe that's a little strong. But it's silly. How much does it take to have a baby?''

''More than I thought I had.''

''You're right.'' She straightened some, but didn't move out of his embrace. ''I'm sorry. I'm sure that was hard for you.''

He shrugged. ''It doesn't matter now. I'm finally going to have a son.''

She reached up and touched his jaw. When he was looking into her blue eyes she said, ''Listen to me carefully. You keep saying 'him' and 'my son.' You don't know if it's a boy or not. Unless that doctor who messed up the tests could tell you only had little boy sperm swimming in your sample, there is a chance that this baby is a girl.''

Never taking his gaze from hers, he slowly shook his head. ''I know it's a boy.''

''You are the most stubborn man.''

''I know that, too.'' He studied her face, counting the freckles on her nose.

''What are you staring at?''

''Your freckles. They're finally starting to grow on me.''

She sighed impatiently. ''You're not taking this seriously enough, Jake. Dammit, we have—''

But he never heard what they had to do. Instead he lowered his mouth to hers. She was shocked by the kiss. He knew by the way she stiffened in his arms. He thought she might want to escape his embrace so he loosened his hold on her and prepared himself for the disappointment.

Instead of pulling away, she nestled closer to him and put her arms around his neck. Her breasts flattened against his chest. He remembered their heavy weight in his hands and the way he'd caressed her nipples into hard attention. He groaned low in his throat.

Wrapping his arms around her waist, he held her as he lowered himself backward toward the floor. When he was stretched out, she lay on top of him, her pelvis pressing against his, her legs between his thighs. She was in control. He wondered what she would do with her power.

She didn't disappoint him. She cupped his jaw and angled her mouth on his. Soft pressure gave way to heated kisses. Her tongue swept across his lips, once, twice, before he parted for her. She tasted faintly of Italian spices, and he grinned as he pictured her sampling the sauce.

As their tongues touched and stroked each other, he moved his hands lower to cup her rounded derriere. He flexed his hips so that his hardness pressed against the soft skin he had touched earlier that day. She rotated in response. A sharp flame of desire licked along him. He caught his breath and resisted the impulse to experience his release right there. He hadn't come that close to embarrassing himself since he was about fourteen.

She held his head and rained frantic kisses on his face.

"Oh, Annie," he breathed.

He felt something moist on his cheek. He opened his eyes and saw her tears.

"Tell me this is about more than the baby," she said softly.

"The baby?" He hadn't even been thinking of their

child. "No, it's about—" He flexed his hips again. "Hell, I don't know what it's about. It seems anytime you and I get within two feet of each other, we risk going up in flames."

She rolled off of him and sat cross-legged on the floor with her back to him. "Jake, this is a cosmic joke or something. Do you like me?" she asked without turning around.

He thought about all she'd done around the house and with Laurel. He thought about the knack she had for driving him crazy. He'd been more angry since he'd known her than he'd ever been in his life. He'd also laughed more, and hungered with a passion he'd never believed possible. She made him feel alive. He hadn't realized how much he needed that until just this minute.

"Yes, Annie. I like you."

"I hope it's enough." She scrambled to her knees, then turned to face him. The tears were gone, but the sadness in her eyes just about tore his heart in two. "I hope we can work this all out. Laurel and the baby. But it's going to be hard. I have less than a month left here."

He didn't like being reminded about the temporary nature of her visit. He hadn't minded before. In fact he'd been waiting for her to leave. But everything had changed since he found out she was pregnant.

"You don't have to go," he said, then wondered what the hell he was thinking of.

"Heather, my assistant, called me. The promotion is mine. I've worked hard for the job. It's what I want for my life. You have your dreams, Jake, and I have mine. They don't connect in any way. I don't deny I want you, but does that mean anything?" She rose to her feet. "I'm lost. I don't know what to do. Laurel already hates me. What's going to happen when she finds out about this?" She placed her hand on her stomach. She swallowed. "I wish—" She drew in a deep breath. "No. I can't wish I'd never met her or you. What I do wish is that someone, anyone, would tell me what on earth I'm supposed to do about all this."

Jake stayed in the kitchen long after Anne had left. He thought about all that she'd said, about her tears, and the way her kisses made him feel. He remembered how he'd hated and distrusted her when they'd first met. He remembered his fears about losing Laurel, and the way he'd resented the changes in his life. In a few short weeks, he'd come so far. Now he trusted Anne. He liked and admired her. And he agreed with her. He wanted someone to tell him what he was supposed to do, as well.

She was leaving. There was nothing he could say to stop her. The thought of her going back to Houston carrying his son was enough to rip his guts out. Yet he had no right to ask her to stay. God, but he wanted to. He wanted to see her growing big with his child. He wanted to hear the infant's heartbeat and feel him kicking. He rubbed the back of his neck, then slowly rose to his feet. First things first. As Anne had pointed out, the baby wasn't going to be arriving for eight more months. However, Laurel was here and a part of their lives.

He walked up the stairs and to his daughter's room. He knocked. Her muffled answer was unintelligible, so he opened the door.

Laurel lay huddled on her bed, her knees pulled up

to her chest, her back to the door. Her long hair spread over shoulders that shook with her sobs. All the women in his house were crying today. How much of that was circumstances and how much of it was his doing? He didn't want to know.

He sat on the edge of the mattress and pulled Laurel close. She didn't fight him as he'd feared; instead, she burrowed close, hanging on desperately.

''Oh, Da-addy.'' She sobbed against him.

''Hush, baby. It's going to be fine.'' But was it? He didn't have any answers. He wanted Laurel and Anne to work this out. They had to. There were even bigger problems to face.

As he held and comforted his daughter, he wondered if he were a worse bastard than he'd thought. Would he be willing to smooth things over if Anne weren't carrying his child? If it weren't for the promised trauma ahead, would he care that they weren't getting along? How much of his desire to play peacemaker was purely selfish?

He didn't have those answers, either. He would like to think that he would have done the right thing no matter what. Anne wasn't the conniving, selfish bitch he'd thought her to be. Thirteen years ago she'd made a mistake. Now he knew how easily that could happen. He also understood her ambivalence about the adoption. There weren't any easy choices anymore. She was sweet and loving, doing more than her part to make it all work. He owed her for that, regardless of what else happened between them.

Laurel's sobbing slowed to an occasional hiccup. He rocked back and forth, smoothing her hair from her face, murmuring her name over and over. He searched for the right words, then realized all he had left was the truth.

"I miss your mother, too," he said, for the first time in two years voicing the words aloud. "I think about her a lot. I think about the way it used to be."

"I want Mommy back," she said, clinging tighter. Her face pressed against his chest and her tears dampened his shirt.

"I know, sweetie. But I can't make her come back. No one can. You must remember that Mommy loved you more than anything in the world."

"I m-miss her."

"I know. And she knows. She'll always know how much you love her."

Laurel raised her head and looked at him. "Does she?"

He nodded. "I promise." Her bangs hung in her eyes. He smoothed them back and smiled. "She's not the only one who cares about you. Anne cares."

Laurel frowned. "No, she doesn't. She's never cared. She's just pretending. I hate her."

"All right. I'll tell her to leave first thing in the morning. Then you'll never have to see her again."

As he'd suspected, Laurel's anger gave way to more tears. "I don't want her to go."

"But if you hate her, why do you want her here?"

"Oh, Daddy." She hugged him tight. Her slight frame shook with the agony of her sobs.

"Hush, baby." He squeezed and rocked her. "I know you're confused. I'm confused, too." He drew in a deep breath. There was nothing left to lose. "When you first told me you wanted to meet your birth mother, I was very angry." She stiffened in his arms, but he continued rocking her, occasionally smoothing her hair.

She was so young, too damn young to deal with this. "I was afraid I'd lose you."

She raised her head and looked at him. Her hazel eyes swam with tears. Hazel eyes. Anne's mother's eyes. It didn't matter what set of traits had created them, he realized. They were his daughter's eyes and they were beautiful. He kissed her cheek.

"How could you lose me, Daddy? I promised I wouldn't run away again."

He smiled. "Not that way, silly. I thought you'd love her more than me. You wanted to live with her in Houston, remember?"

"Yeah." She wiped her face. "I like it here, now. I want to stay. I want Annie to stay. But I was so mad at her." She glanced down. "If I don't hate her, why did I say that?"

"I think you're confused because you really like Anne. It's okay to like her. It doesn't mean you love your mother any less. There's plenty of room in your heart to love both of them."

"And you?" she asked, smiling.

"And me." He touched her cheek. "Anne was only four years older than you are now when she got pregnant, Laurel. That's not very old to make a big decision about what to do with an unexpected baby. I can't be sorry she gave you up for adoption. I know that probably makes you feel funny inside, but it's true."

Her smile faded. "You're glad she didn't want me?"

"I think she wanted you very much. But if she'd kept you, your mother and I wouldn't have been able to adopt you. I wouldn't give you up for anything."

Her smile almost blinded him. She flung herself at him, but this time there weren't any tears. He held her close and realized he'd spoken the truth. Even with all he'd had to go through because of Michael's lies, the one thing he couldn't regret was Laurel. She was his daughter in every way; she made the heartache worthwhile.

He held her shoulders and eased her away. When their eyes met, he smiled. "You and Annie share something very special, something you could never have with your mother. You and Annie are blood relatives. That's a bond that can never be broken."

She cocked her head. "We *aren't* blood relatives?"

He shook his head. "I could prick our fingers and mingle the blood if you'd like."

"Oh, Daddy, gross." She laughed and rolled away from him. Bracing her elbow on the mattress, she propped her head up on her hand. "Thanks for talking to me. I feel better."

"Good."

"Can I—?" She picked at the blanket. Her bedspread and matching curtains hadn't arrived yet. "Can I still go to the party?"

He tried to frown, but he was too relieved to even fake it. "Sure, but only if I take you and then pick you up the next morning."

She thought for a moment. "Okay."

Anne rolled dough into long strips. She brushed the entire length with egg white then loosely knotted it. With a spatula she placed the roll on the cookie sheet next to four others.

"I can't believe I'm making bread by hand," she muttered. "For a bunch of ingrates who won't even notice."

She felt her anger slipping, but she hung on to it. If she didn't stay mad, she would start thinking about what had just happened with Laurel. Then she would cry, then she would want to leave. At this point, leaving wasn't an option, so she couldn't think about it or her daughter's angry words. She'd already figured out the tears didn't accomplish anything, but that didn't stop her eyes from burning.

When had everything become so complicated? She wanted to say that it had all started when Jake had first walked into her life, but she suspected that wasn't true. There had to be a reason she was so susceptible to his formidable masculine charms. It couldn't just be the jeans. Maybe she'd spent too much time alone. Maybe her life was so out of balance with all her energy focused on work that when a good-looking man turned up in her office, she completely lost it.

She rolled out another piece of dough and wished it were that simple. Her reaction to Jake wasn't just because he was good-looking. She knew lots of handsome men, had even dated some of them. But no one had tempted her the way he did. It had to be chemical. Or maybe it was the fierce way he'd protected his daughter from the very beginning. Maybe it was his willingness to admit he'd made a mistake. Whatever the reason, Jake had gotten past her barriers and deep inside her heart. She wanted not to care about him, but it had been too late for that for days.

She was moving the roll to the cookie sheet when she heard a noise behind her. She recognized the light footsteps, but didn't turn around.

"Annie?" Laurel said softly.

"Yes."

"I'm sorry I said those things to you. I don't really hate you."

Anne pulled off another length of dough and started

to roll it. "Thank you for apologizing. I know you don't hate me, honey."

Laurel moved close until she was standing next to the counter. Anne didn't want to look at her, but she couldn't resist a glance. Her daughter's face was pale, her eyes wide and red from tears.

"You're still mad, huh?" Laurel asked.

"I was never mad." Anne hesitated, then decided she was tired of all the lies in this house. She was through with walking around on tiptoe so that no one was offended. The teenager was old enough to hear the truth. "I'm still hurt, Laurel. I appreciate the apology. I'm not going to punish you by pretending to be angry or not talking to you, but I can't act as if nothing happened. Saying 'I'm sorry' doesn't take away the fact that you hurt me."

"I'm sorry." Laurel's lower lip started to quiver.

"I didn't say that to make you feel badly," she said, putting the last roll on the cookie sheet then wiping her hands on a dish towel. "I'm pointing out a fact of life. If you say mean things to people, if you lash out without thinking, you're going to hurt people. They have to live with what you said, and you have to learn to live with hurting them." She placed her hand on Laurel's shoulder. "I have to live with the fact I chose to give you up for adoption. It wasn't a decision I made easily. I have regrets, but I'm not sure it wasn't the right decision. We'll never know. I was very young, but I did the best I could."

"Daddy said that you were only four years older than me when you got pregnant."

"That's true," she said, faintly surprised Jake had been defending her. "I had a college scholarship I didn't want to lose. I talked about what to do with my mother. We decided that giving you up to a nice family would be best for everyone.'' She squeezed Laurel's shoulder, then lowered her hand to her side. ''There hasn't been a day that I haven't thought about you, wondered where you were, what you were doing, what you looked like. Especially on your birthday.''

Laurel smiled. ''You remember when it is?''

''Of course. It's my birthday, too.''

''Really?''

Anne nodded. ''You were born on my eighteenth birthday.'' She remembered that it had been the first time in her life there hadn't been a big family celebration with her mother and Becky Sue. She'd been in that small hospital labor room, fighting the pain in her body as she gave birth, and the pain in her heart as she realized she was going to have to give up her child.

''Did you cry when they took me away?'' Laurel asked, staring at the floor.

Anne reached out and touched the girl's chin, forcing her to look up. She could feel the tears forming in her eyes. She didn't try to blink them away.

''They wouldn't let me hold you,'' Anne said softly. ''I begged them to. They said it was for the best. Later, one of the nurses told me that you were already gone. I felt as if there were a hole inside of me so big I'd never fill it up. And I didn't. Not until I met you.'' She swallowed and brushed away the moisture on her cheek. ''Ellen is your mother. She raised you, taught you, was there when you were hurt or sick. She'll always be your mother. I'm your mother, too, in a different way. I'll always love you, no matter what you say or do. You can be mean to me, if that's what you have to do to survive, Laurel. You can't make me hate you.''

"Oh, Annie." Laurel threw herself into her arms. "I love you."

"I love you, too, baby," she said, holding her close. "Always. No matter what."

They stood like that for several minutes. Finally Laurel eased back and grinned up at her. "I guess I have two moms, huh?"

"I guess so." Anne returned her smile.

"I promise I won't say anything mean again. And if I mess up, I'm sorry."

"It's okay." Anne tapped her daughter's nose. "Don't you have a party to get ready for?"

"Yeah." Laurel started from the room. When she reached the doorway, she turned back. "You're the best," she said and ran down the hall.

Chapter 12

Anne started to turn the page of her book, only to realize she hadn't read a word in the last half hour. Normally she could get lost in a story, forgetting her own troubles with someone else's, but tonight it wasn't working.

She paced the bare living room and listened to the sounds of the evening. The hoots from an owl were drowned out by a car engine, then the engine was shut off. She heard a door slam followed by footsteps on the porch. Jake walked into the house.

"Did Laurel get to the party all right?" Anne asked, settling back on the sofa.

"Yeah." He walked into the room and sat down next to her. He shook his head and grinned. "It turned out that none of the girls were going with boys. This Brad fellow thought he might be able to convince Laurel to go with him because she was new in town. Instead of his father driving, it was his big brother."

"You're kidding? I can't believe he would lie like that."

"Neither could Laurel."

"What did she do?"

He turned until he was facing her. His mouth relaxed into a huge grin. She could see his pride in his daughter's actions. "She gave him a piece of her mind, and his older brother, too. Told Brad he was a lying creep and she never wanted to have anything to do with him. Several of the other girls applauded her. Brad was allowed to attend the party after apologizing. I took him and his brother aside and had a few words with them."

"You threatened him, didn't you?"

Jake didn't even have the grace to look ashamed. "Of course. I told Brad and his brother that if they ever bothered Laurel, I'd hunt them down and beat the—" He paused. His grin got bigger. "Let's just say they got the message."

"The macho solution."

"Hey, it worked, didn't it?"

She shrugged, then gave him a smile. "Time will tell."

He was wearing a long-sleeved white shirt rolled up to his elbows. As usual, jeans and boots covered his lower half. She wished she could look at him without wanting him. She wished he wasn't so protective of Laurel and such a good father. It would be easier to dislike him, and ultimately easier to leave.

Slowly the atmosphere in the room changed. The air grew heavy as if charged with electrical current. Without Laurel in her room playing music or flipping channels on the TV, the house seemed strangely silent. Laurel was spending the night with her girlfriend. Which meant, Anne realized with a sinking feeling, that she and Jake were going to be alone.

She cleared her throat, then didn't have anything to say. She glanced around the room, at the book she'd thrown down, at her athletic shoes, at Jake's boots. The latter was dangerous. She wanted to gaze at his long legs, then his chest, then his face. But that would be a mistake. She could feel it.

"We have to talk," he said. "We have to come to some sort of resolution to our problem."

"Our problem being?"

"Laurel and the baby."

Oh. Of course. It wasn't about them or the desire flickering between them. There was no "them," Anne reminded herself. Jake was barely admitting that he liked her. As for the sexual feelings between them, so what? The sex hadn't been that special.

She cringed in her seat and waited for lightning to strike her dead. It was about the biggest lie she'd ever told. The sex between them had been hotter than a bonfire. She could still feel the heat. But that wasn't what he wanted to talk about.

"I don't see a resolution," Anne said. "You and Laurel live here on the ranch. I'm going back to Houston in a couple of weeks. What do you suggest? I want to stay in touch with Laurel. I thought she could spend time with me in the summer, and maybe on school holidays."

"She'll want to see more of you than that."

"I know. I want to see more of her. But alternating weekends are impractical. They'll also disrupt her life. But that's not what you're worried about, are you?" She risked meeting his gaze.

His brown eyes had been shuttered to conceal his

feelings, but she saw the hints of pain in the straight line of his mouth and the tight set of his jaw. A lock of dark hair tumbled onto his forehead. His shoulders were stiff, his hands balled into fists.

"No," he admitted. "I know that you and Laurel will keep in touch. I think it's a good idea. As you pointed out before, she's going to need a woman in her life. It's unlikely that I'm going to remarry any time soon. I trust you to do right by her."

"Thank you," she said. "So the real question is what are we going to do about the baby?"

His gaze dropped to her midsection. Her oversize shirt hid her body from view, not that there was anything to see. Her stomach looked the same as it always had—not quite as flat or as firm as she would like—but there wasn't any sign of the baby.

He opened his mouth to speak, then closed it and looked away. She ached for him. He wanted so much. But she couldn't give him this.

"I'm keeping the baby with me," she said. "I'm sorry, Jake. I know you want him." She shook her head. "Now you've got me talking like I know it's a boy. I gave up one child. I'm not giving up another one. I know that hurts you, but I don't have another choice. You don't know what it was like wondering all the time. Wishing you could be there, just see your child, or touch her. I missed everything about Laurel. I missed her learning to crawl and walk and talk. I missed her first birthday, her first day at school."

"Now I'm going to miss all that."

Her breath caught in her throat. She hadn't thought of it that way. Oh, God, what were they going to do?

He read the question in her eyes. "You could stay here."

"No." She stood up and walked to the window. When she reached it, she held on to the wooden frame. "I can't. It's not fair to ask me. I've spent my whole life working for what I wanted. I finally have it. I have the job I want, I have friends, a life I'm very content with. I'm not going to give that up and come live here."

"I can't raise horses in Houston," he said. "This is my grandfather's land. It belonged to his father."

"So we're back where we started," she said slowly. "Nowhere. Neither of us happy with the situation." She leaned her head against the cool glass. "You realize we haven't figured out what we're going to tell Laurel."

"I don't want to think about that."

"We have to. There has to be some perfect sentence to explain it and keep her from being hurt." She turned slowly. "Jake, please don't let her hate me."

"She doesn't." He frowned. "I thought she apologized to you for saying that."

"She did. That's not what I mean. When this whole thing comes out about the baby, she's going to be very upset. She's going to feel betrayed. I gave her up for adoption, but I want to keep this child. She's not going to understand that. Be on my side."

"There aren't sides to this. We're all in it together."

"I wish that were true." She walked over to the coffee table and bent down to pick up the photo album. "I've looked at all the pictures. I've seen the evidence of her growing up, but it's not the same as being there. I missed so much." She looked at Jake. He sat on the edge of the sofa, his elbows on his knees, his hands laced together. "I don't want to deprive you of that. I swear I don't. I just want to do what's right for both of us.''

"I wish I knew what that was."

"Me, too." She tried to smile, but her mouth wouldn't cooperate.

He stood up and held out his hand. "Come with me."

"Where are we going?"

"Trust me."

He had that peculiar expression on his face again. The one he'd had when he'd first realized he had fathered her child. She set the photo album back on the coffee table and placed her hand in his. His skin was warm to the touch. Instantly his fingers closed around hers. She felt safe and secure, which was insane considering what they still had to deal with. But she couldn't shake the feeling, so she gave in to it. When he smiled at her, she was able to smile back.

He paused by the downstairs rest room and snagged a box of tissue. "What's that for?" she asked.

He pulled her down the hall. "It's kind of how the day's been going around here. Just in case."

They stopped in the study. He stood her in front of the leather sofa and placed both hands on her shoulders until she sat down. Then he walked over to the bookcase beside the VCR. After fumbling through a shelf of tapes, he pulled one out and put it into the machine. He rejoined her on the couch.

"Ready?" he asked.

She nodded. He settled back next to her, then shifted and dropped his arm over her shoulders. She thought about resisting his embrace, then figured that she was already pregnant. She could hardly get in more trouble.

The scent of his body surrounded her. She liked the

musky fragrance of man and heat and horses. He was hard to her soft. They meshed. She remembered the cold stranger who had come to her office such a short time ago. The result of their chance lovemaking had forced them to deal with each other on a much more immediate basis. She wondered what their relationship would have been like if she hadn't gotten pregnant. Would Jake still be trying to hate her? Would she be doing her best to ignore him? Or would they have become friends with the passage of time? Had they interfered with or created their own destiny?

A soft cooing sound caught her attention. She looked at the TV screen. A gasp escaped her. She sat up straight, her body stiff, all her attention focused on the flickering picture in front of her.

A toddler, two, maybe three, ran through a petting zoo. The assortment of goats, lambs and ponies didn't frighten the little girl. Brown hair tied into pigtails bounced with each step. Her pink shorts and ruffled shirt were covered with dust, as were her tiny white tennis shoes. The girl reached out to pet a duck, but the bird ran off. She looked up and laughed out loud.

"Almost, Mommy," Laurel said to the camera. "A duck."

"You okay?" Jake asked, and placed his hand on her leg. "You said you missed seeing her grow up. It reminded me of these videos. If it's too painful to watch…"

"No!" She gave him a quick glance. "I want to see everything. It hurts, but it's not a bad pain." She turned back to the screen and smiled. "I can't believe how beautiful she is. And so small."

The video continued, showing Laurel enjoying her day with the animals. She petted most of them, chased

the duck, all the while quacking. Anne laughed with
her, vaguely aware that Jake kept his arm around her
in a protective gesture. She wanted to tell him that she
was fine, that the ache in her heart came from bittersweet joy. She couldn't undo what had been done, but
these films allowed her to see pieces of Laurel's life
that she had only imagined.

The picture flickered, then changed to a picnic scene
in a park. Laurel still looked young, but her clothes
were different. The camera panned across the green
grass to the little girl playing with a ball. Suddenly a
woman stepped into view. Anne's breath caught in her
throat. The woman was tall and slender, with stylish
short dark hair. She walked barefoot across the grass,
her narrow hips swaying provocatively. When she
reached Laurel, she crouched down beside her, then
looked up and smiled.

"That was Ellen," Jake said.

"I figured."

Anne wanted to glance at him to try to read his emotions, but she didn't dare. She didn't want to know how
much he still loved his late wife. She stared at the
figure on the TV screen. The photos in the library
hadn't done Ellen Masters justice. She was pretty in a
still shot, but in motion, she was pure elegance. Taste-
ful jewelry glittered from her ears and around her neck.
Her summer dress exposed well-shaped tanned arms
and legs. She had the long neck and elegant carriage
of a fashion model.

Some people joined the picnic, but Anne couldn't
take her eyes off Ellen and Laurel. The woman chatted
with her friends, but kept most of her attention on her
child. When Laurel toddled off out of the camera range,
Ellen hurried after and brought her back. The child's

smiles threatened to turn stormy, so Ellen tickled her belly and blew on her neck until the little girl was giggling.

The scene shifted again. Now the family was at the beach. This time Jake played with his daughter. A younger Jake, looking sinful in swim trunks. The little girl ran toward the waves, then shrieked when the water lapped against her toes. The picture tilted as the camera exchanged hands. Now Ellen appeared, her lean body displayed by a two-piece bathing suit. She took Laurel's hand and led her to the waves. Laurel was afraid of getting her face wet. Ellen crouched down and patiently encouraged her to try until the child was laughing and playing in the surf.

"My mother always did that," Anne said, staring at the screen. "She always told me to try and that it was better to face the fear than let the fear win."

"I wish I'd met your mother," he said, from his seat beside her. She could still feel his heat and inhale his scent; he still turned her on with his mere presence in the room. Despite that, she was less inclined to pursue a physical relationship. Not after seeing Ellen in a bathing suit. She glanced down at her large breasts and generous thighs. She'd never thought of herself as heavy, but she did have curves. Ellen had been a fantasy woman, long and sleek, elegant and well dressed. Anne worked hard to be put together for the office, but at home, she just couldn't bring herself to care if her shorts and T-shirt were in perfect condition or if her bra and panties happened to match. There were too many important things to worry about. But even saying that over and over to herself didn't stop her from wondering if Jake missed Ellen's perfection in his life.

The video came to an end. Jake got up and changed it. When he came back to the sofa, he stared at her.

"You're not crying."

She smiled. "You sound surprised. I'm really enjoying these. You've given me something I thought I'd never have—a chance to see Laurel grow up. As for the tears—" She shrugged. "I think I'm all cried out right now."

He reached for the remote but didn't use it. "There's a bunch of tapes. Help yourself whenever you want to watch them."

"Thanks, I will." She angled toward him on the sofa. "The three of you were a real family. Laurel was well loved, happy and with a good home. I'm glad she had Ellen." Funny the truth didn't hurt as much as she'd thought.

He raised one hand to her face and brushed his knuckles across her cheek. His skin whispered against her, igniting tiny fires in her nerve endings. Then he dropped his hand and the tingling stopped. She wished he would touch her again.

"I admire your generosity," he said. "I'd like to think that I'd be the same, but I doubt it."

"What do you mean?"

"Bobby, her 'birth father' for lack of a better term. I'm not sorry he's gone. The last thing I need is more competition for Laurel."

"Why do you doubt yourself? You're a terrific father."

"You don't know what happened after Ellen died. I—" He shook his head. "I got lost. I missed her so damn much. I know Laurel needed me, but I couldn't put myself together enough to be there for her. She paid a big price for that."

"She's done fine, Jake. You've started to make your peace with Laurel. That will go a long way to making up for the past."

Anne briefly closed her eyes and wondered what it must be like to love and be loved that much. To be part of a family and so important that your passing would leave an empty spot that would last a lifetime. What had Ellen Masters possessed that made Jake unable to stop loving her even when she'd been gone for two years? Could he ever come to care about anyone else, for example her, as much?

The last thought shocked Anne. She didn't need Jake to care about her romantically. They had problems to work out, but none of them required more than a friendship.

Oh, but wouldn't it be perfect if they could just… Just what? she asked herself. Fall in love? Then she would have to make other kinds of choices. Besides, he couldn't love her—he loved Ellen. Even if she'd wanted a chance with him, it wasn't going to happen. There was too much baggage between them.

"What are you thinking?" he asked.

"I was wondering if you would have liked me better if we'd just met as strangers. If we didn't have Laurel between us." Or Ellen, but she didn't say that aloud.

His brown eyes met and held her own. The gold flecks in his irises glowed with a fire that made her want to squirm in her seat.

"Yes," he said, his voice husky. "I would have liked you too damn much."

Despite the tension building in the room, and the night around them and the fact that the house was empty, save for the two of them, she smiled. "How can you like someone too much?"

"Easy." He leaned toward her. "You expose your feelings and they use them against you. They manipulate you or make you feel guilty about something that wasn't even true."

She told herself she should pay attention to what he was telling her, that the information was important. But she couldn't think about anything except the fact that his face was getting closer to hers and his gaze had locked on to her mouth. She licked her lips in anticipation.

The good girl inside her, the one raised in a small Texas town by a conservative single mother, reminded her that this wasn't a good idea. It would only complicate the situation. He was going to kiss her. If he did there was no telling where this night might end. The two of them had a bad habit of burning out of control in each other's arms. The voice in her head mentioned all that, then told her making love could easily turn into *being* in love. She needed that complication even less. Jake was still in love with Ellen. She would regret this come morning. Loving him would make it harder to leave. She *had* to leave. She owed it to herself to follow her dreams.

As if he sensed her hesitation, Jake hovered above her mouth. His breath fanned her face. One strong hand gripped her shoulder, but she could have easily pulled back. The voice in her head ordered her to do just that.

"Go away," she whispered to the voice.

Jake froze.

"Not you," she said, and slipped her hand behind his head.

But he didn't kiss her. He straightened and rose to

his feet. Passion burned in his eyes, giving him the hungry, powerful expression of a predator. He paused and extended his hand.

"I want to make love to you, Annie Jo Baker," he said. "In my bed, with the lights on. I want to touch and taste and see every inch of you."

Instantly moisture dampened her panties. Her breasts tightened. If he'd been touching her anywhere on her body, she would have climaxed right there. Her breathing stopped altogether, then started in short ragged breaths. Their eyes met. He neither pleaded nor warned her away. The decision was hers. It was as inevitable as the tide.

She placed her fingers on his palm and allowed him to help her to her feet. She thought they would walk calmly up the stairs, then undress like civilized people. She'd been wrong.

He pulled her hard against him. Her breasts flattened against his broad chest. Before she could think, he claimed her mouth. Even as his tongue caressed hers, his fingers fumbled with the buttons on her shirt. He didn't bother pulling it off, instead he left it hanging open and expertly unfastened her bra. When her breasts were free to his touch, he lifted them in his hands and used his thumbs to tease her nipples into delicious hardness.

Her thighs trembled, her knees threatened to give out. She had to wrap her arms around him to keep from falling. He tasted of coffee and something masculine and heady. His hair slipped through her fingers like raw silk. She kneaded his shoulders, then gripped him as his fingers plied their wondrous touch on her sensitive skin.

He raised his head and stared at her. "Tell me you wanted me this afternoon. When I touched your belly."

"I wanted you."

"And now?"

"I want you more."

He groaned low in his throat, then bent down and locked his arms below her buttocks. He raised her so he could suckle on her sensitive breasts. His tongue circled around each tip, leaving a moistness that cooled quickly in the night air. The contrast of hot and cold, wet and dry, made her blood run faster. She rained kisses on his head, then wrapped her legs around his waist. Her most sensitive spot rubbed against his erection, the thick fabric of their jeans the only barrier to their mutual pleasure.

He moved out of the room and toward the stairs. On the third step he released her and let her slide until her feet touched the carpeted flooring. He was one step below her so they were almost at eye level. He kissed her mouth, then sucked her bottom lip. She clutched at his shoulders. Her shirt and bra hung open. She wanted to press bare skin to bare skin, so she reached for his front buttons. He reached for her jeans.

He couldn't pull the denim off over her shoes, so he sat her on the stair and took them off. Her socks followed, then he slipped the pants down her legs. He knelt between her thighs and ran his fingertips along her bare skin. From ankle to calf, from knee to hip. Shivers raced through her. She braced herself on the stair and watched him. Their eyes met and he smiled.

"What happened to making love in your bed?" she asked.

"We'll get there." He touched the elastic band of

her panties and followed it from her hips to between her legs. "You're wet. I can feel it through these."

Before she could be embarrassed, he bent down and nipped at the skin right below her belly button. She jumped, then laughed because it tickled. Even as he licked her belly, he moved to one side and pulled off the scrap of damp cotton.

He stared at the exposed femininity. "Auburn," he said, as if he'd just made a wondrous discovery.

"I have red hair. What did you expect?"

He looked up and winked. "Just checking. You have freckles." He touched her chest, then her legs. "And curves." He touched her breasts.

"Jake, we're on the stairs."

"I know where we are."

"But what if someone finds us?"

He slipped his fingers into her damp curls. "The doors are all locked."

"But I—"

"You're talking too much. I must be doing something wrong."

With that, he bent down and kissed her thigh. With his fingers, he gently stroked her waiting heat, then urged her legs farther apart. Despite the stairs and the remote possibility of discovery, she complied with his silent command. Every touch led her closer and closer to her release. When he lowered his head and brought his mouth to her tiny place of pleasure, she had to bite her lip to keep from screaming. He knew exactly what to do, exactly how fast—her breath caught—then how slow—she gasped—to move against her. His tongue slipped over and around, then dipped inside, mimicking the act of love. He left her hanging on the taut edge of ecstasy, then gently sucked her to oblivion.

Jake knew the precise moment she began to climax. He kept his ministrations moving in time with her contractions. When her body ceased to tremble beneath his, he pulled her close and held her. Only when her breathing returned to normal, did he pick her up and carry her to his bedroom.

The place, the bed itself, everything was new. He firmly closed his mind to any memories that might wish to intrude on this perfect time. He placed Annie on the bed, then quickly pulled off his own clothes. She was slick with perspiration. He wiped her with his shirt, then slipped in next to her. Her small hands reached for him, cradling his arousal. Instantly his hips flexed.

She looked up at him. "Something tells me that if I mentioned I had some mending to take care of right now you'd be most unhappy."

"Most," he agreed, and kissed her. Her mouth opened without urging. Their tongues mated, causing him to harden even more. The pressure was uncomfortable, but he didn't want his release yet. He liked being tempted to the edge.

He rolled onto his back and pulled her up against him. Her full breasts burned into his chest. God, she felt good. He traced her hips, then gripped her rear, squeezing the rounded flesh. He liked the curves and the way she tasted. He liked—

He gasped. She suckled his nipple as he had hers. Her fingers brushed his chest, then ran down his belly, tangling with the thicket of hair. His hardness flexed in anticipation. She moved her fingers lower to his thighs, then brushed delicately against his testicles. He parted his legs to allow her to explore that part of him he'd always thought useless. Aching need grew, but he held back, waiting, letting her lead the way.

She raised her head and smiled at him. Moving slowly, she straddled his midsection. Her moist center dampened his stomach. Bracing her arms on the mattress, she slipped back until the tip of him teased at her.

Before she could continue, he gripped her waist and tumbled her to her back. He poised between her legs.

"So you want to be in charge," she teased, her eyes bright with anticipation. Her pale red hair fanned out on the pillow. Her generous breasts moved with each breath. He wanted to kiss each freckle, discover every inch of her, as he had promised, but first he had to be inside her or he would die.

"I can't wait," he said, by way of apology.

"Then don't." She tilted her hips toward him, bringing his erection in contact with her waiting warmth.

"Ah, Annie, how do you do this to me?" He slowly slipped home.

It was as explosive as that night in the desert. There was no time to discover a mutually satisfying rhythm, no conscious thought left to deal with finesse. There was only the feel of her around him, the heat and the need. Her legs embraced his hips. His fingers held her breasts, her hands urged him closer.

When her eyelids slipped shut and her mouth parted, he forced himself to slow enough to take her with him. At her moment of climax, he held back a heartbeat. As his body shuddered and expelled his seed, he reveled in the power of knowing this is how he had created their child. This mystical act that bonded the generations. This moment from which he'd felt excluded and so much less than a man.

As she cried out his name and her nails bit into his arm, he knew that there would never be a more perfect feeling than her body rippling under his, and his echoing the passion.

As clearly as the sensations filling him, he knew the solution. It was so simple he wanted to laugh.

So when their breathing returned to normal and she lay next to him, her head on his shoulder, he took her left hand in his and spoke five words.

"Annie, will you marry me?"

Chapter 13

Annie immediately moved away from him and reached for the sheet. After she pulled it up to her shoulders, she brushed her hair out of her face and slowly sat up. "You don't mean that, do you?"

She didn't sound overly enthused, but he wasn't worried. "Come on, Annie," he said, raising himself up on one elbow. "It's the perfect solution. You can stay here and be with Laurel and the baby. We won't have to worry about custody or visitations. I know the ranch isn't making any money yet, but when I sold out of the construction business, I made a mint. Not to mention the stocks my grandfather left me." He shrugged modestly. "What I'm trying to say is that finances will never be a problem."

She shook her head. "This isn't about money." She stared at him. The color fled her face leaving behind pale skin and the dark spots of her freckles. "It was never about money. It's about different lives and goals. You don't love me."

He fingered the cotton sheet that covered her. "Is there someone else? Is that why you don't want to marry me?"

"No," she said quickly.

He was surprised to find out he was relieved that there wasn't another man in her life. "Then don't you see?" he said, taking her hand. "It'll be good between us. We get along. We both love Laurel. I think we're pretty damn hot in bed." He raised his eyebrows. "Marriages have been built on less."

She sighed impatiently. "You can't marry me just because it's convenient and we happen to have a chemical attraction."

He leaned close so that he could nibble on her shoulder. "Sure I can. Why not?" Her skin grew hot under his touch and her eyelids slipped closed. He watched as her grip on the sheet loosened. The white cotton slipped lower until her breasts were exposed. He stretched so he could gently lick a puckering tip. "It's magic, Annie. It's never been like this before for me."

"Me, too," she said softly. "Jake—" Her voice became a moan as he continued his ministrations.

She tasted sweet, almost like peaches, he thought, deepening his kisses, drawing more of her breast into his mouth. She squirmed, then pushed him away and pulled the sheet up to her neck.

"Stop it," she said. "I mean it. You've made your point about the sex. It's very powerful. But that doesn't prove anything. I'm not interested in getting married so that I can have a good time in bed."

It seemed like a fine idea to him. The first few years with Ellen had been fun, but there had never been this instant heat between them. "Why *are* you interested in getting married?"

"Oh, Jake, don't do this." She drew her knees up to her chest and hugged them close to her body. "You think getting married makes it all work. You get a housekeeper, a lover, another parent to help with Laurel and the baby. You make it sound so easy."

"Why does it have to be difficult?" He rolled off the bed and stood up. "Dammit, Annie, can't you see this is the best solution for both of us?"

"No." She shook her head. "It's the best solution for you. I still have a life of my own back in Houston. What about that? What about the job I've worked so hard for? It's been nine years coming. I deserve this chance and you don't have any right to keep me from it." Her blue eyes flashed with fire, but it wasn't fueled by the heat of passion.

"Are you saying you don't like it here? I know it's not a high-powered job, but neither is trying to make the horse ranch pay. It's different, and in a lot of ways, better."

"That's your dream. Mine is different."

"But it would make everything—"

"No, it wouldn't," she said, cutting him off. "You aren't listening. I won't take the easy way out again. I did that once. My mother and Becky Sue both told me giving up Laurel was the best thing for the baby. I believed them because I wanted to. I was seventeen, and terrified of being alone with an infant. I had a future I didn't want to mess up." She drew in a deep breath. "I'll regret that decision until the day I die."

That got his attention. He stared down at her. "You never told me that," he said softly.

"I never wanted to admit it to myself. I did what

was simplest and best for everyone. Or so I thought.
I'm not doing that again. I'm happy about the baby,
but not thrilled about the circumstances. It was an accident, and we'll find a way to deal with it. That
doesn't mean we have to get married.''

He braced his hands on his bare hips. "I'm beginning to think there are no accidents. You're not going
to marry me, are you?''

"Not like this.''

He sat on the mattress and pulled on his jeans. It
had been the perfect solution. All his elation faded
away, leaving him feeling old and tired. Nothing was
easy, that was one thing he could count on. He thought
about all the years with Ellen, and the way they'd
fought at the end. He thought about the baby. His son.
He turned on her.

"Dammit, woman, you're not taking my child away
from me. You have no right.''

She stretched her legs out in front of her, then raised
her head and looked at him. He'd expected her to be
angry, or at least defiant. Instead her mouth trembled
at the corners and her eyes looked very sad. "Don't
worry, Jake. I'll make sure you get everything you
want.''

Anne threaded her needle and picked up a square of
fabric. The ultimate handicraft, she thought, knowing
it would be faster to use the sewing machine. But she
wanted to make this quilt by hand. She wanted to touch
the cloth. She wanted to feel the different textures and
have it grow slowly from unconnected pieces to a complete whole.

The late-afternoon sun poured in through a freshly
washed window. She glanced down at her hands. When

she'd first arrived on Jake's ranch, her skin had been smooth, her nails long and elegantly rounded. Now she had a few healing cuts from run-ins with the potato peeler or a paring knife. Her index finger was pricked from sewing. She'd long since cut off her nails. When she got back to Houston, her manicurist was going to have a fit.

She picked up the square of fabric and knew that her scarred hands weren't the only changes since she'd left her white-on-white condo. Not by a long shot. She was pregnant. That was certainly a change. And she was hurting.

She'd thought she'd experienced her worst pain when she'd given birth to a baby she'd never been allowed to see. The death of her mother had also been hard. Meeting Laurel, dealing with Jake—that, too, had added to the amount of pain she'd experienced. But none of these events compared to his proposal for a marriage of convenience.

If she lived to be a hundred, she would never forget the flash of joy following his words. Marriage. In that second when she'd stared at him, she'd allowed herself to hope. Worse, she'd allowed herself to admit that she'd come to love him. The thought that he might care about her had been too wondrous to be contained. But she'd forced herself to hold back, even when she had wanted to throw herself into his arms. She'd bitten her tongue until she could get out words other than "Yes, yes, a thousand times, yes." She'd asked if he was sure.

He was. He wanted to marry her because it was convenient, the best solution to their mutual problems. Not because she was special, not because he loved her, but because it was easy. He would have everything he wanted, and she would be left with nothing.

She sighed and began stitching the cow-print fabric. That wasn't completely true, she admitted to herself. He wasn't the only one who would gain by their marriage. She would get to be with Laurel all the time. That would be lovely. She would be part of a family, something she'd longed for ever since she was a little girl.

But what about her career? What about the job she'd worked for all these years? Could she walk away from it? She could find other work, but relocating big companies to Houston, Texas, wasn't exactly a job she could do here on the horse ranch. Would she be willing to give it all up because a man loved her? She shook her head. No, not for that.

She glanced down at the squares of fabric she'd already cut. Several were from the cow-print curtains hanging in the kitchen. A few had been part of a dress Laurel had stained and torn. Five came from fabric samples for curtains now hanging in the mostly decorated house. She hadn't made a quilt in years. Not since high school. She also hadn't baked or sewn or made lasagna from scratch. She wouldn't have given up her job just because Jake loved her, but she might have given it up to stay home with her new family and experience a different, maybe even better, life. She'd never been a full-time mom before. It sounded challenging and more rewarding than any contract. Of course that could simply be a case of wanting what she couldn't have.

She glanced at the clock. Laurel was out riding with her father. They would both be back soon. She put down her sewing and walked into the kitchen. She had a chicken ready to go in the oven. She checked the temperature, then slid the pan inside and set the timer.

It had been a week since she and Jake had made love. A week since he'd proposed and she'd turned him down. A week since they'd had a conversation that was anything but impersonal. She pulled out a bag of potatoes and put several on the counter. If she didn't know better, she would say his feelings had been hurt by her rejection.

That wasn't possible, she reminded herself as she reached for the peeler. He didn't want her; he wanted a solution to his problems and full custody of his child. She could have been anyone and he would have come to the same solution. He didn't care about her. He didn't love her. Thank God he hadn't figured out she loved him.

In another week it wouldn't matter, she thought, peeling the first potato, then dropping it into a bowl of water. She would be gone. Back to her real life. She paused in midstroke and dropped the vegetable onto the counter. She didn't want to go.

Anne leaned her forearms against the counter and closed her eyes. She had to admit the truth to herself if to no one else. She wanted to stay here and be a mother to Laurel and the baby. She wanted to plant a garden and watch it grow. She wanted to make all her mother's favorite recipes, and can berries in August. She wanted to be a part of a family. She wanted to love Jake forever. Most of all, she wanted him to love her back.

The front door opened, then slammed shut. She straightened and blinked to make sure her eyes were completely dry.

"The mail is here," Jake said, walking into the

kitchen. "They left a package." He set a large box on the kitchen counter.

Anne glanced at the label. "It's from the company that made Laurel's bedspread. It's probably the throw pillows."

"I'm sure she'll be pleased," he said, his voice as impersonal as it always was these days.

She almost wished he would get angry at her. Then at least there would be something to react to. This calm, cool stranger had nothing in common with the Jake Masters she knew. He was not the same man who had stood in her office and passionately reminded her she had no legal rights to Laurel. He wasn't the man who had made love to her on a rock beside a trailer park in Paradise, or reverently touched her skin searching for proof of his child. Some of the memories she would carry with her were wonderful, some very painful, but in each, Jake was vibrantly aware of her. He wasn't distant and uncaring.

"What time is dinner?" he asked, picking up the box.

"About five-thirty."

"What are we having?"

"Baked chicken, broccoli and scalloped potatoes."

"I'd prefer mashed potatoes," he said, and walked toward the door.

She almost said fine. After all, she didn't care about the potatoes. But something inside of her snapped. She was tired of being ignored and treated like hired help.

"No," she said, and set down the peeler. She wiped her hands on a dish towel.

Jake stopped dead in his tracks. His eyes met hers. For the first time in a week, something flashed in the brown depths. Something alive and passionate. Even if this fire was fueled by anger, she didn't care.

"Excuse me?" he said.

"No." She smiled. "I'm not going to make mashed potatoes."

He drew in a deep breath, then spoke slowly, as if dealing with a recalcitrant child. "We always have mashed potatoes with baked chicken. Both Laurel and I prefer it that way."

"I figured as much. That's why I'm going to do something different." She folded her arms over her chest and raised her chin defiantly.

He set the box down and approached her. When he was about two feet away, he braced his hands on his hips. "Don't start something you don't intend to finish."

"Oh, but Jake, I *do* intend to finish this. I'm tired of you ignoring me. You want mashed potatoes?" She tossed one of the unpeeled vegetables toward him. He caught it in his left hand. "Go ahead and make them yourself. But if you want me to cook, we'll do it my way. I refuse to live up to the memory of a saint."

"You leave Ellen out of this."

"How can I? She surrounds all of us. To the best of my knowledge, the woman never even lived in this house, yet her presence is everywhere. If you want to live your life in homage to the dead, go ahead, but that's not part of my deal. I'm tired of being compared and found wanting."

"Then maybe you should do a better job."

She told herself he was just lashing out and that it didn't mean anything, but she felt the sting of his remarks all the way down to her heart. She squared her shoulders. "I'm doing a fine job. I've been better to you and Laurel than either of you deserve. I've done my best to fit in. I'm not playing that game anymore. If you want an Ellen clone, go find yourself one. Some dark-haired beauty with the right manners and a perfect pedigree. I'm just Annie Jo Baker, from a trailer park a little east of nowhere.'' She leaned forward and glared at him. ''I'm also Laurel's mother, and nothing is ever going to change that.''

She was finally getting through to him. She could tell by the veins throbbing in his neck. His muscles tensed. ''You shouldn't mind being compared to Ellen. After all you're the one trying to take her place in Laurel's heart and my bed.''

''That's a lie, and you know it. You're the one who wants me to be a replacement. You're the one who wants to get married because it's so damned convenient for you. You're the one insisting I stay. Have you thought about that, Jake? Do you ever wonder why you're so scared of me? I'll tell you why.''

She moved until they were inches apart. Heat radiated from his body. She knew its source was rage, but that didn't stop her body from responding to his. She had to dig deep for her own temper to find the courage to tell him the truth.

''You don't trust anyone to love you enough to stay. You hold on to Laurel so tightly, I'm not surprised she ran away. You're afraid of losing her. You don't have the guts to admit you might need me, so instead of trying to keep me here by caring about me, you talk about 'the perfect solution.' More than that, more than anything, you're afraid of losing your baby.'' She touched her belly. ''It's my child, too, Jake. I'm the one carrying him, and possession is nine-tenths of the law.''

The silence nearly deafened her. Jake's eyes gave little away, save a growing ugliness directed at her. "Damn you," he growled. "Don't you threaten me. I'll never let you keep my son."

A soft sound made them both turn. Anne saw Laurel standing in the door. She must have come in from the barn without either of them hearing her.

"Daddy?" she said, her voice shaking. She turned her hazel eyes on Anne. "Annie? Are you having a baby? A baby you're going to keep this time? How could you?" The question came out as a scream. "How could you?" She turned and ran from the room.

Chapter 14

Jake took off after Laurel, but she beat him to her bedroom. He heard the door slam, followed by the click of her lock.

"Let me in," he said, then pounded on the wooden door. "Dammit, Laurel, I'm not kidding about this."

"Go away," she screamed. "Just go away."

Her voice shook with sobs. He wanted to break down the barrier between them and hold her until this all went away. Instead he leaned against the doorframe and closed his eyes. It wasn't going away. He'd put off thinking about Laurel and how this would affect her. In his happiness about the baby, he'd deliberately ignored her feelings. He hadn't wanted to think about the problems and had instead concentrated on the reality of actually being able to father a child.

"Laurel," he called through the door. He deliberately spoke softly. "Please, honey. We have to talk."

"I don't want to talk to you. Go away, Daddy. Leave me alone."

If she'd claimed to hate him, he would have felt better. Her emotional outbursts never lasted very long. But this uncontained agony was more than he could stand. Determined to give her the time she needed, he turned to leave. Anne stood behind him on the top of the stairs.

"I hope you're happy," he said, pushing past her. "You've just destroyed your daughter's life for the second time."

"Don't you dare blame this on me," she said. "I've wanted to discuss telling Laurel from the very beginning. You're the one who wouldn't listen. You're the one—"

But he didn't wait to hear his part in the problem. He continued down the stairs and out to the barn. He started to go into his office, then realized the last thing he needed was to be cooped up. Emotions bubbled through him. Frustration at the situation, anger at Anne, regret for hurting Laurel, determination to keep his son. They boiled through him until he wanted to put his fist through a wall.

He jogged out of the barn and around to the side. Logs had been stacked, ready for splitting. It was late October. The first snowfall would come with the next storm. They needed the wood for their fireplace. He eyed the ax and the huge pile of wood. Perfect.

He took off his wool work shirt. The late-afternoon breeze cut through his cotton T-shirt, raising goose bumps on his skin. He didn't care. It wouldn't take long for him to warm up.

He positioned a log, then picked up the ax. His stroke was sure and true. The wood split down the center. He left the halves where they fell and reached for another piece.

The rhythmic motions raised his body temperature and cooled his temper. Random thoughts filled his mind. Why the hell couldn't Anne be more cooperative? If she'd just agreed to marry him, everything would have been fine. They could have put off telling Laurel about the baby until she was ready to hear about it.

He must have done something wrong. He hadn't used the right words or something. He would have thought after all those years of living with Ellen and watching her get her way in everything, he would be better at manipulating people. God, he'd hated living in her perfect world. That damned house in Dallas. He grimaced remembering the matching wallpaper and drapes, the furniture that looked beautiful, but untouched. The rose-colored lace in their bedroom. He remembered how she always took so long to get ready to go out, it wasn't usually even worth the trouble to go. Ellen couldn't just take off to the movies or a picnic. Everything had to be perfectly choreographed.

Not like in the early days. His ax cut through the logs, one by one. Sweat broke out on his back and forehead. He remembered when they first had Laurel and had both stayed up all night. Neither of them had known what her crying meant. They'd stared helplessly at their newborn and prayed for someone to give them some guidance. He remembered the afternoons he'd rushed home from work so he could be with his wife and daughter. Of the times they'd spent at the park.

He stopped in midswing and took a breath. The air was crisp and clean, smelling faintly of pine, freshly cut wood and horses. When had she changed? Had it simply been a function of time? Was it when they'd moved to the big house? Had it started the night he'd said they should think about a separation?

Laurel had been five, maybe six. He'd finally realized that even though Ellen was his best friend and he loved her, he didn't want to stay married to her. He sensed there was something missing. Their friendship and youthful feelings hadn't matured into something that would last. Had it started then? Had she changed to keep him, not knowing that by turning into the perfect wife and mother she had killed what he had loved about her? He remembered the pain in her eyes and the way she'd defied him to leave her. She'd said that he owed her—she had stayed with a man who couldn't give her the one thing she'd wanted most in the world. He was the reason she couldn't have a baby.

He'd stayed because leaving had been too hard. He'd allowed her words to build a paper cage around him, closing him inside with a lock fashioned from guilt. He raised the ax and drove it through the logs, one after the other, hating Ellen for what she had done to him. Cursing her name, her memory.

When his muscles trembled and he couldn't raise his arms high enough to split another log, he sank onto the tree stump and struggled to catch his breath. The sweat on his body evaporated, leaving him chilled, but he made no move to reach for his shirt. He prayed she would burn in hell for what she had done to him. She had used him to her own end. And he had let her.

He started to stand up, then sank back to the log. *He had let her.* He dropped the ax on the ground and slumped forward, resting his elbows on his thighs and his head in his hands. Dear God, he had *let* her manipulate him. She hadn't made him stay. He could have left, but he didn't.

Images from the past flooded him. Of course, he thought, startled by the realization. Staying had seemed like the right thing to do at the time. It had also been easier to stay in the life he knew than risk starting over. He'd done what everyone wanted. Just as Annie had done when she'd given up Laurel. But unlike her, he'd done it out of fear. She'd been right when she'd accused him of being afraid of losing it all. If he'd left Ellen, he might have lost Laurel. If Anne went back to Houston, he would lose his son. He would also lose Annie, and he couldn't bear to think about that.

He raised his head up toward the sky, but found no answers in the coming night. He had chosen his own path and now he had to live with the consequences. As Anne had to learn to do. She had chosen this path as well.

He shook his head. No, that wasn't fair. He'd been the one to get in touch with her. He'd been the one to bring her out to Colorado because he hadn't wanted to take Laurel back alone and risk her not forgiving him. He'd been the one who wouldn't discuss the realities of the pregnancy, because he'd been afraid of what would happen with Laurel. Annie wasn't the guilty party. Yet her innocence did nothing to change the fact that they had both hurt Laurel.

He had lost his best friend years before when Ellen had changed. Then he had lost his wife. Annie would be taking away his unborn child when she returned to Houston. He could very easily lose Laurel because he'd put off dealing with the truth. He would be left with nothing, and he had no one to blame but himself. None of this would have happened if he hadn't withdrawn after Ellen's death. If he'd only thought about his daughter instead of himself. But the realization came two years too late. He didn't know how he was supposed to make it all work now.

Anne sat in the hallway and leaned her head against Laurel's door. She hadn't heard anything for almost ten minutes. She didn't know if that was good or bad. It didn't really matter, she thought sadly. She had to try to make Laurel understand.

"I'm sorry you found out this way," Anne said, raising her voice so she could be heard through the door.

"Go away."

At least she hadn't said she hated her. Maybe that was something. "I can't go away until we talk."

Laurel's response was to turn up her stereo until the music pounded through the walls, blocking out any possibility of conversation. Anne waited. She tried to gather her thoughts together and figure out what she was going to say. She should have told Laurel before, when she'd wanted to. At least then she could have planned her words in advance and tried to soften the blow. To hear the truth that way, blurted out in anger.... She winced. She wasn't even sure what she and Jake had been yelling at each other, but she would bet it had been ugly and unsuitable for a thirteen-year-old to hear.

Oh, baby, she thought, touching the door between them. If only it had happened differently. If only she and Jake hadn't made love that night in the desert. She touched her stomach. No, that's not true. She wanted the baby. She wanted Laurel. Her mouth curved up in a slight smile. She might as well finish the list and go for it all—she wanted Jake. But not like this. Not with everyone bleeding inside. She'd come here to make a difference, to make it better. Instead everything was going wrong.

In a few minutes the music stopped. She drew in a deep breath. "You will always be my daughter, Laurel," she said, hoping the girl would at least listen. "I still love you and want you in my life."

The door flew open. Laurel glared at her. "No, you don't. You want your b-baby." Her voice cracked. Her long brown hair hung down in two braids. With her warm plaid shirt and baggy jeans hiding her budding figure, she looked young and fragile.

Anne scrambled to her feet. "I'm sorry you found out this way."

Laurel glared at her. "You're not sorry you're pregnant, are you?"

"No."

"I knew it." Fresh tears formed in her eyes. "You never cared about me. That's why you gave me away. You never wanted me. You only came here because you wanted to get pregnant. You wanted the baby so you could keep it. You're going to keep it."

Laurel balled her hands into fists and struck out. Anne grabbed her wrists, holding her at arm's length. The girl thrashed for a few seconds, before going still.

"You didn't keep me. You gave me away." Her hazel eyes, so like Anne's mother's, accused her of the most heinous crime. "You were supposed to be my mother. Now you're going to be someone else's mother. I can't even hate you anymore. You made me want to have you stay here forever. But it was lies. You lied to me."

Anne pulled her close. Laurel resisted at first, then sagged against her. She wrapped her arms around the sobbing girl and murmured soft, meaningless phrases. "Hush, honey. Hush." She led Laurel over to the bed and sat next to her. "I'm sorry."

"No, you're not."

"I am. I swear." Anne reached out and brushed her daughter's face with her fingers. Laurel flinched at the touch, but didn't pull back. "I wish I could explain, but it's very complicated."

"That's what grown-ups always say." Laurel sniffed. "It doesn't seem very complicated to me. You want this baby and you're going to keep it."

Anne shook her head. "I know this hurts you. It hurts me, too." She held up her hand to ward off her daughter's interruption. "Please listen, honey. I was seventeen when I got pregnant in the back of a boy's pickup truck. It was stupid and I knew better, but I did it anyway. I gave you up for adoption because I thought it was the right thing to do. If I could be that seventeen-year-old girl again—" She swallowed hard. "I want to tell you that I would keep you. I would, knowing what I know now. If I had been smarter, I wouldn't have gotten pregnant in the first place. But given the same set of circumstances, knowing there was a loving couple wanting a baby and not being able to have one, I would give you up again."

Laurel stared at her. Anne could see the pain in her eyes, and the need to believe, but she was afraid to have her trust shattered yet again.

Anne took one of her hands and held it tightly. "There's nothing you can say to me that I haven't said to myself. I never wanted to hurt you. Even though I wasn't with you all those years, I never forgot about you, or stopped wondering where you were or what you were doing. Your dad showed me some videos."

Laurel looked up, surprised. "He did?"

She nodded. "Of when you were little."

Laurel grimaced. "They're so dopey."

"Not to me. I thought they were very special. I got to see you playing and laughing. I saw you with your mom. I saw the way she held you and taught you not to be afraid to try. What would you do, Laurel? If the choice were yours, if you could go back, would you want me to keep you? Would you want to give up your mom and dad so that you and I could live in a trailer like Becky Sue and her kids? I never got married. You might never have had a stepdad. It would have just been the two of us. My mom is gone, and Bobby didn't have much family, either. Would you give up everything you've ever known and everyone who's loved you just so you and I could be together?"

Their eyes met. Laurel slowly shook her head. "No. I love my dad. I miss my mom. Sometimes I cry because I want her back so much."

"I know, honey." Anne rested her hand on her daughter's head and pulled her close. She rocked her back and forth. "I'm not asking you to decide. I'm trying to show you that we all make hard decisions. We do the best we can, then we have to live with it. I'm sorry the thought of my having a baby hurts you. But you'll always be my firstborn. We've found each other now. It's up to us to keep that relationship special or let it die. We can't change the past, but we can influence the future. I love you and want to be a part of your life forever. You decide what happens next." She held her breath and prayed for a miracle.

Laurel drew in a deep breath and sighed. She stiffened, then shifted and wrapped her arms around her waist. Anne hugged her back.

"I love you, Annie."

"I love you, too, Laurel."

"I'll try not to be upset about the baby."

Anne touched a finger to her daughter's chin and urged her to look up. "You can be upset. I'm upset. This changes everything. But we can make it work. I promise."

"I used to want a little brother or sister."

"Your dad is convinced it's a boy."

Laurel frowned. "If my dad's the father of your baby, that means you guys—" She stopped talking and grimaced. "Oh, gross."

Anne bit back a smile. "Maybe it's best if you don't think about that part."

"I guess." Laurel wrinkled her nose. "Does this mean you're going to get married? Don't you have to be married to have a baby?"

"Obviously not," Anne said. "I had you."

"But that was different. If you marry my dad, that means you'll stay here with me. Don't you want to?"

"It's not that simple."

Laurel sighed again. "That means no."

"I can't marry your father. He's still in love with your mom. That would make the relationship hard on everyone. I don't belong here. I have a job, a promotion, waiting for me back in Houston. All my friends. Everything is there except for you." And Jake, but Laurel didn't need to hear that.

"But you have friends here, don't you? I think Daddy likes you a lot. Don't you have to like someone to, well—" She glanced at Anne's stomach, blushed and looked away. "I mean, I wouldn't mind if you married him. Dad says I can love you and Mom. That it's okay."

"Can't you love me if I don't live with you?"

Laurel thought for minute, then nodded slowly. "I guess."

"Good. Because I'll still care about you. We have something very special. It's not about geography or who lives where. I'll always be available to you Laurel. Just a phone call away. We'll work out some way to have visits together. Often, I promise."

Laurel stared at her. Her freckles stood out on her pale skin. Anne counted the dots on her daughter's nose and knew the number and pattern matched the freckles on her own face. They were tied together by more than blood, but it was nice to know the family connection was still there.

"You're leaving," Laurel said suddenly.

"You always knew that."

"But you're leaving now. You're not going to wait until the two months are up, are you?"

Laurel threw herself at her. Anne clutched her. Sometime in the last few minutes she'd made up her mind. It would be easier for everyone if she was gone. Jake and Laurel could get on with their lives, and she could make plans for her maternity leave. She would have to figure out how much time she should take and... She touched Laurel's hair. The details could wait. For now it was enough to hold and be held by the child she'd lost so long ago.

"No, honey, I'm leaving in the morning."

Jake stood on the top of the stairs. He heard the words but didn't want to believe what they meant. She was leaving him. The sharp pain in his chest surprised him. He hadn't realized how much he would care.

Laurel looked up and saw him. "Daddy." She ran

to him and embraced him fiercely. "Annie's leaving. Don't let her go. Please make her stay."

"Laurel, I—"

She tore herself free and raced down the stairs. The front door opened, then slammed shut.

He leaned against the doorframe and folded his arms over his chest. Annie sat on his daughter's bed. Her eyes looked haunted.

"How much did you hear?" she asked.

"Enough to know that you're going to be one terrific mother."

Her smile looked a little ragged at the corners. "Thanks. I don't feel so great right now."

"Laurel knows that you love her. That's the most important thing. The rest of it can be worked out."

She folded her hands together on her lap. Her pale red hair had grown a little since she'd been here. It brushed her shoulders in an unruly mass of waves. The oversize sweatshirt she wore dwarfed her, concealing her generous curves. But he remembered them. He remembered how she tasted and felt in his arms. He remembered the fire that consumed them every time they got within two feet of each other. He knew in his heart it would be like that forever. He thought about her gentleness, her humor, her quick wit and sharp mind. He thought about her half-finished craft projects, littering the house, and the cow curtains fluttering by that damn cow-print table and chair set in the kitchen. He thought about how she had struggled to make it work for all of them, and the fact that she put her needs last. He knew he would be a fool to let her go.

"I don't remember when I first met Ellen," he said quietly.

She glanced up, her eyes wide. "Jake, I don't—"

"Please. Just listen."

She bowed her head and nodded.

"I guess we were babies. I don't remember a time in my life when Ellen wasn't there. We were best friends, all the way through high school. We both dated other people, but we hung out with each other. We could talk about anything. Then I went off to college while she was in her last year of high school. I came home for Christmas break, and something had changed. We thought we were in love."

Anne took a deep breath. "That sounds very wonderful," she said. "I'm sure your parents were pleased."

He wished she would look up so he could guess at what she was thinking, but she didn't. "They were. In retrospect, I know we weren't in love. I think the hormones kicked in and we didn't know what else to call it." He smiled, remembering their fumblings in the front seat of his sports car. It had been an awkward tight fit, but neither of them had minded. "We got engaged, then married. It took me several years to figure out something was wrong."

She looked up then, surprised. "What are you saying?"

"I didn't love Ellen the way you think I did. The woman I mourn has been gone a lot longer than two years. I miss my best friend, the girl I grew up with. Not the woman who died. I keep up the traditions out of obligation and maybe a little guilt. Also because they mean something to Laurel. Not because I care. I—" Now it was his turn to look down. He stared at the pale gray carpet newly installed in Laurel's room, then glanced back at Annie. "I used her memory to make you feel unwelcome. Maybe I used it to hide behind, as well.'' He shrugged. ''I'm not proud of that, and I apologize.''

She didn't say anything. He cleared his throat and continued. ''I care about you, Annie. You've found your way into our lives. I can't imagine this house without you. I need you. Laurel needs you. We're not naked in bed, I'm not drunk or angry or desperate. Please stay and be my wife.''

She reached up and tucked her hair behind her ear. ''Because you love me?'' she asked.

He nodded cautiously.

''Passionately?''

He smiled. ''You can't deny the passion.''

''No, I can't.'' She stood up and approached him. When she was close enough for him to inhale the sweet scent of her perfume, she placed her small hands on his folded arms. Her blue eyes stared into his. ''I love you, Jake. I don't know when or how, but I do. I think it all started when you were so protective of Laurel.''

A fierce gladness rose inside of him. The knot of tension in his gut released. It was going to be all right. She was going to stay. ''Annie, I—''

''No.'' She reached up and touched her fingers to his mouth. Her hand cupped his jaw briefly, then returned to his forearm. ''I won't marry you.''

''But if you love me, why not?''

''Because you don't love me.''

''I do.''

She shook her head. ''I'm not saying I don't believe your story about Ellen. I'm sure it's true. Actually it explains a lot of things to me. But your timing stinks. It's a little too convenient for my taste. I'm leaving in the morning so you happen to figure out that you haven't loved Ellen in years, oh, and by the way, you love me, too? I don't think so.''

He could feel the panic growing. He was going to lose her. He knew it. ''Dammit, woman, what do you want me to say? I've told you I love you, I've asked you to stay. Is it the idea of being married? We can live together, if you prefer. I don't like that, but I can be flexible. As long as we're a family.''

''As long as you have your son.'' The sadness of her face pierced him like a knife. ''That's what this is all about. Whether you're willing to admit it or not, this entire discussion is because you're afraid to lose your son. If you can't intimidate me into staying, you're going to woo me into submission.''

''That's not true,'' he said, but wondered if it was. Was he playing some kind of elaborate game with her? Was he that shallow and unfeeling? She was right about one thing. The timing of his confession did stink.

''I'll figure something out,'' she said, stepping away from him. ''Visits, or maybe I'll look for another job close by. You'll be able to see your son, Jake. I promise.''

He framed her face in his hands, then bent down and kissed her. He tasted her passion and her sadness. Had it been their destiny to break each other's hearts? ''Despite what you think Annie Jo Baker, I do love you.''

Tears formed, but she blinked them away. ''Then let's stay friends. For both our children.''

He pulled her close and held on tightly. Her body felt familiar against his. Familiar and so very right. ''I'm sorry,'' he whispered into her hair.

''I'm not. I found Laurel. I've been gifted with a second chance and a second child. And I found you,

Jake. You'll never know what loving you has meant to me.''

Then why are you leaving me? he wanted to ask. But he didn't. There weren't any words left to convince her to stay.

Chapter 15

The rain fell, obliterating all but the brightest lights in the Houston skyline. Anne stood at her window watching the storm. Through the glass she could feel the damp, cool air. It was early December. In Colorado, they had already had snow. She knew because she watched the weather channel's national report, as if seeing computer images of snow or rain would make her feel she was still living on the horse ranch with Jake and Laurel.

Her daughter also brought her up-to-date, she reminded herself. The twice-weekly phone calls lasted almost an hour with Laurel chattering about her friends and her plans for the weekend. When Anne called, Jake rarely picked up, and when he did, he politely asked how she was feeling, then handed her over to their daughter.

She'd been back over a month, so why didn't the beautiful white-on-white condo feel more like a home?

Anne turned from the window and walked toward her study. She'd brought work from the office, as she did most nights. Her new promotion carried with it a lot of responsibility. She wanted to be accessible to her team during the day which meant her paperwork had to be done in the evening. She had a big raise, stock options and use of the corporate apartment in New York when she went there on business. Heather had taken over her old job and was doing it very well on little more than forty hours per week.

"You don't have to kill yourself to be successful," Heather often reminded her when they went out for lunch. "I might not get the next promotion as quickly as you got yours, but I have a family to think of."

Anne did, too, but she hadn't told anyone about her pregnancy. As she entered her study, she touched her rounded stomach. All but the most formfitting of her suit skirts still fit. Still, she would have to think about buying some maternity clothes soon. And this condo. She glanced around at the perfect decorations. Maybe she would sell it and buy a small house with a yard. She had to think about hiring a nanny to take care of the baby while she was at work.

She sat behind her desk but instead of picking up the file on top, she reached for the photograph Laurel had sent her. It was her school picture. The teenager smiled out at the camera. Her hazel eyes hinted at laughter and a loving spirit that even difficult circumstances couldn't deny. Anne remembered the fight they'd had about what the girl would wear for the photo session. The screams that had led to tears and a deeper understanding of their relationship. There had been so many tears. Later, when Laurel had found out about the baby, and then at the airport, when they waited for her plane.

Anne closed her eyes to block out the visions of the past, but they intruded. Her flight had been late, giving them more time to stand around awkwardly promising to call and write. Jake had looked as if she was ripping his heart out by leaving, but that couldn't be true. He didn't really love her; he wanted his child.

But she still loved him. Not a day went by that she didn't ache for him. Her body needed for him to ignite and consume her passion, her mind and spirit longed to be in his presence, to hear his voice, to love him honestly, as a woman loves a man. She grew sick with wanting, then told herself it was the baby making her feel ill, not missing Jake. Besides she would be seeing him in a few weeks.

She opened her eyes and leaned back in her chair. How was she going to get through that visit? Laurel and Jake were coming to Houston for Christmas, then Jake was returning to the ranch right after the holiday, and his daughter was spending the rest of her vacation in the city. Anne had planned to take several days off. The holidays were always slow around the office. She and Laurel would see the sights; she even had tickets for a Houston Ballet performance. Then Laurel would fly home and Anne would be alone. Again.

But it wasn't the being alone that scared her. She would deal with that when it happened. It was seeing Jake. Being in the same room with him for three days. She only had one spare bedroom so he would be staying at a nearby hotel. When he told her about his plans she'd wanted to offer her couch, but she knew how easily that would lead to her bed, and then they would be back where they had started. She wouldn't be able to leave him again. She knew that now.

"I'm fine," she said, aloud, and reached for the top folder. After flipping it open, she stared at the page in front of her. But instead of words and numbers, she saw Jake's face, the gold flecks in his eyes, and the smile that could melt her bones.

"Stop it," she ordered herself. She didn't need a man in her life. She didn't need Jake. She and her baby would be fine by themselves. Just fine. After all, she'd worked hard for her career and this promotion. She deserved the chance to be successful.

She looked at her hands. Her nails had grown back and her skin was smooth again. Still she missed the baking and the sewing. The quilt she'd been working on lay packed in a box. She hadn't taken it out to finish it. She told herself she was too busy, but she knew the real reason was she couldn't face the memories.

Her gaze swept her desk to another framed picture. This one was of her mother. "You always told me to be the best," she said to the photo. "I'm being the best I can be, Mama."

Her mother had also told her to be happy. That happiness was the most elusive gift of all, and if she found it, she should hold on to it with both hands. Anne reached forward and touched the silver frame. She wondered what her mother would think if she knew her only daughter had settled for being just fine.

The flurry of present opening Christmas morning left the living room looking like a paper storm had blown through. Laurel sat on the floor in the center of the pile of presents. She opened yet another box and pulled out a pale pink wool sweater that matched a pair of corduroy pants Annie had given her.

"Cool," the teenager said, then leaned over and kissed Annie's cheek. "This was some Christmas."

"I think Annie and I both went a little crazy," Jake said, from his place on the white sofa. "We're going to have to be on our toes to keep you from turning into a spoiled brat."

Laurel rolled her eyes. "Da-ad. I'm the perfect child."

"Oh, please," Annie said, reaching for several torn sheets of wrapping paper.

"And you both love me," Laurel said confidently. She scrambled to her feet and crossed over to the couch. "Thanks for everything, Dad," she said. "I love it all."

He held her briefly as she kissed his cheek. If nothing else, she was right about one thing. He and Annie did love the girl. That's why they were going through these awkward three days together. For her sake.

"Is it okay if I call Terry and tell her what I got?" Laurel asked.

"Sure." Annie pointed down the hall. "You can even use the new phone in your room."

"Thanks." Laurel gathered an armful of presents. "Just so I don't forget anything," she said, then grinned and dashed toward the guest room. Her long brown hair fanned over the back of her bathrobe. From behind she still looked like a little girl, but Jake knew his daughter was very nearly a woman.

Annie rose to her knees and picked up several bows resting on the coffee table.

"Let me help you with that," he said, leaning forward. They reached for the same bow and their fingers brushed. He half expected to see sparks fly between them.

She jerked her hand back. "Sorry."

"It was my fault."

They stared uneasily at each other. It was about ten in the morning. Jake had come over early from his hotel room, but Laurel had slept in until almost nine. He'd sat in the kitchen with Annie, talking about the ranch and her work. Everything but what he really wanted to say. Now, alone in her big living room, with the remnants of the holiday around him, he still couldn't find the words.

"It looks beautiful," he said, pointing to the large decorated tree in the corner. "It must have been tough getting it up in the elevator."

She reached for a trash bag and began filling it. "There's a service elevator in the back. They use it to bring up furniture and that kind of thing."

"Oh. Convenient."

"Hmm. Yes, it is."

She sat on her knees, half turned away from him. Her profile was exactly as he remembered. The small nose, the full lips. The freckles. Every time he looked at Laurel's sweet face, he saw Annie's freckles.

A pale peach oversize shirt hung to midthigh. Peach stretch pants covered her lower half. He couldn't tell how much she was showing. He wanted to ask how she felt, but he was afraid she would misunderstand the question.

"It's hard without you, Annie," he said, because he was tired of pretending it wasn't.

She bit her lower lip. "I miss you guys, too."

"I've hired a housekeeper, but it's not the same."

''Yeah, she probably gives you everything you want.''

He leaned forward and rested his elbows on his knees. ''She does. It gets really boring.''

She looked up at him. Her delicate brows drew together in confusion.

''There's no one to argue with,'' he said. ''The house is clean all the time. No projects scattered around. No more sewing or baking.''

''She doesn't bake?''

''I told her not to.''

''Why?''

''Laurel and I agreed it would be better that way. We have too many memories of you already.''

''Oh.''

''How's work?'' he asked, knowing he was a coward. He knew what he wanted to tell her, what he wanted to ask her, but what if his words weren't enough? How could he convince her of the truth?

''Fine.'' She grimaced. ''I'm perfectly fine.''

He swallowed his pride. Without her, what good was the damn thing anyway? ''I'm not fine. I still love you, Annie, and I miss you. That house is big and cold without you in it.''

''Jake, don't.'' She picked up a piece of paper and crumpled it. ''I can't go through this again.''

''I've finally figured out a way to convince you that I want you because I love you and not because of the baby.'' At least he hoped he had.

She looked up, skeptical. ''Oh?''

Here goes nothing, he thought. ''I'm going to sleep with another woman and get her pregnant.''

''You're *what?*''

He fought back a grin. Leaning back on the sofa, he

raised one arm to stretch along the back. "It's the only way. Then I'll have another child of my own."

"That's the most...the most..." She clamped her mouth shut and glared at him. "Don't you even think about it, buster."

"Don't you see? If I have another child and I still love you and want you to marry me, you'll believe me when I tell you it's not about our baby." Then he did smile. "You were right. I was trying to have it all without thinking about you. The timing for my confession was a little too convenient. I've had these weeks to think about all of it. Annie, I can have a baby with anyone. If that was all I was interested in, I'd go out and find a woman who wants to marry a rich rancher, then get her pregnant. I'm not the greatest guy in the world, but I think I'm a pretty fair catch. I'll admit at the beginning I was focused on the baby." His gaze dropped briefly to her midsection. "Our baby. But I've realized it's so much more than that. I want a child, but I *need* you in my life. I love you. Please marry me."

"Damn you, Jake Masters." She threw the crumpled paper at him.

"Is that a yes, Annie?" he asked hopefully. "Do you believe me, now?"

"Do I have a choice?" Her smile was shaky. "If I don't you're going to go knock up some bimbo."

"I have better taste than to choose a bimbo," he said, and held open his arms.

She moved to the sofa and bent down. Their mouths met in hungry exploration. He gripped her hips and lowered her so she settled on his lap.

He looked at her. "Was that a yes?"

She nodded. "Yes, Jake, I'll marry you."

She took his hand and slipped it under her shirt. He could feel the change in her shape, the growing roundness of her belly. He could feel something else, too. The heat of her body and the electricity arcing between them.

"I love you," she murmured, then touched her mouth to his.

"And I love you."

Her breasts flattened against his chest as she leaned against him. Her tongue dueled with his.

"Wow!"

They broke apart. Jake groaned low in his chest, then turned his head to look at his daughter. Laurel danced from foot to foot in the hallway. "You're kissing," she crowed.

"You're interrupting," he said.

"This is good, right?"

Jake looked at Annie. "Very good."

"So you guys are like getting back together?"

Annie smiled at her daughter. "We're getting married."

"All right!" Laurel made a pumping motion with her arm. "That's totally cool." She looked at them both, then her expression changed from childish happiness to adult amusement. "I think I'll leave you two alone and go make another phone call."

"Make it a long one," Jake called after her. He looked back at Annie. "Where were we?"

"Right here." She angled her head, then lowered her mouth to his.

Epilogue

"I told you he would be a boy," Jake said from his place on the side of her hospital bed. He reached out and touched the tiny infant's face.

"You were right." Anne stared down at her sleeping child. Her body ached from the six hours of labor and she wondered if she would ever lose the extra twenty pounds, but none of that mattered right now.

She closed her eyes and savored the feel of the small bundle in her arms. He felt so perfect there, as if they had been made to fit together. Joy filled her, tinged with a bittersweet realization. Almost fourteen years before she'd given birth in a small hospital like this one. It had been Texas, instead of Colorado, and she'd just turned eighteen instead of being thirty-one. But the experience had changed her as much as this child being born.

As she held their son, she fought against the tears. She'd lost this with Laurel and it could never be recovered. She glanced up at her beautiful daughter. "Are you okay?"

Laurel nodded, her eyes wide. "He's so small."

"It's hard to give birth to them full grown."

"I guess, but gosh, I didn't expect this." She peered down at the scrunched-up red face. "He's not very handsome, is he? He's got monkey ears."

Anne laughed, then winced as the muscles in her stomach protested.

Jake winked at his daughter. "It's just how you looked, kid." He glanced at the sleeping baby. "Nah. He's better looking."

"Da-ad." She leaned closer. "Can I hold him?"

"Sure." Annie placed her son in her daughter's arm.

The teenager held him securely and cooed. "Hi. I'm your big sister. Laurel. Can you say Laurel?" She walked around the small room.

Jake touched Anne's face. "You feeling all right?"

"Never better."

"You did great in there. I'm really proud of you."

She leaned back against the pillows and sighed. "We make a good team."

"Well, I'm the team captain and I want to remind you that you promised not to go back to work for six weeks."

"Jake, I'll take the baby with me. The craft boutique has only been open a couple of months. I want to go in and keep an eye on things."

He frowned, then shook his head. "Why do I even bother fighting you? You're more trouble than my most stubborn brood mare."

"Speaking of brood mares, you knew this one was going to be a boy. What's the next one going to be?"

He took her hand and brushed his thumb against the

diamond ring on her left hand. "You'd have another baby?"

"Sure. I thought we agreed on three kids."

"I know, but I thought with the labor and all the weeks you haven't been able to see your feet, you might change your mind."

She looked at Laurel holding her brother. Then she stared at Jake. The love between them was as tangible as the world they lived in. She would do anything for him. Every day she loved him more. He trusted her with his heart, his soul and his flaws. If he wanted another child, she could deny him nothing.

"I liked our plan of three," she said, smiling. "So what is it going to be? A boy or a girl?"

He placed his hand on her stomach and thought for a second. "A girl."

"You're sure?"

"Yup."

"Okay. I'll stock up on pink." She touched his face. He was tired from staying up most of the night with her. The lines around his eyes had deepened, but he'd never looked more handsome to her. The transition hadn't been easy but they were together and they were happy. She couldn't ask for anything more than that. As her mother had taught her, she was holding on to their happiness with both hands.

* * * * *

Thank you, Kerry.
Happy Valentine's Day.

THE COWBOY
Cait London

Dear Reader,

I absolutely love this down-home story, about a guy who always tries to do the right thing, no matter how difficult. In *The Cowboy*, Lucas Walkington is true hero material.

When my editor invited me to write "anything that starts with a dating show scene," I thought about the attraction of opposites. Thus "The Love Bandit" and "Honey" were born, or in their real lives, Oklahoma cowboy-rancher Lucas and Chastity, the dull backroom file clerk.

I love peeling away appearances and revealing the true souls of these characters, and their strengths. With one date and a baby on the way, this confirmed bachelor has to retrieve his Honey from Chicago. This reminder of a knight claiming his lady is so romantic. Also, a writer's life flows into their stories. At the time, my sister had hired a "water witch"— and guess what Chastity's hidden talent is?

Thank you, readers, for my wonderful career and for the suggestions to write about Lucas's twin daughters, Summer and Raven. For more on my books, please visit http://www.caitlondon.com.

Cait London

Chapter 1

Lucas Walkington studied the reflection of the television studio's overhead lights in his polished Western boots. He shifted uncomfortably, preferring his rangeland to Chicago's maze of concrete buildings that encircled the studio. He was picturing his Oklahoma ranch lying cool and springtime-sweet in the pink glow of dawn, when the show's theme song suddenly began. The host of "Heartbeats" took center stage and the crowd applauded loudly, eagerly awaiting the sensual banter between the show's contestants.

Valentine's Day meant Lucas gave his girls presents and they cooked a special dinner for him; it didn't mean he acted like a yahoo, offering himself up on some baby doll's dinner plate for a handful of tiny gold hearts while an entire nation watched and hooted.

The studio chair lacked the comfort of his favorite saddle. His competitors leaned forward, listening intently to the "Heartbeats" host. After a warm-up joke, the host issued the audience's preshow instructions. Ginger, a previous contestant, was unable to return to the show. A new "Heartbeat Goddess" named Honey would take Ginger's slot. Honey was described as every man's dream girl—a delicious blond confection—and after asking questions of each male contestant, she would choose her male "Heartbeat" for a luxurious weekend near Las Vegas.

That male contestant would return, brag about his weekend romance to coast-to-coast viewers, and choose from three new female contestants; thus "Heartbeats" rolled on across America.

Lucas ground his back teeth together and glanced at the other men seated behind the curtain with him. Ten years younger than Lucas's thirty-eight, El Toro's and Dream Guy's expressions lighted with excitement. Wearing winter tans, gold chains and loose designer shirts and trousers, they leaned forward in their chairs. Lucas settled back, crossing his long legs at the ankle. He studied the crease in his jeans and decided to settle back while El Toro and Dream Guy took the lead in the sensual banter with Honey.

He'd waited out droughts and dry pocketbooks, his seventeen-year-old twin daughters' scrapes with life, and fate still wasn't satisfied. Slapped with the stage label of The Love Bandit, Lucas concentrated on his boots; if he had a lick of horse sense, he'd stand up and hightail it back to Oklahoma.

A young woman assistant, a few years older than his daughters, smiled invitingly at him, and Lucas scowled back. The show was saturated with sensual heat, on-stage and off. All he needed was some underage baby doll sidling up to him.

Sweat trickled down the back of his neck into the

collar of his shirt. The glaring lights added to the heat of his shirt and sweater. His daughters had picked out his red designer sweater—after they entered his name in Tulsa's Lonesome Cowboy contest. They had taunted, tormented and teased him into appearing on the television program. To prove to his daughters, Summer and Raven, that he wasn't entirely "out of it," untuned to the pains of living and loving—to prove he hadn't completely turned one-hundred-percent certified old hermit—Lucas had reluctantly submitted to being coached and groomed for the dateable bachelor contest.

The contest promoted Oklahoma tourism and offered a prize of five thousand dollars in return for appearing on the widely televised dating program in Chicago.

Elated when Lucas won the Tulsa competition, the twins were ecstatic when he was chosen as a delegate to "Heartbeats." For the moment, they were angelic, a situation that could revert in half a shake of a prairie dog's tail.

The beautiful, six-foot, lanky twins were destined for trouble from the moment of their conception. Alesha, their mother, decided at the twins' birth that she'd had enough of scrimping and hardships on Lucas's remote ranch, and had yanked them into Tulsa with her parents. Later, when they were three, Alesha did not want the responsibility of "taming the tomboys." When the twins prepared Lucas for his "Heartbeats" debut, he began to understand a little of Alesha's fear. His daughters had tugged the new sweater across his broad shoulders and rumpled his hair, their blue eyes widening. Summer had exclaimed, "Dad, you are really a st— You really look hot!"

Then Raven had added quietly, "Ah...for, ah... someone your age, that is."

His tanned fingers gripped his thighs, and Lucas traced the scar caused by barbed wire. The host—Lyle Drake—ran through El Toro's and Dream Guy's advertising backers. Lucas lowered his jaw into his open collar as Lyle—a man who wore buffed fingernails and shoe lifts—introduced the Love Bandit. The Bandit's skin warmed, and a drop of salty sweat burned in his new razor cut. Somewhere in Lyle's introduction lurked the words "a tall, tanned hunk of Oklahoma cowboy beef."

The "beef" wondered darkly how Lyle would look with his designer rear end squishing a fresh cow pile.

The host of "Heartbeats" listed the show's many sponsors and the prizes awaiting the contestants at the different levels of competition. The Bandit's Oklahoma sponsors received their advertising due, and Lucas concentrated on the amount of interest five thousand dollars in appearance money would draw in the twins' college fund.

Lucas took a deep breath, preparing to shed the inane sensual banter with as much grace as he could scavenge. He would sit back and let the other yahoos take the lead. El Toro and Guy were frothing at the mouth, ready to party.

With a bit of luck, Lucas would be eliminated early in the rounds of questioning. He'd be so dull, so dumb, that he'd be dropped quicker than a cornered skunk.... The Heartbeat Goddess would select a weekend player and he could slink back to his ranch to hole up until the whole mess was forgotten.

While waiting to be introduced on "Heartbeats," Chastity Beauchamp shot an angry glare at her half-sister, Hope.

Chastity inhaled sharply, uncomfortable in the tight, confining bra and low-cut, slinky dress Hope had chosen for her to wear. Black, off-the-shoulder, hugging every curve until the hem touched her thighs, the dress represented everything that Chastity was not—sexy, available and ready to play.

Chastity crushed Hope's prepared list of questions for the waiting dateables. Her sister had drafted the wrong person to fill a vacancy on the show's lineup. Chastity pressed her lips together, then parted them as she remembered her sister's instructions for glamour. Hope had applied gloss and color for "wet, dewy lucious lips."

Adjusting her tightly closed fingers to avoid damaging a false nail that Hope had carefully applied, Chastity duly licked her lips as she had been instructed. In her lifetime role as family supporter, she had played many roles for many disasters, each worse than the last. Hope's latest disaster had laid a guilt trip right at Chastity's practical shoes.

Chastity wished for those comfortable shoes now, rather than the stiletto heels that made her legs appear longer.

"If you don't take the empty slot on the Valentine's Day show, Chas, beloved sister of mine," Hope had finally said after a long argument, "my tush is out the studio door. My job is seeing that the contestants are interesting and that they appear. I can't help it if Ginger got married last night—this is a live show, Chas—have a heart…I've got to pull a sexy blonde out of some closet and you're the only live body I've got to work with. You could have a shape, I guess…with a real effort—if we worked with your…"

At this point, she had examined Chastity from head

to toe, then continued with a frown. "You need makeup, a haircut and lightening, decent clothes, coaching in how to talk and walk, and voilá, a Heartbeat Goddess is born."

Hope had paused, scanned Chastity's loose, earth-colored clothing and tightly braided hair, and scrunched her lids together. "We'll work hard on the body part. You're definitely not built long and lean," she muttered quietly. "Thank God, you don't have to wear glasses for distances." Then she had opened her eyes slowly, smiled sweetly and played her trump card. "I know you love to putter in files and grow plants and all that boring stuff that makes you what you are—sweet. I know you like blah clothes and quiet and I love you with all my heart, Chas…but if you don't help me, I could lose a job that is making my career—change that—my *life,* amount to something. I'll make it up to you, I promise…trust me. I'll love you forever," she had said as Chastity groaned loudly.

In the end, Chastity submitted as she had always done in the face of Hope's disasters.

Then there was the matter of the thousand dollars, which would help clear her mother's last credit card mess. Grace Beauchamp's addiction for ordering television bargains was momentarily under control; however the credit card bills remained, with a sum due on Chastity's grandfather's nursing-home tab.

From the Big Pool Hall in the Sky, the Old Coot's chuckle floated over Chastity. Her grandfather had loved a good con game.

Chastity closed her eyes, aching for her grandfather. As a child, she ran to the Old Coot for love while her mother flitted through affairs and loved the two children she'd had before Chastity. He insisted that she had inherited his special talent, giving her the identity she needed to survive in a hectic, Gypsy environment. Created ''on the wrong side of the blanket'' and ignored as a child, Chastity had always wanted someone to love who was hers alone—her special person who loved her with equal intensity.

Now Chastity stood waiting to be introduced on a show she never watched, primed with directions on how to be appealing and wishing she'd resisted her sister's final coup de grace, ''Please don't cost me this job, Chas. It's my life. Oh, and don't tell anyone that we're related. It's a no-no on the show.''

The long, slinky earrings in Chastity's ears slithered against her neck, tangling in the wealth of newly lightened hair that reached her midback. In the dressing room mirror, her shadowed and mascaraed eyes had seemed enormous. Hope had used cosmetics and brushes like an artist until a gorgeous, sexy blonde named ''Honey'' had emerged.

Lyle Drake introduced Honey, and a roar of catcalls and whistles shot up from the studio audience. Chastity swallowed and reminded herself to walk slowly toward the host. Then Lyle's firm hand enclosed hers and she returned his warm smile, forcing herself to forget her new tight lingerie, which did unearthly, spectacular and pert things to her bosom.

The ''Heartbeats'' host drew her to the two chairs onstage. ''Honey is gorgeous, candidates behind the curtain. She's everyman's dream. Our last winner, Ginger, was unable to play at the last minute and we were lucky to find Honey. As you know, the show's format is that the contestant who is chosen this time will ask the questions on the next show. He or she returns from their exciting weekend, shares the fun with the audience, and then chooses a datemate from a new contestant line-up, allowing the show to continue. Make no mistake, gentlemen behind the curtain, Honey is a knockout, not second choice in any dating book. Come on, Honey, tell us a little about yourself—what's your job, what you do for fun—something to give those guys behind the curtain and our audience a little insight to the real you. For instance, why did you want to appear on 'Heartbeats'? Come on, Honey, sit down…''

Blinded by the lights, Chastity focused on Hope's directions. *Follow Lyle's lead. Read my questions and "ooze" remarks like, Oh, I'd love to share a midnight dinner with you.…*

She repeated the breathless, sexy ''Hi, Lyle'' Hope had designed, and tried to equally lift the corners of her mouth. Hope had forced her to practice equalizing her smile until her cheeks ached. Lyle was a nice man, according to her sister; he needed the show's high ratings to help provide for his three small children. ''Lean on me, kid,'' he had said in their preshow interview. ''It's just a game, and you're perfect for the part. Hope sure knows how to pick 'em. Loosen up, it's just for fun and we're glad you're helping us by filling in.''

''Well, Lyle,'' she murmured slowly, huskily after dampening her lips for the cameras and bringing up that reluctant left corner of her mouth. ''I work in an office. Right now, I'm in-between on the dating scene, and there are no significant others. I just love this show. I watch it every day, so do my friends.''

Between dates? Chastity winced inwardly, then decided the statement was true. Randall had been a steady date for a year…two years ago. In the future, she hoped to have another date.

An expert host, Lyle snared her hand and held it

reassuringly. "You're gorgeous, Honey. To El Toro, Dream Guy and the Love Bandit behind the curtain, Honey is about five foot six inches tall, a leggy, green-eyed blonde with a very cuddly look. She's in her twenties and has never been married. Tell us what you're looking for in a weekend date, that special something that interests you."

Behind a studio camera Hope licked her lips, silently instructing Chastity to do the same. *"Move sensual, sis. Move like you were silk sliding on silk, like every pore of your body enjoys being a woman who attracts men's stares...."*

Chastity smiled gently at Lyle. She carefully tilted her head to one side, allowing a jumble of honey-colored curls to flow across her bared shoulder. She rotated that shoulder slowly, picturing silk on silk, then answered softly in her normal husky, hesitant tone, "I want a man who enjoys spending lots of quiet time with me. One who doesn't need a crowd to make him happy."

Lyle's eyebrows lifted. "I know *I'd* want to be alone with you, Honey," he returned with a boyish grin that had charmed her in their interview earlier. "Whoops. I didn't mean that, Barbara," he said, waving to his wife at home.

Handing Chastity a gold box filled with twenty golden hearts, Lyle said, "Let's get started, Honey. For every answer that appeals to you, drop a heart into the tube marked El Toro, the Love Bandit or Dream Guy. The dateable delectable receiving the most gold hearts on this special Valentine show is your date for that weekend at Casa Bianca. Now, what's your first question for our contestants?"

Honey glanced down at Hope's list of questions for

the contestants. If she had been drafted, the least she could do was save Hope's job and Lyle's ratings. "I'd love to know what each guy would want to do on our first date." She spaced her words slowly, deliciously apart, just as Hope had directed.

Lyle relayed the question to El Toro, who returned suggestively, "Honey, I'd do anything you want."

The audience cheered, and then Dream Guy launched into a lengthy list of a candlelight dinner, a bearskin rug and a hot tub.

The Love Bandit cleared his throat after a lengthy silence. "Maybe a movie. Maybe a dinner later...." The slow, deep drawl intrigued Chastity. The man was reluctant. If she *had* to spend a weekend with a date-able, she preferred a really reluctant man. She dropped a heart into Bandit's tube.

She asked the next question. "Describe what you think you do best...."

El Toro and Dream Guy giggled and joked and suggested a smorgasbord of delights. Chastity found she enjoyed the light banter with the two men. Her masquerade as a stunning blonde had become a game...like playing a Cinderella role. Her friends would never guess her identity—who would know she was just plain old Chastity from Charlie's Auto filing-and-bookkeeping department?

She licked her lips appropriately, adjusted her newly sensual body to the chair and crossed a length of bare thigh. She winked at Hope, whose mouth gaped.

Bandit hesitated again. Then his deep, liquidy voice, marked by a distinct twang, said, "Listening... maybe."

Leaning forward, Chastity found herself waiting for that cowboy twang. *If* she had to spend a weekend with a dateable to preserve Hope's job, she wanted a man who wasn't primed for— "Listen to what, Bandit?"

The silence stretched into two heartbeats. "Listen to the rain. Listen to the wind moving through the grass. Listen to the old windmill catching the wind, moving with it." He was quiet, then said, "It's important to listen to people. Not what they say...but what's inside...."

Lyle made an impatient movement as though the cowboy's answers didn't fit the show's format, but Chastity listened, entranced. The man's wistful, lonely tone struck something soft and cuddly and feminine within her; she wanted to snuggle on his lap and— Lyle glanced closely at Chastity's expression and interrupted. "Bandit, tell Honey and the audience how you would like to kiss her the first time."

A chair scraped immediately behind the curtain and a man's low, dangerous tone snapped, "First, I'd ask if the lady wanted to."

Dream Guy added quickly, "Hot. I'd kiss her hot."

El Toro chimed in, "The neck...I'd start there. Women love it." He entered into a long dialogue with Dream Guy filled with innuendos.

"Where would *you* start, Bandit?" Chastity found herself asking. Parts of her body were heating, shifting and reassembling into one big question mark. Her feminine molecules anticipated Bandit's answer. The audience leaned forward in their seats. Chastity took a deep breath and closed her eyes, then licked her lips, almost tasting the cowboy's mouth.

"Depends, I guess," he returned in that soft, low drawl.

"On what?" she asked, aware that her breathing was uneven. "And where?"

"The lips, ma'am," the cowboy said as though speaking to a slow-witted child.

"I like kissing lips," Chastity said slowly, thoughtfully. She pictured a curvaceous blonde with mounds of curling hair snuggled to a tender cowboy's tall muscular length, held gently in his arms as he bent to kiss her. The romantic scene caused her to shiver, anticipating the man's mouth. She dropped five gold hearts into Bandit's tube and repeated Lyle's question. "Tell me how you would kiss me the first time, Bandit."

Chastity blinked, suddenly aware of how much she fitted into the role of Honey. *Lord, she wanted that cowboy's kiss.*

There was a muffled noise as the man cleared his throat. Then Bandit said uneasily, "Soft. I'd see if you...how you felt. What you smelled like up close.... Just soft," he finished impatiently.

In the audience, women sighed dreamily. Lyle squeezed Chastity's hand, his expression urging her to pursue the cowboy. "What do you think I smell like, Bandit?"

Again, the answer was deliberate, as though he'd thought about her scent. "Sweet. Like raindrops on..."

Chastity could sense him seeking the appropriate word. His sincerity and thoughtfulness was endearing.

"Like roses," Dream Guy supplied in an aside.

"Like orchids," El Toro muttered impatiently.

"Like raindrops on the spring prairie wind," Bandit finished firmly and the women in the audience went wild.

"Whew! What do you have to say about that, Honey?" Lyle asked with a grin that said: *Zinger. Ratings are up.*

Chastity sensed the camera sliding in for a close-up.

She disregarded everything but her blatant attraction for Bandit. For him she wanted to be gorgeous and sexy and inviting. She maneuvered through a series of questions to the men and decided that El Toro and Dream Guy should be tossed back in elementary school, while Bandit was certified "Adult Male, Thoughtful and Sweet."

While the other men might need leashes at Honey's bedroom door, she was positive that Bandit would not place one boot over the threshold unless properly invited.

"I want him," she whispered firmly to Lyle, whose eyebrows shot up. The show's format called for more questions. She dumped the entire box of tiny gold hearts into Bandit's tube. *"I want that man."*

Lyle stared blankly at her and "Honey" fluttered her lashes back at him. For good measure, she found Hope hovering behind the cameras and she fluttered Honey's lashes again.

If she was bound for a weekend with a man, she wanted a real one. A reluctant one with a slow, sensual cowboy drawl. She dismissed a weekend with the raging hormonal boys who needed shots.

Lyle chuckled and beamed. "Honey isn't a woman to waste words. She wants her luxurious weekend in Casa Bianca to be spent with…the Love Bandit," he announced happily. "Honey, let's meet the men you turned down—El Toro and Dream Guy."

Each man cuddled and kissed Chastity playfully. "And now…the Love Bandit," Lyle exclaimed jubilantly. The crowd cheered and Chastity's heart pounded heavily. She took a deep, uneven breath and waited.…

The Love Bandit was gorgeous…tall and tasty. He was worth every gold heart on earth.

He walked toward her in a lithe, slow stride, all angles and reluctant masculinity. There were broad shoulders, gleaming blue-black hair, a vast chest tapering down to long legs sheathed in new jeans.

Western jeans, she noted with a burst of joy, not the designer brands, but the kind that fitted and molded—

Chastity inhaled sharply, ignoring the restricting cloth over her bosom and the way her breasts pushed upward. She gripped her hands together to keep them from reaching toward him.

She closed her lids, relishing the sight of Bandit behind them. She sighed and knew that his wary, don't-touch-me-ma'am look was hers to unravel over one entire, blissful weekend. Bandit was the present of her lifetime and she wanted to experience every little masculine angle—

Just once she wanted to reach out and take something really nice from life and, without doubt, Bandit was that special gift.

Her heart thumped wildly as her eyes slowly ran down his lean body, then traveled upward with absolute delight.

"Oh," she breathed unevenly, drawing Lyle's quick scrutiny. But "Honey" didn't care; she was too busy picturing the cowboy walking toward her wearing nothing but an overnight beard and a towel around his hips. Then she debated jerking the towel away, and whispered a soft "Oh" again.

Bandit hesitated warily, his legs locked at the knee as though he were a gunfighter sizing up dangerous territory. Then he breathed deeply and a muscle moved in his jaw as though he was gritting his teeth. Two tiny indentations appeared in his cheeks, indicating dimples. With grim control he walked toward her, his eyes narrowing on her face.

Chastity sensed Bandit's determination to keep his eyes above her bare shoulders and found that rather endearing.

She wanted to melt into him…wanted to curl against his six-foot-three rangy frame.

Honey wanted to stand on tiptoe, even in her stiletto heels, lift her mouth to Bandit's hard one and let him demonstrate the promised soft kiss. She was on a tight time frame and needed to snare his interest quickly, if she was to experience the cowboy's attentions.

Acting on impulse, Chastity sidled Honey's leggy, shapely body into the rangy cowboy's path, planting her curves firmly against his hard, delectable body. Mere inches from her, he remained gorgeous without the aid of her glasses. His thighs were hard and he smelled like soap and lime-scented after-shave.

Chastity fluttered Honey's lashes up at Bandit, tipped her head back and lifted her full, glossy lips invitingly.

Before her lids closed, Chastity saw the dark heat in Bandit's blue eyes. She saw the tightly leashed hunger and knew that he'd never take anything she didn't want to give. She adored the deepening, serious line between his well shaped eyebrows. Bandit had refused the show's makeup artist, the lines on his tanned face endearing.

Wrapped in the safety of his gentlemanly manners and Honey's sexy blonde image, Chastity placed her hands on his chest, her fingertips exploring the heavy pads of muscle.

They rippled. Hard cords shifted uneasily beneath

her touch and Chastity stared up into Bandit's eyes as her hands floated over the width of his shoulders.

The heat and hunger flared in those dark blue eyes, and she sensed that this was the kind of man who'd pick her up and carry her off—if he were hers. Chastity had dreamed about this man, waited for him, and now he was within her grasp. She'd waited years to taste delight, and now...

Honey wanted to rip off his sweater and shirt and— Chastity blinked. Bandit smelled the way a man should, like soap and low-key after-shave. "You may kiss me, Bandit," she whispered huskily.

"Now, ma'am?" he asked politely, though a flush moved higher on his tanned cheeks. There was an arrogant tilt of his head as though he didn't bend easily. "We're on television...live."

She noted clean waves of hair, the way it just touched his collar. She touched the strands gently, noting with satisfaction that it was naturally crisp. Bandit was a very natural man. A touchable man. One that Honey could cuddle near, and nibble on his ear— Chastity noted the said earlobe. It did look tasty, dark and sweet and vulnerable. "Now, babe," she urged in Honey's husky, sultry tones.

He inhaled sharply, his eyes darkening dangerously. The cowboy was an exciting man with little masculine switches that she ached to flip on. She was pleased with the way she'd tossed the in-word, "babe," at him, thus proving that "Honey" knew how to play.

Chastity decided that there were certain advantages in acting the role of a vamp. She could step out of her shy character and grasp what she wanted—and *she wanted to experience that cowboy*. Beneath his sexy trappings, Bandit wore the wary look of a man who had tasted life and found it sour. Poor man, he needed a tender touch.

Bandit's jaw clenched and lowered into his collar. The grim curve of his hard mouth served as an obligatory smile.

Why wasn't he taking advantage of the moment? What was wrong with her, anyway? She'd taken hours preparing for the moment, including a drastic forty-eight-hour diet-and-exercise plan, and now Bandit wasn't all that eager. Maybe he preferred brunettes or redheads with evenly matched smiles....

Piqued by the brunettes and redheads clustering in Bandit's future, she whispered, "Sweetcakes, the audience is expecting you to kiss me. Do it."

Bandit wasn't just another pretty young cowboy. Anger rippled beneath the surface; his body heat snared her though he hadn't touched her. Blue-black eyebrows and lashes shielded deep set eyes; his squarish jaw bore the tinge of a recently shaved, but heavy beard.

Then there was just the cutest little tuft of black hair at his open collar. Chastity wanted to nuzzle her nose in the fresh soap and male scents.... "Later, ma'am. If it's all the same to you," Bandit said in a low aside.

Lyle took Chastity's hand to draw her away from Bandit. She looked longingly back at the man who moved to her side. He felt so good, standing there, firm and strong, that she leaned a little his way.

Because he was obviously a gentleman, Bandit's arm slid around her waist to support her. She snuggled back against him, enjoying the wealth of taut muscles and clean masculine scents.

A small shudder rippled through his tall length and for just an instant his fingers tightened on her waist, drawing her nearer. Chastity nestled against his hard frame, feeling like a cat who was being petted.

Chastity smiled at Lyle as he described the weekend at a posh resort near Las Vegas. But she was concentrating on Bandit's warm, hard thigh pressing against her backside as the host urged them closer to the other contestants on the stage. She barely heard the final chorus—behind her hips, Bandit's body had responded blatantly to her femininity. After all the insecurities of her lifetime, the cowboy's response was sheer glory. To let him know she appreciated the compliment, she lifted Honey's sultry hot look and traced his rugged features.

Bandit's mouth tightened, and her ego soared higher. For the moment, plain Chastity Beauchamp was disturbing a fantastic man and loving it.

Then Hope was hugging her and staring adoringly up at Bandit. The tall cowboy's brows were drawn fiercely together. He nodded to Chastity politely. "The name is Walkington, ma'am," he said stiffly. "Lucas Walkington. I reckon you're stuck with me for the weekend."

Hope blinked and gaped when Chastity leaned toward Lucas, licked her glossy lips and said, "You got it, sweetcakes. You and me. Together for one heck of a weekend."

"Chas, the man is dynamite. He is such a babe! He's got that untamed cowboy look, like he's been around and wary. Just the kind of man that a woman wants to…oh, you know."

Chastity adjusted her glasses and groaned. Bandit had made her feel just that way. Then Hope continued, "I can't believe how good you were on the show. They put three extra operators on the switchboard. The sponsors want a special show when you come back. They're talking about keeping the audience on hold for one whole month, *then* bringing you and Bandit back to the show. They think there was so much steam between you that, given a month, no telling what could happen!'' Hope almost crowed.

She drew a black lacy peignoir from the mound of clothes on Chastity's bed and folded it into a suitcase with the air of a general packing war missiles. ''There might not be any other games for you and Bandit. Everything just clicked right the first time. You'll cinch this week's ratings. The way you looked up at him and the way he— You sizzled, Chas. Everything is perfect. The audience feedback slips asked if there was a fan club for Lucas.... Trust me, you'll enjoy this weekend.''

''I don't know what came over me. I must be having an identity crisis, and it's your fault, Hope,'' Chastity said as she stared at the clothing Hope had selected. The skimpy black maillot suit was sinful, and one tiny strap supported the sequinned hot pink sheath. The dress represented her emotions when she'd seen Bandit, wary and tough, all broad shoulders and narrow hips.

She'd wanted to pet him, to snuggle against him, to wrap herself along that tall, hard body. Her trademark restraint had snapped and crumbled like a thin cracker. The green light inside her body had flipped on and she wanted whatever time she could pilfer alone with him. She wanted a time and a man of her own, unrestricted by the needs of other people. She wanted to bask in the fire and the hunger in those sky-blue eyes, to tuck reality under a sofa cushion and run with the excitement racing inside her.

Chastity watched as Hope added musk-scented bath salts to a bulging cosmetic bag and said quietly, ''I am sick.''

''No time for that, Chas. Sorry. The show's limo will be pulling up with Lucas in about fifteen minutes.''

''I don't know what came over me…why I let you or any of the family get me into these things,'' Chastity returned firmly while Hope fluffed her jumble of blond curls with a hair pick and adjusted the collar on her jumpsuit. ''It's Friday night and I usually watch television and water my violets. Maybe repot a few plants. Filing is nerve-racking, you know, and auto payments must be entered properly. I'm under immense pressure every day, and Friday is my night to relax.''

She breathed deeply and glared at Hope. Born after her mother's divorce from Hope and Brent's father, Chastity had always tucked her needs away and cared for theirs. With the one devastating lapse of claiming the cowboy for her own, she had never been greedy. ''I've just recovered from getting our brother off the hook. Playing an irate wife isn't easy. Brent should have picked up his dog without the elaborate scene. I'm sure his ex-girlfriend really didn't want his Saint Bernard. Pickles eats a ton. Now you've got me flying off to Las Vegas for a weekend with a man I don't know. Have you noticed that cowboy's hat never falls off, never tips unless he adjusts it? I think there is something genuinely suspicious in that.''

Hope ran a cosmetic brush filled with blush powder across Chastity's cheeks and studied the effect intently. ''They learn that in cowboy school…. Use the Autumn Mauve shade to give that hollow look, Chas.… You're going to have a great time. Trust me. Just act like you did on the show—''

"I'm not a Heartbeat Goddess, not even close. Honey just isn't me," Chastity said between her teeth. "I just got caught up in the moment, that's all. Playing the part you and Brent cast me in as usual.... This is the last time you are going to get away with—"

"You look hot," Hope returned gleefully, lowering the jumpsuit front zipper two inches. She snatched Chastity's glasses away and repeated, "Real hot."

Chapter 2

At ten o'clock that night, Lucas sat watching Honey's progress back to their secluded, candlelit table. He had the sinking feeling that he'd been transported into another galaxy.

Casa Bianca lay miles from Las Vegas, a posh getaway that specialized in romance. The roomy suite he shared with Honey contained a private kitchen, stocked with exotic food for those who wanted absolute privacy. That tiny refrigerator held costly food worth more than several months of his grocery bills. A Jacuzzi with tropical plants and redwood decking sprawled just beyond a sunken living room, which held a fireplace.

Honey moved toward him in the nightclub, drawing male attention like bees to blossoming field clover, and he thought how she belonged in the exotic setting.

Her gold lamé top and slacks shimmered in the dim light. The top was magically supported by a single strap running around her delectable neck. Honey was all woman, her small waist and full bosom matching her soft hips. Beneath the slinky cloth of her slacks, her thighs moved strongly and Lucas found himself gritting his teeth. Drawn to the luscious curves and daring outfit, men traced her path, and Lucas pushed down his irritation as she approached.

He was too old for the reaction he'd had on "Heart-beats."

If ever Lucas read invitation in a woman's eyes, he found it in Honey's. A froth of blond hair tumbled from combs that pulled it back from her face, enlarging those huge, green eyes.

He gripped his thigh hard beneath the tablecloth to remind himself that he wasn't a boy. Honey issued big welcoming signs at every look, every touch.

Lucas pressed his lips together. He might be over-the-hill about the rules of today's dating games, but he wasn't prepared for the open invitation. Honey smiled in that secret way of hers, just the right side of her mouth moving slightly, and Lucas studied those full, glossy lips.

He wondered briefly how many men had kissed that satin-soft, lush contour. With little effort, he pictured what Honey would look like after making love—drowsy, warm, cuddly. Just the woman to make a man forget mortgages, daughters that needed college funding and a ranch that never ran out of problems.

Here he was, lounging around at eleven o'clock on a Friday night, preparing to dance until dawn. The idea grated. A hardworking man, Lucas couldn't reconcile the loss of time and money while indulging himself.

Honey may be used to exotic retreats, but he hit the sack early and got up with the chickens....

As she approached the table he stood and drew her chair back for her to sit down. She glanced up at him appreciatively, the big green eyes dark as jade. "Thanks, Lucas."

He nodded curtly. That hesitant, sultry tone slid right into his stomach with the impact of a satin sledgehammer. He had signed an agreement to see the date through and he would. Lucas sat slowly, fitting his length into the chair and stretching his legs out under the table.

"Lucas?" Honey stretched out her soft hand to rest on the back of his. Her nails were long and bright red, expensive-looking like the rest of her. "Are you tired? Should we go back to the suite?"

Because he wasn't ready to share living space with a woman who looked incredibly soft and warm, Lucas shifted uneasily. The whirlwind trip from Tulsa to Chicago after a night of rescuing his cattle from a sudden late-spring snow didn't leave him much control. When Honey inhaled on "Heartbeats," her pale breasts had lifted upward, the softness had quivered with her pulse—a pulse that would run deep in her warm, curved body—and he'd had to force his eyes away. She seemed oblivious to the way her arms squeezed against the fullness as she stared hungrily up at him. A man would have to be stone-cold dead not to notice those eyes,and that irritated him. "I thought the schedule said dancing until dawn. The photographers will want to start shooting at ten in the morning."

Honey's low laughter stroked him like warm velvet. "Some relaxing weekend. We're scheduled every minute."

A man with spiked hair and loose clothing came up

to their table, smiling at Lucas and Honey. He nodded at Honey and asked, "Dance?"

Lucas took a deep breath, unaccustomed to the freedom of one man to poach outright on another. He listened to the fast beat of the band and recognized it as a favorite song of his daughters. He'd been forced into learning the steps when they primed him for the Lonesome Cowboy contest. He glanced at Honey. "Dance with him if you want."

Her fingers tightened on his hand and somehow he found himself turning his palm and opening to her touch. When he'd sensed she needed him on the show, leaning against him, he'd responded the same immediate way. Despite her now-woman attitude, Honey had a shy turn to her that Lucas found appealing. She glanced at the man and shook her head. "I'm saving myself," she said huskily, indicating Lucas.

Lucas wondered darkly how many times a woman like her saved herself. The phrase "once in a blue moon" came to his mind.

He allowed himself to hold that soft hand within his, and instinctively ran his thumb across her palm. The tiny calluses surprised him.

The band swung into a slow tune and Honey looked at him. "Dance, cowboy?"

"Sure." He didn't bother with the line about stepping on her toes. He'd been doomed since his daughters had entered him in that first contest. Lately, he learned to take his medicine without fighting.

On the tiny floor, Honey moved into his arms as though she'd been there many times. Her arms slid up his chest to encircle his neck and she smiled that soft, one-sided, wistful smile up at him. "You look tired and grim, Lucas. I hope I'm not too much of a burden...."

He concentrated on moving his feet, carefully placing his hands on the small waist that flared into soft hips. He liked a woman with hips, he decided, smoothing the rounded curve. He tried not to think of her breasts nestled against his stomach.

Honey's soft arms tightened and her palm stroked his neck. "You're so stiff, Lucas." She gently massaged the taut cords at the back of his neck, toying with longish strands of hair that curled at his collar. She eased her cheek to his chest and turned her face against his throat. "I love to dance like this, don't you? It's so sweet."

"Sweet," he repeated grimly as her lips brushed his throat. His body wasn't remembering his age, the fact that he had jumped into his daughters' dare with both boots on, trying to placate the tortuous female mind—

Her hair brushed his cheek. Unlike her peers' teased and sprayed stiff curls, Honey's was soft and fragrant. Just the texture a man wanted sharing his pillow....

He glanced down and found his gaze locked to the crevice running between her full and half-exposed breasts. He wondered instantly how they would feel pressed against his bare chest or filling his hand. Forcing his lids closed, Lucas sensed the sweat beading his forehead. He was too old, too worn, and should have more control over his body when it came to women.

His body wasn't taking orders when Honey was near. The thought angered him. He should be long past the age when a woman's come-on could send him over the edge.

"Hold me close. I like being cuddled," Honey murmured against his throat.

"You're plenty close enough," Lucas returned roughly.

She glanced up, wide-eyed. "Touchy, sweetcakes. What's wrong?"

He studied the skillfully applied cosmetics intently before looking over her hair. Beneath the makeup, Honey's features were even, but not beautiful. Her walk and smile and the mysterious look in her sea-green eyes, as if she were waiting just for him—probably for any man—were designed to raise steam. "You wouldn't understand, but where I come from there are still times when a man makes the first move."

Her eyebrows lifted. "Really? When are you making yours?"

He chewed on that, taking her wrists away from his chest and leading her off the dance floor. "I think we're both tired. You can stay here and dance, or you can let me take you back to your...our room...our suite." He hoped she didn't see his face warm in the dim light.

"You're blushing, Lucas," she whispered softly, then ran a fingertip down his cheek. "That's cute. Let's go to *our* suite. You'll feel better after a night's rest." With that Honey turned slowly, shot him a sizzling look over her bare shoulder and winked. He was left to follow in a wake of admiring gazes.

Lucas frowned at her swaying hips. Honey moved in a leggy, smooth stalk that molded the gold fabric to her round hips. Lucas dried his palms against his pants.

He cursed silently as they moved through the foyer and Honey took his hand. She was one touchable woman and a woman who liked touching. The muscles on his neck ached from stress—he was too old not to know the consequences of having his emotional cage rattled.

Honey liked to rattle cages, he thought darkly as she lifted her hand to ease away a curl from her cheek. The movement brought the gold cloth to her breasts, taut as it stretched from tip to tip within the folds.

A businessman in a suit stared at her, his expression showing clearly that he envied Lucas. He raised his thumbs upward in a way-to-go-guy signal and winked.

Honey leaned against Lucas and lifted her face to whisper, "They take terrible care of their plants here. They need repotting."

"Uh-huh," he returned as two men dressed in swimming trunks and towels stared openly at Honey. He nodded to them and noticed that one exhaled, letting his stomach return to its normal paunch.

In the suite, Lucas loosened his collar and opened the patio door to breathe the fresh night air. He should be sleeping now, or working on bills, choosing how much to what creditor. Instead he was thinking of Honey's wide green eyes and long legs.

He was thinking that maybe a man deserved a little soft skin and sweet perfume after years of loneliness. "Heartbeats" required a television rehash after the date, but then he'd never see her again—

Honey's perfume filled the air before her hand touched his back and stayed there. She rubbed his shoulder slowly. "It's only a weekend, Lucas. Try to enjoy yourself, okay? See you in the morning." With that she reached up to pat his cheek. "Sleep tight, babe."

Lucas wanted to sleep tight. Or rather sleep tightly with— He forced his thoughts away from Honey's closed bedroom door and the circular bed with pink satin sheets.

Determined to shuck Honey for the night, Lucas lay full length on his bed and telephoned his ranch. While he was playing at Casa Bianca, the twins could be playing, too.

Lucas listened intently to the sound that had wakened him before dawn. "You're on the prowl pretty early for a city girl, aren't you, Honey?" he asked.

"How did you know that I was here?" she returned huskily from the terrace door.

He turned slowly on the black satin sheets, taking care to cover his hips. As experienced as Honey appeared to be, he didn't want to share evidence of his desire. Standing outlined in the predawn light and a filmy peignoir, Honey's curvaceous body did little to calm an uncomfortable problem that had kept him from sleeping. He yawned and stretched, unable to see her face in the shadows. "I knew you were here when the door latch clicked and your scent filled the room."

The lacy black peignoir floated around her as she moved toward him. She wrung her hands when she stopped at his bedside. "Lucas, we need to talk."

"What about?" He wondered then what that soft body would look like curled between the black satin sheets....

"What's wrong with me? You seem angry that I chose you...."

His thoughts erupted. "I'm a plain-speaking man, Honey. You might not like what I have to say."

"Really?" The tone challenged, and because Lucas was feeling raw, he saw no reason to shelter her.

"I'm thirty-eight, not some kid out on the prowl.

You must be a good ten or so years younger than I am—''

"I'm thirty-four, sweetcakes," she returned sharply, plopping down on the bed. In a huffy movement, she gathered the peignoir around her like a queenly cape. She leaned closer and peered down at him closely. "Try again. Why are you so determined to be Mr. Meatball?"

"Mr. Meatball?" he repeated darkly. Didn't the lady know better than to enter a man's bedroom in the early morning and start tossing taunts at him? He jerked a black-satin-covered pillow to the headboard and propped himself against it. "Listen, lady, I've got a dry ranch back in Oklahoma and two seventeen-year-old daughters who are trouble with a capital *T. What I am not, is a fun date.* Sorry, but you picked the wrong man for games. It goes against my grain to be bought with twenty little gold hearts like some yahoo with no sense. I'm long past this—" He paused, debated the word, and said, "Manure."

"You're thirty-eight, a rancher, and you're determined not to have fun, is that the picture, babe?" she challenged between her teeth.

The word "babe" threw him over the edge. He looped his fingers around her slender wrist and jerked slightly, unbalancing her. Another tug and she sprawled full length beneath him. He expected her to fight and covered her body with his, gripping her wrists in his hands. "You are going to listen to sense, lady...." he began, then realized that Honey wasn't struggling.

She lay looking up at him with those green eyes filling her pale face. In the shadows, her face was bare of cosmetics, her lips more soft and luscious than when covered with gloss. "This is what you want, isn't it?" he asked when he could speak.

Honey was soft in all the right places, he realized immediately. Every bit of her was real and womanly. "Damn," he said quietly, as his body went taut.

"Gracious," she returned in an uneven whisper, staring up at him. She blinked rapidly as though trying to focus better.

Cradled in her long legs, Lucas suddenly forgot his reasons for not wanting her. The heat burning through the cloth separating them had aroused him instantly. "I'm past the fun-and-games stage right now, I reckon."

She lifted her hips slightly, and Lucas pressed into the soft juncture instinctively. He yearned for a moment of primordial heat and passion that would warm the ache he'd carried for a lifetime. The moist aroused, feminine scent of her body swirled around him as she rubbed her thigh up and down his legs. "Reckon you are, babe," she murmured.

"Damn," he said again, fervently, as she grinned and repeated the enticing movement, the cloth between them dampening. "You are really asking for it."

Lucas could not stop tracing her lips. When he did stop, his gaze slid down to her breasts shimmering in a pool of black lace. He closed his eyes.

He'd been years without a woman's soft body, and now the need pushed violently at him.

Each breath raised her softness against him. Each time he breathed, he smelled her scent beneath the perfume. "You just took a bath," he murmured quietly, watching her. A ringlet coiled at her throat and he nuzzled it, smelling the shampoo and the soft skin beneath his lips.

"I'm a morning person, babe. I was too tired last night," she returned absently as she examined his face. "You look great in the morning."

Lucas felt eighteen again and about ten feet tall. "What about that kiss now?" he asked huskily, his fingers trailing down her arm to caress her side.

Lord, how he wanted to touch those soft breasts. How he wanted to taste and roll and— He inhaled sharply, fighting the stark desire. "Kiss me, Lucas," she invited softly, her hands framing his cheeks. "And make it good. I've waited a long time for a man like you."

He tried to think then, tried to make sense of her statement, but her hands were drawing his mouth to hers....

Whatever Honey was, she was sweet to kiss, he thought as he tasted her mouth gently. He nibbled her bottom lip, moving slowly to the corners. Whatever she was, Honey made him forget everything but kissing her, feeling that soft womanly body cradle him invitingly.

She kissed like an innocent. Just the girl-woman that a man wanted to teach for him alone. Her hands smoothed his shoulders and his upper arms. After a long moment, he lifted his head to look down at her. In the dawn, he traced a pair of wide-set green eyes, drowsy with invitation. A bit of a nose preceded a generous, well-kissed mouth.

She made a purring noise that sounded like hunger, and he shifted slightly, pressing deeper into the juncture of her thighs. Satin and lace separated them now, and he could feel her heat, sense her waiting for him. "What do we do now?" she asked hesitantly.

Then her tongue licked her upper lip and Lucas tried

to think of something cute. But all he could think was how much he wanted her, wanted everything she offered, if only for the moment.

"One of two things, ma'am. You figure out which one and let me know. If you choose to stay in this bed with me, you'd better know that I'm not prepared—''

Her kiss sealed the rest of his words away forever. "I want you now, babe.''

He studied her intent expression. "That might not be smart, but I haven't had a woman in a long time. We can wait until we've got protection, but you push me and—'' Somehow it was important that he treat her honestly and gently.

"It's been a long time for me, too." She ran her cheek along his chest, nuzzling the crisp hair and kissing him. "My, you are tasty.''

He chuckled. " 'Tasty.' Don't remember ever being called that before.''

She framed his jaw, nibbling at his mouth. "You're mine, Lucas Walkington. You smiled just then and showed me your dimples. That makes you mine for the weekend. Now make it count, will you, cowboy?''

Nothing could have stopped him, she met him kiss for kiss and then he was pushing against her heat— "What the—?''

Honey breathed quickly, her fingers pressing into his shoulder as she frowned up at him, her thighs quivering along his. "Ah...Lucas...are we having a problem?''

"Problem," he gritted, shaking with the need to enter her completely. He braced his weight on his hands, raising slightly. "You missed a minor detail, didn't you, lady?''

"Detail?" she asked too innocently, then swallowed. "Whatever could that be?''

"Sex," he stated flatly, thoroughly frustrated. His body shuddered, aching to slide deep into her moist depths. The tiny barrier and tight channel had surprised him. "You haven't had a man—ever."

She blinked, wincing slightly as he pushed gently to prove the point. "Of course. I know."

"Hell," he gritted softly as he lowered himself carefully to rest his head on the pillow beside hers. "Give me a minute...*and don't move...quit wiggling*," he ordered against her throat.

"But, Lucas...I want you," she wailed softly, scooting closer.

"You shouldn't say things like that," he said tightly. "I don't want to hurt you."

"Sweetcakes, you and I both know there's no way to avoid it. It's just the first time and then we'll be fine."

He grinned ruefully, enchanted by the way she blithely dismissed her virginity and the way he felt as if some great honor had been bestowed upon him. "That's supposed to be my line, buttercup."

Her small "Oh, I didn't know" caused him to grin wider, despite the sensual urgency driving him.

She bristled slightly. "You can stop feeling superior. I would have sooner, but there wasn't anyone as appealing and it didn't seem worth the effort."

He chuckled, smoothing a long, soft expanse of trembling thigh. She wanted him badly and wasn't afraid to show it. Honey tugged on his chest hair, making him wince despite his utter happiness. "Stop making fun of me."

"I wasn't. A man likes to know he is appreciated. If you're serious, and I hope you are, lady. We'd better do this nice and slow."

Honey tugged him closer. "You're a great kisser. You probably do everything great. Lead on."

Another time, Lucas might have laughed outright. Just now he waited while Honey eased a little closer to him and said wonderingly, "My. Oh, my. Is this going to work?"

Lucas closed his eyes, straining for control. Whatever Honey was, she was sweet and fresh and wanting him. "Are you sure?"

"Sweetcakes, I've never been more certain of anything in my life."

Then he was in her, her soft cry taken by his mouth. He fought the desire taking him over the edge, waiting for her comfort. Then she was taking him further....

Chastity awoke to a gentle slap on her bare backside. Tangled with Lucas's big body on satin sheets was a perfect way to spend a Saturday morning. He was so cute, she decided drowsily as his fingers lingered to caress her hips, holding the softness in his palm.

Then in a quick movement that took her breath away, Lucas hauled her up and over him. She blinked again rapidly, trying to focus on his face. He stroked back a wispy tendril that clung to her cheek and he kissed her nose. "I don't suppose you'd like to explain what happened an hour ago. Why you decided to give me your virginity?"

Chastity kept her lids closed, wallowing in the warm, hard body beneath her and the feeling of being well loved. She squirmed slightly for comfort and grinned when Lucas responded magnificently. He was so sweet, a real Band-Aid on her deflated femininity. "I haven't seen anything appealing to date and I wanted you. What's hard to understand?"

"But the way you look, the way you flirt…a man thinks—"

"Mmm," Chastity squirmed around on the delectable surface that was suddenly tensing. "I think we should practice."

He caught her upper arms and lifted her slightly away. "Oh, no, you don't. You've just gifted me with something pretty special—"

Chastity smiled softly. "That's exactly why I picked you. You're sweet and caring, when you're not grim. I love the way you laugh like just before you slept—"

"Honey," Lucas said gently, kissing her chin. "There's no time—the camera crew will be here in ten minutes. You know this relationship can't go anywhere, don't you? I haven't a thing to offer you."

"Sure," she replied brightly, and a piece of her heart tore away. "It's just for the weekend."

Lucas sat on the edge of the pool and watched Honey walk toward him, the skimpy black maillot drawing interested male stares. The photographers had taken shots of them at their patio breakfast and in various poses lounging around the luxurious suite. At the poolside lunch, they'd requested Honey to sit on his lap and she'd obliged. The soft tangle of arms and legs and the lush contours snuggling against him set Lucas off like a shot.

He'd snapped at the photographers, and Honey had soothed the moment by kissing him. The long, sweet kiss pleased the cameramen and stopped him dead. Lucas didn't feel dead; he wanted to carry her off to a secluded nook and finish what she had started.

When the photographers asked him to oil her back, Lucas sat on the wide lounge beside Honey's stretched-out body and wondered how he was going to live until they were alone. Her sleepy, sated gaze up at him over her shoulder reminded him of her look earlier, after they'd made love. Needing her near him, Lucas nudged her aside and settled down on his back.

Honey had snuggled to his side as though she belonged there and had nibbled on his shoulder when the photographers weren't looking. Her hand found his chest, stroking it, and Lucas dozed momentarily, placing his hand over hers. He awoke to a camera click and discovered his other hand resting possessively on the back of her thigh. The photographers leered when he cursed, and assured him that they couldn't use the intimate shot for the show, but that he might want the photograph for his ''private collection.''

Lucas snorted. As if he had a ''private collection.''

Now Honey glanced at him and blushed wildly before diving neatly into the pool. She swam a half length before she surfaced at his feet. She shook her hair from her eyes and grinned. She tickled his sole beneath the water and sunk to nibble on his toe, then emerged with an impish grin. ''Miss me?''

From where he sat, Lucas had a full view of Honey's curves. He pushed back the thought that he hadn't taken time to explore and taste that lovely expanse of soft flesh. He still had the feeling of falling off the top of a windmill, with the ground far below.

At any moment there would be a rude, painful awakening.

Now Honey looked up at him with those wide, mysterious green eyes and blinked the water from her lashes. Her hands rested on his knees. ''You're being grim again, cowboy.''

"How do you feel?" he asked carefully, still unable to believe that she had chosen him.

"Like eating the whole evening buffet. Are we going dancing tonight at the club?"

"Uh-huh. Have to for the publicity shots. Ed and Jonesy are coming, too." He thought about that willing, tight little body beneath the maillot suit and groaned inwardly. "You ate enough breakfast for two people."

She wiggled her eyebrows lewdly. "Exercise, my good man. It makes me hungry."

He laughed outright. Whoever Honey was, she was good for his morale. "We're not exercising again like that until we're protected, woman."

Lucas touched her lashes, smoothing them dry with his thumb. Just after making love, he'd dozed for a moment and awoke with the certain knowledge that he'd given her a part of himself. The knowledge was elemental, something older than time, but the certainty was there—a part of him had become hers.

"Grr...you've got that closed-in, thoughtful look. I love it when you get all broody and possessive, cowboy," she teased with a grin.

He caught her wandering hand, drawing her up and out of the water. "I want you to spend time in the hot tub, Miss Sassy Mouth. That should take the ache out of—" He found himself floundering as her eyes widened and she began to giggle.

Lucas discovered that he could blush.

Later, as they were dressing for dinner, Honey called him from her bedroom. "Lucas, would you please come here?" Ed and Jonesy winked and fiddled with their camera equipment as he crossed the suite to her door.

He entered the all-pink room warily, then closed the door quickly when he saw Honey. Dressed in a lacy beige bra and panties that his daughters called "French-cut," Honey frowned at the pink sequin-studded garment in her hand. "The hem is coming out of this dress, and I really wanted to wear it. What else would look—" She turned to catch Lucas's hungry stare skimming down her body and added, "Talk about looks. You do things for a woman's ego, sweetcakes."

"They're doing publicity photos tonight, right?" he asked, knowing the answer and angry with himself for being out of control.

"Mmm. We have a minute or two. Do you know what I would like?" Honey began to walk toward him and Lucas's mouth dried, his body tensing immediately as she stopped near him.

"What?" he managed after clearing his throat.

Honey slipped her hands inside his shirt and gently tugged it open to reveal the hair on his chest. She nuzzled his skin. "We could hide."

"Can't. We both signed agreements, remember?" He allowed his hands to slide down her waist and rest on the curve of her hips. "Then, we'll have to improvise...." Honey looked at him hopefully.

He laughed outright, surprised to find himself so much at ease. "You're a scamp, Miss Honey. Reckon I could patch this bit of a dress for you."

"You? Patch? You're kidding." Within moments, Lucas was sitting on her bed, neatly mending the torn dress. He held it up for her inspection, tucked his needle in the traveling sewing kit and stood.

"Well, I'll be horn-swaggled," she said in an exaggerated Oklahoma drawl.

"Beats letting the commoners ogle your sweet hide, ma'am," he returned as she slid the dress over her head.

Before Lucas could move, Honey clicked the bedroom lock and leaped up on him, closing her long legs around his hips. The force of her body took him against the wall, and surprised, Lucas reached to support her body from harm. His palms cupped her lace-covered buttocks. Honey hugged his neck and kissed his cheek. "I knew you were special, Lucas, sweetcakes. How often can a cowboy patch clothes and carry his own little sewing kit?" she exclaimed in delight as she began kissing his mouth in hungry little pecks.

"Ma'am," he felt honor-bound to admit, "my daughters are seventeen. I've had to mend a time or two to keep them in clothes."

She snuggled closer, drawing him into a silky tangle of arms and legs and sweet perfume. "Oh, Lucas. You are wonderful. Do you know what I'd like you to do for me? Kiss my breasts, that's what. We never got around to that this morning, and you just seemed so upset and concerned, that I hated to ask. I really want you to— I'm aching to have your mouth there. Just *aching,* Lucas."

Lucas stared helplessly up at Honey as she somehow levered her breast near his mouth. "You can't wrinkle sequins. Look…" She wiggled slightly and a thin strap slid down her shoulder.

"Do you realize how old I am?" Lucas demanded when he could speak. "Sure too old for games—" But his hand tightened beneath her hips, smoothing the lush contour.

She nodded solemnly, her eyes dark green and mysterious. "Is what happened this morning all there is, Lucas?" she asked hesitantly, sadly.

"Honey," he began firmly, trying to dredge up all the reasons why they shouldn't play a weekend game that was destined for a dusty scrapbook.

Her legs tightened around his hips and Lucas shuddered, desperate for the taste of her skin. "Oh, Lucas," she whispered unevenly as he nuzzled aside the lace to draw her breast gently into his mouth.

"Oh, Lucas," she repeated as he sensed her soft explosion, one that left her limply holding him. She snuggled against him, her heat enfolding them both in a tiny, private moment. He let her legs drift slowly to the floor, then picked her up and carried her to the bed.

Holding her on his lap, Lucas stroked and kissed until Honey stopped the gentle trembling. "There's that, and more," he whispered gently into her ear and wondered dazedly how he was going to live until they were alone again.

Then Ed knocked on the door. "Hey, our dinner reservations are for seven. Hurry up."

Throughout the long evening, Honey's pink-sequin-covered body kept him on a constant alert. She snuggled to him on the dance floor, her expression that of absolute sensuality as she moved closer to him.

"Your chest is so hard, Lucas. I keep remembering—" She stopped, swallowed and pushed her hot face into the shelter of his neck and shoulders. She moved against him and whispered in his ear, "I want you against me, holding me, with nothing between."

Then she sighed wistfully and the sound went through Lucas like the sweet spring wind sweeping the prairie clean.

Lucas closed his eyes and absorbed everything about Honey right into his bones, because he knew dreams didn't last.

Chicago dream girls and dirt-poor Oklahoma cowboys didn't mix.

Chapter 3

Lucas slammed the posthole digger into the soft spring earth, pushed the handles together and lifted out a good chunk of Oklahoma sod. He hadn't slept for two weeks, his bed without Honey as welcoming as a cold rock shelf. Her sweet gasps of surprise had echoed from the last sound of the meadowlark until the morning dove began to coo.

He ran his forearm across his forehead, drying the sweat with his sleeve. He'd worked hard to forget Honey, to get her out of his blood, but she stuck in there; when he could manage to sleep, he awoke to empty arms and the hard reminder that once he'd been awakened by Honey's soft, warm body flowing on his.

She'd winded him, and again he was left feeling as though he'd given her a primordial essence, a tiny piece of himself.

New Angus calves gamboled around the cows, lending a timelessness to the land. Scanning the Oklahoma hills, Lucas concentrated on the rhythm of his neighbor's oil rigs, which stood on the horizon like huge chickens bobbing for grain. His grandparents were born in the Cherokee territory, before Oklahoma became a state. His great, great grandmother had survived the Trail of Tears. The solitude of the land was bred into him.

Honey was a creature of luxuries; her wardrobe alone cost more than his old barn. High heels and country dirt weren't a good blend. Toss in the old house, needing repair, and the antics of two daughters with just one year of high school left, and the situation would make a glamour girl turn tail and run for the nearest city.

He inhaled slowly. Honey was a special female, half girl and all woman. She deserved a man who could give her a good, comfortable life.

He'd tangled with love and dreams and come away with a bad taste in his mouth. Alesha had taken something from him, other than the first three years of his daughters' lives. She'd taken his pride, made him wary, bitter about women's needs, and made him ache every time he saw a boy marry his best girl....

Summer and Raven rode toward him on spirited mares. His daughters knew how to ride, as graceful as Alesha. They slid from their horses before reaching a full stop. Dressed in sweatshirts and jeans, they bore the color and the lanky, tall Walkington build. "Hi, Daddy," they said in unison.

Raven handed him a cold beer from her saddlebag and grinned as he drank thirstily. Summer clasped her hands behind her and matched her twin's grin. Lucas glanced from one girl to the other, deeply pleased by the way they were stamped with Walkington height, black hair and blue eyes. Experienced with their antics, he asked, "What's up?"

"Nothing," Summer said too innocently, her blue eyes widening.

Raven, always more sensible, glanced at her sister and plucked a stalk of dried range grass. "Daddy, we're fixing your favorite meat loaf for supper and scalloped potatoes and chocolate cake with fudge frosting. Summer has folded the laundry and we've cleaned all day—"

"Uh-huh," Lucas said warily. "I asked what's up?"

"Oh, Daddy, we want to go to Chicago with you to meet Honey," Summer burst out.

Lucas tossed the empty beer can to her and tugged up his leather gloves. "No."

Raven thrust her hands into her jeans, locking her long legs at the knee, her jaw set to challenge him. "Why not, Dad?"

There was that ruthless tone, the Walkington temper stored carefully away. Lucas plunged the posthole digger into the ground, reluctantly admiring the way the girls managed to stand up for what they believed. They'd inherited that much from him.

"She's special, Dad," Summer stated. "Honey's got something that makes you laugh. We saw it in the program and in those pictures the studio sent. You looked good together, Dad."

Raven grinned and teased, "Sweetcakes...Babe..."

"Shh. Show some respect," Summer ordered sharply and smothered her grin. "Dad may be just another 'Heartbeats' sweetcakes and babe, but he is our father." The twins began giggling, and launched themselves against him.

"Please, Daddy. Please call Honey. You saw her face on the videotape. She really liked you."

Disentangling himself from hugs and pleading blue eyes, Lucas stepped away. "None of that. It wouldn't work."

Lucas squinted against the bright afternoon sun and thought about the photographs hidden from his daughters. The one with him looking like one pleased hombre lying next to Honey's curvaceous backside, his dark hand on her soft pale thigh, was very private.

"Daddy, what Summer means is maybe you've been out of practice so long that, well...maybe we could help—"

"Lay off, girls. I'm not seeing her again after the last show. There's no point in it."

He wanted to remember Honey's last kiss, not her expression of disgust when she saw his ranch. Working at odd jobs around the country, he could manage to scavenge enough money to pay taxes and support his girls. Honey would want more—like water-demanding bubble baths, a lawn that was watered and green in the summer, and a man who could afford to take her out to dinner. Her long, pretty nails wouldn't last long without a dishwasher, and her sequins weren't meant to flap on a dry Oklahoma wind. Patched muslin sheets weren't pink satin, and his plain oak bed wasn't round.

"We'll be going away to college after this last year of high school, Dad. You'll be left alone. Mrs. Evans says hermits get sour, and now that we know you can get real...I mean have fun...I mean, act like a stu—" Summer stopped abruptly when he scowled at her.

Lucas threw the posthole digger to the ground forcefully and tipped his hat back. He glared at the girls who glared back, unfrightened. After a long moment, he said carefully, "Get this and get it good—Honey and I are not suited for each other."

"That's manure," Raven said with a tight smile meeting his hard stare. "You said the same thing about Wayne, our poodle, when those folks left him to bake in that deserted car. You broke the window, brought him home and made him ours. You threatened them with all sorts of things when they came to claim Wayne."

"Kaspar Percival Reynard de Montchamp? He's some ranch-yard dog, isn't he? Worthless piece of coyote. Cross between a curly coat lamb and a house cat."

"Daddy, he's *your* dog. He loves you better than us. Try again, Daddy," Summer said, bracing her long legs firmly into the Oklahoma sod as her ancestors had done.

"Okay, you're old enough to know why," Lucas said tightly. Since his daughters entered their teenage years, he had tried to cope with a realm of unsteady female emotions. He'd learned a couple of things as a single father: there were feminine cycles in which the girls either cried or raged, and his best safety was quiet. The other thing he'd learned was to spread his cards on the table and await the consequences. He'd discovered his daughters had a good sense of balance despite their years. "Honey isn't the kind of woman who could live on a ranch like this. I tried it once and it didn't work."

"Mother definitely is not country," Raven said thoughtfully, remembering her visits to Alesha's Tulsa home.

"Neither is Honey," Lucas stated firmly. He bent to pick up the posthole digger. "So lay off. Do whatever women do to get over the sulks. Raven, lay out your lacy blouse. I'll patch it tonight.''

This time Raven wasn't to be bought off by mending. ''Daddy, you're not using us as an excuse to hide from love. Something happened when you were with Honey and you've been molding away like a bale of hay in the rain.''

Her twin looked straight into Lucas's dark face. ''She's not Mother. Give it a chance or Raven and I will always feel to blame.''

He knew better than to mix in matters better left alone, but that night Lucas dialed the home number that Hope had given him for emergencies. His fingers shook slightly, fear running wildly through him. He didn't have a lick of sense. Honey wanted him and against his better judgment, he'd initiated her into womanhood. A call to her could break up a romantic dinner....

Lucas's knuckles turned white as he gripped the telephone. The vision of Honey in another man's arms brought anger surging through him, hot and wild.

His stomach knotted painfully. Honey's current man probably could afford romantic weekends in posh resorts, his hands soft on Honey's silky skin—his heart kicked into double-time, pounding like a runaway horse.

Wayne rolled over, presenting his belly for Lucas's nightly toe-rubbing. Excitement quivered over the telephone lines as Hope directed his call to Honey's apartment.

The sweat on his forehead grew cold in his dark bedroom, the muscles in his jaw aching from tension. Taking a fierce, deep breath for courage, he punched out the buttons with one hand and crushed the lace blouse he'd been mending with the other. "Hello, dear heart," an older woman answered in a high, quivery voice.

Without pausing to allow Lucas to introduce himself, she began an involved explanation of why she had burned the soup. In the background, jazz played softly, liquid sloshed, and ice cubes clinked. Gracie, as she called herself, was "tibbling a bit after a bad day," and she was so happy he had called to chat. Her daughter, Chastity, was sleeping, and she, the mother, would take a message.

"Sachmo" revved up his horn as Grace described the horrendous red shade her beautician had chosen for her nails. Lucas sympathized on cue, sensing that when tipsy Grace could indulge tidbits about Chastity. Grace rambled through her family soup recipe, sipped her iced drink, then sighed. "I do hate this shade of red. Chastity seems so tired lately. Of course, I know that a pregnant woman usually just drops into bed almost immediately. Heavens, I wouldn't want to tell my own daughter that she's pregnant before she discovers it herself. That just wouldn't be right. But you know, I spent the first three months of my pregnancy with Chastity draped over every couch and chair I could find, if not a bed. She's got that pregnant look, but I should try a pink shade next time."

Gripping the telephone tightly, Lucas forced himself to breathe quietly while his heart thudded loudly. A shot of sheer pleasure raced through him as he remembered her body opening to his. "She's lucky to have you taking care of her," he murmured.

Grace was like a hungry trout leaping toward a fresh bug as she answered with the slightest "Yes, you're right." Lucas listened intently, forcing himself to breathe normally. "She sleeps—Lord, how that little girl sleeps. Poor thing, poor little innocent girl who went to Las Vegas with some hot-pants young two-by-four—they call them studs, you know. He just took advantage of my poor little plain girl, that's all. Left her in a terrible mess." Grace paused to munch on something crisp and swallowed.

Lucas lay back in his worn armchair, his eyes closed. "Honey" had been so eager, so new— The baby was his. *Baby*. His eyes opened as Grace rambled blithely on. "They ought to do something with those…boys before they allow them to escort ladies to these fancy resorts, you know. Something to drain off all that excessive sexual energy. There she was, alone without me, having to fend off that fiend.…"

Hours later, Lucas inhaled the cold crisp midnight air. At thirty-eight, he was presented with a second round of fatherhood. He turned over the thought of a new baby, of the soft, desirable body sheltering it, and found himself grinning and glowing.

A truck's headlights soared through the night on the neighboring dirt road and Lucas scowled at the intrusion. Honey didn't have to have the baby…or if she did, she didn't have to keep it. The Oklahoma chill settled in his bones and ached. "Damn," he muttered quietly, striding to his corral to saddle his big bay gelding. He eased Duke out into the night, preparing to think through fate's newest present to him.

At a knoll overlooking his house, Lucas braced his forearms over the saddle horn. He'd taken pride in raising his daughters, giving them what he had and loving them. One good disaster could cost everything he'd worked to keep in his family.

He had his daughters and a fingertip hold on his life. Born and bred to Oklahoma dirt, he'd found sunshine for a few hours in Honey's arms.

Fear wasn't new to Lucas. He recognized the giant fist squeezing his entrails and panic pouring into his veins. There wasn't a chance in hell that Honey could be carrying another man's baby. *Damned if he ever wanted her near another man.*

If he had any horse sense at all, he'd leave her alone. The Walkingtons never ran from trouble.

Honey wasn't trouble; she was soft and sweet—

Lucas forced himself to swallow. At twenty-one, he'd reached out and grabbed a dream. The shredded remnants left him living a nightmare, carrying enough guilt inside his gut to last an eternity. Without his girls, he wondered if he would have survived.

To go after what he so fiercely wanted this time was certain disaster.

The picture of Honey with a baby in her arms caught his breath. She was carrying his baby and no other yahoo was taking the right to see her through this away from him.

No other yahoo was sidling up to Honey and claiming her.

With grim determination, Lucas urged the horse to walk slowly back to the corral. Whatever happened, he was claiming the baby Honey carried as his responsibility. "Hot-pants two-by-four," he muttered darkly as he unsaddled Duke and prepared for a long sleepless night.

The next morning, Summer's eyes widened over the breakfast table. "Dad? You're kidding."

He shrugged, cupping his coffee for warmth. When

a man prepared to reach out and snag something good, he'd better lay a good foundation. He'd explained to his daughters as gently as possible, relying on their ranch training to complete the picture. "It's only a possibility. When I see her at 'Heartbeats,' I'll know."

"You're bringing her here," Raven said quietly, watching him.

"Yes," he said firmly, ignoring the twins' cheers. "If I can. If she's carrying my baby, she'll need rescuing from smog and that family of hers. Listening to her mother describe their family, I get the picture that Honey shoulders a heavy responsibility.... Sounds like their lazy backsides need kicking."

"Go get her, Daddy. Do it," Summer said firmly as she washed her breakfast dishes and scooped her schoolbooks off the kitchen table.

"Things are tight enough," he pushed, watching the twins closely. "There will be expenses—"

"Suits me," Raven said, joining her sister at the door. Then, in two steps, she flung herself at him, hugging him tightly. "Go for it."

"I'm talking marriage, tidbits," he said slowly, following their intent expressions. "I'm old fashioned and it wouldn't do to have her here without marriage and my baby is bearing my name."

The girls nodded solemnly.

Lucas fought the tears burning his lids, holding Raven tightly. "She might not come. She might come, have the baby and take off. There are no guarantees for anything."

He struggled with the words, his fear that Honey wouldn't want to see him, nor return to his ranch. "It's hard out here. She's bred to city life. By this time, she may have figured out that a romantic setting can do a lifetime of damage.''

''You can handle it, Daddy. We'll help.''

When Lucas stood alone in the room, he inhaled sharply and watched the girls' old pickup truck soar down the dirt road. They were thrilled with the romantic idea of his capturing a city love.

He was flat-out scared. A thin pocketbook and hard times weren't much to offer a woman like Honey.

The proverbial limb to which he clung quivered threateningly. A second go 'round with a woman wasn't what he wanted.

Three weeks and two days after her beautiful weekend with Lucas, Chastity sipped her cup of jasmine tea and listened to Hope rave about Honey and the Bandit's ratings. On each ''Heartbeats'' show a fresh screen picture of Lucas and herself was presented, á la Ed and Jonesy, reminding her of that beautiful weekend.

The camera men had been ruthless in their pursuit, and when Chastity and Lucas were finally alone in their suite, she'd blown the whole evening by falling asleep on her bed. She had awakened to the delightful warmth of Lucas's bare body spooned against her back, his arm resting possessively across her waist. She loved nestling into the aroused male heat, loved his arm tightening around her.

She'd turned slowly to face a masculine confection of new beard and darkly tanned torso wrapped in pink satin sheets. He snored gently with a look of pure pleasure swathing his dark features. She couldn't resist sliding over him, joining sweetly with him as he slept and awakening him with nibbling kisses.

Clearly Lucas was having a delightful dream. He grinned sleepily and she caught his earlobe in her teeth. Then there was no time for anything but pleasure and with a last soft cry, Lucas gave himself to her.

He had breathed hard, holding her tightly over him until his heartbeat slowed into a gallop. Gently, reluctantly, he eased Honey down to his side, cuddling her against him. "So much for the protection I got yesterday," he had grumbled, forcing one lid open to the blinding morning light. "Sweetcakes, stop complaining..." she'd managed before he began kissing her hungrily.

Then a sharp rap on the bedroom door, followed by Jonesy's barroom bellow, cut through the sweet, lingering kiss. Lucas had cursed soundly and the day began. It ended at O'Hare Airport in Chicago with Lucas's taut expression.

Chastity straightened her round wire-rimmed glasses and discovered that the daydream of Lucas had fogged them. The jasmine tea leaves formed a pattern on the bottom of her cup and Hope was saying, "...ratings are great. The entire world is waiting for Honey and Bandit to relive their weekend...."

"Why couldn't we have just taped the thing the next day? Why did Lyle and the sponsors insist waiting this month?" Chastity asked bleakly. "Everyone else returned to the show immediately following their weekend...."

Hope glanced up from the paper's ratings. "Suspense, Chas. The camera caught the sparks between you, and the viewers loved it. If we polished you and Bandit off too fast, our ratings would flatten to pancake level. The producers say you guys are so hot together that they don't want Walkington to do the customary follow-up show with another woman.''

Another woman. Lucas Walkington's well fixed body and dimples drew women like bees to flowers. The idea that Lucas was endowing his beautiful dimples and lovely, desperate lovemaking to another woman squeezed her heart painfully. If he were so impressed with her as he'd indicated after the virginity episode, he would have called. A note saying ''Thanks for letting me experience your virginity'' would have been nice. He'd probably forgotten the whole thing, riding his precious range with a cowgirl goddess. She discovered that she had shredded her napkin into bits.

''I don't like cliff-hangers. This thing has gone on far too long,'' Chastity mumbled. The twinge of uncustomary jealousy surprised her. If Lucas was passing out samples— Her nails moved on the table, aching to gently claw through that lovely curling chest hair to the dark skin beneath.

''Hey, lighten up. The sponsors sweetened the pot for you and Bandit, didn't they? Another thousand just to wait the month before the final show didn't hurt and you can pay off the Old Coot's nursing-home bill. I have to tell you, Chas. You looked supreme when you got off the plane. The studio audience went wild when they saw you kiss goodbye…although Lucas's cowboy hat hid the real thing.''

''He wouldn't be interested in plain old Chastity Beauchamp,'' Chastity muttered and yawned. ''He thinks I'm a glamour girl. If Lucas got one look at the real me, he wouldn't turn up for the show tomorrow.''

Hope dismissed Chastity's lament and went on with her last instructions, carefully itemizing Honey's beauty tips, then said, ''Chas, you've been filing too hard. You look tired. Remember to use that shadow concealer beneath your eyes tomorrow. For gosh sakes, don't carry that huge canvas tote of yours.''

"He hasn't called. He hasn't written. Gee, he sounds really eager to renew our acquaintance," Chastity said sarcastically. She remembered his heart pounding rapidly after their lovemaking—she hoped it survived the massive overtime when he returned to his ranch and the cowgirl goddesses.

She pictured him riding the range, supremely happy away from her, and hated him down to his boots.

The sharp, bitter emotion stunned her. She'd guarded herself since childhood against reaching out for dreams, only to be loved as desperately as Lucas had taken her.

She wanted to dump linguine over his head and down his well-stuffed jeans. She was very angry for the way he had treated Honey.

A sweet girl like Honey needed protection from dimpled cowboys with slow Oklahoma drawls.

"The guy could have been busy. Maybe his horse or his dog died or something. Who knows what can happen in greater, outer Oklahoma?"

"Women can happen," Chastity answered with all the dark jealousy that had been swirling in her. Lucas's kisses weren't untutored, nor was his lovemaking. She resented every woman who had tasted him. "You forgot that Bandit might have a harem on the range."

"Not a chance. I saw the way he looked at you. Like you were the only woman in the world. You sure are a good actress, Chas, when you try. You awed the guy down to his boots, take it from me."

Chastity thought better of discussing how much sleep she'd been losing thinking of Lucas's lovemaking and his grim determination to leave her as quickly as he could. Clearly he wanted to place the past behind him and return home.

At least he'd never see her as plain Chastity Beauchamp. A woman who made water faucets drip. Her singular talent, according to the Old Coot, was a gift. The sexiest thing about her was Honey's pink sequin dress hanging next to her loose mix-and-match skirts and blouses.

One bitter fact remained: Lucas had not contacted Honey and Chastity hated him down to his boots.

The next day, the studio limousine took Honey, properly dressed in a cobalt-blue sheath with long sleeves and dipping bodice, to the television studio. Chastity's palms were cold and damp as she gripped Honey's small purse and pushed open the door to the studio viewing room.

Anger rode her like a nightmare, the sleepless nights wishing for Lucas in her bed swirling around her. Lucas had treated Honey horribly, giving her a taste of delight, then hoarding himself back in Oklahoma. *He deserved dimple-damage.*

Lucas stood abruptly when he saw her, his eyes darkening into a shade that matched her dress. Clad in jeans, a dress shirt and a Western leather jacket, he walked slowly toward her. He scanned her face intently while she searched her Honey vocabulary and tried to remember to lift the lazy left side of her mouth when she smiled. Her smile attempt flopped belly-up on the studio floor. "What's wrong with you?" he asked urgently, roughly, just as Lyle entered the room with a big grin.

Lucas's blue eyes darkened with anger, the lines on

his face deepening throughout Lyle's happy dialogue about ratings and waiting audiences at home and in the studio. Lucas ignored Lyle's pleasantries, caught Chastity's arm and lifted her chin with the tip of his finger. "You look terrible. What's wrong?"

She frowned up at him. *He* was the problem, all six foot three of him. "I'm not happy," she stated tightly, trying to ease her arm away from his grip.

"So? I'm not either."

"You look tired," she accused, blaming him for her sleepless nights. She'd suffered Hope's beauty administrations for hours, and the footloose cowboy had the nerve to tell her she looked terrible. He could take his long, lean sexy look and—

"Hey, kids…kids…ease up," Lyle cautioned urgently, his expression of glee changed to one of distress. "We've got an audience out there at home and in the studio. They're all anxious to hear about you lovebirds—"

"Shut the hell up, Lyle," Lucas snapped as the studio intercom announced two minutes until the show began.

"Hey—" Lyle began in earnest.

"Let me handle this, Lyle," Chastity ordered. "You have no idea how ill-tempered this cowboy can be." For good measure, she thumped Lucas on the chest with her finger. No one had ever caused anger to surge through her like that dimpled, ornery cowboy. She resented that.

She frowned up at him. It was his fault that she'd become so physical, anyway. Sweet little plain Chastity would have never thought about thumping a man. Or dragging him into the studio's secluded closet and vamping him until he quivered, whispering for rescue—

"Hey, folks, show time," Hope began, then stopped as she sensed the taut scene. "Oh no, oh no...."

"The studio-lounge sink faucet has just begun leaking again," another assistant said to Lyle. "Water running everywhere. Same thing happened the last time these two were here."

"Get a plumber," Lyle ordered, pale beneath his tan and makeup, while Honey and Bandit stared ominously at each other.

"You've lost weight," Lucas said in a tone resembling a growl. "Keeping too many late nights?"

Chastity sensed his jealousy, and it fueled a temper that rarely surfaced. Well, maybe when she discovered that Grace was hooked on charging goodies from the toll-free telephone numbers. Lucas had made her feel as saucy and exotic and appealing as any woman would want to be; then he zoomed off to Oklahoma and forgot her for an entire month. Logically, the deflation should have squelched his appeal, but it hadn't. "What's it to you, cowboy?" she snapped as Lyle began urging them toward the soundstage.

"Take it easy, kids," the show's host urged. "Just a few minutes on the air and you're off the hook. You won't see each other again and your nerves will settle down like *that*." He snapped his fingers, looked at Honey and Lucas, and his hopeful grin died an early death. Lyle tried again, "Remember, our audience has waited an entire month to see what's happened between you. Calm down, take a few deep breaths and everything will turn out fine."

"Like hell," Lucas muttered darkly as they walked onto the stage and his fingers locked around her waist.

No man had ever touched Chastity as though he'd never let her go, but Lucas had left her to deal with empty dreams. The thought plopped down in the pit of her stomach like lead.

"Sweetcakes, pipe down," Chastity managed in Honey's sexy tones. She wanted to strangle him, to drag him off into a corner and give him a good piece of her mind for not calling her once—not once. This ill-tempered cowboy was the reason she'd been making mistakes in filing and bookkeeping. He was the reason her appetite had slipped into the "compulsive eater" zone, though she was losing weight. He definitely was the reason she wasn't sleeping, which was possibly the reason for her sudden light-headed feeling—

Hope made a strangled noise, snatched Chastity's purse away and stepped behind a camera. Lyle patted her shoulder and whispered, "Nerves. Emotions. I've seen this happen before. The show will be great, trust me." Lyle had previously appeared on a children's show and acted professionally in disasters, swinging smoothly into his host routine.

A huge screen onstage televised the dream weekend, filled with Bandit and Honey, eating, dancing and generally enjoying each other's company. The audience cheered as gigantic, full-color Bandit swept Honey into his arms and kissed her hungrily.

Chastity watched the huge screen images of Lucas and herself deepening the kiss and closed her eyes. Her skin was clammy, her bones seemed to turn to noodles and from far away she heard Lucas's sharp exclamation, "What the—"

She had the impression of being carried in strong arms, being stretched out on a couch and having a cold washcloth placed over her forehead. Lucas's dark blue eyes searched hers, his warm hands cradling her cold ones, "Honey?"

Though his face was fuzzy, out of focus, she recognized his concern.

His voice was sweet and tender and everything she'd remembered. Because she'd frightened herself and because she knew Lucas would know what to do, she whispered, "I want to go home."

"Sure, Honey—"

"Maybe we should get the studio nurse," Lyle offered worriedly.

"The warm-up is almost done. They need to be backstage." Hope said.

"Hush up," Lucas bit out. "She's not up to games."

Chastity didn't want anyone but Lucas. She held his big hand tightly. His fingers tightened, his callused palm warm and secure around her cold hand. "Lucas, take me home."

In the next minute, she was lifted, carried, and eased into the studio limousine. Lucas cradled her against him despite her protests.

"Driver, pull over," he ordered sharply as they passed a drug store. Within moments Lucas had entered the store and returned carrying a small sack.

He snapped at the grinning chauffeur and slid next to Chastity. He tested the heat of her forehead with the back of his hand, his expression strained as the limousine began gently swaying. "Come here," he said roughly, lifting her to his lap and tucking her head against his shoulder.

"Lucas, I am fine...." she began as the auto pulled to the curb in front of her brownstone apartment building.

"Uh-huh. Sure," he agreed tightly, easing out of the

deep seat, then turning to lift her out and into his arms. "You're just dandy. Peachy keen. That's why you fainted on the show."

Within minutes, Lucas placed Chastity on her ruffled quilt with an order not to move. In short time, he prepared and served a cup of steaming hot tea and crackers. He leaned against the wall to watch her.

"You're making me nervous," she murmured, noting how out of place he seemed in the feminine room. She didn't want him intruding into her privacy, didn't want him near until she could tell him what she thought about him. He'd given Honey a wonderful moment to remember, then rode off into the sunset without the slightest—

"Okay, I make you nervous," he agreed amiably, not moving while he watched her.

She blushed under the intense blue stare. "You can leave now, Lucas. You've done your good deed for the day."

His well-padded shoulder remained locked to the wall. She inhaled, fighting the distress swirling around her like icy sleet. She eased her legs toward the edge of the bed, anxious to be less vulnerable in front of his grim expression. "Lucas..."

"Get them right back up where they were," he ordered in a no-nonsense tone. "Now."

The telephone rang and Lucas snatched it from its cradle. "Yes?" The raw masculine tone held all the welcome of rawhide leather. He shot a dark look at Chastity and handed the telephone to her. "Your mother. She's ordered more jewelry and an exotic bird from a television auction...something about a credit card. The bird can recite love poems."

Lucas sat on the edge of the bed, watching with interest while Chastity tried without success to end the call. "Call you back later, Mother.... Yes, I paid last month's bill.... No, I didn't see— I'll call you back...."

He picked up a magazine she'd left near the bed, flipped to the label on the cover and studied the address closely. She frowned while her mother chattered and Lucas picked up two envelopes with her name and the same address. He studied the gold-framed pictures of Hope and other family members, then picked up the picture of Chastity and the Old Coot.

Lucas's clear blue eyes swung from her tight braids in the recent picture to Honey's curled hair. Then, standing in a lithe movement, he wandered around her bedroom until he stood facing the closet.

His long legs locked at the knee, presenting a taut backside and the impression that nothing could move him from the spot.

Chastity held her breath, aware of her mother's distress and her own as Lucas extracted the pink sequin dress. He ran one dark hand over it slowly, then scanned the other clothes with interest. He drew out cotton skirts and washable dresses, holding them high and checking the sedate hemlines. There was no question of the direction of his thoughts. Honey and Chastity were the same, yet different women.

He jerked open a bureau drawer, rummaged through the lingerie and extracted her prim **panties** and firm bra. He tossed her flannel granny gown on the chest, his expression thunderous. With care he opened the pair of extra glasses lying near her bed, studied the practical wire rims and looked at her, mentally placing the glasses on her nose.

"I have to go now, Mother," Chastity said firmly

and replaced the receiver to the cradle as Lucas came to stand over her bed.

He placed the glasses on her nose, adjusted them to her ears and studied the effect.

The faucets in her bathroom dripped steadily away, and the clock her mother had ordered during a television auction rampage ticked loudly.

"You…" Lucas said ominously "…are Chastity Beauchamp and you could be pregnant with my baby."

Chapter 4

Chastity tried for Honey's bravado. She wished briefly for all those golden hearts she'd tossed away in Lucas's tube. He stood there in his dimples, *challenging her in her own bedroom.*

"Not a chance, sweetcakes. I'd know—" Then everything came tumbling back, the possibility dawning on her that Lucas had hit the proverbial nail on the head. She jerked the afghan lying at the foot of her bed up to her throat for protection against Lucas. He gripped it, pulling it steadily away and studying her intently from head to toe. She didn't like his predatory smile.

"You could be, Honey. Everything fits. That's why I bought one of those pregnancy kits, to see if you are." The telephone rang again, and Lucas jerked it from the cradle. "Yes?"

His jaw tensed as he listened, his blue eyes darkening with anger. "Listen, bub, you might be Chastity's brother, but where I come from you don't tell a woman to come pick you up from a bar when you've had too many afternoon drinks. Call a taxi.''

Slamming the telephone into the cradle, Lucas smiled coldly at Chastity, showing his teeth like a wolf who had just staked out his prey. He identified the caller curtly. ''Your brother. Hope is your sister and your mother is a credit-card addict. They depend on you. I'll bet you're their Little Miss Fix-it,'' he said between his teeth. ''It all fits now. When Ginger canceled, Hope had to come up with somebody fast, and you became Honey.''

''You can't take over my life like this, cowboy.'' Rigid with fury, Chastity raised slightly, only to be pinned by one big hand on her chest. The sensual tremors began immediately and Lucas's hand slid to cover her breast, his eyes darkening. She resented her body responding so blatantly to his touch, resented his intrusion into the privacy of plain, practical Chastity Beauchamp's apartment. Her refuge had been invaded by a tall, ill-tempered, maniacal cowboy without the slightest concession to her wishes. ''Go away, Lucas.''

She wanted to deal with his suggestion privately as she had always dealt with the events in her life.

''Like hell, lady.'' His words slapped the air in the frilly, delicate apartment, cutting at her. Narrowing his lids, Lucas stared at her grimly, looking as though his boots were cemented to her shaggy cream, washable rug. Her sheer floral curtains seemed to quiver.

She straightened her glasses with the tip of her finger. ''This is very rude behavior, Lucas.''

''Yep. Reckon so. You're needing someone to take care of you. Reckon that's me, so rest a bit and then we'll talk.''

Glaring at him, Chastity breathed quietly.

"Simmer down," he said more gently, running his hand across her cheek. There was something so comforting, so gentle in his trembling touch, that her anger suddenly melted, leaving her drained and tired. She resented the lack of energy to protect herself from Lucas's devastating touch.

"Things are complicated, Lucas."

"Sure are." His fingers played with her hair, brushing it gently.

Chastity closed her eyes, wishing she'd never allowed Hope to enter her as a Heartbeat Goddess... wishing she'd stayed plain old Chastity in filing and bookkeeping. She sighed wearily and wished....

The faucet continued dripping and somehow the noise was comforting. She'd lived with the sound from birth, reassured that however her life had turned over, faucets still dripped when she was near.

"Go to sleep, Honey," Lucas drawled in a deep, soft voice as he removed the glasses. "We'll talk about it when you feel better. Just rest now." Then the soft afghan was replaced, tenderly tucked around her toes, and Lucas stretched out by her side, drawing her gently against him. "That's it, buttercup. Reckon we could both use some sleep."

The bathtub faucet began to drip rapidly when Lucas's big hand slid to test the weight and shape of her breasts. Chastity was too tired to think about the warm, callused palm sliding beneath her clothing to caress her softness. His thumb gently circled the tender tip and she sighed, deeply comforted by his touch. She tried to summon the strength to push him away and failed.

"Yes," he whispered sleepily, reverence in his deep drawl. "There's a difference...."

* * *

Chastity awoke to the scent of coffee and the clatter of dishes in her kitchen. The clock on her bedside table blinked at her. "Seven o'clock… Work starts at eight!"

She whipped off the blankets and stood up to feel the cold air sheathing her body. She glanced at her singular garment, Honey's lacy, French-cut briefs, and suddenly felt woozy.

Lucas entered the room carrying a tray, scowled at her and ordered, "Get the hell back in that bed, lady."

She stared blankly at him. The sweetheart she'd bought with twenty golden hearts had changed into a raw, primitive male with raised hackles. Wearing his jeans unsnapped at the waist and nothing else, Lucas's tanned body caught the morning sun in stripes as it passed through her miniblinds. His chest hair gleamed over a tanned chest.

Chastity blinked, her woozy feeling gone. She tossed away the urge to leap on him, curling her legs around those narrow hips. She'd never had a man in her bedroom and remembered with raging fury the way Lucas had refused to leave. "Get out."

He slammed a low curse into the frothy mauve bedroom and Chastity suffered for the African violets on her window ledge. Poor things, they were used to soft encouragement and loving tones.

"Be nice," she ordered curtly, swaying slightly as the cotton rug began to rise toward her. Perhaps she needed her glasses… All those golden hearts seemed to shimmer in the "Heartbeats" tube, reminding her of the folly of falling for a deep, sexy, wistful, lonesome cowboy voice. They seemed to glow when she remembered the perfect, desperate lovemaking of her dreams that ended with Lucas's body pouring into hers.

"Get back into that bed, sweetheart," Lucas said in a too-sweet tone, as he showed his teeth in a tight smile and placed the tray on her bureau. "Please?"

Determined to hold her own, Chastity crossed her arms over her chest and hunted for her shredded dignity. "That's better, sweetcakes...I...oh, Lucas, I'm going to be ill—"

The violets were destined for another blossom-quaking round of hushed curses as Lucas swept her into his arms and carried her into the bathroom. Minutes later, he carried her back to bed, despite her protests, covered her with the warm blankets, and snapped, "Do all the faucets in this apartment drip?"

"It's a curse. My inheritance," Chastity murmured from beneath the cold washcloth covering her face. She clung to Lucas's hard warm hand, soothed when he lifted hers to his lips and brushed kisses across the knuckles. Being cuddled and cherished in the morning was something she could grow to love, Chastity thought wearily as her stomach began to growl.

"Buttercup..." he began huskily, his mouth against her skin.

Without her glasses, the fuzzy light in his eyes resembled desire. "Lucas, I'll be late for work—"

"Honey," Lucas said firmly. "I called Charlie's. Hope gave me the number. They know you're coming in late. Someone called Sherry giggled when I told her you were sick."

Chastity jerked the cold cloth away. "Lucas, Sherry lives for gossip. She'll be spreading all sorts of stories about me. Your voice alone is enough to set her off—"

He scowled down at her and she explained quickly. "You have a slight accent—a cowboy twang—add that to deep and sexy and Sherry's mouth is off and running.''

He chewed on that while he sat on the bed, watching her drink orange juice and nibble on toast. Reaching to lift a jumble of curls away from her cheek, Lucas watched Chastity's tongue forage for a crumb saturated in honey. His eyes darkened, his chest rose sharply as he inhaled. Chastity focused on that lovely contour and the way the wedge of crisp black hair narrowed down the flat, washboard muscles of his stomach. She forced her eyes to lift to his grim expression, tracing the heavy morning beard covering his jaw. ''Lucas, why are you here?''

''I needed the sleep.'' He bit out the words. ''I've missed a bit.''

''That doesn't make sense, but I'm fine now. You're free to go,'' she said gently, formally. ''There are no obligations.... You've been kind.... Thank you, Lucas.''

The blue eyes blazed and his hand tightened around hers. ''Just like that...thanks and get out, cowboy.'' Then he smiled that cold movement of lips that had nothing to do with warmth. ''Think again, buttercup.''

''I don't think I like the tone of that, babe,'' Chastity returned, recognizing the quicksilver temper that rarely lasted long when she wasn't feeling well.

''Tell you what, buttercup,'' Lucas said as he wrapped a curl around his dark finger and studied the contrast. ''You go to work. I'll be here tonight and we can talk.''

''Don't you have cows to water or chickens to feed, or—''

He smiled again and bent to kiss her parted lips. Against them he said, ''I've got all the time this is

going to take. You do what you have to do, and I'll do
what I have to do. Seems to me like it's an even
trade…for today. There are crackers in your bag. Eat
them if you need to." Then he placed his open hand
on her stomach and rubbed it gently. "Take care of
that."

She jerked away, surprised by the easy way he
touched her. "I don't want you here, Lucas. You have
no right to interfere in my life, acting like a bounty
hunter who's found his prey. Look, we had an experience—" His eyebrows shot up, and his head tilted
arrogantly, challenging her.

Spreading her hands, Chastity took a deep breath and
began again. "You're not obligated. We had a
dream…a weekend away from reality. I'm having a
little flu and I've always managed on my own—"

"Times have changed, buttercup. Now you have
me," he said flatly.

"What did you say?" Sherry asked at four-thirty that
afternoon. "Chastity, you've been mumbling all day. I
think you said…'take care of what?'" Sherry's eyes
widened, her lips parted and she gasped as she glanced
past Chastity's shoulder, her lips parted, and she
gasped.

Chastity followed Sherry's stare to the tall cowboy
opening the door for two young, jean-clad women
dressed in jackets with leather fringes. She removed
her glasses to see better. The girls' straight glossy hair
reached their waists and swung gently as they moved.
They wore their jeans tucked into their boots, while
Lucas wore his on the outside. The trio moved through
the customers' lobby like a Western vigilante gang after bounty. Lucas's black hat almost brushed the tops

of the doorframes as they entered the customer service office. Chastity clutched the thick book of overdue accounts against her for protection as Lucas and the tall girls mirroring his features stopped to ask directions.

Charlie's entire staff traced the Western trio who walked straight to the counter in front of Chastity. Lucas took off his Western hat, nodded, and said in a defensive tone, "Chastity. These are my girls, Summer and Raven. I thought they should meet you. They're ornery as the dickens, but they're mine. Same as I want you to be."

His eyes dared her to challenge him in front of his family. Her nails bit into the account book as she tried for control. It irked her that only Lucas could draw passionate emotions. He caused her to feel as though she was dancing on the line of irratic, irresponsible and definitely unprofessional behavior. He'd invaded her home and her office, presenting her with the prospect of an uncertain pregnancy, and had summoned his family posse from Oklahoma to support his takeover.

"Hello," she managed after a moment, and nodded at the girls who eyed her curiously from their six-foot heights. Six blue eyes fringed with black lashes skimmed the braids wound tightly on top of her head, then slid down her flowing blue primrose blouse and loose, long navy cotton skirt. Chastity blushed when she found Lucas's eyes darkening and touching her lips. He reached to ease a curling tendril behind her ear, then the warm fingertip slid down her hot cheek, lingered and lifted away reluctantly. Hunger, unshielded, tangled and heated the air between them for a moment before Lucas took the heavy book away from her. He placed it firmly on the counter with a look that dared her to pick it up. "Too heavy," he said firmly, placing her glasses on her nose. "Don't lift anything that weighs over five pounds from now on."

Chastity wanted to scream, refusing to adjust the tilted angle of the glasses. Lucas defined rules, intruded and acted as if he had the right to do so. She resented that deeply. While she was thinking about a proper retort, Lucas's dimples played in his cheeks as though he was smothering a pleased grin.

"Nice meeting you, ma'am," Raven said quietly, shooting an impish expression up at her father, while Summer worked to smother the brilliant smile tugging at her lips.

"It's nice to meet you." Chastity touched her braids self-consciously as the girls continued to inspect her, clearly in awe. "I'm afraid 'Heartbeats' wanted me to look…"

She glanced at Lucas. He hadn't said a word about being disappointed. He knew that Honey was a fabricated fluff designed for a camera, *and he hadn't said a word*. The quick flush ran up her cheeks and heated her throat. The poor guy must be laden with guilt, accepting his punishment on those broad shoulders. There wasn't a thing luscious or desirable about her. Then Lucas's blue eyes pinned the heavy pulse at the base of her throat.

His finger rested on it lightly and his mouth tightened. "The word is 'sexy.'"

His expression said he wanted to carry her away that moment. Sherry gasped somewhere in the outer stratosphere and another clerk dropped a stack of papers.

Chastity's lips parted with a thought she couldn't think as Lucas's finger rose to caress her chin. They were alone then, wrapped in something she didn't understand.

Summer elbowed Lucas and his finger lingered, then moved away as if he didn't want to stop touching her. "She's prettier than on television."

Chastity glanced at her sharply, but the girl wasn't teasing, her expression open as her outdoor heritage. "I...I...they lightened my hair...then the makeup and training..."

Lucas glanced impatiently at the clock. "You get off at five. We'll wait in the lobby. I cooked supper while I waited for the girls' plane. They just got in." Then he smiled warmly at Sherry, who was gripping the counter tightly, her eyes jerking between the four of them. "Don't mind us. I'm Honey's—Ms. Beauchamp's intended husband and these are my girls."

Then he reached, cupped Chastity's jaw in his warm, rough palms and drew her mouth to his for a lingering kiss that left her dazed.

Sherry's soft whoosh of air exploded as Lucas shot a hot, meaningful stare at Chastity. He and the girls left to wait in the customer's lobby. Through the windows, Chastity finished her work beneath the girls' stealthy stares.

Later, in the sanctity of her bedroom, Chastity exploded. "Lucas, explain yourself. You walked into Charlie's, started the gossip mill churning, and—"

"Have you taken that test yet?" he demanded, crossing his arms over his chest.

Definitely a challenging male, Lucas was just short of breaking her well-known patience. "No, I haven't had time, and the directions say it's a morning test—"

"You make time in the morning, lady, and we'll take it from there...the four of us, together. If you're pregnant—"

"Lucas!" Her impatient scream drew giggles from the living room.

He jerked open the door and ordered, "Summer. Raven. That's enough. Set the table. We'll be out in a few minutes."

"Daddy, you be nice to her," one girl warned while the other giggled.

Lucas shut the door. "Sassy-mouthed, ornery—" Then he looked at the smile Chastity tried to hide. His expression lit and warmed and suddenly he flashed that devastating all-male grin and drawled sexily, "Come here, you."

Before she could resist, Lucas's kiss melted and heated, filled with hunger and desire and promises. When it was done, she leaned limply against Lucas's hard thighs, his heart racing beneath her hot cheek. Sometime during the tropical storm, the lightning crashing and the hunger racing, she'd locked her hands into his tooled Western belt. Now her fingers refused to leave their mooring. Her glasses were steamed and slanted across her nose. She feared the heated kiss had bent the wire rims.

Poor unsexy Chastity Beauchamp shivered in confusion, while Honey wanted to take Lucas down to the creamy shag rug.

"The way I see it," he said unevenly, his hands trembling as he cuddled her against him, "is this—one step at a time. Take the test, then we'll see what happens."

He bent to kiss the tip of her nose, his eyes very blue behind the steam covering her lenses. "If you don't, buttercup, reckon the girls and I can camp here until I know otherwise." Then he patted her bottom, ran his palm across her tummy and gave her a look that said he wished they were alone.

The next morning, Chastity shivered behind her bedroom door, breathed deep and searched for courage. "Ah…Lucas, could you come in here?" she asked.

The girls smothered giggles when their father halted his long-legged stride across the room to glare at them. "Hush up, tidbits," he ordered gently, his eyes locked on Chastity's face.

Chastity sat on the bed, rereading the kit's instructions, and tried to ignore Lucas's clean, soapy scent. She hadn't slept all night, aching for him to hold her.

This morning her living room couch and floor were filled with Walkingtons; the girls slept deeply, but Lucas's sleepy gaze had stopped her on her way to the kitchen. "Mornin', buttercup," he'd whispered, and the drawl echoed with needs that started her heart racing and her stomach fluttering.

Now he eased onto the bed, placed his arm around her and waited. She liked the quiet way he held her cold hand on his thigh. "We're in trouble, according to this," she whispered after a moment, her hands trembling and cold.

How could she have conceived so soon?

"No, we're not, Honey. Everything is just fine." He tipped her chin up with the tip of his finger and she looked into his clear blue eyes. "I want this baby and I want you."

"But, Lucas, we're so different—" Images of bills, her mother's credit-card gambits, Hope's job, Brent's troubled affairs and the problems of assorted relatives swirled through her head.

"Honey, we'll take it one step at a time." Then he

removed her glasses and kissed her and savoring the sweet, tender taste, Chastity kissed him back.

Then she was lying on her back and Lucas was nuzzling her neck gently. She touched his upper arms lightly, pressing the hard, tense muscles. Running her palm behind his neck, she smoothed the taut power with a caress and Lucas stilled, letting her wander through her thoughts.

She stroked his black waves, waiting for his breath to warm her throat. Lucas felt like eternity. As though he would always be there, solid and close to her.

Lucas Walkington, the babe, the sweetcakes, the one-hundred-percent-certified male, wanted her. He trembled then, the vulnerable movement endearing him to her. Chastity closed her eyes sleepily, warmed by his heat, and stroked his back lightly.

She wanted this man desperately, greedily. She wanted whatever time she could have to hold him just like this. She'd waited for a special man, waited for a family of her own, and nothing could stop her from taking the risk. "Yes," she whispered.

He relaxed slightly against her as if relieved; the press of his chest against her surprised her and she realized that he had been holding his breath. "Yes," she said again, more firmly. "Let's go for it, babe."

Then she yawned, dropping into the sleep that had been closing gently on her.

"One step at a time," Chastity repeated two days later as the big Chevrolet Suburban that Lucas had rented eased out of Chicago. Dawn fought its way through her plants and boxes filling the spacious interior. In the aftermath of Lucas's vulnerability, she realized one poignant fact: she had as much resistance to him as she did to double-Dutch, maraschino topped, triple-fudge cake with walnuts.

She'd grabbed Lucas like a brass ring for a weekend in paradise and now her entire life was out of control. He was a disaster as a gentleman, looping his fingers around her wrist as though he was afraid she would run away at any moment.

He moved quickly, with deadly intent tinged with desperation.

Within the space of a day, Lucas had plopped his daughters on a return trip to Oklahoma and packed her things. When she returned home that evening after giving her notice, he had cooked dinner, laundered and purchased assorted prenatal-care books. Her relatives began appearing and Lucas graciously served them his home-style chili and jalapeño corn bread. He planted gentle, but distinct hints about Chastity needing rest and care, which caused her to want to scream. When her mother protested and cried, Lucas handed her his freshly ironed handkerchief. "I'll take good care of her, ma'am. We're getting married just as soon as possible. But Chastity won't have time to baby-sit your credit-card situation. Reckon you'll have to bite the bullet."

With that he had lifted the back of Gracie's hand and kissed it, totally captivating her. The dimples flashed full force. "It's easy to see that you're Chastity's mother. She's got your beauty and intelligence. Then there's the sweetness, too. You must have been very young when you became a mother. I hope our baby has those same lovely green eyes. Like new spring grass."

Grace had flushed and giggled. She patted her wedge of curly hair and asked Lucas about his ranch. Mildly disappointed when he explained the simple, budget life-style in spacious Oklahoma, Grace was quickly swept under Lucas's charm, which Chastity noted he dragged out when needed. Grace thought it was "cute" and almost swooned with romantic delight when he swept up Chastity, who had been dozing on and off, and carried her into the bedroom.

One startling thought nagged Chastity. Lucas could be devastating, charming when he wanted, or ornery and stubborn when it suited him.

Why was she sitting in a Suburban driven by a cowboy, headed for outer Oklahoma?

She had wanted to protest his takeover, but the incredible fatigue draining her body prevented a mutiny. She dozed through Lucas's cleaning and packing and whirlwind arrangements with Hope's help. Her sister arranged for a temporary secretary to shoulder the remainder of her week's notice. Charlie loved the miniad on "Heartbeats," another trade-off that Hope had arranged. In the end, Chastity slept, tried not to focus on her growing confusion and wondered who was doing what to package her as Lucas's bride-to-be. Everyone seemed immensely happy for her. If she could wake up fully, she would toss him out on his well-shaped rear.

His game plan lacked a few finer points like asking her opinion.

Lucas never mentioned love or commitment or whispered little nothings.

She did not want Lucas to feel obligated to sweep her off her feet, much less marry her.

Once she got control of her tired, drained and sleeping self, she would regain her senses. She'd stepped out for a wonderful, memorable weekend, something to tuck away for her old age and suddenly Lucas was grimly—yes, grimly—determined to pirate her to Oklahoma without a word of love or romance.

Chastity frowned at an encroaching vine of wandering Jew that bobbed on her shoulder. She replaced it carefully. She was a practical woman who knew that love and romance belonged in fairy tales. Some deep, dark, secret part of her must have been inherited from her romantic mother. The whole adventure was doomed for disaster.

Once she awoke fully, she'd weigh the situation and come to a sensible conclusion.

"Bite the bullet," Chastity repeated darkly as Lucas sipped his morning coffee, while deftly steering the Suburban onto an interstate highway. "You evidently called Hope and she maneuvered the rest of the family into thinking this Oklahoma thing was best for everybody…including the show's ratings."

"Something like that." Lucas nodded, watching traffic closely. His profile resembled that of an intent wagon train master plotting his course on the prairie. He'd pulled out the charm and buttered up every woman who could lessen his chances to snatch her away. Brent had tasted a bitter lash of male disdain and Chastity wasn't certain what else, but after a private conversation with Lucas, her brother had shown signs of terror. Now Lucas sat beside her, pirating her away to Oklahoma. Her glasses were safely tucked in his shirt pocket.

"Magic between Heartbeat Goddess and Bandit turns to love, is that right?"

"Yep. She bought it. We won't have to turn up on the show again. Some little clause about relatives not participating—"

"You used blackmail?" The high-pitched squeak

twirled around a huge elephant leaf plant and the boxes, and dropped between them.

Chastity stared at him through the shadows of the cab's interior. A leaf on her lemon tree quivered. "I have no idea who you really are—as a person. Or why I'm sitting here beside you. Or Oklahoma ranching. Oh, Lucas, *why am I sitting here?*" she asked desperately. "You don't have to do any of this. Why are we here?"

He slowly placed his cup in the dash holder, reached out an arm and scooped her against him. "Because we've made a baby. Because I want to take care of you. Because if I left you in that bleeding heart hornet's nest, you might get sick."

"I feel," she said carefully, wearily, "like I am being drafted."

"That's right, buttercup. The only thing you have to do on my ranch is care for yourself. You'll have plenty of fresh air on the ranch and good care. We live simple and I want you to know there's not much excitement or money out on the ranch." He stated the last part slowly, his expression hard, as though it had cost him a measure of pride. "I work away when I can, picking up odd jobs. There's not much employment around Chip."

Chastity thought of spending every waking moment near Lucas. Oklahoma looked marvelous.

He was acting gallantly, paying his obligation to care for her, even plunging into marriage because of a dream weekend. The result would be disastrous. The odds for a successful venture were less than okay, closer to low.

"This is a big mistake," she managed sleepily from Lucas's safe, broad shoulder, afraid that her brief moment of ecstasy could be swept away forever. "I've lived in the city all my life. I quit eating beef when I realized it came from cows with those pretty brown eyes. Maybe I'm not pregnant. We should have waited for a doctor—"

She forced inches between them and blinked up at him, refusing to reach into his pocket for her glasses. "Oh, Lucas, you told Mother that we were getting married. If you want to tell your friends that we are, I won't mind. Or that we're not and I'm a cousin or something. Or you could just put me back on a bus."

She wanted her safe, frilly bedroom, her predictable job at Charlie's, and the never-ending disasters of her family. She was comfortable in her life-style; it suited her to be in control of her emotions. She barely recognized greed, but it was there every time she thought about Lucas. Deep, challenging anger was a new emotion she'd discovered since meeting him.

Living with Lucas would be a disaster. The whole event was a fiasco from top to bottom.

She frowned. *Something was definitely wrong. Lucas was acting out of his sense of honor and obligation. She didn't want a life built on his sacrifice.*

Lucas tugged her back gently to his shoulder and stroked her hair, which helped her growing headache. "It's not likely a mistake, Honey. I've thought about it since I saw you. Making love with you was a natural thing to do. Just like making a baby. I sensed it then, like part of me became yours, like cherishing."

When he said things like that, her skidding resistance rolled over into a pleasant "okay."

"I'm nothing like Honey, you know. I'm just plain old Chastity Beauchamp," she whispered sleepily against a tanned throat that she couldn't resist kissing.

The strong pulse running beneath his warm skin felt like an eternity of sunshine and rainbows. "I'm a modern woman. I can have and raise a baby alone."

"Not likely. Not my baby, anyway, and there's no other yahoo in the picture, the way I see it," Lucas stated flatly as she slid into the safety of sleep.

Chapter 5

Lucas tightened his hand on the steering wheel and cuddled Chastity's soft body nearer his. He'd calf-roped her into moving to Oklahoma, hadn't given her time for second thoughts. He'd reached out and grabbed what he wanted desperately, disregarding the consequences. He wasn't a boy now, polishing his honor and owning up to spending too many nights experimenting in a back seat. He knew he was acting instinctively, grabbing with both fists what he wanted and dragging Chastity into his life. She was the kind of woman to expect love—

Love. Lucas turned the word around, studying the facets. His throat tightened against the thought. At thirty-eight he wasn't likely to experience that kid's disease. He wouldn't let himself get ripped up a second time. More likely he'd found a woman who soothed the lonely ache within him. Marriages and affairs were based on less than love; people worked on relationships, caring for one another.

He wouldn't ask Chastity to take on his problems, he wanted to keep her tucked away, safe and rested.

That didn't explain the savage anger that erupted when he discovered Chastity's role in the family. She was somewhere between a doormat, a banker, a psychiatrist and a mother.

He couldn't desert her in that swamp of users. He wanted to cherish and cuddle and protect her.

Lucas scowled at a young couple kissing in the front seat of a passing pickup. He'd played the love game as a youngster. This go-round wasn't clear yet, but he intended to keep Chastity tucked beside him until the dust settled.

He checked her seat belt, adjusted the angle of her legs against his and settled down to drive the long interstate highway with his hand on her thigh. Traveling down the interstate, taking his woman to his home, was right and inevitable, filling him with a quiet joy. Chastity sighed softly against his skin and the hair on the back of his neck rose immediately. She was sweet and soft, and if ever he'd known a woman to be a good thing—Chastity was that woman. He hadn't hesitated to snatch her from that grasping family mob. The thought of his baby in the midst of that bloodsucking crew—his knuckles turned white on the steering wheel.

Chastity slept beside him, her head resting on a pillow now and Lucas traced the way the spring sun entered the window to glisten in the single braid that lay over her chest. Suddenly Lucas found his finger stroking the thick braid, catching its warmth and fragrance. He ran his thumb across the loose tip, allowing the curls to lick and twine around his hand.

He bore the scars of heartbreak and didn't want to need Chastity desperately, achingly.

Alesha had fascinated him in the wild hunger of youth. Drawn him into a world that shimmered and heated, then ripped him apart as a man. He'd fought to match her needs, the demands of her wealthy family, and lost himself for a time in a social whirl that almost sucked him into an empty abyss. In the end, she agreed to have the twins, then snatched them from his "ugly, broken-down cattle farm" and tucked them into a mansion for three years.

A big semitrailer passed Lucas and the Suburban lurched in the wind's force. Lucas found Chastity's soft hand, drew it to his thigh, and laced his fingers with hers. He'd found her by mistake and pounced with the deadly intent of keeping her near him.

He'd heard how some women slept often during the first weeks of their pregnancy and suspected that Chastity's dozing was that symptom. He wasn't above using her weakness to get her back to his ranch. He was walking on eggs, realizing that she could wake fully at any minute and change her mind. The desperation racing in Lucas frightened him.

He should know better; should know that things were better left alone.

Damn. He wanted her with him. Feared that at any moment he'd lose her.

The whole thing was headed for a cow pile. She'd take one look at his ranch, the house and the way he worked at any job possible to pay bills, then she'd hightail it back to Chicago. The whole thing could fall apart at any minute.

Just past Springfield, Missouri, Chastity grumbled as he carried her into the motel room. When he slipped off her shoes, she roused sleepily and swatted his hands. She sighed as he stripped her down to her panties and tugged his T-shirt over her head. Within minutes, Lucas smiled in the dark as Chastity's soft thigh eased gently across his thigh to rest within his legs. Her arm flung across his chest and she murmured "Mmm" with pleasure as she stroked the hair on his chest. In the next sleepless hour, Lucas tensed each time she moved, nestling closer.

Nothing but soft cotton separated them as Chastity eased over him entirely and settled down to sleep comfortably. Lucas couldn't force himself to place her aside, couldn't stop his body from responding to the soft heat of hers. Within seconds, she tensed, inhaled sharply and pushed her hands against the pillow they shared. He kept his lids closed, feigning sleep, and enjoyed the moment. Confused, she blinked, and eased away from Lucas. He couldn't resist grabbing her wrist, reluctantly releasing her. "Bed hog," he accused, wanting to draw her beneath him—

"Oh, I'm so sorry. I'm...I need the bathroom." She searched desperately for the bathroom, then ran to it, presenting Lucas with the tantalizing view of her rounded bottom where her panties had inched higher.

Placing his hands behind his head, he waited and enjoyed the sound of her bathing. Within a half hour, she called gently, "Ah...Lucas?"

He fought the grin teasing his mouth and remained quiet. She reminded him of a cuddly soft little bunny rabbit, curiously approaching something that fascinated her. After several moments, she whispered, "Lucas? Are you awake?"

She opened the bathroom door slightly and a wedge of light sliced across him. He traced her progress to the bed from beneath his lashes. Draped in the long-sleeve shirt he had discarded earlier, Chastity eased onto the other bed. She sat with crossed legs and clutching a pillow to her chest. The dim light tangled in her loose hair, creating a halo as she studied him and brushed her hair. "What am I doing?" she muttered quietly. "Of course he's delectable. But what am I doing?" After a few more angry strokes, she whispered, "This is all Hope's fault."

"Delectable says get into bed," Lucas said quietly and watched her expressions range from surprise to chagrin.

"You're awake, you jerk!" She launched the pillow at him and Lucas tossed it back gently. "You undressed me!"

"Lighten up, buttercup, I need my beauty sleep. First you roll all over me, trying to seduce me in my sleep, and then you mutter and keep me awake. Get into bed." He anticipated her next move with delight.

"You are a strange man, Lucas Walkington," she said in a hushed, wary tone. "Thank you for your thoughtfulness—setting out my traveling case, but *I am not a buttercup*," she added in a dignified and quiet explosion.

Lucas turned on his side, studying her in the darkness. There were long legs and a frothy mist of hair, the nudge of soft curves beneath his shirt. She looked and smelled sweet. "Buttercup," he said firmly, enjoying the way she cornered her rising temper and pressed her lips together. He felt like a boy with his first girl, tormenting her for the sheer pleasure of getting her attention.

"My hair is not blond, Lucas. It's light, mouse-brown. Buttercup must be some sort of odd family name," she returned haughtily, easing into the empty bed.

A truck soared by on the highway outside, and Chastity said quietly, "I don't like the idea of you acting out of some ancient idea of honor, Lucas. You are not obligated to do any of this."

"A man does what he has to do," he returned, his body rigid. At any moment, she'd say that she was leaving him—

"What do you have to do, Lucas?" she asked in a breath of a whisper.

"Keep you," he said truthfully, realizing that the wrong word, the wrong tone could send her running away from him.

"Why?" The word trembled in the shadows, scurrying around his heart.

"I want you with me," he answered, his stomach hurting with pain.

He waited for her to reply and when she didn't, he closed his lids, waiting. The minutes stretched into a half hour and he realized that she slept. Lucas settled down to sleep with the thought that at least his shirt was snuggled up to her. A half hour later, he eased out of bed, scooped her up gently and deposited her into his bed. Before he slept fully, Lucas adjusted Chastity into his arms, keeping her close, and nuzzled her fragrant, damp hair. She was just what he needed to warm the ache that had been with him for an eternity.

At a truck-stop café near their motel, Chastity replaced the glass of orange juice firmly on the booth's table. Lucas had devoured three pancakes with butter and syrup, six slices of bacon, three eggs and an entire plate of hash brown potatoes. He sipped coffee, oblivious to the waitress in the tight uniform who sidled by their booth with lingering, hungry looks.

"I think," Chastity said calmly despite the raging anger that had brewed in her since they'd walked into the café and Lucas had drawn women's hungry eyes, "that this farce has gone too far." She adjusted her glasses primly. "I think we should call this whole thing off and return to our respective corners. For some unknown reason, you have a disastrous effect on me. We couldn't possibly live together. I am a calm, reasonable woman, and your tendencies to order me about are grating."

That statement drew a masculine brow upward. "We're not suited to each other," she said, foraging for strength that dissolved the moment Lucas touched her. She shivered slightly, trying to place the morning's embarrassment behind her. She had awakened sprawled over Lucas's aroused body. He'd been gruff and abrupt when he awoke, piling her into the Suburban without a drop of the devastating charm he'd spread for her mother. "I don't like..." she began carefully as he scowled at her.

In her lifetime, she'd rarely stood her ground for her own interests. The insight rustled through her, raising an anger that never surfaced when she was plain Chastity. Lucas's ability to unbalance her had to be stopped. "I really don't like being hustled into a temporary arrangement we probably will regret. You feel obligated to do your duty, and while that's marvelous, it's really not practical. I've never been a burden to anyone, and I don't want to start now. We can't ruin our lives for a moment when we..."

Her fingers spread out and she noticed with distress that they were shaking. If Lucas didn't stop shooting her those blue-eyed passionate looks—*Lucas was very bad for her control. She had never met a man who could make her feel so violent, so feminine, so utterly bothered.*

He lounged back in his seat, shot a devastating thank-you grin at the waitress who had just filled his cup, and looked at Chastity with dark blue eyes. Her resolve to grasp control of her life since meeting Lucas began slipping. She spread her hand out on the table's cool surface and hoped that her morning nausea would not resurface. "Look, there might not be a baby. This whole thing is a mistake. I'm not anything near a Heartbeats Goddess. You won't be happy. You'll hate me...*and I'm so sleepy I can't think,*" she finished in a soft plea. "Lucas, this arrangement is not logical. Here we are...somewhere..." She looked desperately for reality and it scurried out into the Missouri sunshine.

Lucas let her sit there in the booth and sink in oozing, cold fear. She could have killed him for that. He was nothing like the gallant who kissed her mother's hand and charmed everyone she knew in Chicago. The sun glittered on the tips of his blue-black lashes and Chastity fought touching them. The thought that he was so beautifully touchable angered her. Beneath that dark skin, jutting cheekbones and the lurking dimples that charmed feminine hearts at will, was a dark moody temper, a possessive streak, a chauvinistic steel will and a man who kidnapped her out of Chicago's safety. Chastity took a deep breath, tried to ignore the way those blue eyes jerked immediately to her sensitive chest, and rummaged for all the drama she had learned from Old Coot. *Play it to top, wring it for every drop.* "I am not going to let this happen. You are not ruining your life, nor mine, for some antiquated masculine, chauvinistic idea of male honor. Put me on a bus for Chicago.''

Lucas's smoky blue eyes locked with hers, and his fingers gripped her wrist. "Like hell, lady."

Her control slipped slightly. "You are not lassoing a cow, Lucas—''

"Heifer," he corrected with a sexy drawl. "Top grade."

Chastity tossed her head, ignoring the wispy tendrils that refused to stay confined in her braid. "Whatever brand of cattle you want to name is fine. The point is, you can be mean and ornery. Quite unlike any man I want to live with, let alone…" Reaching for an expression, Chastity sailed out a hand and found her other wrist snagged firmly. She realized that her lenses had distorted the distance and she had almost toppled over a pitcher of syrup. "This is just too fast—"

"You're cute in the morning," he drawled while she tried to find a dram of sanity from the moment she posed as Honey.

"Cute?" Chastity shook her head, dazed. She'd been labeled "well-groomed," "neat and dressed sedately," but no one had ever referred to her as anything but plain Chastity Beauchamp.

"If the baby is a boy, we could name him 'Beau' for Beauchamp. That way your family name would be carried on, too." Then Lucas drew her palms to his mouth and licked each center gently. While something inside her turned to sunlight, butterflies and spring rain, Lucas suckled her fingertips. "Your eyes just turned to evening meadow green, buttercup. There are gold flecks around the black, and that's filled with me," he whispered huskily. "Sure takes the years out of this old man."

Poised to pour more coffee, the waitress gasped, and Lucas hauled out two adorable dimples, catching Chastity in midbreath. "We'll do fine," he said.

Scrimmaging for control, Chastity gripped his hands tightly. "Lucas, I haven't the foggiest about farm life," she managed desperately. "Clearly this is a mistake. I'm not ready to make this commitment. I've promised myself a marriage based on love, not convenience. Please put me on a bus. We'll correspond if you like."

"I'll take you back to Chicago and that bunch of freeloaders you call family," he said, playing with the tip of her fat braid, watching the light turn it to gold. "But I'm staying wherever you are until a doctor says that you're pregnant—and you are, buttercup. I know it in my bones. I knew when I gave you my baby. The choice is up to you. We can turn around right now—"

"You have a ranch, responsibilities and the girls." She couldn't force herself to ask if he felt one tiny, itty bitty bit of love for her, if he could possibly dredge up the enthusiasm to perhaps slip a little romance into the adventure. Of course she wasn't a romantic woman; she was practical and faucets dripped when she was near. Maybe he thought that once back in Oklahoma, he could transform her into Honey forever.... Her stomach contracted and she yawned, filled with a sense of disaster.

Lucas was pure common sense. "Summer and Raven wouldn't like it if I came home empty-handed. They're pretty happy to have another female to bear the burden of an old hermit daddy."

"Old hermit daddy," she repeated blankly, trying to fit the description to Lucas's vibrant, sexy image.

''Buttercup, don't leave me to face those monsters alone,'' he cajoled in that deep, sexy Oklahoma twang. ''They're mean, ornery and have half the boys in Oklahoma stirred up.''

He tugged her braid, ran a fingertip slowly across her mouth and said, ''I'm just a rangy old cowboy looking for a little warmth in his remaining years. Buttercup, I purely want what we've got together and maybe with God's blessings, what we've made together.'' The dimples deepened and Chastity fought not to touch them. Lucas removed her glasses and tucked them in his pocket with the air of a man successfully completing a mission.

By the time she recovered, she was tucked safely in the Suburban and too drowsy to rally a good mutiny. She dropped off to sleep with Lucas holding her hand and whistling ''Home on the Range.''

Chastity felt like a princess scooped away by a dashing prince. The wrinkle in the fairy tale was Lucas's desperate sense of old-fashioned obligation and the fact that he could be in love with Honey, not herself.

She dozed, awaking just as he slid into the driver's seat after filling the gasoline tank. Shaking her head slightly, Chastity spoke the thought that had been worrying her for miles. ''Lucas, don't expect...we're not going to...ah, you know....''

Apparently Lucas had been circling the same thought. He nibbled on her lips. ''Wouldn't think of doing anything before you asked me, buttercup. You have my word on it. You let me know when you think the time is right. To make sure I don't jump the gun before you're ready, you're going to ask.''

Hours later, Chastity awoke slightly as Lucas eased her into his arms. The crisp night air swirled around him, cows mooed and two girls whispered in hushed excitement. "Put me down," she ordered, thrashing her way free of the soft blanket in which he had wrapped her. She blew a row of curling tendrils from her forehead. "You've got to stop carrying me everywhere."

"Buttercup, we're home," Lucas stated with deep pride, placing her on the linoleum floor of his kitchen.

A dog yelped frantically, bobbing around Lucas's long, jean-clad legs. When he bent to rub the poodle's white, furry head, the dog licked happily at his hand. "That's Wayne," Lucas said, tossing his hat to the table. He adjusted her glasses and grinned.

Chastity blinked, looking up at the two teenage girls who stood in disreputable sweatpants and Lucas's old shirts. He tucked her against him, one hand resting lightly on her hip as he faced the twins. "Have you girls stirred up any trouble since we parted?"

"No, Daddy," they chorused innocently, studying Chastity closely. She blushed under their intent blue eyes.

"Did Mrs. Biddlecomb call?"

"Yes, Daddy. She's been over every day checking on us," Raven said with a defensive edge to her voice. "I told her we could manage for these few days, but she insisted on coming anyway. Her and that snoopy sister of hers. They want to meet Honey."

When Raven floundered, Lucas glanced quickly at Chastity, then said, "My future wife, that's what she is. We'll arrange it tomorrow."

"Lucas…" Chastity pressed her hand against her stomach, which had been growling slightly. She didn't want to upset his children by expressing her doubts. Nor mentioning the way he hadn't stopped to ask her opinion along the way. She immediately sympathized with the girls, whose expressions said they thought the whole adventure was romantic.

Summer reached to touch her hand, blushed and whispered reverently, "Oh, gosh, Daddy. This is so exciting. We're going to have our own little baby."

Looking up, Chastity was amazed to see Lucas blush beneath his deep tan. "Yep. If things work out."

Both girls giggled and leaped on him, the impact taking him back and down to the couch. Lucas struggled amid a web of long limbs and then he chuckled. The brief, deep sound enchanted Chastity and she listened for another, which did not come. Amazingly the trio rolled to the floor without interrupting the giggles. The girls scrambled to their feet, and Lucas lay looking up at Chastity. He looked rumpled and adorable, his shirt opened to expose his stomach, his hair tousled. Wayne managed to scoot under his hand for petting. Lucas's dimples deepened amid dark stubble and he said unevenly, "Welcome home, buttercup."

Both girls pivoted toward her, their eyes widening. "Buttercup? Daddy calls you 'buttercup'?" they chorused, bending to take Lucas's boots and drag him a short distance.

"Lay off," he said, grinning sleepily and looking marvelously all-male. "Watch your manners. She's half-ready to run away now. If you two start acting like savages, she might take off."

Summer and Raven straightened slowly and frowned at Chastity. "You wouldn't take our baby away, would you?" Raven asked cautiously. She glanced down at her father, who lay there watching the females with interest, his hands behind his head. "Get up and behave, Dad. Your horseplay might scare her away."

Her sister glanced from Lucas to Chastity with interest. "Dad, you just laughed for the first time in years," she noted in a startled tone as the kitchen sink began dripping steadily.

Lucas rose slowly to his full height and tugged Chastity's braid. "Go lay down. The girls and I will bring in your things. We'll take the car back to the rental place first thing in the morning." When Chastity glanced at the cozy living room and the doors leading from it, Lucas nodded toward a bedroom. "That's my room. We've got one bathroom."

When she hesitated, determined to salvage a tiny dram of her pride, he looked at the girls and nodded toward the Suburban. "Git."

Chastity swallowed uncertainly as he glanced at the television set. The girls had been replaying tapes of Bandit and Honey, school books and a bowl of popcorn lay on the floor. On-screen Honey slid into the tall cowboy's path, demanding her kiss. Her eyes were green and hungry, her mouth glossy and parted. Standing behind her, Lucas wrapped Chastity in his arms and swayed gently. He fitted his chin on top of her head and watched Honey's hungry expression. "We're home now, buttercup," he whispered gently. "I haven't got much to offer you but two ornery daughters, and clean air and sunshine. We'll take care of you."

Chastity fought fatigue and the urge to punch his dimples. "Lucas, I'm used to taking care of myself. I take care of other people."

His big hand covered her stomach and he soothed it as he swayed her in his arms. She could have stayed like that all night, warm and cherished, wrapped in Lucas. "We'll manage, at least until we know about the baby. We'll work it out after that. I won't hold you if you want to go, buttercup...."

The ache in his voice wound around her heart and Chastity closed her eyes. Lucas rocked her gently, his body tense behind her, his hand firmly on her stomach. "This is wrong—"

"Can't be. Nothing can be wrong that feels this right," he said simply as he kissed her temple.

"Lucas," she began again, staring at the open bedroom door, which symbolized her life with him. Somewhere in greater Chicago, her mother, Brent and Hope needed her care. The faucet dripped in her apartment bathroom without anyone to scowl at it. "I don't know."

"Hush up, buttercup," he whispered unevenly. "Bed down in my room for tonight and I'll take the couch. We'll get married in the morning, when we return the car. After that, reckon we'll take it a step at a time."

"Lucas, marriage is a little drastic for the situation. Marriage for convenience is worthy in some cases, but not necessary with me. Marriages are for love and commitment—"

"I'm committed, buttercup," Lucas stated tightly. "Love is a dream. We can make things work."

"I am so tired," she whispered drowsily. Any minute Lucas would wake up and accuse her of entrapment. Of presenting a luscious dream girl as bait, then sticking him with a woman with short, practical fingernails.

"Lady..." Lucas lifted her gently into his arms and carried her into the dark bedroom. "Get this straight. You worry too much. That's what I'm for, to worry and to lean on. You take it easy from now on."

"If I weren't so tired, I'd argue," she returned with a yawn. "This won't work. Will you stop carrying me?"

His arms tightened and she realized that no one had cuddled her for an eternity. In the morning she'd wake up, find reality and save them both from disaster, but just now she nestled against him.

The room smelled like Lucas, safe and warm and dark. The furniture was sturdy, made from oak that would last like steel. There was a scarred desk with boxes of papers stacked beneath it. Photographs of his daughters and old brown-tinted pictures studded the tan plaster walls. Lucas held her as he walked to the wall, nodding to a framed picture of the twins as babies. "Twins," he said slowly, watching her expression in the shadows.

"They're beautiful," she said, admiring the fat cheeks and masses of black hair.

He held her a moment longer, as if he wanted to say something more, then decided against it. Gently Lucas placed her on her feet. He swallowed, ran his hand over her cheek and hair, and bent to kiss her. "You rest, buttercup. The girls and I will take care of you."

Too weary to debate his orders, Chastity waited until the door closed, then sat slowly. "Here I am in Oklahoma. Why?" Then she looked at the comfortable, clean white pillows amid the huge wood-frame bed and decided all decisions could wait until the morning.

Morning lurched at her in blinding sunlight, and beyond the bedroom door, a hushed Walkington argument was brewing. "Git," Lucas said in the same no-nonsense tone as he had used the previous night.

"We want to stay home from school today, Daddy. Chastity needs help, and you're grouchy and tired...."

Chastity waited for traffic sounds to begin, for the scurry of people going to work passing her apartment doorway. She hugged the warmth of the old bed, stretching beneath the weight of the quilt, which smelled like wind and sunshine.

A dove cooed beyond the window and the smell of fresh coffee slid through the wedge of sunlight crossing to the bed. She felt thrillingly awake and alive, stretching again and wiggling her toes.

"You're going to school today," Lucas said more firmly over the clatter of dishes.

"I've never been in a wedding. Daddy, it's early yet. No one knows that this is a shotgun wedding—"

"Hush," Lucas snapped.

"I want to show her my new calf," Raven said. "Rosebud is pretty."

Wayne barked wildly and somewhere in Chicago a taxi cab driver cursed and honked at blocked traffic.

The Oklahoma dove cooed again and Chastity whispered, "Shotgun wedding."

Lucas's flannel robe lay across the foot of the bed as a reminder of his possession.

She eased to her elbows and closed her eyes. "Heartbeat Goddess...Charlie's bookkeeper...the bride in an Oklahoma shotgun wedding..."

Lucas had kept her moving, carrying her where he wanted her. Her hands closed into fists. He'd picked her up and plopped her down in his ranch, moving with certainty while she dozed. Using his dimples when she faltered, Lucas had made her lose control of her life. She wanted it back and she wanted Lucas in it. Because he was an old-fashioned guy, loaded with hang-ups about modern relationships, she would have to marry him to soothe his inhibitions.

No other man had ever affected her the way Lucas could, making her feel alive and passionate, riding on the cusp of happiness so close she could taste its sweetness. While she sensed his fear of their relationship, she couldn't allow his shyness to crush the future she wanted.... When it came to Lucas, she was a very greedy woman.

Smoothing her stomach, Chastity smiled slightly. She'd love the fantasy to be true, to carry Lucas's child tucked within her.

The cold air hit her bare legs as Chastity slipped into the soft flannel robe and tied the sash with a jerk. She had been pushed enough. Lucas's worn moccasins looked warm and comfortable and she slid into them, padding across to open the door.

The three tall Walkingtons pivoted to her, their expressions tight with a temper she suspected was a family trait. "Okay, I'm awake now," she said warningly, meeting Lucas's scowl. "I'm not falling asleep at the drop of a hat anymore. I am fully, truly awake and I really don't like confrontations."

With a small degree of pride she acknowledged that she'd managed to keep her temper and voice controlled. "Hustling poor, sleepy Chastity into Oklahoma is kaput. My wedding day is next Saturday, Lucas. If you don't stop antagonizing these girls, you can forget playing the groom," she said, fighting the tug of warmth in her lower stomach as Lucas's dark gaze slowly prowled up her bare legs where the robe had separated.

She inhaled, drew herself up to every centimeter of her five-foot-six frame. She had once extracted Hope from a love-stricken, beefy wrestler using the same menacing technique. "Summer…Raven…if your father insists on marrying me—a sacrifice he seems honor-bound to make—then *I* insist that you act as bridesmaids at a church wedding. I've always said, if you're going to do something, do it right."

"It's Tuesday morning," he stated flatly. "It's four days until Saturday."

"I said I'm awake. You're not calling my tune on some royal male whim. That's four days of the couch for you," she returned hotly. Lucas had pushed enough; now it was her turn to set terms. A thrill raced through her—Lucas didn't want to be apart from her.

He was hers, and she was his, but there were rules. "I'm no longer so tired, Lucas. I believe that any decisions concerning our lives should be made jointly now. Isn't that right?" she challenged.

Raven giggled and hugged her father, who stared at Chastity blankly. "Dad, you should see your face," Raven chirped happily before Lucas stalked out the door and slammed it behind him.

Chastity smiled tightly, surprised at the simmering temper within her. Then she tightened the huge robe, shuffled the comfortable moccasins to the table and picked up a slice of toast. The girls stared as she nibbled on a corner and shot a dark look at the closed door. "That man," she muttered, "can be difficult."

"Yes," the girls echoed at once.

Chastity held up a firm finger. "But. He can be sweet."

"Uh-huh. Sure." The twins' tones lacked sincerity.

"Last night was the first time we've heard him laugh for years," Raven muttered.

Jerking the robe sash tighter, Chastity luxuriated in

regaining her control. She nibbled on the toast and regretted the loss of poor, quiet, amendable Chastity. Lucas would roll over her like a bulldozer—she debated the term, ''roll over her'' and blushed. Lucas dismissed conventional romance with a sweep of his Stetson.

She wanted the whole enchilada with Lucas. She would drag love and romance out of him while he worked on old-fashioned obligation.

She wanted Lucas Walkington from his battered cowboy hat to his dusty boots.

Then she smiled the perfect smile, controlling both corners of her mouth to lift them equally.

''We'll work on your father's laughter. Tonight we'll work on the wedding, after your homework is done. Please tell your father on your way to school that he is to reserve the church for Saturday afternoon at one o'clock. I'm sure there is a white country church around here and that's where I want the wedding. I'm wearing white. A friend gave me her gown and veil and I'm wearing it.''

Chastity breathed deeply, power surging through her. Maybe it was the clean air in outer, greater Oklahoma. Or maybe it was Lucas Walkington, waiting to be challenged. She doubted that many women had challenged Lucas. He was in for one memorable experience. If he thought he could withhold romance and love from *her* marriage, he was off base. If she was pregnant, she wanted her baby to be in a real family embroidered with love. Chastity dusted crumbs from her hands and lifted her head. Lucas needed taming and she, Chastity Beauchamp, had found the challenge of her lifetime. ''I've always wanted a Saturday afternoon, one o'clock wedding. If the church isn't free this Saturday, then we'll wait for an opening. Your father is used to having his way. If I stay—if I marry him—things will have to change.''

"Go, Honey!'' the twins cheered.

Chapter 6

Lucas watched Chastity walk slowly toward the ancient oak tree that had marked Walkington land since his great-great-grandparents had settled on it.

Wearing loose cotton slacks and a city maxi-style coat, she looked tiny against the vast rolling prairie that baked in the summer and froze in the winter. The wind pushed at her, making her lean slightly against it while Wayne yipped and played at her side. Amid the dead stalks, new spring grass began to show, the March air heavy with the scent of the land just turned by his tractor plow and waiting to be seeded.

His cattle spread across a knoll, watching Chastity move toward that single huge oak reigning like a monarch over the land. Lucas ran his hand across Duke's muzzle as the horse whinnied, his nostrils catching the woman's scent.

Squinting against the early afternoon sun, Lucas stood trapped in the magic of inevitable time and his deep emotions. *He wanted her like that, walking straight and proud across the land of his birth, the land he hoped to leave his children.*

This morning she'd startled him, those green eyes hot with anger, challenging him on the spot.

Lucas patted the horse's muscled neck with his glove, pleased with Chastity's temper flash. With narrowed eyes, he traced her walk to a knoll, where she stood in the sunlight amid the sun and the wind as though she already belonged to the land...to him. He liked discovering that grit beneath the soft, loving ways. Liked that she wasn't afraid to put him in his place. Whatever he wanted from a woman it was the truth.

Alesha had walked to that same knoll, making her choice to leave him and take the girls to her parents'.

Three years of driving to Tulsa, spending two hours each weekend with his growing daughters, had stretched Lucas and his beat-up farm pickup to the limit. He'd lost four calves and three cows because of fatigue or because he wasn't there for them.

The twins were three when Alesha had called suddenly, asking him to take custody. She wanted a new life with a man who didn't want children. "The twins are just like you, Lucas. There's no possible way they can ever be civilized. I can't afford to throw my life away after them when they're never going to be anything but Walkington tomboys," she'd yelled. "I don't know why I ever spoiled my body bearing them...."

Lucas's jaw ached and he forced his teeth apart. His heart had been racing with the memory and the fear that Chastity would react as Alesha had years ago.

"Let's go see just where I stand with the lady now,

boy," he murmured, tugging his hat down against the wind.

She stood against the old tree, surveying the miles of prairie, broken only by electric poles and dirt roads. The wind colored her cheeks, tugging strands of her hair free from the braid and curling them around the rough bark. She held a dried stalk of milkweed pods in her hand, her eyes almost closed.

In profile her jaw promised strength, her lips the softness of a woman, the gentle sweep of lashes the innocence of the child-woman he'd taken. "Hello, city woman," Lucas said softly as she watched his approach from those mysterious, half-closed eyes.

She smiled, enchanting him with the lift of those sweet lips at one corner. "Hello, cowboy."

Lucas shared the tree with her and wished she shared his life. "So you'll marry me Saturday. The church is free."

Her head turned slightly against the bark, eyes marking each feature of his face as though she were tucking it inside her forever. "Don't press your luck. I'm not happy with you now."

Gathering the coat closer to her, Chastity stared at his Angus cattle. "A temporary marriage isn't for me."

"Temporary?" Lucas fought the terror sweeping through him. His hand wrapped around her wrist, her pulse beat steadily beneath his fingertips. Shrugging her shoulder with elegant meaning, Chastity closed her eyes. "Annulment, divorce, estrangement. I've never stepped out on a ledge before, Lucas, and I'm frightened."

Twisting a wisp of silky hair around his dark finger, Lucas leaned closer. "You think I'm not?" he asked huskily, sensing that this moment would determine if she stayed with him.

When she lifted her head, her eyes were clear and green, filled with his reflection. "Lucas, people don't get married because of a fantasy weekend. They don't change the course of their lives on a whim, and they don't get married without love."

Pain shot through Lucas like a cold iron. His tense muscles ached. "I married once for love. It's a cow pile in the back lot."

"But you want a marriage?" she asked disbelievingly.

This time Lucas stared at his cattle. "I'm not a man who jumps around. I won't put my boots under any other woman's bed while I'm married to you."

"It isn't enough. There's tenderness and a partnership involved." Chastity's tone had risen defensively. "You acted impulsively, Lucas. A sense of honor won't be love, and you'll feel cheated in the end. You'll look at me one day and wonder how you could have married me. Now is the time to change your mind—"

He looked at her sharply. "Are you saying you're hightailing it back home?"

Her eyebrows shot up with the challenge. "I'm saying that you'd better think before marrying me, Lucas."

"Are you saying no?" he pressed, his heart aching with heavy, pounding heartbeats.

Her head tilted, her eyes focusing slowly on his face. He recognized the slow blink as though she missed her glasses. "Are you?"

"It's right, buttercup. You're what I want," he said tightly.

"That's nice," she returned in the same tone. "You're what I want."

"It will work," Lucas said finally, slowly, thinking how green her eyes were, how warm her lips were beneath his. *God, it had to work, but he couldn't give her love. Love for a woman wasn't in him. Alesha had taken his love and buried it in a nightmare.*

He leaned down, nuzzled the wind and sunlight tangled in her hair and prayed for the moment to last. "It's hard out here," he whispered as the wind tossed a curl against his cheek and it caught in the stubble he'd been too angry to shave. "Hard on women."

The Chicago pawnshop ring in his pocket was a good introduction to his finances. Thin, gold and hocked by someone needing cash, it bent Lucas's pride. He pictured placing a tiny diamond on his wife's slender fingers and the hurt went deeper. "What do you think about the place?" he asked, expecting a list of what she needed.

The small house and looming, ancient barn were surrounded by barbed-wire fences and electric poles zigzagging off into the horizon. Battered by time, the old windmill clattered away in the wind, a monument to his lost dreams.

Scanning the small frame house with a large back porch and larger front porch, Chastity's mouth eased into a tender, one-sided smile. "It's beautiful and warm. Like a jewel on a green ocean. Oh, Lucas, the air smells so clean." He liked that, sharing the timeless tree and the sun with her, her voice husky with sleep. Unable to resist, he turned her cheek with a finger and bent his head for a light kiss that lingered.

Her lips followed the gentle pursuit of his until Lucas asked, "Still mad at me?"

"You…" She searched for the word, her eyes half-closed and her breath washing sweetly across his lips.

He kissed her again. "Stir you up?"

The half smile returned and Lucas kissed its warmth. "Are you sorry?"

She leaned against him slightly, raising her face for his kisses like a kitten snuggling to a petting hand. "None of this makes sense, Lucas. There is no need for you to marry me. Nor to feel any obligation. I'm perfectly capable of handling my life, my way. I have no idea why I permitted you to take over.… Everything is happening too fast."

He chuckled at that and her lashes fluttered. "What?"

"Some things aren't happening enough," he teased as a fragrant curl slid across his lips.

"Lucas," she whispered in that sad way that made him ache everywhere. "Haven't you realized that I'm nothing like Honey?"

"Nope."

The sea-green eyes darkened and she breathed lightly. "You take my breath away."

"I'd like to. The girls are at school," he offered, testing his luck and sliding his hands beneath the heavy coat. Beneath it, she was round and soft, her waist an indentation that just fit his hands before they smoothed the flaring curve of her hips. He caressed her ribs, running his thumbs along the outer curve of her breast.

"Lucas, you are impossible," she whispered, desire flushing her cheeks.

"Hungry is the word, buttercup," he corrected, nibbling on her bottom lip with his teeth. His hand slid under her sweater and upward, caressing her breast.

"It's cold out here," he murmured, thinking of the warmth of her body waiting for him.

He'd been cold for years, he realized suddenly as the sun tangled in her hair, the wind whipping it gently. He'd acted instinctively, grasping the woman who warmed him, who made him feel like a man.

Then she was curling against him, lifting her arms to lock behind his head. "Poor baby," she teased, the half smile dying as his aroused body locked with hers. Lucas cupped her hips, raising her to him hard. Heat shot between them, and Chastity's eyes widened in surprise. "My," she whispered.

He grinned when she shot a shy glance downward. "My goodness," she whispered, looking up at him.

A red-tailed hawk squealed overhead and a rabbit scampered into the brush. Wayne barked at sparrows and pranced about with a stick in his mouth. Rummaged by the wind, a dead leaf on the oak sifted down to settle at their feet.

Pushing his luck, Lucas slipped his hand to unhook her bra. Her breasts were soft, filling his hand with gentle weight as a blush began in her throat and worked up to her cheeks, flushed by the cold wind. "You're changing, buttercup. Ripening—"

"Goodness, Lucas, you make me feel like a tomato or a melon." Chastity buried her warm face against his throat and held his arms. "This is all so fast. My head is spinning."

Then he was kissing her, taking what he wanted, and her arms were locked around him, keeping the cold wind away. "I need you," he said roughly, meaning it. Then deeper, rougher, "You're mine."

Fear raced around him as Chastity raised her eyes

slowly and they filled with his reflection. Lucas's stomach hurt, his heart pounding.

Then Chastity's soft mouth began to curl, that gentle mysterious smile snared him in a soft web, easing the terror. ''Don't worry, babe,'' Chastity whispered, licking the dimple groove beside his mouth. ''I'll take care of you.''

Four days later in outer, greater Oklahoma in a small town named Chip for buffalo chip, Chastity spoke her wedding vows to a man she'd barely seen for days. Beside her Lucas wore his Western-cut, blue-gray church suit, and a grim expression.

Throughout the day and the country-style reception, he'd snapped at Summer and Raven, who were spending the weekend with a girlfriend. He barely noticed Chastity's gown, a soft white cotton with lace and long sleeves. When he jammed the thin gold band on her finger, his bitter expression had frightened her.

By eight o'clock that night, Chastity fought the simmering anger that had been brewing since he'd dropped her off in front of the house with a grim ''Git.''

''Git,'' Chastity muttered as she waited for her groom to complete the chores and stalk his cute little rear end to her wedding bed. In the four days she'd been dozing and getting acquainted with the Walkington family, she'd found that Lucas deeply loved his daughters, but didn't know how to communicate with them. Crossing her arms over the black lace peignoir, Chastity tapped her foot.

She closed her lids and remembered his worn wallet, Lucas opening it to pay the minister for the church, then turning to give his daughters each a bill. Because money had never mattered to Chastity, she found her pride scratched. Lucas could have used her savings, if she had them. She'd watched his mouth tighten and suddenly realized that the Walkington's trip to Chicago for her and the rented Suburban had cost money he could ill afford.

"Git," she repeated, jerking a cold-cut dinner from the refrigerator and plopping a bottle of red wine on the table. She sloshed the wine into a glass and glared at the lights in the barn as she sipped it. Husbands didn't keep to themselves. She would not have a husband who blew hot and cold in their relationship. He might be Mr. Lord of the Plains to his daughters, but he was just so much good-looking sweetcakes to her— he was a babe and he'd better not forget it. Babes had responsibilities to the women they chose to gift with their babe-ness. Like cuddling and—

At her feet, Wayne tilted his white curly head and whined sympathetically.

Striving to push down her rising anger, Chastity glanced around the Walkington home. Lucas's home was cozy, beautiful in its practical mix-and-match furniture. Her plants swallowed a corner by a window and her framed family pictures rested on a buffet that had crossed the plains in a covered wagon. A rocker that had belonged to Lucas's great-grandmother waited in the shadows to rock sleepy babies. She ran her finger around the Old Coot's picture lovingly. "You would have loved Oklahoma, Old Coot. It would be a real challenge. Lucas certainly is."

Sensible area rugs covered a gleaming hardwood floor; the big family kitchen with a washroom and pantry slid into a spacious living room. The gas cookstove and refrigerator were ancient, but a new washer-and-dryer set dominated the washroom. Surprised when she

first learned that dishwashers weren't a standard house-
hold appliance, Chastity discovered that people in
Oklahoma dried dishes on a rack-thing. Sometimes
they dried clothing on lines strung from poles in the
ground.

She sloshed wine into her empty glass and studied
the clothes neatly arranged on hangers by the washer.
Last night the washer and dryer had run past midnight,
and she noted the basket of towels waiting to be folded.
In the days prior to their wedding, Lucas had not made
one move toward her, other than those dark blue eyes
making promises that no righteous man could keep—
she desperately wanted that wild, heated freedom of
Lucas's lovemaking and it was her night to howl, darn
it.

She rephrased that mentally, remembering the small,
hungry noises she'd discovered she'd been making that
night at Casa Bianca. The proper term was swooning
noises. Maybe she had purred later.

Chastity plopped her glass on the table, jerked her
maxi-coat from the hook in the pantry, grabbed a beer
from the refrigerator and braced herself against the
wind on the way to the barn.

He'd hustled her out of Chicago against her better
judgment. If he changed his mind about trapping a
plain woman in lieu of a goddess, he would have to
tell her outright.

Lucas watched with interest as she fought the wind
and the huge board door, finally opening it and squeezing through the narrow passage. "You could have used
the door," he drawled, looking up from polishing his
leather saddle.

"Door?" Chastity found it immediately and whirled
to him, her anger raging. "I see no reason to dillydally,

Lucas Walkington. 'Git' isn't a word that a groom uses to his bride on *their wedding night*.'' She tossed the beer to him and adjusted the maxi-coat around her with dignity, then plopped on a square hay-thing. A horse whinnied in the looming darkness of the barn and she jumped, frightened at the noise.

Lucas sipped the beer and leaned against the rail, which supported his saddle. ''What's up? You look like you're in a tizzy.''

''Tizzy?'' The casual remark caused Chastity to narrow her eyes at him. ''You've been hiding out for days, Lucas. Avoiding me. That romantic kiss at the wedding may have fooled the others, but it didn't me. You've changed your mind and should be man enough to admit it. You've found yourself in a mess with a woman that doesn't suit you and are taking your punishment like a man.'' She jerked her thumb to her chest. ''*I* don't want to be that punishment. That cross to bear…that albatross around your neck, the old lady—''

His eyes slid from her face to the part in the coat, then down the long length of her legs. She inhaled sharply, fighting her temper and the rising need to— ''Typically a groom is interested in his bride on their wedding night, Lucas,'' she reminded him stiffly, looking at him from his arrogant black hair to the tip of his polished, dress boots.

She pushed back a bobbing curl that detracted from her forceful impact. His light blue shirt was open low and a bit of pink confetti nestled in the crisp hair covering his chest. Chastity closed her eyes against the hot wave of desire taking her breath. ''Being dropped like a stinky sock doesn't do much for a girl's ego on her wedding night,'' she said, her words dropping off into the barn's spacious gloom.

"Uh-huh. I said you'd have to ask. What are you wearing under that thing?" he asked, placing his beer aside to walk toward her. Lucas stood over her, forcing her to look up. The stark light of the single bulb swaying overhead hit his grim expression, changing his face into sharp planes and dark shadows. A tense muscle moved on his upper cheek, running down into the dark shadows of his evening beard. "Marriage can be hell," he stated in a cold tone that cut Chastity's heart, as though speaking his thoughts out loud. "I promised myself I'd never step in that cow pile again. There wasn't much left of me after the last time. That ring you're wearing is pure pawnshop."

Uncertain of his mood, Chastity watched his face harden, his hand reaching out to wrap in her curls. "All this is natural, isn't it?" he questioned in the same musing tone. "You've got a few cosmetics in the bathroom. *All* of you is natural, isn't it?"

"Oh, Lucas," she whispered, her throat tightening with emotion. "I'm not a bit like Honey. I'm just practical, plain old me. Except my hair was layered and lightened for the show and now it won't stay in my braids. It's a curse. I think annulment might be in order if you've changed your mind, and I think you should."

His hands wrapped in the coat's lapels, drawing her to her feet. "You keep reminding me that you're not Honey. Why did you come out here?"

"Out here in Oklahoma, or out here in the barn?"

The warm fingertip prowling her hot cheek slid to her earlobe and tugged. "The barn. I didn't give you much rope to do anything but come to the ranch with me."

"I made that decision myself, thank you," she returned loftily. There was danger dancing in his blue eyes, challenging her. Chastity's body ached, his heat and scents driving into her. Then she caught the amusement flickering beneath his lashes and it set her off. The muscles in her cheek locked with anger. "I came to thank you for the nice time today, Lucas. I loved meeting the people of Chip. That's why."

"Uh-huh. I don't buy that."

Chastity stood, too filled with anger to care about the consequences. He wanted the truth slapped across his hidden dimples, did he?

She jerked open the maxi-coat, dropped it to the hay and pushed Lucas's chest hard with her open hands. "You jerk. I came because I wanted you. Because wedding nights are supposed to be romantic, simmering with romance. But oh, no. I spent a full hour in the bathroom, waiting for my impatient groom to tap on the door. But oh, no, not this groom—" With that she poked his chest. "But now I've changed my mind," she stated airily, reaching to replace the coat. "It's your loss," she managed with as much dignity as a woman who has offered herself and met rejection.

The tiny straps supporting the black gown snapped easily beneath Lucas's hands and it slipped, pooling at her feel. Grabbing the transparent negligee closer, Chastity scowled at Lucas. "Babe, that wasn't nice."

Her hopes for the evening soared higher. Tearing her clothing off was just the right cure to her unstable, wild emotions. She needed to know that he wanted her as desperately as she wanted him.

"I love it when you get tough, buttercup," he drawled, running a finger around the dark tip of her breast and watching with interest as it peaked. He bent to kiss it through the sheer material without laying a hand on her. While Chastity dealt with the melting hunger skimming down her body and circling in her lower stomach, he grinned wickedly and the dimples appeared.

She pushed at his chest again, wanting to physically...physically do something. To show him she wasn't a simpering woman of yesteryear, Chastity took his lapels in both hands and jerked his shirt apart. Buttons flew into the barn dust, clinking and rolling and setting her temper aflame. She hadn't ever really exposed the world to the temper she controlled, but Lucas Walkington—her alleged groom—was testing her to the limits. "This is my wedding night, sweetcakes, and I want the whole enchilada."

Deep inside her, sweet little shy Chastity Beauchamp, shivered in confusion. Reaching out and taking wasn't in her gentle nature.

Chastity Walkington decided that lust was a good place to start. Wrangling Lucas into committing his heart was a serious matter and she intended to turn on the heat.

She thought of the heat she'd experienced twice and started to sizzle.

"My, my," he drawled, flicking a glance down at her nails, which had been gently clawing his chest. That hungry, dark blue stare at her body stroked Chastity's ego like a match to tinder. Throwing away caution, Chastity allowed the negligee to slide to the floor, leaving her standing pale and nude beneath the stark lighting.

Lucas's gaze slid down her curves slowly, intently.

"This barn isn't heated, is it?" she asked uneasily. No man had taken her apart inch by inch, making her feel soft, feminine and desirable as a beautiful woman.

Now Lucas inspected every trembling inch with deep interest.

"You're not lean," he said quietly, inspecting her breasts, which had started to ache for the warmth of his mouth. He traced her stomach, and Chastity fought her blush as he stared intently at the shadows above her inner thighs.

To her distress, the soft flesh quivered.

"No. I've never thought diets were sensible," she said tightly, intensely aware that she stood unclothed, bared to his scrutiny, while he remained fully dressed.

She wanted him stripped and in bed. Chastity glanced around the shadowy barn.

"Bed isn't the only place I'll want to make love, buttercup," Lucas drawled as though he followed her thoughts. He watched her expressions, then reached to tug the light bulb's string and the barn went dark.

Maybe the pickup truck's bed? she offered silently, desperately wanting his heat, wanting that exquisite joining of his body with hers. *Or the pickup's long front seat?* Good Lord, where did people in Oklahoma make love?

When he chuckled, toying with a curl swirled around his fingers, Chastity glared up at him. "You're enjoying this, babe."

"You got that right, buttercup. Your expressions tell me just what you're thinking. It's pretty complimentary to have a lady come calling—"

"Hush," Chastity ordered sharply. "And lay down on those square hay-things—"

"Bales—bales of hay," Lucas said when he stopped grinning that devastating, all-cocky, arrogant, desirable male grin.

"Whatever. Git. Just do it." Good Lord, if she didn't

have him near her, holding her, wrapped around her soon, she would burst.... "You are a difficult man, Lucas Walkington," she said, her words sliding off into the howl of the night wind as he began undressing.

Placing his shirt carefully beside her coat on the hay bales, Lucas reached into the back of the pickup and shook out a blanket. "Make-do," he explained simply, covering the bales.

"Lay down, sweetcakes," she ordered tightly, needing him desperately. Clearly her body wouldn't allow her to be the blushing, reluctant partner. Lucas seemed to enjoy her ploy and, encouraged, Chastity pushed him slightly.

His broad back tensed, the muscles rippling. Straightening, Lucas unfastened his belt and slacks and shucked his shorts in the process, presenting her with a wonderful view of broad shoulders and ridges and cute little dimples low on his spine. She touched a devastating little indentation experimentally and the sheer need to swathe his body with hers enveloped her. He stood tensed as she swept her palm over the ridges and planes of his shoulder, skimming the muscles of his upper arms. Her tiny, awed gasp and the sound of her heavy heartbeat filled the airy barn.

"You're the boss," Lucas said in a low, husky, uneven tone. "What now?"

"Lay down—no...." Chastity wrapped her arms around him, and pressed her body to his back. It was warm and deliciously hard. Then, without mooring, her palms slipped a little on his flat stomach and she jerked her hands back, flushing as she realized there was an anchor of sorts available. "Ohh!"

Lucas moved forward suddenly, unbalancing her and turning to catch her as she sprawled over him on the bales. He locked her to him with one arm, cupping her bottom with his hand, while his other hand prowled her curves. Taking his time, Lucas lifted her breast to his mouth, licked the area around the center and whispered against her skin, "I'm here. Now what are you going to do with me?"

Fighting to think, to stop the coils of desire centering low in her stomach, she clung to his shoulders with all her strength.

"This?" he asked, lifting his hips slightly and easing into her. "Or this...." Then she was filled, heated, pulsing around him.

Moments later, she lay draped over Lucas's warm body, the coat covering her as he waited for her to recover. He chuckled in her ear. "That was some compliment."

She roused long enough to whisper against his dark warm throat. "What?"

"I turn you on, buttercup. You were already on the edge, waiting for me. A man likes to know he's attractive for his wife. What do we do now?" She sensed the humor, the deep hunger riding him, the tense muscles of his thighs lifting slightly to press deeper within her.

"Oh, Lucas, I don't know anything about this wife business. I don't know anything about raising a family, or your daughters, or—" His kiss stopped her.

"One thing at a time," he whispered in the dark, rolling gently over her. "Let's work on finishing the current project.... Tell me what you want next..."

Then he moved deeply within her and Chastity knew what she wanted.

Later Chastity was surprised to find that her babe knew how to walk and make love, too. The process was incredibly erotic. Lucas swathed her in her coat, ordered her to lock her legs around him and stood with her in his arms. At the barn door, she couldn't stop the quiet scream of pleasure.

He was naked and magnificent, his body damp and cold as he entered the night. She whimpered softly again when he opened the house door. Then Lucas placed her on the washer. Chastity looked at his stark features, at the slightly swollen curve of his bottom lip, and moved closer to him. She nestled her breasts against his hairy chest and luxuriated in the rough texture. "I can wait until we're in a bed," Lucas said tightly as she bent to lick his nipple, suckling it gently as he had her.

The challenge was too much. Chastity launched herself at him, determined to keep their beautiful joining through the night. "Don't leave me, babe," she whispered before tracing the whorls of his ear with the tip of her tongue.

"Oh, damn," he whispered hoarsely, gathering her closer and moving with her flow. Minutes or an eternity later, Lucas cuddled Chastity's warm, limp body with big, unsteady hands. "We just made love on the washer, buttercup." He sounded incredulous.

She nestled in his arms, biting his shoulder sleepily. She'd really gotten the hang of loving Lucas and though part of her wanted to play into eternity, part of her wanted to roll herself around him and sleep. "The dryer is close. You wouldn't have to carry me far...."

Lucas snorted at that. Chastity had the impression that she had bruised his dignity, his ability to control the moment. That sound reached into her ego and jerked it two stories high. "Let's eat," she whispered, suddenly filled with energy that had escaped her for over a month.

"Eat. I'm lucky to be breathing," Lucas stated in a dark, irritated growl and glared at the washer. "Git," he ordered Wayne, who was watching with interest. The dog sulked into Summer's room to hide.

Elated with her first success as Mrs. Walkington, Chastity patted his stubbly cheeks and kissed the lips that responded nicely to her nibbling prompts. "Sweetcakes, there are cold cuts on the table. I'll be right back."

He snared her wrist and stayed her for a moment, reluctant to let her go. Chastity loved the uncertain, primitive, incredulous, macho expressions shifting beneath his dark skin. She truly loved the wary look in his blue eyes; he seemed dazed by her attempts at passion. She hummed in the shower and got that little peremptory rap on the door that she had wanted earlier.

"Yes?" she asked innocently, studying the chafe marks Lucas's beard had made in the steamy mirror. "Who is it?" A snort of male disgust raised her hopes for a lovely evening. Lucas entered the small room when she opened the door, shot a wary glance at her and stepped into the shower.

Lucas Walkington, Oklahoma babe, was just the man she'd been waiting to try out all her life. That thought warmed her through their brief candlelight dinner. Wearing a pair of worn jeans, open at the waist, Lucas concentrated on his cold-cut sandwich. A deep flush of red ran up his tanned cheeks when he glanced at her breasts covered by another gown with tiny straps. Chastity slathered mustard on her sandwich while little pings of pleasure shot off inside her. No doubt Lucas was thinking of the straps he'd torn earlier. "I'm thirty-eight," he said suddenly, startling her. "A man takes pride in his control."

His eyes jerked down to her bosom and lingered in the deep crease covered by black lace and pink satin. "You are one well-developed woman. Hungry, too."

Chastity chewed on her sandwich and his comment. She decided it was a compliment and that he liked her curvaceous body. In a few words, he'd erased the lifelong doubt she'd had about her sensuality. She didn't feel pink-pastel sweet and blushing bride-like; she felt like a beautiful, red-hot, desirable woman. The passion humming through her like electricity skimmed along her skin, and she wanted to toss Lucas's six-foot-three body on the floor and have her wicked way with him. Whatever happened between them later, she was having a wonderful, exhilarating wedding night to remember forever. She loved the stunned expression in his blue eyes as she stood and slipped the gown off, tossing it to a chair. Lucas stared at the tiny black-lace strip serving as briefs, then up at the hunger in her expression. "Lady, you are really asking for it," he warned as she slid onto his lap.

Closing her eyes, Chastity thought how she'd like to try with Lucas all the sensual how-to's she'd read about in contemporary magazines. Lucas sucked in his breath as her fingers wandered over him, testing the zipper— "Easy. That could be dangerous," he warned sharply when she tugged it experimentally.

She nestled on him, squirmed to get more comfortable on his hard body and grinned when his hand slid to cup her breasts. He trembled then, his fingers smoothing the lace covering her heat. "You're ready again, aren't you?" he asked in a startled tone, as though speaking his thoughts aloud.

"Just for you," she urged desperately. "Oh, Lucas, take me now."

They were on the couch suddenly, the springs creaking with their joined weight. Lucas's jeans opened magically while Chastity kissed him on the mouth—she loved the taste of Lucas on her tongue. Then she was settling down on his aroused length and in a quick jerk, Lucas tore away the lace separating them.

"I think we're going to have to work on our timing—like taking things nice and easy," he murmured as he scooped her up later. Chastity poured her well-sated body into his keeping and snuggled into his arms.

At the doorway to his bedroom, she threw out a hand and caught the doorframe, bracing a foot against it, stopping him. She asked the question that had tormented her for days. "Lucas, I have to know. Did you share that bed with your wife?"

"No." He eased her through the doorway and stood holding her, his body tense. "Bought it at an auction. The mattress and springs are new. Got them before coming to get you."

"Good enough." Chastity didn't want to know anything else. She just wanted to sleep, wrapped in Lucas's safe arms.

Something hard and warm shifted beneath Chastity, rousing her as the catcalls, car horns and pounding began. Lucas rumbled and growled, pushing his chest against her breasts. He snorted and lurched and reached out to hold her protectively against him. She turned her head slightly on the pillow to watch Lucas awake with a curse. He wiped his hand across his face, blinked several times and snatched the clock from the bedside table, holding it near his face. "Damn. I'm too old for a shivaree."

"Shivaree?" she asked, aware of the instant heat between them.

Lucas shot a hard look at her, eased from beneath her leg and tugged her arm gently from him. "Just a lot of sh—manure. People with nothing to do stand around and harass newlyweds—" He stopped, glanced down at her grin as though surprised.

"That's right, Lucas. You qualify as a newlywed."

"I'm a little past the prime picture," he shot back, then ran a possessive hand down her backside, cupping her bottom.

The hooting and banging grew louder, circling the house. Wayne barked and bounded up on the bed. He stood on Lucas's flat stomach, clearly defending his master. Car lights cut through the curtains. "Hey, Lucas! Whatcha doin'?" a man called out as the noise rose above the howling wind. "Come on out and say howdy," another man yelled.

"Hey, Lucas, remember the time you shivareed me and my Betsy? Your turn now."

A woman's voice slid through the night. "Git on out here, Lucas Walkington. We've got the wheelbarrow ready...."

Lucas continued a steady stream of curses, standing up and jerking a clean pair of jeans from the closet. He paused, ran his hands over Chastity's clothing next to his and shook his head as if dazed.

"Hey, Lucas! You left the barn door open. Guess what I found inside," a younger man yelled.

"That would be James Lexington—"

"Daddy? We're waiting." Summer's voice swept into the room. "Time to push the wheelbarrow."

Lucas shook his head. "That girl is going to get her backside paddled—"

"Lucas, my old bones can't stand this night wind much longer. Get yourself out here now," an older woman demanded.

"Hattie McCord. Tough as old leather," Lucas muttered. He glanced at Chastity, who had snuggled down to watch his warring emotions. "Get up. They won't leave us alone until we pay our dues."

"I'm too comfortable. You go." She grinned, snuggled down deeper in the quilt and sniffed the pleasant scent of his body on the bedding. "I'm tired."

His grin was slow, disarming and deep with dimples. Scooping her from the bed, Lucas tossed her lightly in his arms and said, "Are you getting dressed or do you want the whole countryside to see you in the raw?"

"You wouldn't." Chastity's smile died as he began to walk toward the living room. She caught the doorframe a second time that night. "Stop. What do I wear?"

He lowered her to her feet and patted her backside. "Anything, a pair of jeans. Get a move on. I want some sleep tonight."

"I don't have jeans. What about cotton slacks and a sweater? Or maybe a matching blouse and skirt? Or…"

"This isn't a fashion show, Mrs. Walkington. It's a damned circus," Lucas snapped impatiently. Then Chastity caught the dark hunger in his eyes before he shielded it.

Skimming down his body, she noted the heavy arousal thrusting at his worn jeans. Because he was in a snit, impatient and arrogant, Chastity wriggled slowly into cotton slacks and a sweater. Lucas needed tempering and when she looked over her shoulder at him, his face was dark with desire.

He might hide his love away, protect it ferverently, but he desired her and for now it was enough.

Minutes later, the wind swirled Chastity's hair around her as Lucas tucked her close to his side. Wayne bounced from friend to friend, holding court happily. Spotlights pinned them, cowbells rang, and wooden spoons banged on pots. "To the barn and back," the crowd ordered in a chant.

He squinted against glaring headlights. "Hey. I'm an old man. I've got two of the orneriest daughters this side of Tulsa. Save this stuff for the kids—"

A man's barroom voice cut through the wind. "Are you saving it?"

"Hell, he had to go across three states to get him a woman. He's scared all the rest off. He's been saving it for years," Hattie McCord taunted.

"Maybe I'm not anymore," Lucas returned smugly and Chastity hoped the wind would account for her hot flush. He bent to kiss her passionately, lifted her high in the air and swirled her around until she grasped at his bare shoulders. "We're having us a baby. No reason to go careful now."

"Oh dear, oh my," Chastity whispered between her well-kissed lips when the horns stopped and the crowd's eyes swung at her, pinpointing the area of her flat stomach beneath the coat.

Then Lucas laughed outright, the wind whipping at him, his face dark with a new beard.

The noise and the catcalls continued until Lucas placed her in a wheelbarrow and began pushing it toward the barn. Cattle lowed in the distance and a drop of rain touched Chastity's cheek as she held tightly to the bouncing old wheelbarrow. The crowd cheered loudly, confetti mixed with the light rain, and Chastity forced a wide smile.

Lucas had a few things to learn. Like waiting for a doctor's examination. Like asking her if she wanted the entire world to know she'd grabbed him in Casa Bianca.

Lucas ordered Summer to take Wayne, then pushed Chastity back to the house. He scooped her into his arms and ran into the bedroom, kicking the door shut.

Chapter 7

Lucas's grin slowly died. Shimmering in volcanic fury, Chastity leaped to the bed, placed her hands on her hips and glared down at him. Her curls bobbed, glistening in the dim light as she stepped around the tumbled bedding. She pointed her finger at him. "You. You are the most infuriating man, Lucas Walkington."

Alarmed, Lucas snared her wrist only to be shaken loose. "Honey, be careful. You could hurt—"

"The baby, Lucas? The baby we don't know medically exists? The baby you just announced to the entire city of Chip?" she demanded in a soft explosion.

"Get down. You could hurt yourself," Lucas ordered tightly, but Chastity was past listening.

"Sweetcakes, don't you know that people actually converse, decide together about tossing personal information around Oklahoma?"

Unaccustomed to being dressed down, Lucas narrowed his eyes, staring the few inches up to her face. "I called it. I stand by it."

For a moment her eyes widened as she digested his statement. Then her chin jutted out and she snapped her fingers. "Huh. Just like that. You decided to inform everyone about something so…so personal. Don't you know that anybody with a brain can…?" She floundered a bit, slashing out her hands as a blush rose from her throat to her cheeks.

She kicked a pillow, looked at it, then bent to scoop it up and throw it at him. Lucas caught it and dropped it to the floor, uncertain about the illogical creature who had just thrown another pillow at his head. He dodged it, shot her a scowl that always calmed his daughters, and waited for the tempest to cool down. It didn't.

"I have to face everyone and they'll all be wondering. No, they'll *know* that I dragged you into bed right away. You just flopped it out in public. You just stood there and… Oh, this is really wonderful. Now everyone will know that you married me because you felt duty-bound—"

"Shot the honeymoon to hell, didn't it?" Lucas grated out.

She blinked, frowning. "What do you mean?"

He pushed his hands in his back pockets to keep them from trembling, fearing the worst. "I did something you don't like. Therefore, logically, it's the couch for me. Or a cold back." Chastity stared at him blankly, jammed her glasses on and leaned closer to see his face. "I don't know what you mean."

He smiled tightly with the fear racing inside him. Happiness wasn't meant to last a lifetime. "I've been through this routine before. Wife gets ticked and sex is out the door."

"Sex?" Chastity's voice was low, uneven and dangerous. The sea-green eyes shimmered with tears. "You think this is a matter of sex? Ohh!"

Then she was in front of him, thrusting her hands at his chest. "I want you to know that I have never…ever lost my temper. I've always used reason… You are impossible, Lucas Walkington." With that, Chastity reached up, grabbed his ears and tugged him down for a hard kiss. Her tongue pushed inside his mouth and she bit his lip before stepping away.

Lucas faced a trembling, angry woman who asked, "There. Does that feel like I'm ready to turn you away when you act like a…a yahoo?"

He tested his burning lip with his finger and tried to keep the foolish grin inside, warming away the fear.

"Sex!" she continued hotly, throwing out her hands. "Oh no, you couldn't say making love, or lovemaking. No, you said sex. Well, I've got news for you, Lucas. I like…" He noted with satisfaction that a rosy blush spread across her face.

He eased a clinging curl away from her cheek and she swatted his hand away. Taking a deep breath, Chastity said tightly, "You and I will talk—repeat—talk about personal things before we spread them from here to China. I've noticed serious gaps in our relationship. While I'm at it, since we're going to be a family, let's get some things straight."

Fascinated, Lucas watched while Chastity began to pace the length of the room, concentrating as she undressed, tossing her sweater at him as she passed. "This cow thing and horses. I want to understand farm life better, but if you keep sulking and hiding and working and staying away from me, I won't learn anything. Listen up, Lucas. I'm only going to let you keep pressure-lipped for so long—''

''That's 'tight-lipped,' honey,'' he corrected quietly from the shadows.

Chastity kicked off her shoes and glared at him, continuing as though she were Sherman marching through Georgia. ''Then there's the matter of the girls.''

She paused, unsnapped her cotton slacks, stepped out of them and tossed them to him. The soft quiver of flesh above her bra drew Lucas's attention. His jeans were suddenly uncomfortably tight as she continued. ''We're getting to know each other and you're avoiding the inevitable. Those girls want to date and they will eventually. In the short time I've been in the Walkington family, I can see there is work to be done in your relationships. You're all so alike.''

Chastity ignored his snort of disbelief. She unhooked her bra, slid free and flopped it over his shoulder. ''The thing is, we've got a task cut out for us, and if there's one thing I'm good at, it's making lists. Well…there's that one other thing that I can do, but it's not important…a little gift I inherited from the Old Coot, but haven't really put to the test.''

Lucas caught her discarded briefs, wrapping his hand in the warmth. ''I've never been extremely passionate, or self serving. *Or violent.* But you set me off, Lucas Walkington,'' she muttered, glancing at him. ''I never show temper and I'm always considerate of others almost to a fault. I wanted you and went after you. You were the first thing that I've ever wanted selfishly, without reservation. I liked—correct that—*like* how you make me feel…feminine and desirable. Oh…''

Chastity yawned, looked down at her socks and sat wearily on the bed. She yawned again, and murmured drowsily, "A garden. I want a real garden with big, fat juicy tomatoes and cucumbers, maybe snow peas and bok choy. Maybe kumquats or kiwis. Definitely mushrooms in that old root cellar."

Lucas swallowed the wad of emotion tightening his throat. He knelt slowly and began peeling off her socks, aware that she watched him drowsily. Her fingers combed through his hair soothingly, and with a sigh, she bent to kiss him. "My, I've never spoken like that to anyone. You're marvelous for inhibitions, Lucas. A real pressure valve. Thank you for listening, though I'm still rather angry about your announcement. I wanted a doctor's exam to back up the test—I feel glorious, Lucas." She was asleep before he lowered her head to the pillow.

Lying near Chastity, remaining still as her soft thigh crept between his and her arm began sliding across him, Lucas breathed shallowly. In moments, the soft fragrant curve of feminine body would begin inching over him.

His tears surprised him, warm on his lashes. Whatever, whoever Chastity was, she clearly wasn't tossing him out of her bed. Nor were her demands unreasonable.

He swallowed, shifting more comfortably as Chastity pushed her face into the hollow of his throat and shoulder. She nuzzled him and purred.

Not once in her tirade had the lady mentioned money, or rather, lack of. She wanted to learn about cows.

A soft curl caught on his beard, swirling its clean fragrance around him. Lazily caressing the sweep of his wife's back, Lucas fought the swell of emotion pressing against his chest.

Everything was just too damn good. It couldn't last.

He dozed, cuddling Chastity's soft body against him. Lucas awoke from his passion-filled dream to find himself already sheathed within her, her lips nibbling hungrily at his....

After his morning chores on Monday, Lucas packed Chastity into his pickup and drove fifteen miles to Chip. While Lucas pointed out various ranches, Chastity absorbed the tone of his voice, the deep pride and love ringing through it. Country music played from the radio, and somewhere in outer Oklahoma a boy advertised for his lost dog with brown spots and a mangled ear. Chastity sat close to Lucas, ignoring his grim expression and let Oklahoma seep into her bones. A vast state, filled with various Native American nations, it resembled Chicago's mixed nationalities.

The local supermarket was a combination gas station and feed store, since most residents purchased groceries forty miles away at a larger town. While Chastity hunted for broccoli, cauliflower, grapes and tofu, Lucas loaded grain sacks into the pickup. "What's wrong?" he asked, noting her few purchases as he took the basket from her.

"Lucas, they don't have pasta. Spaghetti and basic macaroni, but there's not a package of linguine anywhere. *Lucas, there's no fresh pasta. Not even tortellini. Where's the fresh-fish counter?*"

He tossed a package of spaghetti into the basket, his expression wary and grim. "This is meat-and-potato country, city girl. Most folks do their heavy shopping in Muggins. Beef and pork are in the freezer on our back porch. Fish are out in the lake waiting for a hook."

"A hook?" she screamed softly as Nellie Black-feather grinned nearby. "They don't net them?"

Lucas shot a dark stare at Zeke Farris, who was snickering by the vegetable oil. "You want that garden? The onion sets and planting potatoes are over there. Get whatever seed you want. There's not much free water in the summer, so keep that in mind." He wandered off, pushing a dinky grocery cart with one bad wheel.

Chastity scooped onion sets to her heart's delight, then moved down the rows of bulk seed, filling tiny brown sacks with spinach, beans, lettuce and cucumber seed. A young pregnant woman with one child on her hip and holding a toddler's hand suggested that Chastity wait to purchase the cabbage and tomato plants that would arrive soon. "You're Lucas Walkington's new wife, aren't you?" she asked, kissing the ten-month-old baby straddling her hip, and tugging the toddler away from the bin of potatoes. She smiled shyly, her Native American features timeless and beautiful. "I'm Melody Bearclaw."

"Hi, Melody. Yes, I'm Lucas's wife." Little pings started shooting off in Chastity's stomach when she looked at the girl's rounded stomach. Then she knew—this baby may have startled them, but the next Walkington child wouldn't. She wanted children with Lucas—black hair, blue eyes, with streaks of pride running deep.

Meanwhile, he had lessons to learn.

She found Lucas instantly, standing a head above the aisle display and studying fabric softener. He tipped his hat back with his thumb, his black brows meeting as he concentrated.

"You've got your work cut out for you," Melody

whispered with a grin. "He's been dodging women for years. Except for the things he attends with the twins, he'd hole up on that spread forever. No one could believe he entered that Lonesome Cowboy contest, or that he went to Chicago. I'm so happy for you. Lucas must have known what he wanted right away, with the baby coming so soon."

Chastity smiled warmly, meeting Lucas's sky blue eyes across the aisle. She wanted to pelt him with the onion sets and drag him behind the sacks of cow feed and lecture him on starting gossip. "We're not exactly certain about the baby."

Melody's grin widened. "If Lucas snatched you that quickly, he knew a good thing when he saw it. It's all so romantic. He's so proud of you. Goodness, I didn't think Lucas Walkington would ever marry. He's been like a wily old wolf for years. I heard the Walkington twins took away the ladder from the hayloft and stranded him until he agreed to listen to their idea about the Lonesome Cowboy contest." Lucas's expression shifted into arrogance as he smiled quickly, flashing his dimples.

Chastity returned the smile with a challenge. A dimple display over fabric softeners did not wash away his premature announcement. "Drop over for coffee, Melody. I'd love to learn more about Lucas."

The girl erupted in giggles. "I've never seen him smile, or look that innocent…. He's such a babe."

"A regular sweetcake," Chastity added darkly and plopped her basket on the counter. The owner and clerk, John Blue Sky, shot an appraising glance at her stomach.

The cart with the rattling wheel banged into the counter and Lucas glared at the change John had counted into her hand. "After this, John, if my wife wants anything, add it to my bill."

Scratched by Melody's reminder of Lucas's bold announcement at their shivaree, Chastity reached down to pinch his hard bottom. He jerked away, scowling. "I'm not without funds, Lucas dear." While Lucas's blue eyes promised revenge, John laughed. "Looks like you got a whole houseful of women now. Forgot something, didn't you, Lucas?"

"Yes, his coupons," Chastity said firmly. "Lucas, where are the coupons?"

He snorted and met John's amused eyes over her head. "He means something else."

Cursing softly, Lucas stalked down the aisle containing over-the-counter medications and returned with packages of feminine supplies. He jerked out a few bills and tossed them to the counter, slapped the worn wallet shut and jammed it into his back pocket. His grim determination not to show embarrassment caused Chastity to giggle and temporarily forgive his abrupt behavior at the store as they walked to the pickup. She scooted next to him, edged beneath his arm and grinned. "You're cute, Lucas Walkington. I bet you can't drive this pickup and kiss me, too."

He lifted a speculative eyebrow. "You keep it up, Miss Sass, and we'll likely to end—" He sucked in his breath as she snuggled close to him and caressed his thigh....

Raising himself off her later, Lucas looked stunned. He peered out the steamy pickup windshield and swore. "We're parked behind Fanny Simmon's barn like a couple of over-heated kids."

The day was wonderful, brimming with sunshine and discoveries as Lucas wheeled the tractor into the yard and turned over the old family garden that hadn't been used for years. Chastity slipped off her shoes as she had been aching to do and experimented with the damp spring earth. It was soft and unbelievable. She wiggled her toes and sighed, smiling up at Lucas, who had been watching her. "I've never put my feet on real dirt," she explained shyly.

Chicago did have dirt, but not the freshly tilled, waiting-to-be-nourished soil. Lucas watched her, his eyes shadowed by the brim of his hat. For a moment, their eyes locked, tenderness flowing between them. The tangible emotion swirled around in the clean sunshine, warming her. "Barefoot and pregnant," Lucas said quietly. "You are a sight, Chicago lady."

She wanted to hold him, to wrap her arms around him and soothe away the pain that always seemed near him. Whatever his scars were, they ran deep. Another woman had shared him, wounded him and taken the love Chastity wanted desperately.

She eased her toes into the cool soft soil. Then something wiggled beneath Chastity's sole and she screamed. Lucas laughed outright when Chastity spotted another earthworm in the freshly turned earth. "Night crawlers," he explained, fascinated as she picked a cautious path to him.

"Snakes. Baby snakes, Lucas." With that she leapt for him as though he were a safe tree in a swamp filled with alligators. Lucas's laughter didn't stop until he lowered her to the ground.

"Those snakes are fishing worms. There's crappie and bluegill down at the lake." Then his lips tightened, his gaze lifted to the swelling horizon. "On the old place."

She sensed pain, running deep, swirling around him with memories, and waited for him to explain. Lucas looked down at her, the lines deepening in the shadows beneath his hat. "We're short of water here. Keep the garden small. The stock takes every drop in the summer. I'm helping Seth Jones lay fence until nightfall. The girls will be back after school. Better rest."

Then he shrugged and walked toward the barn, locking her away from him. Chastity stared at the closed door and knew that though Lucas shared his body with her, he wasn't sharing anything else. "Lucas Walkington, you are packing around a big bundle of pain by your little old lonesome."

That night Chastity turned her backside to the bedroom mirror and studied the tight-fitting Western jeans. A bridal present from Summer and Raven, they were perfect. They were worth every squirm, lying flat on the bed to squeeze into them. The girls explained how it was important to start Western jeans tight so that they wouldn't sag after wear.

Working as a team in the kitchen, Lucas and the girls had shooed her away. Chastity drew her hair up into a ponytail. She fastened it with a rubber band, then thrust combs into the sides to keep her hair from curling. The jeans protested tightly as she tied her joggers and stepped into the living room.

"You look great," Raven exclaimed, running to Chastity and turning her around. "Doesn't she, Daddy?"

Lucas straightened to his full height, his eyes flicking over her. "Whose damn idea was that?"

Wayne whined once, quietly, then slid off to his cushion near the couch.

"Stop cursing, Lucas," Chastity ordered softly as both girls turned toward him, their eyes filled with tears. If he wanted to point out her plainness to her, he could have chosen another time. "I'm probably not built right, anyway. Jeans look best on the leggy, lean type."

"You're built just fine. That's the problem," Lucas stated stiffly, placing a huge beef roast on the table. The meat had been simmering in a slow cooker all day and Chastity swallowed, suddenly aware that hunk of cooked, red meat was dinner. She closed her eyes and tried not to think of Rosebud's beautiful big brown eyes and long lashes.

"Daddy is old-fashioned, Chastity," Raven said in a bitter tone. "He won't let us date until our senior year in high school. That's only five months away, and Mel Jones wants to take me out now."

"Mel Jones." Lucas snapped the words between his teeth. "He wants to take you out drag racing on Melody Flats."

Raven lifted her chin. "To a movie, Dad. In Muggins."

"No."

Summer shot a dark look at Chastity. "All Daddy thinks about is money, grades and college. We want to be like everyone else. Just because he had to sell off part of the farm to keep this and couldn't go to college doesn't mean we have to live like prisoners. We're the only kids in school who still have to be home early after a game."

"'Prisoners.'" Lucas's snort indicated he wasn't investing time in the matter. Clearly he'd made certain rules and expected his daughters to keep them.

Three sets of stormy blue Walkington eyes fastened

on her, each waiting for her to choose between them. "What do you think, Chastity?" Raven asked after a tense minute.

"She agrees with me," Lucas snapped. "Let's eat."

"I think…" Chastity said slowly, fighting to control the irritation that Lucas could easily arouse "…that we need to work on communication."

"'Communication.'"

"Lucas, stop repeating everything in one-word sentences."

He glanced at his daughters, who were watching the scene with interest. His expression changed to smothered, wary frustration. "Bet you can't sit in those tight jeans," he returned darkly. "Don't wear them outside the house."

"Sweetcakes…" Chastity began too softly, then remembered they were not alone. Because the girls were fascinated with the exchange, she decided that several matters would be resolved behind their bedroom door with Lucas's new lock. She sucked in her breath and pushed down the impulse to dump the roast, gravy, mashed potatoes and carrots over his head.

"Do the dishes. Then do your homework," Lucas ordered the girls immediately after dinner. He jerked on his hat and stalked out the door, slamming it behind him.

Raven threw a dish towel at the closed door. "I just might not want to go to college, Daddy."

The tears that Summer had been withholding throughout the meal began to drip into her plate.

Wayne howled softly from his safe cushion.

Chastity placed her hands flat on the table and studied the short, practical nails. Adept at smoothing family waters, she let her instincts take over. "Okay. He says dishes and homework."

Raven sniffed, wiping her sleeve across her eyes. "Daddy can be so grim."

"After dishes and homework, I say we party," Chastity continued with a bright grin, despite her breaking heart. The picture puzzle wasn't complete, but she saw Lucas struggling to hold on to everything he held dear, to manage as best he could. She ran her hand across her stomach. If his child rested there, Lucas would have another responsibility.

"Will you show us Hope's makeup tips?"

"Oh, my dah-lings," Chastity cooed. "She sent tons of makeup and perfume samples with me. There's nothing more relaxing than a good makeup session."

"Nails, too?" Raven asked and began stacking the dishes rapidly.

"My dears, we'll pedicure our hearts out. While we're at it, we'll plan an open-house party—"

Raven's grin died. "Daddy won't like the expense. He had to sell cattle for our Chicago fare."

The quiet statement slammed into Chastity's heart. Then Summer said, "Daddy said you were worth it. A good investment, he said. He said he'd mortgage the ranch to get you here."

Those words kept Chastity going full blast until Lucas settled into the bed beside her. He lay there stiffly in the moonlight, arms behind his head and staring at the ceiling. "The girls need their rest," he said in a tone resembling a bear inviting a fight. "The music was loud enough tonight to raise the dead."

"You should have joined us. The girls said you can dance."

Lucas snorted. "Self-protection. Had to learn to enter that Tulsa contest. They were on me like ticks on a dog."

Chastity sucked in her breath. Lucas could bend when necessary; it was a start. "We're having an open house here Friday night. You're cooking a pot of something. Maybe chili and make some of that jalapeño corn bread. The girls are making two chocolate cakes and—"

Lucas flipped onto her, covering her with his body. "You're taking over, are you, Miss Smarty-Pants?"

Because he was hurting, because he said she was worth mortgaging the ranch, Chastity gave him a respite from the pain. She gave him a nibbling kiss, massaged the taut muscles of his neck with her parted lips and wiggled beneath him. The distraction worked, and a short time later Lucas's kiss swallowed her soft scream of pleasure.

He levered his head down to her shoulder and fought to breathe evenly. "Primed...."

Nuzzling his hair and stroking his back, cherishing the way he'd given himself to her, Chastity hated to move. "Mmm."

"You are always primed, buttercup. Sweet and soft—"

Chastity shifted beneath him, holding him when he would have shifted aside. "Dear, I hope I didn't make too much noise."

Lucas's rich chuckle filled the room. "Scared the birds out of the trees outside."

"Goodness. Lucas, we've got to do something."

"Yep," he whispered hoarsely, moving deeply within her.

Then she laughed, holding him closer. He wanted

her urgently and when she held him, stroking his hard shivering body until he slept, Chastity smiled in the darkness. Lucas Walkington would share more than his body with her, he would share his life.

''A man doesn't have to be social to love his daughters,'' Lucas snapped as he lifted Chastity up to the saddle. The Saturday after the Walkington's first Friday-night party was wonderful, filled with blue sky and Chastity ready for anything. Then the horse shifted and she screamed for Lucas, falling down into his arms.

He eased her back up into the saddle with a sharp, ''Sit and hush up. You scream and Liz might run or buck.''

''It's so far down to earth,'' Chastity whispered, gripping the saddle horn with both hands. Lucas swung up behind her and Chastity turned to wrap her arms around him. His legs tightened and the horse began to walk slowly.

His lips brushed her temple and stayed there, his arms strong and secure around her. ''I managed to live through that party last night. You can manage this.''

''Lucas, he's so wide! What if we fall?'' she asked from beneath his chin.

''Liz is a she, Raven's horse. You won't be able to ride for long with the baby coming. Tell me what you learned about having a baby from the women Friday night.'' The horse walked slowly toward the grazing cattle.

''Uh...Lucas, I'll make an appointment with Dr. Blackwell in Muggins when I can find transportation. We've ridden enough, haven't we?'' she asked hopefully. Liz stood near a cow, and Chastity clutched Lucas tighter. He probably wanted her to fall in a pit of cows to repay her for last night. She had worn the jeans, and when no one looked, Lucas's hand had smoothed her backside, a flush running beneath his dark skin, promising a long sensual night.

Lucas had taken her almost the minute the bedroom door closed that night. Of course he hadn't had a choice really. High on the party's success, she'd leaped on him, kissing him with all the joy in her. Duty-bound to respond, Lucas had answered the call magnificently.

"You wanted to ride," he said flatly. Then, "Transportation. Like the local transit system? I'll take you."

"The saddle is squeaking. Maybe you should oil it."

Lucas kissed her hard. "Oil that, buttercup. Stop talking. You rattle like a jaybird when you're scared."

"You're frightened, too. Your Code of the West, or almighty male rules, prevent you talking about it."

Lucas scowled down at her, his old Stetson shading his face. "That's bull—" Her set expression stopped him from finishing the word. "You're pushing, lady. Leave well enough alone."

"Leave well enough alone," Chastity repeated darkly after Lucas's pickup soared off into the night. The storm had been brewing all day. Raven and Summer stared at her, their young faces white beneath green mud masks. Chastity shook with anger that only Lucas had been able to raise. "Just where is he going at ten o'clock at night?"

"Maybe you shouldn't offer to help Daddy do the bills," Summer hesitantly suggested.

"Or ask what he's done about college preparation or looking into grants and aids," Raven added. "Telling him that not using coupons was like throwing away money could have riled him a little."

"Your father isn't an easy man, I'll admit that."
Chastity inhaled, counted to ten and repeated her question, "Where is he going?"

"Mike's probably. It's a tavern in Chips. He hasn't been there for ages, but he's been looking like he wants to hole up."

"Hole up. Hide. From me. In a corner pub." Chastity was too angry to be hurt. "Help me pick out something to go with my new jeans, then take me to Mike's."

She paused, then said, "His hat never leaves his head unless he takes it off. Does the wind ever...or a limb...?"

"Daddy's hat never comes off unless he wants it off," Summer said flatly.

"Hmm." Just once, she promised, Lucas's hat would tumble away without his consent.

Nothing could have stopped her from dressing like Honey. She knew how to act like a barroom sweetie; once she had to track down a con man who had taken the Old Coot for a hundred dollars. She patted her flat stomach. "Daddy has a few rules to learn, sweetheart. If he wants to socialize, he can do it with us."

Lucas sipped his beer and sulked. He'd missed sulking since Chastity had arrived. A man deserved a real good sulk once in a while, especially since he'd found his brand-new wife could throw herself at him and every lick of horse sense he'd ever had sailed out into the night.

He stroked the cool perspiration on his beer mug thoughtfully. Chastity fascinated him, and if he were a kid he'd probably be in love with her. Soft and warm, she eased away the pain of his life. He'd have to gain some control or he'd fly apart when she left.

When she started talking about coupon savings and saving money, his pride had lurched. He'd wanted to take care of her, take her burdens; then suddenly she was exploring cost-saving ideas at the dinner table and riling him. He wanted to swathe her in care, keeping away the burdens she'd taken from her family.

Chastity deserved real parties, not put-together open houses with the neighbors pitching in casseroles and Jethro Ferguson's harmonica solo. Chastity's jeans had set him off, and he'd been in a froth from the moment he caught her body's sweet scent.

Chastity deserved more than part of a family ranch, a budget that didn't stretch and a man going nowhere fast.

A low wolf whistle and two catcalls brought Lucas's head up from his mug of beer. In the dark, smoky room filled with tables, chairs, a bar and a jukebox, a curvy blond woman with tight-fitting jeans walked toward him. The dim light traced a halo around a mass of curls that lay on her bare shoulders, then slipped down to touch the black knit top with long sleeves. The jeans hugged her waist and molded her hips and thighs, sliding down to her high-heeled boots.

She placed one of those high-heeled boots between his feet as he sprawled in a chair. "Hi, babe." Honey's sexy voice wrapped around him like a soft glove.

Lucas slashed an angry glance up at her as she sat on his knee. Every head in the tavern turned to them. Honey traced his lips with her tongue and her mouth slid into that mysterious, sloping smile.

"Hey, Lucas," Brad Koenig yelled. "Is that your wife?"

Honey waved airily, identifying herself. She draped her arm around Lucas's shoulder and waited, green eyes challenging him beneath her lashes. She ran a finger up his taut neck, scooped his hat off and placed it on her head.

Lucas wanted to sink into his sorrows, sulk and wallow, keeping the pain from his family. But there Honey sat, tilting his too-large hat back on her rippling, dark blond curls and surveying her new kingdom from his knee. He bounced that knee to jostle her and found himself meeting her grin. "You're ornery, woman," he muttered, suddenly happy and unwilling to show it.

"This is nice. I like this," she said, nodding as she looked at the various couples dancing and the usual byplay of single men and women. "The Old Coot, my grandfather, used to take me to places like this when I was little. He taught me how to play pool."

"Is that right?" Lucas had the feeling that no matter where his wife found herself, she could manage.

"Mmm. He felt sorry for me, I guess. Mother was so involved with Brent and Hope. Old Coot kept me so busy that I never missed being included…well, later, they needed me and things changed. He made me feel special, like I had secret talents all my own."

Pris Perkins eased her way to stand next to them. She moved the tray of empty glasses to her other hand and tugged down the tight, red satin blouse over her jeans. She skimmed Chastity's outfit, obviously comparing them mentally. Her glance at Lucas invited and challenged. "Does the lady want a drink, Luke?"

"Mineral water with lime, please," Chastity said, watching the other woman closely. Pris's painted eyes were hostile, her mouth tight beneath the glossy red-red lipstick. Unable to bear the thought of another woman in Lucas's arms, Chastity's fingers tightened almost painfully on Lucas's shoulder. "So, the first good tiff we have you run to one of your ex-loves, huh? That will have to stop, babe."

"Yes, ma'am," Lucas drawled, setting back to watch Chastity. She fascinated him, a creature who moved between people and worlds and sensed pain, probing it out with soft, delicate fingers, then stroking the wounds until they eased.

Chastity's fingers drummed his shoulder, her lips tightening. "Yes, I suppose that what's in the past is done. You would have had relationships...." She chewed on that, glanced at the jukebox and stood, tugging him to stand. "Let's dance, babe. You've done enough sulking."

Lucas lay tangled with his sleeping wife hours later and wondered what hit him.

Wiggling up and over him, Chastity yawned. "I've never made love in a sleeping bag before, sweetcakes. We're lucky you had one in the pickup."

He stroked her hair, savoring the fresh clean scent that blended with the smells of the earth and new grass. "Your experience is limited."

Kissing one side of his mouth, then the other, Chastity tugged his hair. "You should know." Then, for a long time, Lucas's world was soft and sweet, easing away the years of strain.

Chastity rubbed her cheek against his chest. "Babe, I'm ready to listen."

Lucas caught her head, held her lips against him, her body tight. In a matter of days, they would know about the baby. Whatever happened, he didn't want to let Chastity leave him.

"I'm not going anywhere, Lucas," she whispered, stroking his shoulder.

"The Walkington land was once four hundred acres," Lucas began slowly, nuzzling the fragrant curls that drifted around him on the midnight breeze. His arms tightened around her, keeping her close to soothe the pain. "My great-grandparents claimed it in the land run on Oklahoma territory. My grandparents added to it, and my folks died holding hands in a blizzard while I was off sowing wild oats. The sod house my great-great-grandparents built was on the land I sold when I was twenty-one and trying to impress Alesha. It seemed right back then. I couldn't handle the stock, the land or a high-priced girl who wanted to play."

He closed his eyes, the tear trail cold on his temples. "Someone should have put me out of my misery. When I dropped off the roller coaster we were on, two hundred acres were gone, oil rigs bobbing up and down on the old Walkington spread. By the time I came to my senses, Alesha was pregnant."

Chastity's hand was soft against his cheek. "You were young, Lucas. You can't blame yourself for eternity."

"I didn't buy much with the money, but hard times. Most of it's gone now and my daughters' heritage with it.... Hard thing for a man to swallow...that he had sold away his family's future."

"Oh, sweetheart, you were young."

Lucas swallowed, his throat hurting with emotion. He hadn't shared the pain, and now he found himself trembling. "The water went with the land. We're on the dry side. In the summer I haul water for the cattle."

"Shh." Her fingertip sealed his lips and Lucas kissed it. "Everything will be just fine."

"Uh-huh," he tossed back, disbelieving. "Sure."

"One thing at a time, Lucas-babe," Chastity mur-mured, moving over him.

He remembered laughing before the tropical storm took him.

Chapter 8

The moment Lucas placed Chastity on her feet behind their bedroom door, he started unbuttoning her blouse. He hadn't said an entire sentence on their way home from the doctor in Muggins, and Chastity fought her tears. She wanted him to do all those fabulous, endearing things expectant fathers did, but not her babe.

The bright April morning sunshine shot through the windows and Wayne whined beyond the closed door. Lucas tipped back his hat and unbuttoned the front of her skirt, almost tearing the fabric.

"Well," she exclaimed in a soft whoosh as he tugged her slip, panty hose and briefs to her ankles. Bracing her hand on his shoulder as he jerked her undergarments off and tossed the bundle into a chair, Chastity drummed her fingers on the solid muscle. "Well," she said again when he stripped off her bra. "This is nice. Yes. Very nice indeed. Classy. Cowboy learns for certain that he's going to be a father again after many years. Cowboy takes wife home and strips her.''

Chastity crossed her arms across a swelling bosom that Lucas bent to study intently. ''It's all the same basic equipment you married,'' she said between her teeth as his open hand skimmed down her stomach, flattening over it.

''Hush,'' he ordered gently, turning her around to study her backside. Two big hands slid down her ribs to her hips, his thumbs stretching to touch in the center. Then turning her slowly again, Lucas lifted her hair back from her throat and pried her arms away.

''This isn't quite how I thought you'd react, babe,'' she muttered as he traced her jawbone, sliding his hands down to cup her breasts. He concentrated on the rounded weight, lightly running his fingers across her sensitive nipples.

''Mmm?'' he asked in a distant tone, continuing to study her stomach, probing it gently with his thumbs.

''Sweetcakes, you don't act extremely happy,'' Chastity said evenly, despite the anger and fear raging inside her.

To balance her simmering emotions, she tossed at him, ''Do you know that your hat always stays on until you take it off? I mean the wind never moves it. It never falls off. That can be very irritating at times.''

When she had cornered him in a stall, the hat had tilted awry as they made love, but remained in place.

''Stetson,'' he returned in a distracted tone, as if the brand name explained everything.

''Oh.''

Lucas flattened both hands low on her stomach, frowning. ''Babies kick at four and a half to five months, the doctor said.... You're just six weeks along— It's real then,'' he whispered huskily, lifting his eyes to hers.

She loosened her fists. One more minute of Lucas's grim treatment, and she was prepared to hit the nearest dimple. Not that he'd been showing them lately.

The wonder and excitement she'd wanted shimmered in the tears shining in Lucas's dark blue eyes. Every dram of the sweet new father expression swirled around Lucas's face, lifting his mouth in a silly, boyish, dimple-creasing grin. He spanned her waist with shaking, callused hands. ''It's true. I was afraid.... A baby. It's going to kick, right there in your soft little belly.''

Chastity began to smile, then Lucas's face paled. ''I...I feel weak.'' Before she could grab him, he sprawled backward on the bed.

''Lucas!'' As she bent over him, Lucas snared her hand weakly.

''Where are the girls?'' His voice was weak, and a fine perspiration glowed on his forehead.

''In school. They'll be home in a few hours.'' Badly frightened, Chastity leaned over him to place her hand on his cold, damp forehead. She smoothed a thick wave back from his brow. ''What's wrong, sweetheart?''

''Let me lay here a minute. I'm winded, that's all. Don't let the girls see me like this,'' he rasped unevenly, then closed his eyes. His lashes lay black and lush against his paling complexion.

''Lucas, you're scaring the daylights out of me! Wake up!'' Chastity slapped him hard, trying to remember where the emergency telephone numbers were located.

''Hey! Lay off,'' Lucas mumbled, rubbing his damaged cheek. She noted that like that of a true cowboy,

Lucas's hat had remained on his head. His fall had merely tilted the angle.

His grin was devastating, all tanned angles and dimples and shining blue eyes with black lashes. The room's filtered sunlight bounced off his teeth in a blinding ray. Chastity jerked his belt buckle upward hard. "You low-down yahoo. You're scaring me to death."

"Must have had too much sun.... You, Mrs. Walkington, are one-hundred-percent certified pregnant with my baby."

"Of course I am. That's no reason to faint. Lucas, you need a doctor."

He drew her palm to his lips and kissed it. "I didn't faint. Just feeling a little tired. Ever slap a man before?"

The delicate nibbling around her palm excited and soothed. "I've never had reason to, Lucas."

He tugged her down beside him, laying on his side to study her. Running his thumb along her jawbone, he noted, "You've gotten a little rounder here."

His hand opened, running along her throat and down to cup her breast. "Why did you slap me, buttercup?"

"I once had to save Brent from a mean, muscular bill collector. We faked his fainting spell to get Brent to safety. I had to slap him quite hard to make it believable."

"So I got the slap of experience, right?"

Chastity snuggled up to him, slipping her hand inside his dress shirt to stroke his broad chest. "Only because I care, babe. Now tell me why you acted like Granite Man at the doctor's."

The seconds stretched into her heart, making it ache. She'd wait until forever to understand his pain. Lucas studied the shafts of afternoon light crossing into the room, his lashes catching it in blue-black tints. ''After Alesha found out she was pregnant, we never made love again. Had the devil's own time persuading her to keep the babies. When she found out she carried twins, all hell broke loose.''

He turned slowly to her, his expression tight with pain. ''She was gone to her folks more than not. Wouldn't let me touch her, or see the changes in her body. I couldn't live with a woman carrying my baby and not share the experiences as it became real.'' The grim lines settled around Lucas's mouth.

Chastity removed his hat and tossed it to a bedpost. ''Learned that from one of mother's beaux.'' She pushed her fingers through Lucas's hair, letting the texture and warmth slip along her skin. ''I'm not Alesha. You're sweet, Lucas.''

He snorted at that. ''The hell you say. When we made love that first time, I gave a part of myself to you. That's why I pushed so hard to get you back here with me. There's not much here, but what there is belongs to my children, all of them.'' He rubbed her stomach, bending to kiss it.

Her fingers tightened in his hair, keeping him near, and Lucas lifted his eyes questioningly. She wanted to tell him she loved him, to ask if he might care, but the dark blue eyes were heating, flowing over her breasts hungrily. Could he love her? Could he tuck his first experience at love in a drawer and open his heart? ''Lucas…I…''

He kissed her stomach again lower and Chastity sucked in her breath, tensing.

The third kiss sent her into trembling shudders while Lucas watched intently. When she blushed, he chuckled. "Sweet bit, maybe we'd better start taking walks after supper. The doctor said to exercise...." The wicked look in his eyes deepened her blush.

"Wicked man," Chastity mumbled at seven the next morning, long after Lucas had gone out to check on the cattle. Later he would help Orvy Holiday lay bricks and pour concrete for an addition to his house.

While Lucas worked and the girls were at school, the echo of her soft scream had clung to her for hours. High and quivering it had swept through the damp night air hovering over the meadow, startling her. She glanced darkly at Wayne who sat amid piles of papers near the bedroom desk. Chastity balled another scrap of paper and tossed it at him, which he dutifully caught in his teeth and placed in a growing pile of wadded balls.

She jotted a number on a column in Raven's discarded notebook. "I am to rest. I am to put my little feet up, take vitamins and rest. I am not a partner in this marriage. *I am a love-toy for a babe*. A cowboy whose hat never, ever tips or tilts or leaves his head unless he wishes. *He* makes decisions for me, just as though I was one of the twins. *He* says..." she lowered her voice in mock male tones "...'Stay in the house, take your itty-bitty nap while I fight the world and take the bruises on my big wide cowboy shoulders.'"

Had she told him she loved him in the night's passionate heat?

Wayne, a good listener, tilted his head and flopped to his feet with a snort. Chastity continued to sort, file, and jot figures into the notebook. Lucas's bookkeeping consisted of his mysterious notes, a drawer of canceled checks and an assortment of coupons from magazines, clearly clipped by young girls wanting cosmetics, body waves and perfumes. Chastity checked the expiration dates on the coupons, sorted them into neatly marked envelopes and addressed an envelope for a rebate ticket. Stacking Lucas's farm, seed and cattle magazines neatly, she carried them to the kitchen and began clipping coupons and rebates.

By the time Melody arrived, without her children, to share morning coffee, Chastity was picking through cereal boxes and peeling labels off detergent bottles for coupons. "I've never gotten into that, but they say you can save a lot if you work at it."

Chastity blew back a curl and snipped around a discount coupon for men's jeans. She'd been couponing since Old Coot bought her a special pair of non-sharp children's scissors. Until his last years in the nursing home, the Old Coot was the guardian of the coupons, a task she had inherited with his talent. Necessary to balance her mother's poor management, the coupons provided everything. As a child, Chastity accompanied the Old Coot to various waiting rooms with the sole purpose of snipping coupons. A child went unnoticed, and the task occupied her for an hour or so until Old Coot delegated another waiting room. She spent many hours happily clipping the coupons that the Old Coot had stealthily noted. "The trick is in organizing. I'm sending off for an organizer that comes with this coupon for soap."

"Mmm…what does Lucas think about coupons?" Melody asked cautiously over the rim of her cup.

"They're great. What else would he think?"

"That man has too much pride. He needed help watering stock a few years ago. The only way he'd take help was if he could pay them back. When he lost that hay crop two years ago and the girls had complications from the flu, we thought he would kill himself working to pay everyone back. He did look real cute behind John's counter measuring out laces and ribbons. He's stiff-backed, Honey. You might work up to the subject and see what he thinks, before you act.''

"Rubbish. Coupons are an American right,'' Chastity quoted Old Coot.

"You might ask, just the same. Lucas might consider it some kind of charity.'' Then Melody went on about her children and marveled at Chastity's plants. Encompassing an entire corner, they would be moved to the porch in warmer weather. The new friends spent the next hour visiting over seed catalogs, which Chastity thought was a marvelous Oklahoma right.

Longing for a garden, Chastity asked the younger woman's advice, and together they walked around the new garden plot. "It needs volunteer plants like garlic and winter onions. Maybe sage... There are things that come up every year. How about a ladies' coffee some morning, and I'll ask everyone to bring a plant or something for the garden? Maybe some berry starts and daffodils. That old elderberry bush down by Lucas's windmill always has berries. You need water for other berries, Honey, and this land is dry. In the summer, we use every barrel, every kiddie pool, to hold water for our gardens.''

She grinned widely. "You'll have a pool in the yard, just like everyone else before long.''

Chastity returned the grin, running her hand down her stomach. "I just can't believe it. The baby is such a long time away. Nothing seems real yet.''

"Better enjoy it. Lucas is walking on air, but he needs to stop working so hard.'' Melody shrugged, running her hand down her rounded tummy. "Doctor and hospital bills are high. Marlene Kleinhoffer is a great midwife, has been for years. She'd love to work with you and whatever doctor you're using."

"Lots of neighborhoods in Chicago have them. I'd love that."

Chastity spent the afternoon alternately coveting seed catalogs with fruit trees and berries and developing a clear picture of Lucas's finances. He paid cash, tossed receipts into boxes, wrote few checks on a small account and contributed irregular deposits to the twins' savings.

Tapping a pencil on her bottom lip, Chastity walked around the house and thought deeply about her relationship with Lucas. He kept his fears neatly tucked away, growled at those who came too close and was frustrated by the growing breach between him and the twins. Clearly Lucas was deeply tired, physically— well, not always, she allowed—and mentally. The baby and herself would be added expenses if he were to have his way.

Chastity frowned and adjusted her glasses. She had never been anyone's excess baggage and she wouldn't let Lucas take that away from her. No babe was going to stand in his well-fixed jeans and— She inhaled slowly, forcing her anger away, and thinking logically as the Old Coot had taught her to do when planning scams. She, Lucas, the girls and the baby were a family and a family shared responsibilities. She would not live on the borders of another family as she had in Chicago, existing when they chose to recognize her.

"Daddy won't like it," Raven said firmly, hours later.

"Daddy hasn't had time to go to school. There are

financial aids and grants available for us. We brought home the forms, but he seems to think college is a cash basis only. The other kids' parents went to the advisor and worked with him. There's stuff available if you send off for it," Summer added. "But Daddy is always tired and we—we argued a lot before you came. We want to date, Chastity, and Daddy is acting like an old—"

"Fuddy-duddy?" Chastity supplied, and grinning. "He's not at all. He loves you and he wants the best for you." She suspected Lucas's fears ran to seeing the girls make his youthful mistakes.

Over sandwiches drinks, and clipping coupons the girls chattered about school events and the special boys they wanted to date. The boys were interested, but Lucas stood between young love like an enraged, battle-wise sheepdog tending lambs. Later, as they showed Chastity how to milk a cow, they talked about clothes and how they wanted to dress. "Clothes shouldn't be a problem," Chastity said, concentrating on a plump, milk-filled udder.

"Jeans are practical. There are skirts and blouses, too. Mother took us shopping, but we left those things at her house. They weren't our style, anyway. Daddy would know how much brand-name clothing costs and it might…well, hurt him."

Chastity tried to avoid the cow's swishing tail. "What about thrift shops or garage sales? I always loved the things from used clothing stores. They didn't cost that much and you could make them over to be just great. I worked at a dry cleaner's after school for an entire year and learned how to tailor." She omitted the family obsession with stylish clothes and how she had altered endlessly.

"There's a used clothing store in Muggins," Raven ventured. "But won't people recognize their own throwaways?"

"Nope. Not after refashioning and dyeing. Why does that calf keep mooing?"

"That's Lacy's calf. She has plenty of milk, but Angel doesn't want to share." Summer lifted the bucket, scanning it. "Dad gives the cream to Mrs. Nelson for butter. She took care of us last year when we had the flu. Daddy worked right through his flu."

Chastity stood and rubbed her hands on her thighs, scanning the calves playing in the fields. Her babe, her sweetcakes, had a mountain to learn about sharing and giving and relationships and loving.

As if on cue, Raven warned, "Daddy won't like you organizing his business desk. He likes to keep that stuff to himself."

"Not anymore," Chastity promised flatly.

At ten o'clock that night, Lucas's pickup stopped in front of the house. Wayne barked frantically, wagging his tail, and barreled out of the door the minute Chastity opened it. Lucas entered the house, his hat dusty, his jeans and workman's boots gray with concrete dust. Carrying Wayne on his hip, he sighed, slid a one-dimple smile in her direction and opened the refrigerator door, scanning the contents.

When he tipped back his hat, the appliance's light spread across his face. Beneath the dirt, lines of fatigue ran deep.

"Hi, Daddy." Raven and Summer looked up from stacks of clothing, the old portable sewing machine reigned over a jumble of thread and cloth on the kitchen table.

Chastity stood in the shadows and ached. Barely

standing upright, Lucas eased Wayne to the floor and patted the dog's curly head. Then he found her in the shadows and his eyes lit up. "Hi, Mrs. Walkington," he said in that low, intimate twang.

"Hi, babe," she returned, her stomach contracting painfully, while her heart raced as the dark blue eyes slid over her.

Lucas's gaze seemed to inhale every inch of her body beneath his oversize shirt. "Come here."

The gentle command spoke of hunger and need, and Chastity could not refuse. Standing in front of him, she lifted her lips and kissed him with all her heart amid the twins' catcalls. When the kiss was finished, Lucas closed his eyes and leaned his forehead against hers.

Vulnerable and weary, he nuzzled her cheek and Chastity wrapped her arms around him tightly. "I missed you, babe," she whispered against his lips and nibbled at them until she felt the tug of his lazy smile.

She rubbed her hand across his back and Lucas sighed, his body rippling beneath her touch like a big cat being petted. "If you shower, I'll fix dinner."

"I meant to start stew this morning, but had other things on my mind," he whispered huskily. "You shouldn't be cooking. You should be resting."

She grinned while Lucas showered. No matter how tired that Oklahoma babe was, he always made her feel desirable. He grumbled at the dinner she had warmed, a mock beef Stroganoff with noodles, and ate half the coffee cake she had baked that morning. While he was grumbling and managing a conversation with the girls about schoolwork, Lucas rubbed Wayne's belly with his toes. He toyed with her fingers as he ate and finished his iced tea, the area's standard beverage. In a weary voice Lucas informed her that before dawn, he would rise to help Sam Ledbetter fertilize a south pasture and repair fence.

He looked so tired and sweet, she didn't have the heart to tell him that coupons, financial aids and grants, and boyfriends for his daughters lurked in his future. Or that she had organized his desk and the twins and herself were shopping at the Muggins used clothing store next Saturday. Or that John's grocery, feed and grain had acquired an at-home, Johnny-come-lately Chicago-bred bookkeeper.

Or that she loved him very much.

"What the hell happened to my desk? Where are my papers?" Lucas's indignant roar shook the bedroom before dawn. He ripped open the scarred desk's drawers, glared at the neat arrangements and opened a shoe box filled with alphabetical envelopes that were stuffed with clipped coupons. "What is this?" he asked between his teeth, thumbing through the coupons.

Struggling up from the tangled bedding, clinging to Lucas's pillow and keeping his scent close at hand, Chastity blew away the curls from her face that he had nuzzled sweetly throughout the night. She struggled with the sweet tingles Lucas had created with his love-making sometime during the night and the scowling cowboy glaring down at her.

Legs spread wide, his jeans unsnapped and his shirt unbuttoned, Lucas didn't look sweet and vulnerable. Not at all the man who had held her as if she were a part of him, not the vulnerable man who had let her comfort her with caresses and soft kisses. She cleared her throat, pasting an innocent baby-doll expression on her face, and wished that she had told him everything last night.

"Now, sweetcakes. The girls are still sleeping." She smiled the Honey smile à la Hope's instructions.

"I can understand the sewing mess and the girls wanting to show you off at school and meet their teachers. I can understand chaperoning the school prom two weeks away. Females are likely to be in cahoots. I expected that from the start. Women make nests. There's female bonding and such…but, by God, you will leave my desk alone!"

Chastity shifted on the bed, covered her bare shoulder with a blanket and couldn't keep the baby-doll smile from slipping. She bit her lower lip to keep it from trembling. Lucas sat on the bed, jammed his feet into socks and never let his sizzling blue stare leave her face.

His silent challenge was too much. "You needed help," Chastity explained. "Organization. I'm a book-keeper and—"

"Git." Wayne's wagging stub of a tail stopped and he slunk into the living room.

"Be reasonable, Lucas—" Chastity began when Lucas stood and began buttoning his shirt in angry, jerking movements. "I'm only two months' pregnant. I've been an active, useful person my entire life. You can't expect me to live off you without—"

"I take care of my family, lady. Since you snooped, you probably know just how little we have."

"I've lived on the outside of one family, Lucas," Chastity shot back, aware that no one but her babe and sweetcakes had the ability to draw anger out of her like wildfire igniting tinder. "I will not be less than I am with my own husband, low-down macho cowboy, dimpled cheeks and devastating charm, ornery as you are, Lucas Walkington. Your finances are my finances and they're not that bad. A little reorganization can help you save time and money. Using coupons and investing the girls' savings accounts into better-earning interest accounts is a simple matter.''

He grabbed the Stetson, plopped it on the back of his head and stared at her.

''Don't try to frighten me like you do your daughters, babe,'' Chastity said grimly.

''You messed up my desk.'' The quiet accusation was a roar of anger and indignation.

''Organization. Files. I'm good at that.'' She omitted the singular talent the Old Coot had bestowed upon her. If Lucas couldn't digest organization, he certainly wasn't ready for a water witch. Of course she had brushing up to do before trying her abilities. Lately forks had been quivering in her hand when she concentrated on the dripping faucet and...

''Lady, you are to rest and let me take care of you,'' Lucas began heavily.

''I have been taking care of myself for years, Mr. Walkington. I have capabilities and talents you haven't even guessed,'' she tossed back, jerking on his T-shirt, which had been tossed aside during their tender lovemaking.

''Uh-huh. Troublemaking and what else?''

The challenge was too much and Chastity hit him with a pillow, lunging for him and taking him down to the bed. She climbed over him and held his wrists to the pillow like a wrestler pinning an opponent. When he grinned, pulling out the dimples, she realized that he had fallen too easily. The words she had been holding sailed out into the pink dawn beyond their room. ''I'm clipping coupons, managing *our* records, working as John's part-time bookkeeper, growing my garden and loving you.''

She hadn't noticed Lucas's body tensing beneath her, the sudden, dazed surprise in his expression, nor the way his fingers had curled around hers. She took a deep breath and released her untried secret into the sweet, morning air. ''Lucas, I am a water witch.''

''You love me,'' he repeated unevenly, his expression stunned as he ignored the admission of her lifelong secret.

''Of course. True, you're not a logical choice. Entirely too proud. But I do and that's that.'' Chastity blew a bobbing curl away from her left eye. She hoped she hadn't frightened him with her water witch admission. Any minute he would suggest therapy. She could tell by the sweet, dazed, confused expression on his bearded face.

The telephone by the bed rang and Lucas reached for it, at the same time jamming a pillow behind his back. His gaze ran over her face and Chastity inhaled sharply. Learning that one's wife was a water witch— true, an untried water witch—could be a shattering experience for the poor dear. A sinking-ship feeling centered in her chest and slid slowly to the pit of her stomach. She swallowed as he frowned, listening to the caller. ''She's right here.''

Placed at a time when she was most vulnerable, the call was from her mother. Chattering about Brent's love affairs and bill collectors and Hope's quest for Lyle, because his wife didn't understand him, nor his three children, Grace took a breath and asked, ''How are you, precious?''

''Precious'' was hauled on her new husband's lap and being cuddled and being kissed sweetly. No doubt

Lucas wanted to calm her before suggesting an analyst. While she tried to concentrate on her mother's delicate pleas for help in managing another credit card fiasco, Chastity focused on Lucas's dimples.

He nibbled on her earlobe and whispered, "You tell her she can go to—"

"What?" Grace squawked while Lucas nibbled his way to Chastity's throat. "Is Lucas saying something, dear?"

Chastity tried to concentrate. The task was difficult. Lucas was unwrapping her from blankets and sheets as though she were his special birthday gift. Poor dear, he hadn't realized that she wasn't lean and leggy yet. "We'll go the coupon route and you can file to your little heart's content," he whispered, studying her body in the morning shadows, his expression filled with wonder as his thumb traced her hipbone.

Her heart quivered, pounding rapidly. Tender and vulnerable, Lucas placed his dark hand across her stomach, moving it gently around the smooth contour.

"Mother, buy a calculator," Chastity said huskily, enchanted by Lucas's expression of awe. "I'll write you when we're more settled. Oklahoma is wonderful—yes, I said get a calculator. Hope can balance your checkbook. Check the expiration date on the coupons. Bye."

Chapter 9

Chastity inhaled the clear May air and wiggled her bare toes in the dirt of her Oklahoma garden. She pushed Brent's plea—rescue from an adoring redhead whom he had promised to marry—into the clear blue sky. Her mother's voluminous package of overdue bills and various notices from credit-card companies rested in the Walkington's rural mailbox. Chastity had returned the packaged clutter with a simple note: "Mother, do not charge anything. Ask Hope or Brent to help you."

Then, because she loved her family, she'd managed to add, "You're a woman of courage. You couldn't have raised the three of us and managed Old Coot without a talent for balancing figures. A little patience and practice and you'll be fine. Tell Hope and Brent that I'm fine and I love you all."

She frowned at a tiny weed invading her precious piece of Oklahoma and bent to pluck it from her carefully planned rows of green beans. The garden was small, a delight to manage. Sage, garlic and winter onions nestled against an old picket fence that had stood in Lucas's great-grandmother's time. Wayne basked in the sun, annoyed by the calves he was not allowed to chase. He growled at the cattle, demonstrating his poodle ferocity. His nails gleamed with Summer's new Adorable Pink polish.

Chastity tenderly smoothed Lucas's worn shirt over her stomach, then hugged herself, keeping him close.

The Walkingtons were facing each other like dogs over a bone. The girls wanted to date, wanted all that they deserved as young women meeting life's trials. Lucas wanted to protect them from bruises. While the Walkingtons' love ran deep, a frontier showdown could occur if the matter weren't resolved and soon.

Construction of a new gym had begun, and Lucas had taken a job as a workman. Tired and snappy, he checked the stock before dawn, left for work and returned at nightfall, barely able to shower and fall into bed. The temporary job paid well, and Chastity sensed Lucas's desperation to provide for his family.

She'd watched him stare at the rise separating his ranch from the old one. At those times, his pain swirled around him like a dark, aching cloak, his expression grim.

The old windmill caught the wind, clacking away with three missing blades. The budding elderberry bush shimmered in the sun. Chastity stepped from her garden and wiggled her toes on the hard-packed earth. "It's a good scam, Old Coot. I'm just where I want to be. Though Lucas-babe is one tough nut to crack. He has far too much pride, and I suspect he is deeply afraid of losing this last part of his heritage."

Lucas's lovemaking was contained, gentle and beautiful. She wanted the desperation, the intensity and the flame of his desire before the doctor's examination.

The wind riffled through the elderberry bush and Chastity stroked the baby who lay cradled in her womb. Lucas had given her his child and he would give her more—a life filled with happiness and love.

That night Lucas walked into the house, slammed the door behind him and ordered Wayne to "git."

Raven and Summer slid wary looks at Chastity, who took a deep breath and launched herself at him. She managed to tilt his dusty hat, the force of her body taking him back against the wall. While he tried to avoid her tiny kisses, she persisted and received a one-dimple smile. His hand stroked her back gently. "I hear the Walkington females have been busy."

The drawl sounded like a warning growl of a cornered wolf. One who wanted to fight.

Chastity patted his dimple, meeting his stormy blue stare innocently. "Things to do, people to see."

"John Blue Sky has a brand-new, nifty, bona fide Chicago bookkeeper. Says she works part-time, building credit on her account."

"That's me, Lucas. I told you I had taken a job—"

He swept that bit of information away like a clinging straw. "There you stand, barefoot and pregnant and *working when you shouldn't be.*" Lucas's indignant tone raised Chastity's hackles.

She smiled, wiggled her bare toes against the cool linoleum and forced the corners of her mouth to lift equally. "I'm used to working, Lucas. The girls pick up the invoices and cash tickets on their way home from school and deliver my work in the morning. It's a few hours spent punching a calculator on the kitchen table. I'm capable and there's no reason on earth why I shouldn't be working now.''

Lucas's jaw, dusted with concrete and rough with a day's stubble, locked in place. ''There's me. I say you take it easy.'' He glanced at the girls lying on the floor and watching television. ''While we're on the subject, who is doing all the cooking around here? Raven, Summer, you will not let—''

Both girls rose to their feet. The tall Walkingtons glared at each other over Chastity's head. ''Honey likes to cook, Dad,'' Raven said tightly.

''We like casseroles and pasta dishes, Dad. When her spinach comes in, we're having salad from it,'' Summer added.

''Uh-huh,'' Lucas returned in the same tone, unimpressed with Chastity's fresh spinach salad. ''I'm going out to the barn. Summer, fold those towels I washed this morning.''

''I folded them, Lucas,'' Chastity said quietly.

His blue eyes sliced down to her with the hardness of steel. ''You are to rest, lady, and quit that damn job!''

''You're cheating Honey, Dad,'' Summer stated flatly, tears brimming to her eyes. ''She's a modern woman, just like *we* want to be.''

''She knows things that could help and—'' Raven stopped when Lucas shot her a hard stare. She inhaled sharply, clutched her school notebook in her hand and said, ''Dad, if anyone is doing wrong by Honey, it's you—''

The whirlwind discussion slashed over Chastity's head and she fought for a way to smother it gently.

''Wrong by me? What do you mean?'' Lucas ripped

off his leather gloves and tossed them on the counter, glaring down at Chastity.

Wayne whined and Chastity's heart thudded in the stark silence. "Ah…dinner is waiting. It's a lovely tuna casserole." Chastity hoped that the tension would settle over her special tuna-noodle bake. Emily Newcomer's homegrown tarragon sprigs rested in her new batch of vinegar— "Honey is talented, Dad," Raven stated flatly. "She's a modern woman who rises to her challenges, just like we could be…*if you ever let us start dating.*"

Summer stood stiffly, tears dripping from her cheeks. "Dad, you've got to let us be us. Everything isn't always money and hard work, there's more…and if you don't stop acting like an old bear, you're going to lose Honey," she wailed, jumping over a stack of clothes and running into her room.

Raven straightened her shoulders, looked straight at Lucas, sniffed once and followed her sister, walking very straight. Lucas stared at the twins' closed bedroom door, his expression taut. He swallowed, ran his hand over his stubbled jaw, blinked and asked, "What happened?"

Chastity decided that the matter of shopping at Muggins's thrift shop could wait. She gripped her hands tightly. "I'm afraid I said we needed to express ourselves more…to work on our relationships—"

"Relationships? Communicate?" Lucas slashed at her. "Lady, I can communicate. *What I say goes.*"

The lordly tone settled on Chastity like spiny thistles on silk. She smiled tightly. "Is that so, Mr. Lucas-babe Walkington?"

"Are you checking out?" he snapped back. "Getting too rough for you?"

She tapped her toe. "Lucas, please don't make me lose my temper."

"Fine," he returned impatiently. "Look, this is the way it is. You need to rest—"

"I am so tired of that phrase, Lucas-babe," Chastity cautioned. "And the last time I rested, I found myself being stampeded into Oklahoma. I'm awake now and you have got to stop ordering me around." Her soft tone rose, the quiet yell infuriating her. Only Lucas could make her lose control, and she resented it.

"They are too young to date," he snapped doggedly, ignoring his campaign to lasso her.

"If they don't date here, Lucas, they will away from home. It might be wiser if you let them try their dating wings while living at home."

Lucas shot her a look of enraged fear. "You seemed happy enough. I thought puttering in that garden made you happy. Are you leaving me?"

She ached for him, the rigid pain digging into the lines on his face. His fists clenched at his thighs.

"You need me, Lucas, to keep you from getting old and set in your ways," she whispered softly, then stood on tiptoe to kiss his tight lips. She nibbled a bit at the hard contours until they softened slightly.

"Everything happened so fast," he whispered huskily, his hands smoothing her waist. "First they were little tadpoles and now…" The helpless tone slid inside her heart, causing it to ache.

Sliding her arms around him, Chastity held him tightly. "Everything will be just fine, Lucas-babe. Would you take a walk with me?"

The bedroom door jerked open. "Can we have dates for the prom, Dad?" Raven and Summer asked at the same time.

Chastity cuddled closer. "Say 'yep,' babe."

* * *

Lucas adjusted his tie, then jerked it loose while he watched his daughters dance in the boys' arms. "They're plastering themselves against my little girls," he muttered darkly as Chastity slipped into his arms to dance. He continued watching the twins over her head, his jaw moving as he ground his teeth. "Pimply, skinny things with *their hands on my girls' waists.*"

Chastity jerked him closer. "Raven and Summer want to date those pimply things."

His eyebrows shot up. "That Brewer kid and the Jones boy? I remember when they were born. That Brewer kid got stuck in a pipe when he was four and I had to haul him out. That Jones boy has never had a lick of horse sense."

"What do you think about the girls' dresses?"

Lucas continued to stare at the boys dancing with his daughters. "Told them to get one out of the catalog and charge it."

"You made them feel wonderful tonight, Lucas, when they were all dressed. They were proud of you, too," she began, wanting to tell him that the dresses would not appear on his charge card. "You were gallant, making them feel like princesses."

"They're my little girls. Scared me to see them all fixed up like grown women. Damn…look at that…"

Just then Mel Jones's cheek pressed against Raven's, and Chastity had to grip Lucas's belt to keep him against her. The time was not ripe to tell him that Raven and Summer wore gowns, purchased on discount and refashioned with satin and lace found in the bottom of a thrift-store box. The pink sequins splashing the gowns were pirated from Honey's dress.

Later, Lucas jerked the curtain away from the window and peered into the night. "It's late. Where are they?"

Chastity leaned against him, rubbing his taut rear end affectionately. "There's a breakfast at the Brewer's house after the prom."

"Stop that." Lucas pressed his hand over her roaming one as it slid inside his jeans.

"I'm proud of you, sweetcakes," Chastity whispered, cuddling against his broad back. "You only shot a glare or two when the four of them left."

"Those Brewer and Jones boys have been away at college for a year. No telling what they've learned."

Chastity nuzzled his muscled arm, loving to comfort him. "You're the one with growing pains."

"All this goes against the grain. They won't need me at all before long," Lucas muttered.

"They'll always need you and so will I," Chastity whispered against his mouth. "Come let me show you how much."

The first week of June, Lucas slapped his severance paycheck against his dusty jeans and settled back into the pickup seat to overlook the starry night. The construction had swung into another phase and the company used its own men to finish the building. All local work force was given a thank-you-very-much and a fat severance check.

"Lucas, your middle name is hard times," he muttered. With dry weather at his doorstep, a pregnant wife and looming doctor bills, his daughters needing dental care, he was out of work.

He'd swept Chastity from her safe job, her relatives, into another pit of needs.

Dreams really didn't last. He started the pickup, jammed it into gear and drove slowly into the ranch yard.

He managed to eat Chastity's pasta salad despite the hard lump in his stomach. The weed lurking in her special vinegar didn't make the spinach salad taste better. The twins' stories of boys, clothes, and cars slid off him like rainwater. When dinner was finished, Lucas sipped his iced tea, stroked his thumb over the beads of moisture on his glass and said, "I lost my job."

He explained briefly about the company using its own crews and petted Wayne, who had hopped up on his lap.

Chastity gripped her fork, which was shaking violently in the direction of the dripping water faucet. She placed it carefully on the table and reached for Lucas's hand. The twins avoided looking at him, waiting for the worst.

"Lucas, don't worry so. This would be a perfect time for you to enclose the porch for another room."

"Money, Chastity. Boards and nails cost. Feed costs, gas and food—"

"My garden is doing beautifully. We've got time to enlarge it. I've always wanted to preserve food. It's much more healthy."

"Water, Chastity. A large garden takes plenty of water. Then there's the baby—"

Raven lifted her head. Fear quivered in her voice as she said, "You're not selling Rosebud."

"Of course, he's not. Rosebud is too precious," Chastity said as Lucas took a deep breath. "He hasn't even thought of selling your calf, Raven."

"He's selling Rosebud," Raven said flatly. Then,

when Lucas did not deny it, she jumped up and ran to her bedroom.

"Not Rosebud," Summer said quietly before following her sister.

"That heifer will bring good money at an auction," Lucas said doggedly when Chastity turned to him.

"Lucas, surely there's another way...."

"Not likely. Lady, you married a loser," Lucas bit out as he stood, reaching for his hat. Then Chastity was at the door, holding her arms across her chest, blocking him from licking his wounds alone.

"You haven't discussed alternatives with me, Lucas-babe. You just drop your decision on the table like a piece of muscle-tissue-meat-roast, and expect us to accept it. Perhaps you should have shared this problem with me before upsetting Raven. Husbands and wives do communicate, you know."

Because he was hurting, Lucas hit hard. "We sure did. Look where it got you."

"Maybe I'm happy here. Except for your stubborn streak, everything has been just lovely."

"You traded one bunch of needy relatives for another—" Lucas stopped, blinked and picked up his hat, which Chastity had neatly knocked off his head. "Why in the hell did you do that?"

"If you're going to feel sorry for yourself, you might as well do it without your hat. I've been wanting to do that for ages. Another thing..." She took a deep breath and propped her hands on her waist before continuing. Lucas had the feeling that she was winding up to hit him. He peered down at her cautiously. For a gentle, understanding woman, his wife could launch attacks that frightened him.

"Another thing that bothers me, since we're finally

conversing, Lucas-babe, is that you have been holding
back—emotionally and physically. I want you to talk
to me, actually share your life—is that asking too
much? And another thing, *I am not Alesha.* I will not
break. I do not want to be treated like her.'' Chastity
brushed her hands as though she had just tossed a dirty
ball to him. ''There. We're conversing. See how simple
it is? I've laid out my problems. What are yours?''

'''Physically,''' Lucas repeated in a snarl. ''You
mean I'm not good in bed. Add that to losing my job
and you—''

''You are too careful, Lucas-dear.''

''You are pregnant, Chastity-sweetheart.''

She lifted her chin, determined to challenge him. Despite his pride, Lucas admired the fine anger brewing
within her. Chastity's cheeks turned pink, her green
eyes glistening. ''You've lost interest. You've taken
your punishment, lived up to your honor by bringing
me here and marrying me, and now *I'm not exciting to
you.*''

A tear shimmered on the tips of her lashes and
dripped to her cheek. ''Honesty, that's all I ask. Admit
you made a mistake and we can—''

''Don't say it.'' Lucas thought that she had never
been more lovely, more feminine. Her lips trembled
with emotions. ''You're the most exciting woman I've
ever known. You're so luscious and exciting I can
hardly keep my hands off you.''

Her expression lit up. ''Really, Lucas?'' All the tenderness was there, the sweet emotions tangling around
his frayed nerves. ''If you mean it, take me to the
barn,'' she challenged softly. ''But first tell Raven
she's not losing her calf.''

* * *

For days Lucas dealt with the echoes of Chastity's soft cries, the hunger on her lips and her body flowing into his. She loved him, gave herself fully to him, and he treasured each touch, each soft sigh, each scent. Fearing to love her fully, Lucas took what he could and gave it back twofold. He regretted that fear, damning Alesha for his scars.

The baby deserved parents who loved each other, and Lucas feared that he would fail again, unable to love Chastity. Fascinated by her warm, womanly instincts, he treasured her with his body and prayed that she would stay.

Two weeks later the well pump made odd grinding noises and he discovered that Chastity had watered her garden.

Chastity straightened from plucking a weed in her peas, slid her hand over the slight bulge in her abdomen. The baby had caused her to unsnap her cotton slacks waistband, and her tender breasts had enlarged. She scanned the Walkington land, smiled at the cattle and reveled in her happiness.

Lucas had begun taking time to talk to her. In fact, at every turn he told her exactly what bothered him.

The previous night he stared at her over a beautiful tossed salad and said flatly, "I like meat and potatoes. Salads don't cut it. A man's stomach can't be filled on fodder."

According to Lucas, the new fabric softener she had purchased with two detergent coupons smelled like flowers, and he wouldn't get caught in public wearing the scent. She learned that freshly ground pepper and coffee was for "people who have too much time." Hot tea was for sick people and elderly ladies. A new brand of soap bar caused an angry glare and a curse, something about being surrounded with women and flowers.

When she, Raven and Summer trimmed Wayne's curly coat to a proper poodle cut, Lucas held the dog on his hip. He plucked away the blue satin bow from Wayne's topknot and tossed it to the counter. Shooting them a menacing glare over his broad shoulder, he took Wayne with him to check the calves. "Don't ever sissify him again," he had ordered, holding the poodle like an endangered baby against him. He bent, sniffed Wayne's newly fluffed topknot and bit out, "Real dogs don't smell like perfume.

As he approached her now in the afternoon sunshine, Lucas's expression bore that same indignant look. He stopped at the end of her garden, tipped his hat back on his head with a jerk of his thumb and crossed his arms over his bare grease- and dirt-stained chest. "Having fun, lady? Watering your little garden to your heart's content?"

"Actually I watered this morning before the sun rose too high. The beans were looking droopy—" His scowl deepened and Chastity frowned. "What's wrong, Lucas?"

"Water gets tight out here. You're not in Chicago using a block hydrant. You've just washed clothes, taken a long shower and *you watered the hell out of the pump. The well is dry.*"

He jerked his thumb toward the patch of green grass in front of the house. "We've never had a grass yard before now. You know why, Miss Chicago Lady? Because of water. Of course there's one good thing, the faucets in the house will stop dripping."

Raven slid around the house to turn off the sprinkler

and Summer's worried face peered out of the open kitchen window.

"According to the predictions, there's a drought coming. A bad one," Lucas continued, wiping his hand across his jaw and leaving a grimy streak.

"Lucas, you're in a dither. Calm down. Summer, bring your father a glass of iced tea," Chastity called.

"Save the tea," Lucas ordered tightly. "We'll need it to water the grass.

Raven touched Lucas's arm, her eyes brimming with tears. "Dad, I just took a bath and used a whole tub of water."

But Lucas was centered on Chastity, who began picking her way toward him over the beans and fresh green lettuce. "Lucas, you are much too excited," she began.

"Excited?" he repeated nastily. "Tell the cattle that this summer when they want water. We buy it in barrels and haul it in dry weather."

"You're selling Rosebud," Raven said quietly, tears streaking her pale face.

"No, he's not. There's plenty of water and I've just been offered two more part-time bookkeeping jobs. The girls want to help and they're re-designing fashions from Muggins's thrift store for resale. Remember that chambray dress Raven wore to church? She made it out of two of your old shirts."

Lucas lifted his hat and ran his fingers through his hair with an air of deep frustration. "I don't know where you get the idea that there's water aplenty hereabouts. Whatever weird ideas you may have, *no Walkington female sleeping under my roof is going to take in work.*"

"Babe, I'm already working," Chastity sweetly reminded him.

"Then quit," he snapped, the muscle in his jaw working beneath the day's beard.

"Daddy!" Raven sobbed and ran toward the house.

Chastity angled her face up toward his. "I don't suppose you would like to retract that statement, would you, babe?"

He plopped the hat back on his head. "No."

"There is plenty of water here," she repeated quietly, despite the need to turn on the hose and cool Lucas from dusty hat to battered boots.

"Says who?" he shot back.

"The pregnant lady. I am a water witch, Lucas. There are three fingers of water beneath your land. Of course, you're so set on dishing out orders that *you're not listening to a word I say.*"

He stared down at her, clearly thinking the pregnancy had affected her mental processes. "Buttercup, maybe you'd better go lay down a bit. We can manage…. Maybe I flew off the handle—"

"The neighbors say that we're called dowsers in Oklahoma, but the principle is the same. Old Coot said I had his gift and I feel like there is water here, though I haven't had the time to research it properly." Chastity closed her eyes and wished for the control she possessed before Lucas entered her life. No one had ever stirred her into such a froth as her husband.

He lifted one eyebrow. "Are you serious? Have you told anyone else about…" Lucas cleared his throat "…about your gift?"

"Melody. She's promised to keep it a secret until you adjust to the idea. I thought I'd mention it again after you accepted the use of coupons and my other part-time jobs.''

"You're quitting John's. Don't take on any more. All this has been too much for you." Lucas rubbed his hand against his jeans to clean it of dust and touched her hot cheek.

Now was no time to fall before Lucas's disarming tenderness. Chastity slashed his hand away and pushed her damp curls back from her cheeks. "No Walkington female who works can sleep under your roof, is that so?"

Forced into a corner, attacked by a woman who didn't like confrontations, but who had evidently been affected by her pregnancy, Lucas muttered, "Yep."

That night Lucas lay alone in bed, his hands behind his head because there was no sweet, soft, cuddling pregnant female to hold.

Chastity had installed herself in a tent in the shade of a maple tree. The large, airy tent was one he and the girls had used years ago. His wife's grim determination to work had unsettled him. Raven and Summer had helped her, lugged one of their mattresses into the tent and ran an electric cord from the house for a lamp.

Lucas answered the soft knock on his door and his daughters entered, wearing his discarded and patched cotton shirts for nightgowns. "Daddy? Were you sleeping?"

"Not rightly."

The twins moved to his window and looked at Chastity's tent. "Daddy, you've got to do something," Raven whispered.

"She's alone out there," Summer added unevenly.

"She'll cool down," Lucas said, though he feared that Chastity would pack and leave at any moment.

"You're so…so unromantic, Dad," Raven said, holding the curtain away from the window.

"Pregnant women are emotional," Lucas returned huskily. "She's a practical lady. She'll sort things out and come back inside."

"No," the twins answered at the same time. "We wouldn't."

The night had been long and in the morning, Chastity poured his morning coffee. The shadows under her eyes said she didn't sleep any better than he had. Lucas couldn't find the words to soothe her, and in the next two days, the house and the meals were weighted in tense gloom.

Hattie McCord's dented, dirty pickup soared down the dusty lane to his ranch. She drove right up to his tractor, surged her two-hundred-plus pounds out of the cab and stalked toward him. "So you're making that nice little wife of yours sleep out in a tent. What's wrong with you, Lucas Walkington? Don't you know a good thing when it's right under your nose?" she demanded, shaking her finger at him. "You ought to be ashamed. Getting that girl pregnant and not letting her be herself. She's a hardworking woman who wants to fit in. You keep tossing that Walkington temper at her and she's bound to head off for Chicago town. You'd better bend, Lucas. Before you lose that sweet little thing and that Walkington baby she's carrying."

Lucas stared at the dust cloud trailing after Hattie's pickup, jammed his hat on tighter and flooded the old tractor.

Chapter 10

Lucas crossed his arms and leaned against the horse corral. He stared at Chastity's defiant little tent. The shadows of the trees danced around it in the moonlight, presenting a fortress that needed a siege. He knew better than to scoop up Chastity's soft body and plop her back in his bed. For a woman who professed to be calm and reasonable, his wife had issued a challenge no righteous Oklahoma rancher would turn down.

In the house, they skirted around each other warily and the twins found reasons to stay out of their path. Wayne deserted him for a soft, musical feminine voice and plates of special doggie goodies. Lucas considered the dog's desertion. He tried a low whistle that Wayne would recognize immediately.

The tent flap moved and a ball of white fluff hovered in the opening. He whistled again and Wayne barked sharply. The poodle ran outside, stood in the moonlight, then ran back into the tent. "A man's best friend,'' Lucas scoffed, jerking down the brim of his hat.

Damn. He'd always taken care of his family, working hard to provide for their needs.

The well had filled slowly, but to save water Lucas had taken their washing to the laundry near John's. Hattie caught him adding fabric softener and had raked him again about treating his family like some ''foreign sheikh.'' She informed him loudly that women had rights and if working pleased them, then it was their God-given right to work.

While Chastity tended her garden and lived in her tent, Lucas chewed on being the laughingstock of Chip.

''Water witch.'' The word slapped the cool night air. ''A Chicago water witch…a pregnant and barefoot one.''

His cattle lowed in the moonlight and Lucas checked the starry sky for clouds. With luck a good thunderstorm would move through; then Chastity Beauchamp Walkington would have to head for the house. He pictured her in clinging wet clothing and groaned. Her swelling breasts and the tiny mound caused by his baby sensually stimulated him to a painful realization: Since they were married, Chastity and he had made love one or more times a day.

She said she loved him. Lucas had lost parents who loved him, and his daughters were growing away every day. He wanted that stubborn little tent-squatter to love him until eternity.

He kicked a rock across the corral. His wife made the world perfect when she wasn't holed up in that tent and her pride.

The next two days, the clear sky and a steady stream of visitors to Chastity's tent challenged Lucas.

The third night, Lucas ripped off his blankets, jerked on his jeans, plopped on his hat and walked out to his wife's new residence. The lamplight traced Chastity's silhouette on the canvas walls of the tent as she sat, working on her bookkeeping. Wayne barked excitedly, sliding through the flap and running toward him. Side-stepping the excited dog, Lucas's bare heel hit a rock and he swore, hopping the remainder of the distance to the tent. He waited for Chastity to invite him into her canvas boudoir. When she didn't, he cleared his throat and waited.

After two minutes in which his temper started to rise, Lucas asked, "Chastity?"

"Who is it?"

Lucas inhaled, pressed his lips together and rubbed his injured heel against the mat that served as his wife's doorstep. "Lucas."

"Please come in." The formal invitation did nothing to soothe his wounded pride.

He pushed aside the flap, bent to enter the tent and stood inside it. Dressed in a light cotton nightgown with ruffles that touched her ankles, Chastity was beautiful. Freshly washed, her hair hung in long, natural sausage curls. Behind the round wire-rim glasses, her eyes filled with him, soft and mysterious. Moisture glistened on her lips and Lucas badly wanted to taste them.

To keep from reaching for her, Lucas jammed his hands in his pockets. The interior of the tent was as comfortable as his home, a small fan humming on a table that served as Chastity's desk. Several books and a lamp rested on another table near the neat bed. A bra strap escaped a pillow and Lucas suspected that Chastity hid it before he entered.

A pang of sweet pain shot through him—he missed the sight of her practical underwear.

Chastity poured him a glass of water from a covered pitcher and handed it to him as though she were entertaining company. That nettled his pride. "Please sit down, Lucas, you're…" Chastity glanced down his tall body, blushed and looked away. "You're so large, you fill the tent."

He stood there holding the glass of water and feeling like one-hundred-percent yahoo. "Where?"

Chastity sat on her bed, crossed her legs and adjusted her nightgown over them. "On my desk chair."

Lucas recognized it as one discarded and left in the barn. He eased into the wooden chair warily; it squeaked, protesting his weight. The night sounds of the crickets and tree frogs threaded the silence between them. Lucas cleared his throat and he glanced at Chastity, searching for a sign that she would yield. She stared back, smiled tightly and waited.

Lucas shot her a frown, eased his long legs out in front of him and took off his hat. "I hear you took on two new accounts."

She nodded solemnly. "Business is good."

"John Blue Sky says there's extra bookkeeping in the coupon business. Seems like folks around are doing more of it lately."

"Waste not, want not," she returned, tucking her bra strap beneath the pillowcase. The motion stunned Lucas; her breasts were warm and free beneath the light cotton. His hardening body reminded him that he had been days without Chastity's sweet love.

"Nice breeze tonight," he said, aching for the heat of her. Aching to be held and cuddled and knowing damn well he'd better skirt the issue of the extra book-keeping jobs.

"Very nice." She lifted her arm to push back a jumble of curls and Lucas's body went taut. The pink rosebud spray across her breasts tightened, her nipples dark beneath the cloth.

"The well has filled back up."

"That's good." Chastity met his eyes, hers glittering and bright, reminding him of how he had jumped her for the dry well.

The thought that he had acted out of anger, hurting her, ripped at him. "Are you moving back in or do you like the Walkingtons being the gossip of the county?"

She sniffed, tilted her head defiantly and asked coolly, "So you haven't come to apologize, Mr. Walkington?"

"Not likely, Mrs. Walkington. I am concerned for you and for my baby. I want you to move back into the house. The problem with you is that you're used to taking care of other people. You're not letting other people—namely your husband—take care of you."

"*My* problem?" She inhaled sharply, spreading her fingers apart on the papers. "Your problem, Lucas Walkington, is that you do not trust anyone but yourself. I think it's time you change and share your life and responsibilities," she stated with an indignant little sniff.

"I've been sharing plenty. Come back to my bed," he returned warily, wanting to scoop her up and carry her into the night.

Chastity smoothed the gown over her crossed legs, and Lucas's throat went dry. "Clearly we are at an impasse."

"Reckon so."

Chastity's eyes slid away from his into the night beyond the flap. Her chin trembled and she hugged herself as though chilled. "Lucas, I think we both know the real problem. You made love to a Heartbeat Goddess and ended up with plain, practical me. Your pride won't let you admit that you've been cornered into marrying a woman you detest. A woman you have to force yourself to make love to—"

Lucas's roar shot out into the night. "What?"

She sniffed once, lifted her eyes, brilliant with tears, and continued in a husky, halting tone. "It's quite evident to me. You forgot yourself with Honey and ended up with me. I don't excite or satisfy you."

While Lucas thought how she excited and satisfied him until he couldn't think, her hands twined restlessly and she plucked at a ruffle swirling near her delicate arch. Lucas ached to stroke that arch, to kiss it and work his way upward— "I'm inexperienced, Lucas, but I want romance and love."

"Who the hell is going to romance and love you?" he demanded tightly, desperate with fear. If she left him for another man, he'd come apart.

Chastity adjusted her glasses primly. "I'm sorry that you don't find me desirable without my Honey disguise. Perhaps in the future there will be a man who—"

Lucas tried to cope with this development in his marriage, staring at her pale, averted face. He shook his head. "I don't find you desirable?"

"I'm just practical me, after all. I'm a woman who has always worked and I won't stop now. I won't be catered to, pampered and be kept outside my husband's heart because of another woman. You want Honey, pink sequins and all. I'm not willing to live with you while you love another woman. Except for Old Coot, I've never been a part of a family, not really...only when they needed me to get them out of scrapes. I grabbed the brass ring, greedy for you and a family to call my own, a family that I could love and cherish and share good and bad.... If you want to keep me outside your family, keeping the problems away from me that are a part of living and marriage, then I may as well stay here.''

Stunned, Lucas stared at her, trying to form reason in his thoughts. ''Damn,'' he said quietly after a long moment in which Chastity fiddled with her pencil. The pencil snapped in two as he continued to look at her. ''I'm out of work, woman. That doesn't do much for a man's pride. You deserve more than what I can give you. That's a pawnshop ring you're wearing.''

''Romance and love and a man's pride are all separate factors, Lucas. Since I can't help you in the romance and love mode, I've decided to help you as best I can. Maybe I can find a place in Chip, but I will not be a burden to you. I can support the baby and myself. Amazing things can happen with proper bookkeeping and filing.''

Lucas thought about amazing things. Like her body fitting against his. He stared at her small foot, watched her toes and wondered if he'd ever sucked them one by one. Chastity inhaled, the motion drawing the light nightgown tightly against her breasts.

The image of the dark pink nubs pushing against the soft cloth remained with him long after he lay in his bed, staring into the moonlight. His wife wanted romance and love. Lucas flopped to his stomach and jammed his fists into the pillow. Chastity's warm, curved body nourished his baby and Lucas wanted her safe in his bed.

Lucas pushed his fingers through his hair. He'd played an honest game with Chastity, letting her know that he wanted her. While pregnant women had peculiar fancies, at four months Chastity wanted romance and love. Some women wanted pickles and ice cream, others craved midnight Chinese dinners. Chastity wanted romance and love.

He circled the thought. The soft pregnant little squatter living in that tent had slept throughout his maneuvering back to Oklahoma. He'd watched for cravings, prepared for them, and Chastity had blithely kept a healthy diet. He frowned, cuddling the pillow closer. Chastity had not shown signs of any unusual cravings...unless... Lucas slid his hand under the pillow to withdraw the practical cotton panties he'd just laundered.

They'd skipped a step from that "Heartbeats" weekend until they married. Every woman deserved her courting time filled with romance, flowers and sweet little nothings. Then there was dinner and dancing....

Short on money and facing a drought, he'd have to come up with unique proof that he loved Chastity. He wrapped his fist in the panties, an idea slowly taking shape as he pulled on a pair of jeans and went out to the porch.

For the next hour, he gripped the panties possessively and sat in the moonlight watching Chastity's tent. One thought kept returning: *Chastity had said she loved him.*

Wayne trotted down to the house, carrying a doggie chew bone. He dropped it at Lucas's bare feet. "She loves me, Wayne. It doesn't make sense, but she said she does.''

The small warmth curling around his heart grew. A big neon arrow soared through his thoughts and pinged softly into his heart. Lucas said slowly, ''Reckon I love her back.... Reckon I'm craving a little romance and love myself.''

He grinned widely, tilting the chair back against the porch wall. Chastity Walkington wanted romancing and love and she was getting it. He would find a way to tell her that he loved what she was, who she was, not Honey on a ''Heartbeats'' weekend.

Within minutes, Lucas found himself standing in front of her tent. Banishing Wayne to the house with a pointing finger, Lucas eased inside the tent.

Chastity stirred in the shadows, nestling on the narrow bed. Both hands rested over her stomach and the child they had created. Lucas swiftly spread a quilt on the tent floor, stripped off his jeans and lowered his sleeping wife carefully to the pallet. She protested in a whimper, holding him tightly as he drew her to him.

Taking his time, Lucas nuzzled her throat, catching her sweet scent.

Chastity's fingers tightened on his shoulders, her nails gently, restlessly clawing. She sighed as he nibbled her mouth, tasting the sweetness clinging to the corners with his tongue. He smiled slightly as Chastity began moving over him, easing her knee across his thighs, sliding until she rested fully on top of him.

Closing his eyes, he stroked her back, cupped her bottom as she began rhythmically nudging her hips against his. A woman of action and purpose even in her sleep, Chastity ran her hand slowly down his body, nestling her face in the hollow of his shoulder. Lucas almost bolted when her hand curled around him, stroked and guided him inside her moist warmth. Afraid to move, fearing Chastity would awake and end the moment, Lucas shuddered slightly, holding back his pleasure as Chastity moved over him.

When he opened his eyes, dark green eyes stared down at him, her mouth curved in that mysterious half smile. "I won't break, babe," she whispered against his mouth.

Lucas lost himself in her sweet, hungry kiss, in the blending of her body with his.

He forgot why he couldn't open his heart to love.

With soft touches and heated kisses, Chastity pushed them over the edge, the flurry of heartbeats blending with the wind pushing against the tent. Her hand ran between them, touching him, then his cry of release met her soft sigh, the fever burning as they soared. At the last, his blood pounding violently, Lucas caught her near him. She lay by him in the aftermath, stroking his chest as the dawn sent streaking fingers against the night sky.

Unwilling for the dream to end, Lucas caught her to him desperately, his arms trembling as they enclosed her, fitting her spoon-fashion into his body as he drew a blanket over them.

Chastity snuggled into the cove of his thighs, turned slightly to brush a kiss across his lips and sighed sleepily. "Love," she whispered in a sigh almost covered by the sweeping wind.

Dozing in her warmth and fragrance, Lucas awoke in early morning. Chastity lay watching him, her chin braced on a hand resting over his heart. Her eyes came into focus slowly, a tendril of hair dancing with her breath. "Lucas, have you ever heard of double-coupon day?"

"No, but it sounds good," he returned huskily, aware that nothing separated them. Soft, warm flesh lay against him, her lips curving in a smile.

Taking his time, Lucas turned her beneath him, lowered his head to suckle her breasts and smiled against her scented skin when she arched against him. However angry Chastity was at him, she wasn't turning him away.

Her arches rubbed his calves, then stopped as he moved swiftly inside her, claiming her. Lucas kissed her hard, lifted his head and whispered, "You're mine, Chastity. Every ornery inch. We'll work out our problems and you'll have what you need...."

"Yes," she returned huskily, her body tightening immediately around him. "I'll have what I need."

She laughed later as Lucas stood at the tent opening and looked down at her curled in the bedding. One dainty arch raised to rub his jean-clad leg. "You'd better go."

Lucas cursed, scowled at the house and wondered why he bothered to shelter his daughters. Certainly they were old enough to know about romance and love. Distracted, wanting to stay wrapped in his wife's arms, he clasped the teasing little foot and bent to kiss her arch. Chastity gasped, her eyes darkening. "My, that was romantic, babe," she whispered in an awed tone.

His good mood didn't dim when Raven caught him crawling into his bedroom window—he'd been locked out of his bedroom. During the day he concentrated on his emotions, focusing on opening his heart and swapping his stiff-necked, old-fashioned pride for genuine acceptance of his wife's talents.

That evening Lucas slapped his saddle on Duke, tightened the cinch and began another moonlight ride. Sorting his life out in the midst of the girls' busy schedule and the various neighborly visits—which had increased since Chastity's little tent had appeared—wasn't easy. He listened to Raven, Summer and Chastity sing camp songs around a tiny fire, their voices settling around his lonely ache like a gentle balm.

He wanted his family all under the same roof. Wanted Chastity back in his bed. Impatience wouldn't solve their problems, it could threaten their marriage. He tugged at Duke's reins, seeking the shelters of the giant oak's shadows from the moonlight.

The country was dry, headed for drought— A series of feminine giggles drew his attention. Raven and Summer performed a cancan dance in the moonlight, Wayne leaping and barking around their legs. Directing the dance, Chastity stood in the moonlight, lifting her long cotton gown to lift a leg high. She pivoted, bent and motioned as if lifting the cancan skirts high.

Leaning his forearms on the saddle horn, Lucas watched her dance. A city woman dancing a cancan in a nightgown on an Oklahoma ranch was unique. The perfect candidate for his lifelong partner in romance and love.

Why hadn't he recognized that her pride equaled his own?

Who was he to take her pride from her?

Chastity wanted to fit into his life, not remain protected and apart from his heartaches. If he wanted to keep her and his baby near, he'd better move fast.

Chastity watched Lucas pry a board from the old shed with a crowbar. The wood was seasoned oak, gray with weather and locked around its nails. Carl Murphy had arrived with his teenage sons at dawn, their pickup beds loaded with lumber. Immediately Raven and Summer had joined the work crew, dressed in their best jeans.

Their father, stripped to the waist and bronzed by the sun, was gorgeous. Chastity ran the flat of her hand across her stomach, calming the little twinges of happiness and the baby. For a woman who had never been stirred before her husband appeared, she found his nightly trips to her tent intensely romantic. Lucas always brought a small present—a bouquet of flowers from Hattie McCord's garden, a start of an herb, an antique canning jar for her collection or a discarded pioneer chest.

The past week they lay wrapped in each other's arms every night, exploring each other. Lucas told her about his parents, and the deep love of the land he had inherited. His boyhood was rich in love, his parents respecting and loving each other. He entered marriage with visions of the same happy life and found the dreams crumbled within weeks of the elegant wedding.

Then the twins, wanting a mother, had shopped throughout the county and had placed an ad in a singles column. Lucas had scampered around marriage-minded women for a year after the ad. Insecure at a young age, the twins needed Lucas's complete attention and he took them on special camping trips. When Raven was seven, she was certain she was adopted, though Summer was her exact image. They visited their mother and returned feeling gauche and ugly; Lucas's expression tightened when he relived Alesha's slap to Summer's cheek.

He taught them what he knew; how to change spark plugs or plow a field. He taught them the dances he had learned as a boy, to walk straight and proud. Then they moved into womanhood and Lucas floundered, the uncertain feminine temperament stunning him. He'd spoken too soon, or too sharply, frightened by the widening gap between himself and the twins.

Chastity had smothered her giggle against his bare shoulder when he told about lowering hemlines and ordering catalog dresses. She cried, learning of the young man saddled with guilt, working to keep the remainder of his inheritance and care for his children in the midnight hours.

She learned through Hattie of Lucas's deep pride in her adjustment to rural Oklahoma, in his daughters who were setting a fashion pace with refashioned clothing.

The weathered boards of the shed slowly became a pile as the men and the twins worked. When Chastity took iced tea to them, Lucas looked at the leaf of lemon balm herb in his glass and winked. "My wife's tea is the best in the county," he said quietly, his eyes warming on her. "She's starting an herb garden."

Chastity remembered when Lucas had placed aside his tea in her tent and had slowly kissed his way from her feet to her—she suddenly discovered that she was too hot, trembling as he bent to kiss her with icy moist lips. "Sweet," he whispered. "You're sweet all over."

After she shivered and wrapped her arms around her chest to hide her reaction, Chastity asked, "Why are you tearing down the shed?"

Summer and Raven took the empty glasses, grinning at her. "It's a surprise."

The next morning several neighbors arrived before dawn and Lucas pulled on his jeans with a curse. He bumped his head against the top of the tent and swore again. The tent threatened to topple and he gripped the center pole, steadying it. Chastity gathered her clothing desperately as the horns and the yells grew louder. When Lucas stepped outside the tent, wearing his jeans and a dark scowl, Hattie McCord shouted, "Honeymooners, get on down here. I'm starting coffee and breakfast. The whole county will be here at sunrise."

By late morning, the side porch was enclosed, the shed's weathered boards acting as paneling for "Chastity's business room." In quick slashes of conversation, Hattie informed her that siding and lumber were Lucas's as payment for his help with her cattle. "Hell," Hattie snorted. "You can even sleep in it if you want. Might save old Lucas from crawling through his bedroom window before the girls wake up. He can't figure out why the lock is sticking, but I'd say there are two girls who know why...they've been locking it every night from the inside and crawling out the window to come back in the house."

She winked and continued while Chastity blushed. "Found that out from Sam Fitzhugh, who came over to see if Lucas would help build fence. Sam saw Lucas crawl through the window and asked the girls about it. Old Lucas must be in love for sure to be sneaking flowers from my garden for you."

"Oh my," Chastity sighed, tears welling in her eyes. The next instant Lucas's arms were wrapped around her, his chin resting protectively on the top of her head. With trembling hands, Lucas smoothed her back, gathering her closer. "Buttercup, what's wrong?"

"I'm just so happy," she wailed, holding him to her with all her might.

After the immense potluck dinner, Lucas drew Chastity into the bedroom. He kissed her hungrily and picked her up in his arms, sitting on the edge of the bed. "I missed you, buttercup," he whispered in her ear. "Come back to me."

She leaned back, adjusting her steamed and tilted glasses to better see him. Stroking his jaw, loving him, Chastity whispered unevenly, "Oh, I miss you, too."

Nuzzling her neck and freeing tendrils from her braid, Lucas ran his hand slowly across her breasts and stomach. "How's the water witching business? I see you practice down by the elderberry bush."

She stiffened slightly, allowing his hand to rest over the baby. "Lucas, there is water there. I've followed Old Coot's instructions with a willow and a peach branch. Apparently my gift uses a peach branch, though the willow did tremble a little. Maybe I'm just not up to willows. Old Coot had a device that twirled, but I can't remember enough to make one."

"You're certain then?" he asked, nibbling on her ear.

"Positive."

"That's good because Harley Jones is on his way with well-digging equipment."

Chastity cradled Lucas's jaw with her hands and he kissed each palm, his expression tender. "What did you say, babe?"

"Harley Jones is a well-digger. You mark the spot and he'll dig," Lucas said, his palms cupping her breasts. "Are you nursing our baby?"

"Of course, but, Lucas, a well-digger...isn't that expensive?"

"Yep, reckon so. Can I watch you nurse the baby?" He lifted away her blouse, studying her breasts with the tip of his finger.

She flushed, uncertain of him and trying to balance well-diggers with Lucas's tenderness. "I...oh, Lucas, you realize that all the neighbors are outside, waiting for us...they'll want to see proof of my abilities—"

"Told them my wife was a gifted water witch. They're waiting for the show. Reckon they'll talk about it for years. Our son will be hearing about it in school—"

"Daughter," she corrected breathlessly, filling with happiness. "Oh, Lucas. You believe me."

Then he was kissing her with heart-stopping gentleness, cradling her and the baby. "More than believe, buttercup. Reckon I'm in love with you. Reckon it's time I told you so."

Her heart pounded, racing with emotions. She'd dreamed of his deep, sexy voice drawling those words someday. Her throat tightened, her fingers trembling as they stroked his warm cheeks. "Reckon?" she asked huskily, unevenly.

"Reckon I do, buttercup." One dimple enticed her exploring fingertips. "It's been a long time coming, hurt like sin paid back, but it was there, even when things were tangled. I knew inside that you were my heart, my dream, the day I met you."

The other dimple deepened. "Buttercup, I've been loving you without knowing it. Reckon I know it now."

"Oh, Lucas...." she whispered before his mouth closed over hers and he lowered her gently to the bed.

The exploring, sweet kiss promised a lifetime of tenderness and love; it whispered romance and excitement and curled around their hearts—

"Mr. and Mrs. Walkington," Hattie shouted beyond the locked bedroom door. "I got milking to do. If there's water-witching to be done, let's get at it.'' Lucas snorted, gathered Chastity tighter in his arms and lifted slightly to retort. Her finger pressed gently to his lips and he kissed it, distracted instantly. "You're certain, Lucas?'' Chastity whispered, easing her fingers through his black hair.

"Love. One hundred percent, Mrs. Walkington." Then he grinned that dazzling high-voltage grin. "Buttercup, they're waiting for a water witch. It's been years since there was a dowser with a divining rod in the countryside.''

"Oh, Lucas. What if I'm wrong? What if I've forgotten everything that Old Coot told me?''

"You believe in you, buttercup. I do.''

"Oh, Lucas. Can we afford a well-digger? They must be expensive.''

"Reckon Harley Jones is counting on a water witch. He thinks if you can find water, he'll be busy for a long time. It's an investment—he's got the idea that you're a working woman and might be interested in working part-time for him...when there's a need.''

Her sea-green eyes widened for a minute, then her laughter curled warmly around him. "How I love you, Lucas-babe. You were worth every gold heart.''

Chastity loosely held the forks of a vibrating, freshly cut peach branch. Old Coot had instructed her to concentrate, hold her breath and begin walking with her left foot.

The soil was dry beneath her feet, the grass tickling her arches. The silent populace of rural and Chip proper stood back from her. Looking tall and locked to his land, Lucas's hat shaded his face. She turned to him for a second, losing her concentration and winning a long, tender expression of love from her Oklahoma cowboy.

The wind rose suddenly, claiming her hair, sweeping the freed curls up and away from her face and caressing her skin. Chastity straightened her shoulders, ran her palm across Lucas's baby and closed her eyes, forcing her attention back to the stick in her hands. The peach branch jerked slightly just as the Old Coot said it would when water was near. She held each prong of the Y-shaped stick, allowing the end to lead her.

Lucas's heart pounded heavily against his chest. He'd forever remember Chastity poised in the sun and the dry June wind, her hair flying up and away from her face like a sunburst.

The wind pressed her clothing against his baby, a child made with desire and love.

There was learning and sharing to be done, long days and nights of opening his heart and telling Chastity of his love. Lucas inhaled the fresh air, realizing with pride that his actions—sweeping Chastity from Chicago to his ranch—were destiny. He had feared to love again, denied in his mind what his body defined for him.

The future waited, dressed in joy and love, sharing the hard times with Chastity and reveling in the good. Lucas glanced at Summer and Raven, at their intense young faces. With Chastity's help, he'd learn to bend, to understand his daughters' pride and needs.

Chastity allowed him to touch and explore her changing body. A gifted woman of tenderness and warmth, she had taken away his pain and given him love.

She followed the branch now, walking slowly toward the old elderberry bush. He walked a little ahead of the crowd, realizing that he would follow her path into eternity. The wind tugged at his hat and Lucas glanced at the clouds gathering in the horizon. Then Chastity stopped, the end of the stick bobbing toward the ground, and Harley's rig growled, moving closer to the spot.

Lucas moved quickly then, reaching his wife in four long steps and lifting her high into his arms, keeping her from harm. For once Chastity did not protest, curling her arms around him tightly as they watched. The boom on Harley's rig lowered slowly, the bit sinking into the ground.

After a few moments, Lucas settled in the shade of the old oak tree, holding Chastity on his lap. "It's deep, but a bigger vein than your well," she said finally, tiredly. "You'll need a pasture for the sprinklers."

"If we have the grass and the water, we can run more cattle...." Seeking to soothe her and ease his tension, Lucas rocked her in his arms and told her how he had bargained with Harley Jones. How Harley had refused at first, then reluctantly admitted that a success could bring business to his doorstep. Harley also had two left feet and needed help courting a reluctant schoolteacher who loved to dance. If ever Lucas felt like a yahoo, it was dancing in Harley's arms, issuing instructions and protecting his feet.

Hattie puffed up to them, carrying a small, rusty box. She handed it to Lucas. "This is yours, boy. It was just under an old root, wrapped in leather and old cloth. Got to get back," she said, returning to the crowd.

Lucas forced open the small box only to find another. Taking care, he snapped the rusty lock with his knife. The box opened and inside were small, carefully wrapped cloth bundles. The old gingham, rotted with time, fell away to reveal a woman's simple wedding ring. In another bundle ten large gold coins fell to the ground. "That's my great-grandmother's ring," Lucas whispered when he could talk. "Those ten coins were her dowry. My great-grandfather died years before she did…before she died, she was missing for a day…she must have come here, burying it. They say this was where he asked her to marry him…"

With trembling fingers, he lifted Chastity's finger and removed the pawnshop band to replace it with his great-grandmother's gold ring. "For my wife," he whispered unevenly.

"Love," he whispered slowly against the curling tendril brushing his face. The word was sweet and new to him, just like his wife. "Love," he repeated, and received a soft kiss.

Looking into his wife's teary willow-green eyes, Lucas barely heard the crowd cheer when Harley struck water.

Epilogue

Valentine's Day evening Lucas watched Chastity tuck Spring, their daughter, into her crib. His wife bent to kiss the baby good-night and Lucas enjoyed the soft rise of her backside beneath his long T-shirt.

Chastity's freshly washed hair, lightened by the sun and free from her daytime braids, now curled almost to her waist. The nursery's light outlined her curved body beneath the T-shirt. The clown lamp, earned with coupons, grinned knowingly at Lucas.

Standing by his daughter's crib, Lucas rested his hand on Chastity's waist and counted each day with her as a blessing. He kissed her temple, adjusted the glasses that had tilted, and shared the sweet moment with her.

Spring had arrived in the middle of November, delivered by Lucas. The midwife's car had stalled and at three o'clock in the morning they drove toward Muggins's hospital. He had pulled to the side of the road when Chastity had shuddered and said too quietly, "Lucas-babe, our baby is arriving—*now*."

Within half an hour, Spring arrived squalling hungrily. In another half hour, Chastity and the baby were in the hospital and Lucas had fainted into the bed next to his wife. Nurses hovered around him; Lucas could barely see his wife in the next bed. Easing to her side, he had bent to kiss her. "I love you, buttercup," he'd said, meaning it.

"I love you, too, babe," she whispered drowsily with that mysterious, intriguing, sloping smile.

"A sweet little girl—black hair," he remembered saying before he fainted again.

Now their daughter lay on her stomach, diapered bottom high in the air, and Lucas wiped away the tear that had been trailing down his cheek. With black curly hair and bearing the Walkington dimples, the baby added to their happiness. Love filled the house now, Summer and Raven laughing, preparing for college and meeting their challenges with his advice. They would enter college in the fall, and with Chastity's budgeting skills, they could continue.

He'd learned to open his heart, to share his fears and to bend his pride, though the task was often difficult. He'd learned that love worked both ways; love would build on trust and time.

Deep in his thoughts, Lucas straightened suddenly when Chastity's hand patted his backside, smoothing it. "Mother called today. She's learned how to balance her checkbook."

Within minutes, she turned the lock on the bedroom door. "Raven and Summer are staying with a girlfriend after the fashion show. That gives us the night, babe," she informed him as she removed her glasses.

The next instant, Chastity launched herself at him, her legs curling around his waist. The impact of her soft body caused him to brace one hand against the wall, the other cupping her soft, bare bottom.

"Oh, Lucas, I'm so happy. You were worth every gold heart."

Within minutes, Lucas lay tangled in her body, winded by the quick, hungry lovemaking they had just completed. He lowered his head to the pillow, kissed her damp throat. "Buttercup, we've got to work on our timing. I had a long, romantic Valentine's evening planned," he protested with a wide grin. "Every cowboy deserves a little romance."

She stirred beneath him, stroking his back. "We've got a lifetime to practice, babe. Tell me you love me again."

"Yes, ma'am, buttercup," Lucas whispered unevenly, obediently.

He whispered his love again during the night. Chastity hadn't lost the habit of inching over him in her sleep.

*   *   *   *   *

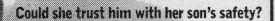
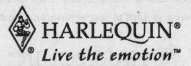

Say "I do" to this fun new anthology
about three couples (finally!)
finding happily ever after...

Always a
Bridesmaid

RITA® Award-nominated authors

Jane
Sullivan

Isabel
Sharpe

Julie
Kistler

Being a member of the bridal party brings more than wedding
favors for these three heroines...it also brings their own groom!

Coming in April to your favorite retail outlet.

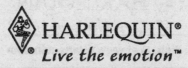

HARLEQUIN®
Live the emotion™

Visit us at www.eHarlequin.com

PHAAB

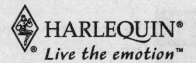

Coming in April 2004
to Silhouette Books

USA TODAY BESTSELLING AUTHOR

INGRID WEAVER

Never leave a man behind.

THE
INSIDER

Gideon Faulkner had lived a life in captivity,
kidnapped and brainwashed years ago by the
Coalition. But he had found a way to sneak
into the outside world, and finally had a chance
to find his real family...and true love!

Five extraordinary siblings.
One dangerous past.
Unlimited potential.